ONE
LAST
BREATH

GINNY MYERS SAIN

G. P. PUTNAM'S SONS

G. P. PUTNAM'S SONS
An imprint of Penguin Random House LLC, New York

First published in the United States of America by G. P. Putnam's Sons,
an imprint of Penguin Random House LLC, 2024

Visit us online at PenguinRandomHouse.com.

Library of Congress Cataloging-in-Publication Data is available.

ISBN 9780593625453

1st Printing

Printed in the United States of America

LSCH

Design by Rebecca Aidlin
Text set in Apollo MT Pro

For my mother, Anna Myers,
who believes the two most powerful forces in the world
are love and story, in that order. Thank you for gifting
all three of your children with plenty of both.

ALSO BY GINNY MYERS SAIN

Dark and Shallow Lies

Secrets So Deep

"There are more things in heaven and earth, Horatio, /
Than are dreamt of in your philosophy."

—*Hamlet* by William Shakespeare

ONE

USUALLY, IT'S THE soft sound of the knife that wakes me. The noise it makes when it slices through the canvas. Like a whisper. I roll over to ask Celeste what it was that she said, but she can't answer because she's already dead. Staring and bloody.

So I run.

Other times when I imagine myself as Bailey, it's the crunch of leaves or the snap of a twig that makes me sit up straight in my sleeping bag.

I stare into the dark, not realizing that the rest of my life can be measured in minutes.

Even in my dreams, though, that night always ends the same way. With me dead. Floating on the surface of the spring. I fade into the blackness, my hair spreading out around me in a sea of blood, without ever knowing that Celeste and I have become the most famous citizens of Mount Orange, Florida.

But then I wake up. Take a deep breath. Hear the hum of the air conditioner. I count the old glow-in-the-dark stars on my ceiling and feel the softness of clean sheets against my skin. I inhale the mountain breeze dryer sheets my mother uses, even though neither of us have ever even seen a mountain in real life. Every time, I'm hit with this rush of relief. Because I'm not Bailey.

I'm not Celeste, either.

I'm Trulee.

And instead of bleeding out in the water, right now I'm standing on the courthouse lawn while the high school choir sings a memorial song for two long-buried girls who have always felt more alive to me than any of the people standing here dripping in the late-May heat.

I squint and glance up toward the sky. All that smooth, endless blue reminds me of the surface of the freshwater springs that lie right outside the city limits. It's the perfect day to be free diving out at Hidden Glen, but I felt like I had to be here. So did everyone else, I guess.

Downtown Mount Orange is a three-block strip of insurance offices, real estate offices, and four or five junk stores that like to be called "antique shops." Other than the memorials to Bailey and Celeste scattered around town, and the old crime scene out at Hidden Glen Springs where they died, the only real things of interest are an old-fashioned ice cream parlor called The Cone Zone and a beauty salon called Kurl Up and Dye. Every business sports a dark green awning out front, and big planters of ferns and pink hibiscus line the sidewalks. It would be picturesque, probably, if you didn't live here.

But I do.

I wipe at my sweaty forehead and glance up at the Florida flag flying over the courthouse.

My home state is known for four things.

Alligators.

Beaches.

Theme parks.

And serial killers.

There's Ted Bundy. Danny Rolling. Aileen Wuornos. The legendary Glades Reaper. He's maybe the worst of the worst. The things he did were so unspeakable that the mention of that name is enough to stop a conversation in its tracks. The original Florida boogeyman.

But I'm not thinking about him as I stand in the baking afternoon sun, struggling to fill my lungs with thick, wet air that feels more like warm oatmeal than anything else.

On a little stage at the front of the crowd, our illustrious mayor, Knox, is rambling on about the new memorial fountain in the town square. I'm not thinking about him, either, though.

I'm thinking about Bailey and Celeste again, our own local horror story.

The anniversary of the murders out at Hidden Glen is coming up in just a few weeks. It happened almost twenty years ago, but it's clear that nobody has forgotten about what went down out there that night, because everyone has gathered here in the hellish heat to see yet another memorial dedicated to our dead girls.

When we were little, my friends and I used to pretend to be them. We didn't understand that they were dead. Murdered. We only knew they were famous, their pictures framed in our school hallways and their names written on plaques all over town.

Once we understood the gruesome truth, we found other games to play. But I never lost my fascination with Bailey and Celeste.

Especially Bailey.

When I reenact the murders in my mind, I always play her role. It's her eyes I see it all unfold through. Her panic that swells in my chest. Her last moments that play over and over in my head.

I look around the crowd. There are a lot of true-crime people here today. A couple hundred, at least. Podcasters and writers. Plus their fans, creepy murder enthusiasts who travel the country visiting beautiful places where ugly things happened. These are the kind of weirdos who get off on playing detective as they pore over clues on internet forums, and there are so many more of them than any normal person would think. That's why we need another memorial. Because the lines get too long at the first five. The murder ghouls might have to wait a few seconds to snap their selfies, which might piss them off. And we can't have our guests leaving town dissatisfied. What if they didn't stay for pie at the diner and antique shopping on Dickson Street? That would be a real tragedy for this town.

I glare at a woman who steps right in front of me, blocking my view. She doesn't even offer up an "excuse me" or a "sorry." She's too busy fanning herself with her hat as sweat soaks through the back of her fancy silk blouse. She's an out-of-towner. I can tell because they're always dressed too formally. The uniform of choice in Mount Orange is shorts and a swimsuit paired with flip-flops. Put on anything else, and you're gonna stand out.

It isn't only the tourists who turned out today. There are

plenty of locals, too. I wave at some girls I know from school. And the lady who cuts my hair. But my eyes keep searching the crowd until they land on Celeste's mom. She skipped the last few memorial dedications, but today she's standing off to one side, staring up at the courthouse windows. When the mayor points her out, the crowd offers up a polite round of applause for the murder victim's mother. Her shoulders tighten, but her face never changes, and she never looks anywhere but up at those empty second-floor windows.

Knox is bellowing from the podium now, giving his best impersonation of a Southern Baptist preacher getting really worked up on this Sunday afternoon. "This mystery will be solved," he promises us, one hand raised skyward like he's waving a Bible. "The guilty will be punished! Someone knows who did this. And nothing stays a secret forever. The killer is someone's son. Someone's father. Someone's brother." He pauses for effect. "Maybe even yours."

Knox narrows his eyes at his captive audience, and a low murmur swells from the crowd, because, in this town, speculating about the Hidden Glen murders is every bit as much a local pastime as watching the high school football team lose championship after championship. We still eye each other with suspicion after all these years, and whispers are always hanging like water droplets in the humid air. When we're waiting behind our neighbors in line at the grocery store or the bank, there's always a part of us that wonders, *Was it you?* It does something to a person, always thinking that the person holding the door open for them could be a murderer, but none of us can give up on the guessing game. After all, there are only three un-solved murders on record in Mount Orange.

Celeste and Bailey.

Plus my sister, Dani.

Although most people think Dani's death was just a tragic accident. Not worth obsessing over. Which is kind of a relief in one way, because it means there's no opportunity for this town to make a buck off her memory. An accident victim's photo won't pull in tourists with cash to spend on pie and postcards. That also means there are no memorial ceremonies or golden fountains for her, so sometimes I feel like I'm the only one who notices that Dani's gone.

A breeze tickles the back of my neck, and I'm grateful for that little bit of relief from the heat. Everyone in the crowd tips their bright red faces toward the sky to find the cooler air. I shiver as it moves across my slick skin, and for the briefest second, I sense someone standing right behind me. Someone I recognize by the sound of their breathing.

"East," I say with a sigh. "I know it's you." I spin around, expecting to find my boyfriend, grinning and ready to wrap me up in a hug, even though it's a hundred and twenty degrees and my shirt is soaked through with sweat.

But no one is there. At least not anyone familiar.

The mayor pushes his cowboy hat back on his head to reveal a few wet curls that hang like limp macaroni above pinprick eyes. He fans at his red face with a yellow legal pad, then ends his speech the way these things always end, with a plea for information. "If anyone knows anything, or if you have any clues, no matter how small, please reach out," he thunders at us, and my hand immediately moves to cover the zipper pocket of my backpack, almost like Knox's beady little eyes have X-ray vision. "One of you out there could hold the key to solving these murders and finally bringing peace to our community."

His words strike the proper somber tone, if you don't pay attention to how fake they sound and how he's mostly focused on making sure our local newspaper editor, Jon Boy Westley, gets plenty of good photos of him for the front-page story we'll run next week.

Jon Boy is my neighbor, plus I work for him part-time at the *Mount Orange Star* in the summers. I'm grateful to have the afternoon off, otherwise it might be me up there gritting my teeth when Knox waves me in for a closer shot.

When it's all over, I take my turn filing by the new fountain. The lady in the sweaty silk blouse leans over me to snap a selfie, and I can't help laughing when she slips and drops her phone in the water. Before I move on, I pause for a second and run my fingers over the lettering on the gold plaque.

DEDICATED TO THE MEMORY OF
BAILEY ALDERSON AND CELESTE WOODWARD,
THE LOST GIRLS OF MOUNT ORANGE,
ON THE TWENTIETH ANNIVERSARY OF THEIR DEATHS

Even though most of them wouldn't even recognize Dani's name, I fight the urge to remind the people around me that

Mount Orange has more than two lost girls. Instead, I watch as melting tourists drift toward The Cone Zone for ice cream.

I'm desperate for some air-conditioning, so I make my way through the crowd to my truck. As I reach for the handle, I feel it again, a whisper of breath on my neck. Someone I can almost name standing close behind me. It slides across my skin like the touch of familiar fingertips, and I break out in goose bumps. I scan the crowd for East again, or maybe my mom or Jon Boy. But they aren't there. This time, all I see is a flash of short, coal-dark hair disappearing around the corner of the drugstore.

Nobody I know has hair like that, so I turn back toward my truck. That's when I notice Celeste's mother leave her spot and head toward the fountain. She's waited for the crowd to disperse, I guess. And now she's standing there alone. I stop with the truck door open and watch her pause for a few seconds to run her hands over the engraved plaque. Exactly like I did.

She looks up and catches me staring at her. Her eyes are fixed on mine, and it makes me uncomfortable. I've been watching her since I was a little girl, always checking for a glimpse of her in the garden when we'd drive by her house on the way to school or, when I got older, looking for a bit of her faded blond hair when someone hurried past the newspaper office windows.

I don't like the idea of her watching me, though.

All I can think is that she has no idea how often I wake up worried about her daughter, because I'm always Bailey in my dreams, but it's always Celeste I'm calling out for.

I climb into the truck and get the AC going, then lean close to the vent and let the cold air kiss my sunburned cheeks. I take a

few seconds to shoot East a text while I wait for the traffic jam
to clear up.

> Hey, baby. You downtown
> at the dedication?

His reply is immediate.

> Nope. Waiting at your place.
> Thought you might want to go
> cool off together. Or maybe
> get a little hotter . . .

That last line is followed up with four kissy-face emojis, a
neon-green penguin, and a bright blue ocean wave even though
we're an hour from the closest beach. On my way, I tell him, and
I relax a little as I slide the truck into reverse and back onto
Main Street. East always has that effect on me. He's a source of
instant calm and comfort, like slipping on an old T-shirt that's
gone all soft from wearing it so much. Or hearing your favorite
song on the radio. The two of us have been best friends since we
were four, and everyone always said that we'd get together as a
couple eventually. So we did, I guess.

On the way out of town, I pass the cemetery. A group of people
is gathered around a little grave that lies off to one side. Right up
against the rock wall. At first, I think maybe a funeral is going
on, and then I realize who that particular grave belongs to.

It's Celeste's.

Bailey is buried up near Tallahassee, where her mother's people were from. But Celeste's final resting place is here in Mount Orange.

I grip the steering wheel as anger builds low in my stomach and quickly moves up into my chest where it sits like a hot coal. The true-crime ghouls have invaded the cemetery. I slow down to watch them jostle and push for their chance to take a picture. After all, why be content posing for selfies with a fountain when you can flash your best smile over the grave of a real murder victim.

I'm not sure why it bothers me so much. I just know I have this sudden urge to roll down the windows and yell something awful. But I can't think of what to yell. So I grit my teeth and keep driving.

When I make it home, East is sitting on my front porch. He waves as I climb out of the truck and leave the cool of the cab behind. The afternoon heat breathes me in and swallows me up again. Like some kind of lazy monster. By the time I make it to the steps, I've surrendered to the constant sweat running down my neck in tiny rivers. I'm not even trying to wipe it away at this point.

I sit down beside East, and he reaches up to push my damp hair back off my forehead—strands of stringy red—as I lean in for a kiss. His lips are soft, and his blond waves glint in the sunlight. I inhale a lungful of him. Mango shampoo and coconut sunscreen. He smells like a potluck fruit salad. The little blue sailboats on his swim trunks make me smile, and I trace the outline of one with my finger.

East grins. "Watch it there, missy," he teases.

"I looked for you at the fountain dedication," I tell him, and East lets out a long sigh.

"Yeah," he says. "I wanted to be there, but I had to work." He gives me a slightly embarrassed grin, like he just got caught sneaking a cookie before dinner. "And then Paz and I went for a dive out at the Well." He pushes his hair out of his eyes, and I try to fight back my jealousy. I've been thinking about free diving all afternoon. I crave the cold, clear water of Hidden Glen Springs the same way our old hound dog craved bacon. It's a constant hunger that hums just under my skin every moment I'm awake. Even in my dreams, I find myself below the surface more often than above it.

Right now, I need it more than usual. I'm anxious to slide into that deep blue and wash the heat of the day from my body.

To see how deep I have to dive before I forget about the smiling tourists at the cemetery.

"Besides," East adds, "I wasn't in the mood to deal with Knox. Especially after last weekend."

Our red-faced, cowboy-hat-wearing mayor is East's uncle, but they don't share much of a bond.

"What happened last weekend?" I ask. Knox gets up to so much shady shit that East hardly bothers to tell me anymore, unless it's something really big.

"Nothin' new." East shrugs. "He got drunk off his ass at Nana's house. Broke a damn window in the front room."

"Jesus," I mutter. So much for the dignity of our high-and-mighty mayor. "What had him so pissed?"

"Who knows?" East shakes his head. "You know how he gets when he's been hittin' the bottle. He's meaner than a hornet with a headache. Maybe Nana didn't make his favorite kind of pie for Sunday dinner." He stops for a second, and his jaw tightens. "Anyway, I'm the one she had to call to clean up the mess. Her standin' there cryin', wringin' her hands, and him passed smooth out in the side yard."

"I'm sorry, baby," I tell him, and I run my fingers through those beautiful blond waves. He just shrugs again. East is no stranger to his uncle's shenanigans.

"Nah. Don't be sorry," he murmurs as he leans in for another kiss. "I'm the one who's sorry for diving without you." He grins. "How about I make it up to you?" I let myself enjoy the feeling of his lips pressed against mine. His fingers in my hair. Our relationship is so easy, worn smooth like the wooden porch steps underneath me. No bumps or rough places. "I thought maybe you and me could squeeze in a dive out at Hidden Glen before dinner."

"I wish," I say, "but I'm supposed to have dinner with Dad." I can't help but roll my eyes.

East frowns. "What's he doin' in town?" He's known my piece-of-shit father his whole life, too, and his opinion of him isn't any better than mine.

"He's coming through on his way back down to Miami."

"Well damn. Tomorrow evening, maybe." East is busy nuzzling me with his nose and pressing his lips to my neck. "I missed you," he whispers against my collarbone. "Sorry I couldn't make it to the memorial." His voice is low and gravelly. Soft and slow like wild Florida honey in my ear.

I'm so hot. Sticky. I fight the urge to move away, to let some air circulate between us. All I can think about is how much I want to be in the water right now. Out at Hidden Glen Springs. And that has my mind drifting back to Bailey and Celeste.

How they died out there in the woods.

"What if the killer was there today?" I ask. It's something I've been thinking about since I stood in that jam-packed town square earlier. East pulls back to look at me. "Down at the courthouse. In the crowd. Watching the spectacle."

East just shrugs.

"What?" I ask him. "You don't ever wonder about stuff like that anymore?" I nudge him in the ribs with my elbow. "I thought maybe we could do a little poking around out at the campsite tomorrow after we get off work."

East and I used to go clue hunting out at the murder site all the time when we were kids. We'd spend the morning trampling through the scrub looking for anything that might point to the killer's real identity. Then we'd spend the afternoon in the water, splashing each other and goofing off and practicing our dive breathing with Dill.

"I don't know." East rubs at the stubble on his chin, and it makes me want to plant little kisses along his jawline. "It's comin' up on twenty years, Tru. All that shit went down before we were even born. And we've been all over back there. It's time to let it go."

It's my turn to shrug, but I don't meet East's eyes. "You sound like your mom," I say. East's family doesn't like to think about what happened that night. Knox was one of the original suspects. But he was cleared.

Now he's the mayor.

"Every time we go poking around back there, all we ever get is ate up and scratched up." East reaches out and touches my cheek. "You're never gonna find anything."

"Never say never," I tease him, and I reach for my backpack so I can unzip the side pocket to reach in and run my fingers over the secret treasure I keep hidden there.

A sudden honk makes us both jump, and I'm careful to rezip the backpack pocket, because what's tucked inside is so tiny. So easily lost.

"Hey! Lovebirds! Y'all wanna come for supper at our place?" East's best friend, Paz, has pulled up in the driveway, and he's sticking his head out the driver's side window, grinning in our direction. "Ma's making ropa vieja!" My mouth immediately starts to water. Paz's mom is Cuban, and she makes the most amazing food. I mean, my mom is an okay cook, but she thinks pepperoni pizza is super spicy. And we've been eating microwave dinners more and more often the last couple of years.

East jumps on the offer immediately, but I say that I can't because I'm supposed to have dinner with Dad. It makes me irritated with my father all over again, because I know eating with Paz's family would be way more fun. Besides, Dad's probably gonna blow me off. He usually does.

Before he leaves, East pulls me in for a goodbye kiss. "I love you, truly. Truly, dear." He half hums, half sings that old song into my ear like a secret, and my whole body is covered in goose bumps. We heard it years ago, on a Bing Crosby record his grandma had, and it's been his song to me ever since.

I hear an impatient cough and look over to Paz, still hanging out the car window, making kissy faces at us like an overgrown second grader.

"I better get going," East tells me, and he promises to text me later. "Paz's mama may be a better cook," he teases, "but you're for sure a better kisser."

I snort as East climbs into his truck and raises one hand to me in a lazy wave. Then he takes off after Paz and I watch until they disappear in a cloud of dust.

When I step inside our tiny living room, I head straight for the stairs. I try not to make eye contact with the two girls in the giant portrait that hangs on the wall just above the TV.

Me and my big sister, Dani.

When I reach the safety of my own bedroom, I unzip my backpack and carefully take out what's hidden in the side zipper pocket: a tarnished best-friends locket on a broken chain. I hold it in my hand, feeling the weight of all the questions it surely knows the answers to, and I wish for like the millionth time that I could absorb its secrets directly into my skin.

I know for a fact the necklace belonged to Bailey, because she's wearing it in the picture they used in all the newspaper articles that ran after the murders.

The other half shines from around Celeste's neck in her photos.

I found it a couple of years ago. Half a heart mostly buried in the sandy soil at the edge of the Well, out at Hidden Glen Springs. I should have turned it in to the sheriff. I know that. But as soon as I touched it, I knew it was meant to be mine. Even before I turned it over, I somehow knew about the engraved *B* on the back, although I'd never seen that mentioned anywhere.

I take the necklace and lie down on my bed to let the air-conditioning wash over me like cool, clear spring water. I'm exhausted from standing in the heat for so long, and I have an hour before Dad is supposed to pick me up.

I don't intend to let my eyes drift closed, but it's almost two hours before the ping of a text message wakes me.

Sorry, baby. Car trouble. Next time, okay?

He could at least have come up with an interesting excuse.

I have a few missed messages from East, so I return those.

There's one from Mom, too. Out late.

It's already dark, so I decide to call it a night. I change into a clean T-shirt and crawl under the covers, then I close my eyes and try to slip away again in the darkness of my bedroom. I imagine myself diving. Calm and focused. Free. Floating in an endless deep.

But I keep hearing a sound. A swish that's barely audible under the loud hum of the AC and the barking of our neighbor's dog. A noise that sounds like a whisper.

Or a knife cutting through nylon.

Before I can figure out what it might be, I fall asleep with a dead girl's treasure clutched tightly in my fist.

TWO

AS SOON AS I open my eyes, the need to dive is humming through my veins the way the constant droning of the window air conditioner hums in my ears. My whole body is pulsing with it.

I only have an hour before I have to be at work at the newspaper office, and I'd be cutting it really close. So I lie there for a minute and try to shake that desperation off. But it's like lying in bed knowing you have to pee. I can't think about anything but diving, no matter how hard I try to distract myself. Until I get in the water, I won't be able to focus on the rest of my day.

East won't be able to dive with me this morning. He's probably already at work. But I know somebody else who will be up and ready to go, so I change into my swimsuit and hide Bailey's necklace away in my backpack for safekeeping. I grab a muffin and my dive bag before I head out the door. Less than five minutes after I wake up, I'm already in my truck and following the highway out of town toward Hidden Glen.

Dill says I was born to breathe water, that my soul should've dropped to earth as a carp, or maybe a striped bass. But my wires got crossed somehow, and that's why I ended up with lungs instead of gills. Every time he says it, I think he's probably right. If I had the chance to pick, I'd choose being a fish over being a human any day of the week, because I pretty much live to dive.

It scares my mom. She won't watch. All she can think about is what if I never come up? And I understand why; she's already lost one daughter. But I've never been afraid of the deep. That's always been the one place that feels safe.

I've never been afraid of the gators, either. If you grow up in Mount Orange, Florida, you learn early on that they aren't any more inclined to mess with us than we are with them, so the big snaggletoothed fellow sunning himself near the turnoff to Hidden Glen Springs barely gets a glance from me as I pull into the parking lot. Let him hiss and bellow. I don't give a shit.

Today is Monday, and we're kicking off the first full week of summer break. The days are already unbearable—ninety-four degrees and 300 percent humidity—which means, even at just past nine o'clock in the morning, the picnickers and partiers at Hidden Glen outnumber the horseflies and no-see-ums.

I park the truck in the last open spot and pick my way toward the swimming area, stepping over blankets and around stacks of inflatable tubes. There are already people everywhere. Setting up their grills and umbrellas for the day. Listening to music in the sun. Snorkeling with their kids. Waiting for the Dive Bar to open so they can buy overpriced Frito pies and ice pops.

Some of them are out-of-town day-trippers drawn by the promise of our cold, clear water. Others are true-crime fans, like the ones at the memorial yesterday, who've come to check out the decades-old murder site hidden back in the scrub. But most of them this morning are locals, people I've known my whole life. They wave and smile. Shout questions at me.

"You still headin' to FSU in the fall?" Mrs. Bernson wants to know. She was my fourth-grade teacher.

I nod and shout back, "Leaving in August." Her broad smile makes my stomach tighten at the lie I just told.

A group of preteens turns their music up, and I think maybe I'll get away with just one question today, but then somebody else stops me.

"How's your mama doin'?"

And somebody else.

"Missed you in church last Sunday . . . ?"

I grit my teeth at that, because me and Mom haven't seen the inside of a church since Dad left. That was his thing, not hers. Especially after what happened with Dani. But people still ask all the time, like maybe I forgot to show up for Sunday school the last five thousand weekends in a row.

As for how my mama's doing, Mount Orange is a tiny place. Everybody knows everybody else's business, so they all know good and well that she stays out at the Wild Clover a little too late. Dances with too many guys. Drinks a little too much. Nobody ever mentions it because they all know why. Besides, it doesn't stop her from being the top-selling real estate agent in town. Not that we're rich or anything; commission on rundown mobile homes isn't much money.

I've already had enough questions to last me until fall, and summer is just getting started, so I bypass the crowded main spring and follow the wooden boardwalk up the run a couple hundred yards to a second, smaller spring called Elijah's Well. It's a dark blue circular hole, only fifteen feet wide, but almost a hundred and forty feet deep. A liquid elevator shaft running straight down through the limestone, all the way to the Floridan aquifer. If you stand up top and look down into it, it's like staring into a bright blue eye.

I raise the little lever to push open the gate in the chain-link safety fence, and it swings closed behind me. I hear the click of the latch.

Just inside the gate, there's a plaque dedicated to Celeste and Bailey. The Rotary Club put it there years ago. Today, two middle-aged women in murder podcast T-shirts are posing for selfies in front of it, and I fight the urge to push them into the water. Just to see if they can swim.

Instead, I set my bag on the rocks, slip off my shirt and shorts, and wait. I don't figure it'll be long, and sure enough, it's only a few minutes before I hear a familiar voice call my name.

"Mornin', Tru! You're out early today!"

I look over my shoulder to see Dill scampering across the rocks toward me. Derry is following along behind him, picking her way and holding up her long skirt.

Dill moves like one of the little lizards you see everywhere down here. He's nimble. Fast. Sure footed and fearless. But Derry's cautious. Thoughtful. You can see her considering each step before she takes it.

Dill and Derry are permanent fixtures at Hidden Glen. They're modern-day hippies with an off-the-grid camp back in the woods, on the opposite side of the springs from the murder site. Summers, Dill works the crowd out here the way a politician works the room at a campaign rally. He spends the long, hot days chatting people up, telling jokes, showing off with backflips and jackknife dives into the blue of the main spring. Right now, it's clear he only has one thing on his mind.

"We gonna go below?" Dill asks me. He's crouching on a rock, practically levitating with excitement. Dill's little and wiry. Permanently tanned. He's all taut muscles and energy, with dirt under his fingernails that not even the springs can wash away. He's wearing raggedy cutoff shorts. No shirt. No shoes. His everyday uniform.

"You bet," I tell him. "That's what I came for."

The light is flashing in Dill's eyes, and he runs his fingers through his dark tangled curls. I know that urge, the need that gnaws on you with sharp little teeth. He's already digging his gear out of a beat-up backpack while he whistles a little tune—some sea shanty he loves about a dead sailor and the women who mourned him. He pauses to wink at me before he starts spit-cleaning his mask.

Derry's found herself a shady rock to perch on, and she's lost in the pages of a tattered paperback romance. I watch her absentmindedly shoo away a horsefly, then look up to give me a friendly wave.

It feels good to be a part of their little family this morning, especially since Dad no-showed on me last night, exactly like I figured he would.

"You goin' first?" I ask, and Dill nods.

"Age before beauty." He gives me another wink, then pulls

on his gear. Dill lives to shoot the shit most of the time, but when it's time to dive, chatting always takes a back seat. "You ready to get deep?"

"Always," I tell him.

I know my job. Stand up top. Keep watch. Be prepared. Ready to go in. Just in case.

Dill is already poised at the edge of the Well in his mask and fins. He's breathing slow. Eyes closed. Stretching. It's a weird kind of yoga he made up for himself. His face changes completely as he relaxes. He's an artist preparing to pick up the brush. Or a writer just before the first stroke of the pen.

Dill is always so intense, like a struck piano string. Or a live electrical wire. I love to watch the change that comes over him when he's getting ready to go below. All that wild, pent-up energy flows out his fingertips. He becomes this other version of himself. Still. Focused. He's completely calm. It's the opposite of watching someone transform into a werewolf.

Then he's gone. Vanished. He disappears from the rock in the blink of an eye. No splash. No ripples. He slips below the surface of the Well as silently and gracefully as the sunlight.

I watch him move through the water, and I think back to that summer Dill first started teaching East and me to dive. We were ten years old. Dani had died a few months earlier. Mom and Dad were after each other all the time, and I could tell Dad was on the brink of bailing. East's mom was pregnant with Seth. Her latest boyfriend had already ditched her, and she was always busy working two or three jobs. So East and I were just kind of drifting along by ourselves. We'd ride our bikes out to the springs every day, and Dill and Derry were always here.

I don't know how I would have made it through all that without them.

Dill pops up out of the water and swims toward the side of the spring. He gives me a thumbs-up, then pulls himself onto a rock and collapses. I watch his chest heaving up and down. Big breaths to fill his starving lungs. A huge grin on his face. That's the free diver's high. Soul-shattering euphoria. The danger of diving without an air tank is worth that feeling of indescribable joy.

When it's my turn, I slide into the water and let the spring swallow me whole. I know from the beginning it's going to be a good dive. I'm in complete control of my mind and my body. The space inside me feels so big. It's like I have enough air to last forever. I go down and down and down and down.

One by one, I'm letting go of all the thoughts that've been eating at me—

How Mom doesn't know I never sent my application in to FSU—

All the things I wish I had the guts to say to Dad—

How it's my fault Dani died—

How I love East with all my heart, but sometimes I wonder if maybe there might be some other life out there for me—

I do like Dill taught me. I imagine each of those thoughts floating up and away toward the surface, like air bubbles. I watch them drift out of sight until the world goes still and I'm finally left alone with just myself. And even though I'm holding my breath, I feel like I can finally breathe.

Below me, on the bottom, I see the vent—a curtain of bubbles streaming out of a crack in the rocks. The perfect clarity of the water plays tricks on my eyes and my brain. It looks like no more than a few feet down to the bottom, but I know it's over one hundred.

An almost unbearable urge pulls me toward those bubbles. It's a constant tug, that desire to push myself harder and farther. To dive deeper. Go longer. I feel it even when I'm lying in bed at night, or when I'm working in the overly air-conditioned newspaper office.

No matter how much time I spend in the water, it's never enough, because when I dive, there is no good or bad or right or wrong or should or shouldn't or happy or sad. Or even up or down. I'm not thinking about Mom. Or Dad. Or what happened to Dani. Or East or college or how messed up everything feels sometimes. There's just weightlessness.

Peace.

Before I know it, I'm farther below the surface of Elijah's Well than I've ever been before. The depth markers scratched into the soft limestone tell me I'm at about seventy feet. Halfway to the bottom.

I want to get deeper. It's the worst kind of craving. I turn my face up to find Dill so I can signal to him that I'm okay, and when I look down toward the vent again, someone is swimming toward me. My muscles tighten and my mind locks up.

This is impossible.

No one else went into the water.

There shouldn't be anyone down here.

But there is.

A girl is coming up fast from below me. Long brown hair floats around her face, hiding her features. She's wearing a short white dress. Definitely not dressed for swimming.

She grabs me by the wrist and panic strikes right though me like summer lightning. My heart rate skyrockets. My pulse pounds in my ears and my lungs immediately start to ache.

Then she's pulling me down. Not like sinking and dragging me with her. This girl is swimming hard toward the bottom of the spring, jerking me along like she's the kite and I'm the trailing ribbon.

I kick hard. Claw at the limestone wall with my free hand, hoping for something to grab on to. All I can think about is my mom. And East. How they'll feel if Dill has to tell them I'm dead.

I blink hard. Force those thoughts out of my mind.

I have to think clearly.

I have to—

I have to breathe.

It's the only thought my body knows now.

I have to BREATHE.

HAVE to breathe.

I HAVE TO BREATHE.

My lungs are desperate.

I'm going to die. We're both going to die. In the deep. The cold.

Together.

Just before everything goes blurry, she peers up at me through the curtain of bubbles streaming from her mouth.

I know her. The thought slams into me like a runaway truck.

Suddenly the pressure on my arm is just gone. I don't waste any time wondering what happened. I don't give a shit, to be honest. All I can think about is air. Every instinct I have is telling me to open my mouth and breathe in. But I know that's a death sentence.

I'm kicking hard for the surface, but my movements feel jerky. Chaotic. I try to count fin-kicks so I can keep my rhythm steady, but my heart is hammering inside my chest. I can't focus. I'm using up too much energy. Too much precious oxygen.

I'm not going to make it.

Oh God. Please don't let me—

Everything goes dim, and the next thing I know Dill has me. He's holding my head up out of the water, yelling at me to breathe.

I'm coughing and choking. Vomiting. Clutching and clawing at his chest like he's some kind of human life raft.

Dill isn't much taller than me. Maybe an inch or two at the most. I bet he doesn't weigh any more than I do, either. Yet he hauls me over to the side and up onto the rocks like I'm made of paper. Before I can even get my eyes to focus, Derry has me wrapped up in a towel. She's stroking my hair, telling me to look at her, while Dill pounds me on the back.

I'm still spitting up water.

Shaking.

"Where'd she go?" My throat burns something awful, and I barely manage to get the words out between coughing fits. The confused look in Derry's eyes and a quick glance toward the spring bottom tell me what I already know.

The girl didn't go anywhere. She was never there.

"You're okay," Derry reassures me. "We've got you."

I nod and lean forward to rest my head on my knees.

"Too deep." Dill isn't pounding me on the back anymore, but his words hit hard. "Too fuckin' deep, Tru."

He's right. Prolonged oxygen deprivation is dangerous. It can mess with your mind, cause hallucinations.

"Yeah" is all I can get out.

"This ain't the Olympics," Dill tells me. "There ain't no gold medals out here." Dill's voice is trembling, and that frightens me more than anything else. Dill never gets scared.

I look down at my left hand and see my broken, bloodied fingernails.

I shiver and lean deeper into Derry. She takes my hand and laces her fingers through mine.

Sometimes I wish she was my mom.

Or my big sister.

All of a sudden, I'm hit with that same feeling I had at the memorial yesterday. Someone I know is standing close by. Watching me. I can almost hear the sound of their breathing.

When I look around, I can't see anyone, so I relax against Derry again. I'm letting my imagination get the best of me.

I stay like that for a long time. Struggling to catch my breath. Trying to convince myself I'm wrong about what I think I saw under the water.

Who I think I saw.

Finally I glance at my watch. "Shit," I say. "I gotta get going. I'm supposed to be at the newspaper office by ten."

Derry helps me to my feet. She holds on to my elbow as I step back into my shorts. I slide my feet into my flip-flops and pull on my T-shirt.

"You sure you're okay to drive?" she asks, and I nod.

"Yeah. My head feels a lot clearer. Really."

"It's gonna hurt like a bitch later," Dill warns me, and I know he's right.

I let Dill and Derry steer me across the slippery rocks toward the safety gate. But I'm already thinking of my hallucination again.

It's her face I can't get out of my mind.

Because I'm pretty sure I just stared into the eyes of a dead girl.

THREE

BEFORE I EVEN make it into town, Dill's prediction has come true. My head does indeed hurt like a bitch.

It's a million degrees outside, but when I push open the door to the newspaper offices, it feels like it might snow any second. Jon Boy keeps the thermostat set on negative fifty. He says the cold keeps the Florida humidity down, and humidity is bad for old newspapers. I tell him that freezing to death is bad for humans, but he just shrugs and tells me to wear more clothes.

Jon Boy has been my next-door neighbor since I was born. He's a smart guy. Talented. I used to think he'd leave town eventually. Most of the smart people do. But the *Star* runs too deep in his blood for him to be happy anywhere else. Or at least that's what he always says.

His dad ran the paper when Jon Boy and his older brother, Reese, were growing up. When their father died, Reese took over as editor. Then, when Reese died in a boating accident not long after we lost Dani, it was Jon Boy's turn to carry on the family tradition.

When I walk in this morning, he's leaning on the counter staring at his laptop and nursing a (probably ice cold by now) cup of coffee. He doesn't say a word about me being fifteen minutes late.

He never does.

And I almost always am.

"Good news, Trulee Bear." He grins and offers me a strawberry donut. "I stopped at Wendell's Bakery on the way in this morning."

"Thanks," I say as I snag Jon Boy's offering, along with an old cardigan of Reese's that still hangs on a coatrack in the corner. His name tag is still pinned to the front. R WESTLEY, EDITOR, MOUNT ORANGE STAR. "You workin' on the article about the new fountain?"

"Yeah." Jon Boy is looking back down at his laptop screen. "Trying to edit the photos from yesterday so our great and glorious mayor looks a little less like a side of raw beef."

I laugh and start downstairs. "Good luck with that. I'm gonna finish reorganizing the nineties. Unless there's something else you need me to do."

I'm halfway to the basement before Jon Boy even thinks to answer me. "Nope. Not a thing. You just keep at it down there."

I hold the donut between my teeth and slip on the ratty gray sweater. It's damp and scratchy, and it makes my skin crawl in the same way walking through a spiderweb does. But it's better than freezing to death. I feel around on the wall for the switch, and when I find it, the basement fills with a flickering, buzzing yellow light.

The archives are a disaster. I started pretending to reorganize the 1990–1999 issues at the end of last summer, but I never got past 1992. I should try to get some actual work done today, but I have another project in mind first. I keep thinking about that girl—the hallucination—in the Well this morning. Every time I blink, I see her on the insides of my eyelids.

And I'm on a mission to prove myself wrong.

I drag a rickety chair over to one of the huge metal shelves against the back wall. There are two dusty boxes on the top shelf marked DO NOT THROW AWAY in big, bold letters. Jon Boy calls them the cold case files. The first one holds a bunch of articles and research about the Glades Reaper, Florida's most infamous serial killer. The second one is full of stuff about the Hidden Glen murders. And that's the box I'm after.

I pull it down, then slip off my flip-flops and settle on the floor to dig through the contents. Articles from other newspapers around the country. Photos Jon Boy took out at the campsite after the crime scene tape came down. Scribbled maps and scrawled interviews he did with friends of Celeste's and Bailey's.

Jon Boy would have been about my age at the time. The exact same age as Celeste and Bailey. Not editor of the *Star* yet. He was freshly graduated from high school, a small-town reporter working for his dad and trapped in his superstar older brother's shadow. But what happened out at the springs was big news—national news—and some nights, when he has a few beers in him, Jon Boy still talks about how cracking the case would've earned him a ticket straight to the big time. Some New York City newspaper. Or the *Chicago Tribune*. Or at least the *Tallahassee Democrat*.

But he never cracked it. Nobody did.

I look through the yellowing articles. Run my eyes over the words.

MURDER AT THE SPRINGS.

Local teens dead.

Multiple stab wounds.

Surprise attack.

Throat slit.

I already know all the information by heart. It's the photos of the girls that keep pulling me back. Bailey and Celeste captured in smudgy newspaper black and white. Those side-by-side senior pictures.

Bailey with her neat brown ponytail.

Celeste with her blond curls.

Those half hearts winking around their necks. Each a perfect mirror image of the other.

Best friends forever.

The girls in those photos had no idea how little time they had left.

I'm staring at Bailey when this overwhelming sense of loss washes over me, and I have the clearest feeling that something really beautiful was just about to happen. Like I was just at the edge of discovering the most incredible secret, but now it's been swept out to sea, and I'll never know it.

I shake that sorrow off and keep digging through the pile, but I don't know exactly what I'm looking for until I come across the big brown envelope at the bottom of the box.

I hold it in my hands. Feel the weight of it. The words CRIME SCENE PHOTOS are scrawled across the front in red ink. Jon Boy told me once that it's a collection of eight-by-ten black-and-white photos, copies of the ones taken by the crime lab investigators immediately after the murders were discovered. Before the bodies were removed by the coroner. I've never known how Jon Boy got hold of them. *A reporter never reveals his sources* is all he said when I asked. They were never published, of course, and there was never an opportunity for them to be used in any trial, so most folks have never seen them.

I've never seen them.

I've been tempted a few times, but I remember the warning Jon Boy gave me back when I first asked about that envelope. *Don't ever open it, Trulee Bear*, he told me. *Not ever. You can't unsee that stuff, and it changes you.*

But I'm not a little kid anymore, even if Jon Boy does still insist on calling me by the nickname he gave me when I was five. Besides, it won't be the first time I've seen a dead person. I saw Dani. Up close and personal. I glance back over my shoulder before I run my fingernail under the flap to break the seal. Then I let the photos slide into my lap.

The first one is of Celeste. She's half tangled in her sleeping bag. Blond curls splayed behind her in a matted mess. One muddy foot sticking out.

Empty eyes. Arms and legs bent at weird angles.

The tent is slashed to ribbons. So is the sleeping bag.

It takes me a few seconds to realize that the black stuff smeared everywhere in the photo is actually blood.

For just a second, I stop breathing. I run my fingers over Celeste's face. Even like this, she's still so beautiful.

She wouldn't want me to remember her like this. The thought materializes in my mind like a ghost. It comes from nowhere. *She was always so vain about her hair.*

The donut in my stomach sours, and I think I'm going to be sick. I shudder before I move on to the next photo.

Bailey.

My hands are shaking.

Here she is, in black and white. One last photo captured not long after her soul left her body.

She's floating on her back on the surface of Elijah's Well. This was before the safety fence went up. The water around her is black with blood so dark it looks like an oil slick, and her eyes are wide and staring.

I'm used to seeing her with a neat ponytail in the newspaper pictures, but in this photo, her long brown hair is loose. It drifts and floats around her head while her white nightgown swirls around her body like the petals of a water lily.

It wasn't a white dress.

It was a white nightgown.

Suddenly my head is spinning. I sit there, trying to breathe. It's her. The girl from the Well. The one who tried to pull me down to the bottom.

Suddenly I'm gasping for air. The scent of pine trees fills my nose. I manage to get to my feet, but instead of the cold tile floor under me, I feel the grit of sand. The crunch of leaves.

Pine needles.

A terrible crushing fear consumes me. I'm paralyzed by it. There's only one thought in my brain.

Run.

Run.

Run.

But I'm too confused and afraid to move.

My fingers search for a half-heart necklace that isn't hanging around my neck.

My lucky charm.

"Dammit, Tru." I jump when I hear Jon Boy's voice behind me. Photos and papers go everywhere. "I told you never to look at those."

"Yeah," I say. "I know, but—"

"But you don't listen. I know. Believe me." Jon Boy's voice is sharp and scolding. But there's something a little bit proud there, too. "You'd make a good reporter." He squats down to help me gather up the photos. "I should have fed all this stuff to the shredder years ago." He sighs and shakes his head. "But I couldn't." Jon Boy glances at the photos before he slides them back in the envelope. Then he takes a long look at me, and when he speaks again, his voice is gentle. "I don't blame you for being curious, Tru." He shrugs. "We all want to know what really happened out there."

I put the last of the papers in the box and Jon Boy sticks the manila envelope with the crime scene photos back inside. Then he tucks the collection into its spot on the top shelf before he leaves me standing there in that dusty basement and heads up the stairs. He's almost to the top when he turns back to look at me. "You okay?" he asks, and I nod. He doesn't look convinced, though. I see the way his eyebrows are all drawn together behind his glasses. "That's awful hard to see, Tru. Those photos. If you need to take—"

"I'm good," I tell him. "Promise."

Inside, I'm reeling.

I must have seen the crime scene photo of Bailey before. Otherwise, how could I have a hallucination that exactly matched it?

I spend the rest of the morning and the whole afternoon trying to sort out the mess that is 1993, but I don't make any real progress. I'm too distracted to keep the dates straight. I keep getting June and July mixed up.

My mind is constantly flickering back to Bailey. I keep feeling her cold grasp on my wrist.

That pit of fear in my stomach reminds me of the morning I found Dani. I remember seeing her lying in the ditch— strangely still—knowing she was dead but begging God to let me be wrong.

My eyes drift toward another stack of newspapers, and it would be so easy to go over there and find the one I'm thinking of. I have the exact date memorized. I could pull out the one with the headline just above the fold on the front page. LOCAL GIRL DEAD IN HIT-AND-RUN ACCIDENT. But I don't give in to that urge. I see Dani's face every time I close my eyes. I don't need to see it in black and white today. Or ever again.

I never look at the articles about Dani.

Ever.

Instead I turn to a happy memory. It's my secret trick to make myself feel better. Something I think about a lot when I'm sad. Or scared. Or anxious.

When that crushing guilt comes creeping in.

I'm leaning over Dani's shoulder. I can never see her, but I know it's her, because everything about her is familiar. Safe. She's sitting at a table and I'm watching her pencil move across the paper.

She's sketching a horse. Strong legs and a long, flowing mane braided with wildflowers. And he looks so real that I almost expect him to take off running and escape the page. The memory is hypnotic—the way her pencil moves across the paper—methodical and perfect and with just the lightest touch. Little pieces of that horse appearing as she works. It's magic and it calms me. Every time.

When I get off work at three o'clock, I head out to the springs. Normally, I'd be meeting East and Paz for a dive, but they're seeing a movie in Gainesville this afternoon. So I have some time to kill.

I didn't come out here to dive, anyway. I have something else in mind.

I make my way through the thick crowd and avoid the swarm of little kids flocking around the Dive Bar, jostling each other for Skittles and ice cream sandwiches.

I follow the boardwalk up the run to Elijah's Well, but I don't head into the fenced-off diving area. Instead, I hop off the wooden walkway and skirt around the outside perimeter. I stop at the edge of the trees and scan the shadows. I don't see anything moving. Not one single murder ghoul or rabid podcast fan. Not even an armadillo or one of the fat-ass raccoons that are always hanging around.

I unzip my backpack and pull out Bailey's half heart. I clutch it in my fist and feel the weight of it in my hand. The metal is warm against my skin. Almost electric. I take a deep breath and step into the dense scrub.

Immediately, the sounds of people down the main spring are muffled. The light filters through the trees and everything is bathed in a soft yellow glow. The air has shifted; it's thicker. And the whole world slows.

It's claustrophobic, the way the trees and vines and shrubs all press in on me. Tangled and overgrown. Like they're squeezing the breath out of my lungs.

That feeling doesn't freak me out. I'm used to working without oxygen.

I head deeper in, and I'm immediately battling the plants. Scrub holly snags at my shoelaces and Adam's needle rips at my T-shirt sleeves. It's like being grabbed by a hundred sharp little fingers.

The attack on Celeste and Bailey started at their campsite. Fifty yards back into the scrub. That's where Celeste died. Someone slashed through their tent and tore into her with a hunting knife. Stabbed her so many times and with such force that the knife tip broke off inside her body. She never had a chance to escape.

Bailey ran.

That's what the reports all say. She ran toward the water.

The killer caught her there, at the edge of the spring, though. He slit her throat before he tossed her body into the Well.

The best-friends locket burns in my palm, and I feel sick all of a sudden when I picture Bailey seventy feet below the surface of the spring. Grabbing at me. Trying to pull me down to the vent at the bottom.

My mind playing tricks on me, I remind myself.

A hallucination that happened to look exactly like a dead girl in a crime scene photo that I would have sworn I had never seen before.

I give my head a shake and keep walking, focusing on the act of putting one foot in front of the other, counting steps the way I count fin-kicks when I dive.

One—

Two—

Three—

Four.

My breath catches in my throat when I reach the sandy little clearing where the tent stood. My heart pounds and my stomach flutters. I shiver in the sticky heat. Because I feel it.

I always do in this place.

All the explosive energy from that night is trapped here somehow. It's like the terror and the desperation and the sheer will to live tangled in the brambles. Like the scrub canopy held that panic down and wouldn't let it dissipate. Even twenty years after the murders, there's still enough of that lingering here, soaked into the dirt like blood, to set my pulse racing.

I move around behind the clearing. Just to the east of where the tent would have been set up. I wonder if I'm standing where the killer stood. If he leaned against this same scrawny pine and watched Celeste and Bailey that night. Biding his time until they turned off the lantern. Waiting for the whispering and giggling coming from the tent to stop. He wouldn't have been far away, but it had stormed earlier, and there were thick clouds blocking out the moon on the night of the murders. They never would have seen him in the pitch dark.

If they'd listened carefully, though, they could have heard him breathing.

He was that close.

I always wonder if it was the rustle of footsteps on dead leaves that woke them up.

Or if they slept right up until the moment the knife sliced the tent wide open like the belly of a gutted fish.

I hear the lonesome call of a whip-poor-will. It's getting late. In the last few minutes, all the yellows have turned to blues. I should be heading home.

My skin prickles. Someone is behind me.

"Hey, Tru."

I whirl around, almost expecting to see Bailey standing there. White nightgown dripping. Blood pouring from the wound at her neck.

But it isn't her. It's a girl I don't recognize.

"Did I scare you?" she asks.

Her voice has a soft Southern lilt to it, the kind we don't really have in Florida.

Georgia maybe.

Or Tennessee.

"Not really," I manage to say. Even though that's a pretty obvious lie.

We're eyeing each other warily, almost like two different species meeting for the first time.

And, I mean, we might as well be two different species, honestly. A gopher tortoise and a sandhill crane. I'm powerful, but short. Muscled from years of diving. Blue-black eyes and stringy red hair that falls at my shoulders. A ratty pair of shorts and an even rattier old soccer T-shirt of East's. Grimy from digging around in the woods. Sweat running down my face.

This girl is perfect skin and long legs. Eyes like emeralds and coal-colored hair cropped in a trendy pixie style. Cutoff shorts and a sunflower-yellow bikini top.

She takes a few steps toward me, and it hits me how graceful she is. I always feel so clunky on land. In the water, it's different. I'm like a dolphin. But, on land, I don't have that kind of willowy grace. And I know it.

"I'm Rio," she says, and it strikes me as funny when she holds out her hand like we're two businessmen meeting for lunch down at the Kiwanis club. A nervous chuckle bubbles up in my throat, but when I feel her fingers in mine, I instantly relax. The warmth of her skin soothes my uneasiness. I glance down at our hands and we fit together perfectly.

"Like the city in Brazil?" I ask over the handshake. Her grip is strong. Confident.

She laughs. It's an easy sound. "Like the song. You know?" She sings a few bars for me. "'Her name is Rio and she dances on the sand . . .'"

"What are you doing wandering around back here?" I ask her, and she tilts her head to one side and wrinkles her nose in my direction.

"I could ask you the same question," she teases. When I don't respond to that, she narrows those bright green eyes at me. Then she grins. "The truth is, I was waiting for you."

FOUR

"WAITING FOR ME?" My brain is running through the list of things I should be saying while I'm standing there swatting away mosquitoes. Questions I should be asking. But the only thing I can get out is "Why?"

She shrugs and gives me a long look. Like she's sizing me up. I see her take note of my sweat-damp hair. The scabby bug bites on my arms. "I asked around about a dive partner. A couple of people told me you were the girl to see."

That sends a little zap of confidence through me.

"You're a free diver?" I ask, and she nods. It's my turn to look her up and down now. "Are you any good?"

She wrinkles up her nose again and I notice the little freckles scattered there. "I've never had to be pulled out of the water like a dead fish."

My face flushes as I remember Dill hauling me up onto the rocks this morning, pounding me on the back while I coughed and sputtered. I must have looked like a total amateur.

"You from around here?" I ask.

"Not really." She's studying me like a starfish she's dissecting in biology lab. I shift from foot to foot.

"So, is your family on vacation here or something?" I'm

suddenly feeling awkward. "Because if you're looking for Disney World, you're about a hundred and fifty miles off."

She gives me a funny look. "It's just me. No family."

"Oh," I say. I'm not sure what to follow that up with.

"I took off last week. Right after graduation. The day before my eighteenth birthday." She moves to lean against the trunk of a scraggly looking tree. "I figured it was time to do a little exploring."

"Where've you been staying?" There's only one motel around here, the Paradise Motor Court. It's a sagging collection of little cabins left over from the 1950s, before the interstate bypassed the town. To say it's sketchy would be an understatement.

Rio glances around the tiny clearing. "I've been camping back here."

My mouth falls open.

"You're staying back here?" I hear the way my voice sounds. Like I think she's lost her mind.

Rio runs her fingers through her short dark hair, and it falls right back into place. I'm half-hypnotized. She gives me a little smirk. "Is that a problem?"

"No," I tell her. "It's just—" I stop myself. If she's staying back here, I don't want to freak her out.

"It's just what?"

I shrug. "Snakes and stuff." I'm not lying about that. Coral snakes. Cottonmouths. Pygmy rattlers. Plus it's hot as hell. Even without a history of bloody knife murders, I wouldn't want to be sleeping rough in the scrub this time of year.

She laughs at me then. "Snakes." One raised eyebrow. "I'm not worried about snakes."

It's starting to get dark. Out here, the night always comes with a ferocious suddenness. All the blues are deep purple now. "But you better be gettin' home," she teases. "Before the snakes come out." That Southern accent of hers is floating on the thick air. It blends with the humming of the nighttime insects and the chirping of the frogs. Like it's part of the same summer symphony. "Come back tomorrow morning. If you wanna dive."

"Okay," I say, but she's already walking away from me. Back toward the edge of the clearing. Disappearing into the edges of the gathering dark like a spirit.

I stand there for a few seconds. Like maybe I imagined the whole encounter. But her voice floats back to me across the creeping black. "'Night, Trulee."

"'Night," I say to the nothingness. Then I turn to go.

I use my cell phone flashlight to make my way back to the boardwalk and on toward the parking area. My truck is the only one in the lot now, and it looks lonely sitting there by itself.

I climb in and feel around under the seat for my keys. I'm trying to figure out what I'm gonna tell Mom, because I know she'll be pissed that I'm late for dinner.

Outside the old Paradise Motor Court, the meth-heads are sitting in lawn chairs in the parking lot, watching the cars whiz past on the highway. They shout something as I blow by, so I give the truck a little gas. I hear the engine roar, and I feel it shudder underneath me. Rio's probably better off out at the springs, taking her chances with the pygmy rattlers and the cottonmouths.

When I get home, Mom has the table set for dinner, like she always does on the nights she's not out drinking. Even though it's just the two of us now. Two place settings at a table meant for four. Half a family. It's her one clinging, desperate attempt at normal, setting the table. Cloth napkins and everything.

She's sitting on the couch, still in her clothes from the office. A rumpled blazer is slung over the back of a chair and she's nursing a glass of whatever. Jack and cherry Coke, probably. It's her bedtime go-to. An infomercial flickers across the television screen with no sound.

"I made spaghetti," she tells me. "It's on the stove."

"I'm not hungry yet," I say, on my way up the stairs, and I hear her sigh long and deep. The clinking of ice cubes in her glass.

"Trulee. Where've you been?" she shouts.

"With East," I tell her, because I figure that might get her off my back. I'm pretty sure she started planning our wedding when we were in third grade. Now she's over the moon because we're going to FSU together in the fall.

Only one of us never sent in the application.

"You can take the time to sit down and eat," she calls out. "I took the time to make dinner."

"I will," I promise. "I'm gonna take a shower first."

I make it to my room and close the door before she can say anything else.

I take my time getting cleaned up, and I'm relieved that Mom's already gone to bed by the time I head back downstairs to warm up my dinner. She's left my plate on the table, so I take it to the stove and scoop up the cold spaghetti.

I pop it in the microwave, then carry my dinner outside to sit on the front steps. As soon as I open the door, the sudden heat hits me in the face like I'm walking into a kitchen sponge—solid and wet at the same time. But sometimes being in the house is suffocating. It's crammed too full of old stuff. Knickknacks and memories. Mom's empty glasses and stacks of faded real estate magazines. That big portrait of me and Dani on the wall over the television. It gives me the same feeling as the newspaper office, so full of Jon Boy's dead brother, Reese, after all these years.

His coffee mug in the breakroom cabinet.

His awards on the wall.

That ratty sweater with his name tag still hanging on the coatrack.

Most nights, I'd rather sit outside and battle the heat and the bugs. At least I can breathe out here.

I let my eyes travel across the grass. Or what passes for grass in our yard. It's mostly stickers and sand with patchy bits of green. More weeds than lawn. If Jon Boy didn't help us out by mowing it every so often, it'd be grown all wild and tangled, just like the scrub.

I look up at the sliver of a moon hanging low in the sky over the house just across the road. The blinds are open and I can see Mr. and Mrs. Binger sitting in their matching recliners watching TV.

I wish I'd grabbed a drink. Some iced tea to wash the spaghetti down with.

I turn to the west of us and take in Jon Boy's manatee-shaped mailbox. The rusting golf cart parked in his carport, even though he doesn't play golf. Reese did. And their dad. The two of them used to organize a big tournament every year for the Florida Press Association.

On the other side of us, in a sagging trailer my mother sold them, are the Keppers. Their front porch is strung up with Christmas lights, just to add that festive touch of year-round cheer.

I stare at the blinking red-and-green bulbs, because I don't want to look out past our driveway to the drainage ditch that runs along the side of the road. To the place I found Dani. Wet with early morning dew. Bits of fresh-clipped grass in her hair. Legs twisted and eyes open.

I manage to choke down one more bite of spaghetti before I give up and head inside. Back in the kitchen, I notice a letter from FSU lying on the counter. It probably starts the way the last five have. *We noticed you never completed your application for admission . . .* I take it and toss it into the trash, then scrape the rest of my spaghetti on top of the envelope. I gather a few empty glasses and put them in the sink, then turn off all the lights and head up to bed.

My head is heavy, and my eyelids flutter closed, but sleep doesn't find me. I'm thinking about Bailey and Celeste.

And Rio.

And always, always Dani.

I focus on that drawing of the horse again. Dani's hand moving across the page. Taking her time with each tiny flower braided into his mane. Petal by petal. And I let that memory work its magic until my sister finally lulls me to sleep.

The next day, I wake up extra early because, if I'm gonna dive with Rio, I want to do it before the hordes and masses descend on the springs midmorning. Besides, I promised Jon Boy I'd be on time today. He wants me to help him repaint the front counter at the newspaper office.

East works mornings at the Sno Shack, and Mom is still asleep. I don't have to answer any questions about why I'm up at the crack of dawn for the second time in two days, which is definitely out of character for me.

The parking lot is empty when I make it out to Hidden Glen, so I take a second to pause at the split rail fence to take it all in. The emerald-green lawn sloping down toward the main swimming area. The almost impossible blueness of the water. Huge old live oaks dripping with Spanish moss. The dark jungle of palmettos and giant ferns, like something out of a dinosaur movie. Hundreds of ghostly white spider lilies blooming along the edges of the spring run.

When most people think of Florida, they think of ocean waves. Or cartoon mice. But this is my Florida.

I follow the boardwalk back toward Elijah's Well, and Rio is already there, waiting for me. She's stretched out on one of the big rocks, and I think maybe she's asleep, but when I lift the safety latch and push open the gate, she sits up to look at me. One hand shielding her eyes from the sun. We stare at each other for a few seconds.

"I didn't know if you'd show," she says.

"I didn't know if you'd be here," I tell her. But that's a lie. I knew she would be.

I'm pretty sure she knew I'd come, too.

I pull off my T-shirt and slip out of my shorts. Rio's already shed her clothes. She's got on a bright turquoise bikini top and boy shorts that almost match the blue of the water. I watch her dig a mask and fins out of her bag.

"You wanna go first?" I ask, but she shakes her head.

"Nah. It's your home turf. Besides." There's that teasing sound in her voice again. "I wanna see if you're as good as I've heard."

I push the memory of Bailey—what happened all those feet below the surface—out of my mind. I can't afford to get rattled right before I hit the water. And there is no way I'm going to admit I'm afraid. Not of a figment of my imagination.

Not to some stranger I just met.

I pull on my fins and my mask, then stand at the edge of the Well and look down into the bottomless blue to start my breathe-up routine, beginning with a body scan to focus on re-laxation. I imagine a warm, pulsing ball of white light traveling up my body. It starts at my toes and works its way toward my head, and every muscle along the way feels the warmth of that ball of light and relaxes.

Then I work on my breathing. Dill taught me to always start with some deep belly breaths to lower my heart rate and blood pressure.

Usually, once my bones feel like they're made of eelgrass, I know I'm ready to take my final breath and dive. But this morning, nothing is working for me. I keep thinking about Bailey.

I can feel Rio's eyes on me. So I turn to something I know will work. My fail-safe relaxation technique.

Dani and the horse.

I let that memory wash over me until I'm wrapped in a blanket of calm.

There's nothing but peace.

My heart rate slows.

My breathing evens out.

I'm ready to dive.

Once I'm in the water, instinct takes over and the fear vanishes.

It's a good run. Not my best. But respectable. When I pull myself back up on the rocks next to Rio, she grins at me and nods. "Not bad" is all she says.

When it's her turn to go below, Rio stands motionless in the sun. Her skin glows in the morning light like she's been lit on fire. I watch her breathe. Deep and slow. Until she finds her rhythm. My lungs sync with hers. In and out.

She raises one long arm in a stretch. Then the other. Her back arches—her neck rolls—in a kind of minimalist ballet.

Reach. Breathe. Stretch. Release.

It's such an intimate process for a stranger to witness, and I feel a little like a Peeping Tom.

She slips into the Well.

I stand at the edge and watch as Rio cuts through the water like some kind of mermaid. That grace she has on land is multiplied by a million beneath the surface. She barely moves a muscle as she slides through the blue. I admire the way she changes direction with the slightest twitch of her fins. That economy of movement is what marks a really good diver. You save so much energy that way.

Rio isn't just graceful. She gets deep, too. I watch her swim down and down and down. She has to be eighty feet below, at least.

One minute passes.

Two. Then three.

Four.

Finally she starts her ascent.

Her eyes flash when she breaks the surface and spring water slides down her cheeks and her neck. She's radiant. *I never get tired of seeing her like this.* I know we just met, so that thought is completely ridiculous, but there's something about her face. Those eyes maybe.

"Four minutes, thirty-seven seconds," I tell her. I wonder if she can tell by my voice how impressed I am.

"Not my best," she tells me, and that makes me smile.

If she can do better, I'd like to see it. And I don't mean that in a sarcastic way.

The two of us watch each other for a few seconds. Her bobbing in the water. Me standing at the edge, shielding my eyes from the glare.

She climbs onto the rocks to join me. She's still grinning. All lit up. High from the dive.

"Where'd you learn to dive like that?" I ask her.

"Wakulla Springs," she tells me. "Up near Tallahassee. Deepest freshwater spring in the world. One hundred eighty-five feet to the vent. Now, that's something. And it's dark. Really dark." Rio shivers like she relishes that dark with every inch of her soul. "You just go down and down and down and you never even get to see the bottom. It's like being in outer space." She dries off her mask and tucks it back in her bag. "When I was a kid, I used to hang out there watching the divers every weekend. I kind of picked it up." She turns to look at me. "You ever get to dive there?"

"Yeah," I say. "A couple times." East drove me and Dill up there once or twice. The three of us all crammed shoulder to shoulder on the bench seat of his old pickup.

Rio gives me a funny look. "Maybe we've seen each other before."

"Yeah," I say. "You're really good."

"Not as good as I'd like to be." She pulls her knees up to her chest and hugs them tight. She's looking out at the water now. "There are these people called the Bajau. Somewhere in Malaysia. Nomad fishermen. The world's best free divers. They can stay down twenty minutes, some of them, on a single breath. Two hundred feet or more down." I'm still feeling the euphoria of my dive, so I relax into the warmth of the day. The sun is bright on my shoulders, and Rio's voice washes over me like cool water. I think that's what seems so familiar about her. The sound of her voice. Or maybe the rhythm of her words. "Their bodies, after all these generations, they've evolved for that. Larger spleens. More flexible chest muscles. And their minds, they're different, too. Calmer. Without any words for fear. Or panic. They're just part of the sea, you know." She sighs. "That's what it is to be really good."

I try to imagine that. What it must feel like to experience that kind of deep. Dill's always telling me how people evolved from sea creatures. It's weird to think about evolving back into them.

Rio reaches up to brush the hair away from her eyes. "Did you know that human beings are sixty percent water?" she asks me. Her voice is low and hushed. Reverent, like we're whispering in church. I lean in closer, just to hear her. "When you think about it, each one of us is our own little ocean." She pauses for a moment, and I can see her thinking. "Maybe that's why we need the deep. Why it tugs on us like it does."

It knocks the wind out of me when she says that, because that's exactly what it's always felt like to me. A relentless tugging. Like Hidden Glen has a rope tied tight around my soul, and someone on the other end is always pulling with everything they have.

I've never heard anyone else use exactly those words to describe it.

Not even Dill.

Other people are starting to arrive now. A handful of guys from the local dive club are prepping on the other side of the Well. Showing off. A little crowd has gathered to watch. Their wives and girlfriends mostly. Everyone is laughing and carrying on. It's gonna be a busy day at Hidden Glen.

I want the quiet back, that early morning magic. Some more time to sit and talk before the heat of the day gets to be too much. Beads of sweat are already gathering on my forehead. Prickling at the backs of my knees. The damp breeze that slips between me and Rio like a whisper does absolutely nothing to cool us off.

We pull on our clothes and gather up our things. Then we follow the boardwalk back toward the main spring. Along the way, we talk a little more about diving. Other favorite spots. How long we've been doing it. The way guys sometimes write us off, until they see what we're capable of. She tells me she was born in Nashville, Tennessee. That's where she lived as a little girl, which explains that soft musical accent, but she mostly grew up in Crawfordville, Florida. Just outside Tallahassee. When I ask about her family, though, she dances around the question.

She doesn't ask about mine.

Once we reach the big swimming area, we pause to stare down into the blue together. Below us, bubbles stream from a deep fissure in the rocks.

"There's a party tonight," I tell her. "Our friends have a campsite. Back in the scrub." I point. "Over that way." I don't know what else to say, but for some reason, I'm already wanting more time to talk to Rio.

She tosses her hair out of her face and narrows her eyes at me. One corner of her mouth twitches into the beginnings of a grin. "Are you just sharing that information?" she asks. "Or is that supposed to be an invitation?"

"It's an invitation," I admit. "It just wasn't a very good one."

Rio laughs at that. "I'll meet you in the parking lot," she says, and I nod.

"Cool." I nod again and shove my hands into the pockets of my shorts. "About nine o'clock." We both stand there staring down at the bubbles.

"Think of all that water," Rio finally says. "Blows your mind, doesn't it?"

"Hidden Glen's a first-magnitude spring," I tell her. "That's over one hundred cubic feet of water per second coming up through the main vent. From here it flows down the spring run and out into the river. Then on to the ocean."

Rio turns to look at me. Her face is flushed from the heat and I see the ghost of a smile on her lips.

"But it starts right here," she says.

"Yeah." I nod. "This is where it begins."

FIVE

THE TRUCK HANDLE burns my palm when I reach for it, and the inside of the cab is hot enough to melt my teeth. I should've left the windows cracked.

The whole drive into town, I'm thinking about diving with Rio.

It was so different from diving with East, or even with Dill. With East, I'm always the one wanting to go deeper. To take it further. And no matter how good I get, Dill will never really consider me an equal partner. He'll always be the teacher. The mentor. I'll always be the protégé.

But Rio and I are a good match.

I pull into a parking spot directly in front of the *Star*. Inside, Jon Boy is putting down painter's plastic to cover the old wood floors. He looks up and waves me in. I brace myself before I push open the door, because I know it'll be like walking into the Arctic.

"Goddamn," I mutter. "Aren't you worried about the paint freezing solid?"

"Trulee Bear," Jon Boy says. "Cold is good for the soul."

He points me toward a bucket of bright white paint, then hands me a screwdriver and tells me to pop the lid off and pour it into a tray. Once I've gotten that done, we start rolling it onto the old counter, an olive-green monstrosity that stretches across the whole width of the front office. It takes me less than two minutes to realize it's gonna take about a million coats to hide that ugly green color and all the decades' worth of grime that keep bleeding through. I sigh and pour more paint into the tray.

"How's your mama doin'?" Jon Boy asks. He's bent over the far side of the counter, and somehow, his old blue dress shirt is already covered in white splatters.

I shrug. "Not too bad." I run the roller through the tray again. "I haven't had to go and pick her up in a week or so."

He nods. "Yeah. Me either."

All in all, that's a pretty good sign. When my mother gets a little too far gone out at the Wild Clover, they call me or Jon Boy to haul her outta there.

"Maybe things are getting better," I say.

"Maybe," Jon Boy says, and he switches on the radio. We sing along to the oldies station, and Jon Boy is off-key. I don't mind, until my stomach starts to grumble. "It's almost noon," I finally say. "We gonna stop for lunch soon? I'm starving."

"Crap." Jon Boy glances at his watch and sets his paint roller in the tray. "Is it that late already? I forgot there's a damn podcaster stopping by today." He reaches up to adjust his glasses and smears paint across his cheek. "Dammit," he mutters. I hand him a paper towel and he swipes at the white streak on his face. "She's probably gonna be here any second."

This happens every year around this time. When we get close to the anniversary date, someone comes poking around asking about the Hidden Glen murders. Usually some true-crime podcaster wanting to see that box of research tucked away in the basement.

Jon Boy stands up to go wash his hands, but his foot gets caught in the plastic and he knocks over the paint can.

"Shit!" we both say, in perfect unison, as a river of white makes its way toward the wood floor. I jump up and tell Jon Boy I'll run and get some more paper towels. I'm on my way downstairs when I hear the little bell over the front door jingle.

"Come on in," Jon Boy says. "You must be Lisa. Sorry about the mess." I hear a muffled reply, but I can't really hear anything else until I start back up the stairs, paper towels in hand.

"Just a quick peek," a female voice is saying, and the slow Southern accent is dripping with Tennessee honey. Rolled in sugar. "Then I'll get out of your hair. Cross my heart."

I hit the top of the stairs and look across the office to catch a glimpse of short hair, dark as coal.

Rio stands across from Jon Boy, batting her long eyelashes and leaning casually against the still-unpainted half of the counter. She blinks when she sees me, but other than that, she doesn't react.

I freeze, though. Rio's got her eyes turned toward Jon Boy again. She looks so different from just a few hours ago. Older. More sophisticated. She's wearing makeup. A pair of black shorts and a white summer sweater.

Jon Boy turns to me. "Trulee," he says, "this is Lisa Brown. Ms. Brown, this is my assistant, Trulee. She'll show you down to the archives." He gestures around to the paint disaster. The big puddle pooling on the plastic. The white footprints where he's tracked it onto the wood. "I'm gonna see if I can get this mess cleaned up."

"That's fabulous," Rio coos. She bats her eyes again. First at Jon Boy. Then at me.

Jon Boy nods and turns back to give me a frazzled little smile. "Show her the Hidden Glen research, Tru. You know where the files are."

"Sure," I say. Even though we both know damn well there are no "files." There's only that sad, dusty box stuffed with scraps and bits. Pieces of an investigation that never quite came together.

Rio crosses around behind the long counter and Jon Boy goes back to dealing with the oozing white paint.

When we start down the steps to the basement, Rio beams at me. "Nice to meet you, Trulee," she says, loud enough for Jon Boy to hear. "So grateful for your help."

"Nice to meet you, Ms. Brown," I say back.

When I flip on the buzzing overhead light, Rio's eyes sparkle in the flickering yellow glow.

"What the fuck is going on?" I ask her. My voice is a whisper now.

Rio glances back toward the stairs. "I didn't know you worked here. I swear."

"Okay . . ." I still feel like I'm about a hundred steps behind in whatever game we're playing. "But what are you doing here?" A sudden anger bubbles up inside me. It lodges in my chest and simmers there, like when I saw those murder tourists flocking around Celeste's grave. I take a step back from Rio. "Are you really a true-crime podcaster?"

"No way." She shakes her head. "I just wanted to see the evidence." Rio sighs then. It's a low, breathy sound that floats around us like fog rising up in the damp basement. "I have a lot of questions. About Celeste and Bailey."

The way she says their first names strikes a chord somewhere in my chest. It vibrates against my ribs and reverberates around my heart.

She says their names like they're friends of hers.

"How do you even know about them?" I ask. The basement is freezing. Dripping and musty. But the air suddenly shifts with a kind of electricity. The hair on my arms stands up, and a realization arcs and tingles in the back of my brain. This is what feels familiar about Rio. It isn't her eyes. Or the sound of her voice. It's a feeling. The way everything is more exciting when she's around. The way I want to know all her secrets and, even weirder, the way I want her to know all mine.

Even though we just met.

"I saw something about it on TV when I was a kid. One of those true-crime shows." She reaches up to brush her bangs out of her eyes. "I guess it got under my skin."

"Oh," I say. I want to tell her that I get that. That sometimes it seems like Bailey and Celeste are so deep under my skin that they've become an actual part of me.

I don't because she's staring at me. Waiting. Impatient. "So," she says. "Where's the file?"

I lead her over to the shelf at the back of the basement and point up at the moldy cardboard box.

"It's not so much a file," I warn her, "as it is a mess."

Rio stretches up on her toes. Her legs are so much longer than mine. She has no trouble grabbing the box and setting it on the floor.

"Holy shit," she whispers as we both stand there staring at the box between our feet. "I've been wanting to get a look at this stuff for years." The two of us drop down to sit cross-legged on the floor and Rio holds her breath as she lifts the lid off. "I've had so many theories," she says, and her voice has that same hushed and reverent sound as when she talked about diving out at the springs. Like maybe this is another of her churches. "When I was a kid, I actually thought maybe one of my foster dads was the killer."

"Seriously?" It's the first hint she's given me about her life.

"Yeah. This guy, David." She shudders. Chews on her lip. "I know it sounds wild. But he was such an ass. Rattlesnake-mean. I knew he liked to camp. Hunt and fish. Stuff like that. He would've been about the right age . . ." She trails off. Still staring at the box.

"Wow," I say. I can't think of anything else.

"It wasn't him." She raises her eyes to meet mine. "Turns out he'd been locked up when the murders happened." She blows out a long puff of air. "They should have kept him in there. Thrown away the key when they had the chance."

She reaches for the battered spiral notebook crammed full of Jon Boy's quick sketches and scrawled thoughts. Crazy theories that never held water. List of possible other suspects that didn't pan out. Her face lights up when she realizes what it is. "This," she tells me. "This is what I've always wanted to see."

"How'd you even know it existed?"

She raises an eyebrow at me and one corner of her mouth twitches up. "Your friend up there is active in a couple of internet sleuth groups. He likes to brag about all the research he has into the case."

"Really?" That shocks me. I've never heard Jon Boy brag about anything, and he never talks to me about the Hidden Glen case unless I'm pestering him about it. I guess everyone has some kind of secret life.

Rio flips open the notebook. "He's super closemouthed about what he has, at least online, so I figured I'd come see for myself." She's flipping through the pages of tiny handwriting. "It's so wild that it's coming up on twenty years, and it's still unsolved."

"The anniversary is in less than two weeks," I tell her, and she nods.

"June ninth. That's why I decided to go ahead and come now. I mean, I've been wanting to come down this way forever. But I really wanted to be here for the anniversary." She pauses and I see her weighing the notebook in her hands. Feeling the heft of all that useless information. "Twenty years. That's a long time." She looks up and studies my face. "A lifetime for you and me. More than a lifetime."

"I thought you came here to dive Hidden Glen," I say, and she stares at me. There's a little almost-smirk on her face.

I know that look.

"People are allowed to want more than one thing, Tru. Anybody ever tell you that?"

It's quiet for a few minutes while Rio looks through the notebook and nibbles on her bottom lip. She mumbles to herself every so often.

"Holy shit."

"Jesus."

Finally she reaches up to push those stubborn bangs out of her face, then asks me, "Do you have a phone? I wanna take some pics of this stuff."

"Sure." I wonder why she doesn't have one, but I hand over my phone, and she snaps photo after photo of the notebook and the typed-up interview notes. The sketches. All of it.

"Have you read all this?" she asks me, and I nod.

"I have most of it memorized," I tell her. "I can even tell you the dates he talked to different people." She looks up at me with those glowing green eyes. In the dim basement, it's like seeing the shine of some nocturnal animal.

"This interview with Celeste's boyfriend is crazy," she says. She's staring at Jon Boy's notes again.

"Knox." I nod again. "Yeah."

"He comes off as super jealous. Like, possessive. It's kind of unhinged. And he's your mayor now. Right? I read that online somewhere."

"Yeah." Rio is staring at me. "Plus he's my boyfriend's uncle."

"No shit." Rio glances at me. "It's wild how tangled up things get in these tiny towns."

She's right about that. In Mount Orange, all our stories are knotted like mangrove roots.

Rio reaches into the box and pulls out another stack of

papers. Diagrams and drawings of the campsite. She's staring at Jon Boy's sketches of the little clearing. The location of the tent is marked with a red X.

The color of blood.

"That's why you've been hanging around back there," I say. "Why you picked that spot to camp." Rio reaches up to play with a short piece of hair that's curling at the back of her neck.

"I needed to be there," she tells me. "To, I don't know. Feel the energy or whatever." She gives her head a shake. "I know that sounds strange. I just—"

"It doesn't." I reach out and take the sketch from Rio's hands. That blood-red X seems to glow against the white of the paper. "It doesn't sound strange at all."

"Plus I did really want to dive the Well." She gives me a little shrug. "Then I saw you, and . . ." There's a pause and she shifts her attention to the box.

"And what?"

"And I knew we needed to dive it together."

Rio's holding the manila envelope of crime scene photos now. She starts to undo the flap, but I reach out and put a hand on her wrist.

"Don't," I tell her. "You don't wanna see those."

Rio hesitates.

"Trulee!" Jon Boy is shouting at me from up above. "Everything okay down there?"

I get up and move to the bottom of the stairs so I don't have to shout back. "Yeah. All fine. I think we're almost finished."

"I'm good, actually." I turn back to look at Rio and she's

sliding the box back onto the top shelf. Then she adds a little louder, for Jon Boy, "I think I have everything I need."

I let Rio go up the stairs first, then flip off the light and follow her up. She tells Jon Boy thank you. That she'll let him know when the podcast posts.

He nods and tells her he'll look forward to it.

"Thanks for your help," Rio says to me. "What did you say your name was again?"

"Tru," I tell her, and I try not to smile.

"Well, Tru," she says with bright eyes. "Maybe I'll see you around."

When Rio leaves, Jon Boy starts rolling up the plastic sheeting. "They always think they're gonna solve it." He shakes his head and looks down at his paint-covered shirt. "But they won't."

After that, he makes some excuse about needing to check his email, then disappears into his office and I'm left to clean up the rest of the paint mess.

When I finally leave the *Mount Orange Star*, it's almost two o'clock. I push open the door and run straight into Knox. Our noble mayor. The city offices are right next door to the newspaper, and Knox spends most of his time standing outside smoking and looking over Main Street with an expression that makes it clear he considers himself more of a king than an elected official.

"Watch it there, Trulee girl." Knox's smile is broad, and he takes one last long drag off his cigarette before he drops it on the sidewalk and grinds it out with the toe of his boot. He winks at me before straightening up his stupid cowboy hat. When Knox got himself elected mayor a few years back, he traded in his FSU Seminoles ballcap and started wearing the Stetson instead. I figure he thinks it makes him look like a Wild West sheriff. "Boss man in this afternoon?" he asks me.

"Yeah," I mumble.

Knox nods. Then he pushes open the door to the *Star* offices before he turns back to look at me. "You keepin' that nephew of mine out of trouble?" He follows the question with a wink that makes my skin crawl.

"Doin' my best," I tell him, and I escape to my truck before he can say anything else creepy.

After I leave the *Star*, I swing by the Sno Shack to pick up East. He's grinning when he climbs into my truck. His arms go around me, and he feels like home. I breathe him in, and when he kisses me, his lips taste sweet. Like strawberry snow cone syrup.

We pick up Paz at his house, then the three of us head to the Dairy Barn for fries and shakes. East and I slide into one side of a peeling red booth, and his arm snakes around my shoulders. I nuzzle into him, and he plants a kiss on my neck.

Paz is leaning across the table with a big shit-eating grin on his face. "Heard we're having a little get-together out at the homestead this evening. I already talked Mannie into hitting the liquor store for the five of us."

Mannie is Paz's oldest brother, and he's been buying us cheap beer since we were in eighth grade. His mom would murder him twice and bury him in the backyard if she ever found out.

"The six of us," I tell them, and Paz and East both stare at me, because it's always just Dill, Derry, Paz, East, and me. "I met this girl out at the springs." I snag a fry off the huge pile and nibble on the end. "She's a free diver. From up near Tallahassee." That gets their attention. "We did a dive run together this morning." I reach for the crusty ketchup bottle. Squirt some onto the plate. "She's really good."

"Huh." East is sucking back the last of his chocolate shake. "That's cool."

"I think she's kind of on her own," I tell them. "So I invited her to the party tonight."

"If she's cute," Paz demands, "put in a good word for me." He drags a fry through the ketchup and stuffs it in his mouth. "Unless she's annoying or something."

"No," I tell him. "She's awesome, actually. We get along." I reach for my shake. Chew on the straw. "Or we will. I think."

East smiles and tucks a strand of red hair behind my ear. "You get along with everybody, Tru."

He's mostly right. It's really simple to get along with people. As long as you follow their rules. Only show them the easy parts of you. The parts they want to see.

The three of us spend the rest of the long afternoon hanging around East's house. When Paz gets up to make popcorn, East pushes me down into the soft couch and kisses me until my lips are bruised. "I love you, truly. Truly, dear." That song, plus his hot breath in my ear, makes me shiver.

"I love you, too," I whisper against the skin of his neck. I kiss him back. Just as hard. His proximity anchors me, makes everything more normal.

Paz comes back with the popcorn, and we all settle in on the couch for another bad horror flick. Something about zombies. Paz and East keep a running commentary that makes me giggle, and East won't stop sneaking kisses. It's like any other long summer afternoon the three of us have spent together.

Familiar.

Safe.

Easy.

Except I keep glancing at the clock. Darkness is creeping closer and closer.

And I can't stop thinking about Rio.

SIX

WHEN WE SHOW up at Hidden Glen that night, Rio is perched on the split rail fence in the parking lot. She's swimming in moonlight and I hear Paz suck in his breath when he catches sight of her. "Holy shit." He hands me the cupcakes his mom sent for the celebration. "*That's* the new girl?" he whispers to me as he and East are grabbing the beer out of the back of my truck. "I was not properly prepared, Tru."

I don't blame Paz for staring. Rio's changed again since her Lisa Brown appearance at the *Star*. She's wearing tiny cutoff shorts and a seashell-colored bikini top, and she has some yellow wildflowers tucked into her hair. She looks like a princess—a wild and free, Florida-summer kind of princess. My heart skips a beat, and that strange tickle is back. Like fingertips brushing my skin. Or the brush of eyelashes just before a kiss.

I look down at my own outfit. White shorts and a navy-blue tank top. An old plaid shirt of East's tied around my waist. It's a look he loves on me, but I suddenly feel like I should have tried a little harder.

I handle the introductions, and Paz manages to get control of himself long enough to spit out a couple of funny lines. Rio laughs and he absolutely lights up.

"You ready to party Hidden Glen–style?" East asks her, and she looks at me with that little smirk pulling at her lips.

"I'm ready for anything."

The four of us make our way back to Dill and Derry's campsite. It's a collection of leaning tents and improvised shanties they call "the homestead." No running water. No electricity. An outhouse Dill dug and an ancient camp stove salvaged from the dump.

Dill and Derry were "off the grid" before it was cool. The forest service used to run them out every so often, but they always came back, and now they pretty much leave them be. East says it's because they keep the forest service guys supplied with weed, which everyone knows they're growing back there. I figure it's because they aren't hurting anyone. Besides, everybody loves them. They're local legends. The unofficial ambassadors for Hidden Glen Springs.

They have a fire going and some overturned five-gallon buckets that double as camp chairs have been pulled up in a circle around the flames.

"Hey, hey!" Dill says when he sees us, and he raises the joint he's holding in a kind of Hidden Glen salute. Hand grown. Hand rolled. I think Dill loves the ritual of it almost more than he loves the high. I know he used to smoke cigarettes a long time ago. Before he started to dive. He gave it up so he could get deeper. "Check it out, Derry!" He whistles a few bars of "Pomp and Circumstance." "The graduates have arrived!" Then he notices Rio. "Who's this? New friend?" Rio's smirk spreads into a genuine grin, because Dill is impossible to resist when he's at his most charming.

"My name's Rio," she tells him.

"Cool name," he says. "You visiting from somewhere?"

"Not really," she says, and Dill raises his eyebrows at her. Rio doesn't seem bothered.

"Rio's a free diver," I tell Dill. "She's really good." He practically levitates off the ground at that bit of news.

"No shit!" He looks from Rio to me. "Why haven't I met this mystery girl before?"

"I haven't been around long." Rio turns to look at me. "Tru and I just met."

"Well then you've already met the best diver out here," Dill says. "Welcome to Hidden Glen Springs, New Girl." He gives Rio a wink. "I'll be looking forward to seeing what you can do." He throws an arm around my shoulders. "Any friend of Tru's is a friend of mine."

Derry gives me a big hug and I hand her a few things I scavenged from home. Some chips and a bag of marshmallows. A little bit of beef jerky and a few cans of tomato soup. Three tins of Spam that have been sitting in our pantry since before Dad left, probably. I know she and Dill survive on almost nothing out here. Picnickers will slip them leftover sandwiches or hot dogs occasionally. Sometimes Dill does odd jobs around town for a little cash, and Derry's super creative. She makes jewelry out of Mountain Dew cans she digs out of the recycling barrels. Every once in a while, she'll sell a tiny ring or an ankle bracelet to one of the out-of-towners for a couple of bucks. She even writes poems on demand. Busy days, she'll set up shop at the main spring with a rickety card table and an old-fashioned typewriter that Dill got her their first Christmas together, more than thirty years ago. It was probably fifty years old already when he bought it secondhand, but it works. For a couple of bucks, Derry will use it to knock out an original poem about anything you want. Your boyfriend. Your kids. The sunshine. The state of politics. Whatever.

I'm sure they sell some weed, too. Although most of what they grow in their tiny patch seems to be reserved for personal consumption.

Paz is handing out beer to everyone now. He makes a big show of wiping Rio's off on his T-shirt before he pops it open and hands it to her. They're standing together under the glow of some little battery-powered Christmas lights that Derry strung up between two palm trees. Paz says something I don't catch, and Rio throws her head back and laughs.

Jealousy bites at me like a little red ant, and I wish I was in on the joke.

Derry is sitting on Dill's lap. They're sharing some of the beef jerky I brought, and they both look so happy. So in love—completely content with nothing but each other—even after all these years.

East comes up behind me. His arms go around my waist and I lean back to relax against his chest. I tell myself to breathe.

The fire crackles and pops and everyone moves to gather

around it, even though we're already sweating. We watch the dancing flames send sparks into the night sky while we all finish our first beers and start on a second round. Dill passes the joint.

"So you're a diver, too, huh?" Derry is still sitting on Dill's lap, but she's focused on Rio now.

"Yeah," Rio tells her. "Been diving up at Wakulla Springs since I was a kid."

"Tru says she's really good," Paz offers. He scoots his seat a little closer to Rio's, but she doesn't notice.

"Doesn't it scare you?" Derry asks. She has one arm slung around Dill's shoulder and he's got one hand snaked up the back of her shirt.

"It did at first," Rio admits. "But once you let go of the fear, it's the best feeling in the world. Nothing holding you up. And nothing holding you down."

"Nothing holding you up," Derry repeats with a shiver.

"But nothing holding you down," Rio adds.

We all raise our beers in a little toast to that. Wipe the sweat from our foreheads.

"It scares me," Derry admits.

"It's okay to be scared if you're watching," Paz tells her. "Just not when you're diving."

"You can't take fear into the water," Dill says. He's finishing off what's left of the joint. "Gotta let it go."

"I'll never understand it," Derry says, and she runs her fingers through Dill's wild, tangled curls. "That obsession you have."

"It's like flying," Paz tells her. "You gotta try it for yourself sometime, Derry."

"'Once you have tasted flight,'" Rio says, "'you will forever walk the earth with your eyes turned skyward—'" She's looking at me across the fire now. I see the green of her eyes flashing between the flames. "'For there you have been, and there you will always long to return.'"

A longing wells up thick and heavy inside me. It fills up my chest cavity with what feels like mud and makes it hard to breathe.

All I want in the world is to fly.

East gets up to get us two more beers. This is my third, I think. They're warm now. But it doesn't really matter. "Who said that?" he asks when he comes back to the little circle.

"Leonardo da Vinci," Rio answers.

The beer and the weed are making my head feel funny. Everything is soft and fuzzy around the edges, and I can't quite find my footing. Even East's arm around my waist doesn't make me feel secure; I'm drifting.

Floating.

I try to anchor myself with words.

"I had an argument with my mom a couple years ago," I tell them. "After my sister died. She was like, 'No sport is worth risking your life for.' But she doesn't get it. Free diving isn't a sport."

Nods from all around the circle. Murmurs of agreement. Dill holds up his beer like it's a prayer offering. The party has become an old-fashioned revival.

Testimony by story.

Baptism by alcohol.

Pass the weed. Take communion.

"That's right," Dill says, and he nods at me.

"Soccer is a sport," I go on, and I lean down to flick away the tiny ants that are crawling up my shins. "I played when I was little. It was fun. But I didn't mind giving it up." I tilt my head back to study the stars through the thick canopy of trees. "But diving, diving is so much more than that. It's pure. Not just the rush of it. It's like, that's the only time I can be really in the moment, you know? It's like underwater is the one really, truly quiet place on earth."

It's silent for a few seconds except for the snapping of the logs and the night sounds back in the scrub. Frogs and bugs. The bellow of a gator off somewhere in the distance. Then Dill leads the boys off into the dark to gather more firewood, like he's some kind of pied piper. Derry steps away to search their tent for a few birthday candles to put on the graduation cupcakes Paz's mom sent.

Rio moves to sit on the bucket closet to me. Our knees are touching.

My head is spinning.

"You okay?" she asks me. The smoke is drifting around us like fog.

"Who wants to know?" I can't help but giggle. "Rio the diver? Or Lisa the podcaster?"

Rio throws her head back and laughs. It's a sound as dark and rich as the night that threatens to swallow us whole. "Definitely Rio," she says. Her eyes are glassy and her cheeks are flushed in the firelight. Little freckles stand out like pinpricks across her nose. She pauses and runs her fingers through her hair. Black as coal. "I'm all Rio tonight." She finishes the beer she's holding and tosses the can into the fire, then glances around the campsite. "Nice place. How long have these two been living out here?"

"I don't know," I tell her. "Forever, I guess."

Rio raises an eyebrow at me. "Were they here when the murders happened?"

"I mean, yes and no." It's hard to think. I'm distracted by Rio's bare knee against mine. "They'd already set up camp here, but they weren't here that night. A storm was gonna be blowin' through." I'm trying to remember how the story goes. I've heard Dill and Derry tell it a million times, but tonight the details are slippery. "So they spent that night with Derry's people."

Her folks live in a decrepit trailer down behind the Piggly Wiggly. They sell tomatoes and okra at a roadside stand and take in stray animals. There must be a hundred bobtail cats and three-legged dogs running around their place. But they're Mount Orange people through and through. Have been from the beginning. When Derry took off down south for a while, and then hitchhiked her way back up here, with Dill in tow, the town just took him in, too. No questions asked.

The boys are making their way back in our direction. They're laughing and singing and carrying on. Flashlights blazing. Beer cans shining in the moonlight. They dump the wood next to the firepit and grin like cavemen back from taking down a mammoth.

Rio moves to let East have the spot next to me, and I wish we had a few more minutes to talk. Just the two of us.

Dill and East are both good and buzzed, but Paz is shit-faced. He shows off for Rio, cracking jokes and trying to make her laugh, while the other two tend to the fire. Rio just looks at me and rolls her eyes.

Derry comes back with four half-burned birthday candles she unearthed from somewhere. All different colors. One for me. One for East. One for Paz. And one for Rio, since we told them she just graduated, too.

Dill makes a little speech, and when he mentions me and East heading to FSU together in the fall, East slips his arm around my shoulders and pulls me close. I feel like throwing up. Dill leads us in a toast. "Fight for your future. Live in your present. But never, ever forget your past, my friends." We all raise a beer to that. "This place," he tells us. "Right here." He looks around the circle at each of our faces. "This is where you come from."

Derry sticks the used candles in the chocolate cupcakes, and then hands one to each of us. The frosting is melted from the heat. Mine has a bug stuck to it. But nobody complains. Dill lights the candles, and we blow them out. There's a round of applause.

We spend the next few hours swapping stories. More beer and weed and laughter. The glow of the campfire. My head is heavy. It rests on East's shoulder. Now and then he bends down to press his lips against my forehead.

Paz is the first to pass out. No surprise there. When he falls asleep on a big flat rock near the fire, Derry raises his head and slides one of her sweaters underneath. Watching her gives me this sudden yearning for a mother with soft hands and a soft voice. Someone to make sure I'm okay.

That I'm not hurting.

Dill and Derry are the next to call it a night. "We're getting old," they remind us before they head into their tent, and we laugh because that's such bullshit. Dill and Derry don't seem to age at all. They keep staying the same while the rest of us grow up. I figure we'll be older than they are eventually. And they'll be our kids then.

There are two old cots sitting off to the edge of the clearing, in an area Dill and Derry call "the guest room." It's tradition for us to spend the night out here on evenings like this. Or at least part of the night, until someone has sobered up enough to drive home.

We pull off the tarp spread over the top to keep them dry, then drag the cots closer to the fire. Away from the tree line. Out of the thick shadows and into the small circle of light. One for me and East to share. One for Rio. Then we curl up on our backs and look at the stars.

My arms and legs are heavy, like I'm made of stone. I let myself sink into the softness of the cot mattress.

The firmness of East's body.

The fire is burning low and the dark is creeping in closer. Like a wild animal that's stalking us.

Circling.

Waiting.

I think about that other watcher in the woods. The stranger who paused at the edge of Bailey and Celeste's campsite. Leaning against a tree. Knife in hand.

Patient. And ready.

I shiver and East pulls me harder against him. His breath is hot in my ear. "Sleepy?" he murmurs.

"Uh-huh," I manage to mumble, and he presses a kiss to my collarbone.

"You sure?" he asks me, and I can hear the smile in his voice. Feel his fingers at the waistband of my shorts. I know what he's thinking. A night together. In the woods. And the dark.

Not an opportunity to be wasted.

His lips are on my neck now, and I hear myself moan. East slides a hand inside my shirt. I feel his palm resting on my stomach. The heat of him.

He's waiting. Asking for permission.

I can hear Rio breathing a few feet away. I don't think she's asleep.

I shift in East's arms. Roll so that I'm curled on his chest. "Is it okay if we just sleep for a bit?" He's right there, but I suddenly feel so far away from him. From everything. "I'm so tired."

"Yeah." He moves his hand to brush the hair out of my face. "Sure, baby." I barely feel the kiss he presses to the top of my head before I fall asleep.

It's hours later when my eyes flutter open. I'm covered in a film of sweat and about ten million mosquito bites. I'm trying to remember where I am. What it was I heard. What woke me up.

The rustling of leaves. Or the snap of a twig.

Someone breathing in the night, maybe.

There's so much to listen to.

East is snoring beside me, and I untangle myself from him—wincing as I separate our skin where the heat and sweat have sealed us together. I sit up as quietly as I can manage on the creaky cot.

Paz isn't on his rock anymore. He's gotten up and moved to Rio's cot, but she isn't asleep there. She's sitting on a bucket by the fire, poking at the embers with a stick. Coaxing them back to life. I see flames beginning to lick at what's left of the wood.

"Hey," she whispers when I get up and move to the bucket next to hers. "How you feelin'?"

"Okay," I tell her. "My head hurts."

"Yeah." She gives me a little smile. "Mine too."

I reach up and stretch, and my back snaps and pops like the fire. "Those cots aren't the best," I say, but Rio shrugs and pokes at the coals. She's got a pretty good little blaze going now.

"I've been sleeping on the ground. In a sleeping bag. So . . ."

"Right," I say.

I'd forgotten that.

"You wanna take a walk?" Rio's slow, sweet Southern accent seems even thicker tonight. It's like honeysuckle on the night air.

"A walk? To where?"

"I wanna see the water," she says. "In the moonlight." She stands up and pulls a little flashlight out of her pocket. Her hair is fire licked. Dark and glowing. Her eyes burn like the hot coals she's been stirring at.

I follow her down the narrow footpath toward the main spring, but neither of us speak until we're standing on the boardwalk looking out over the swimming area.

There's no color at night. No blues. No greens. Everything is painted over with iridescent pearl. It's like the photographic negative of the spring I'm used to seeing in the daylight.

Rio turns to look at me. "Worth the walk. Right?"

"Yeah," I say. "Definitely worth the walk."

"I wish we could dive it," she says. "The way it is now. All dark and empty."

"You wanna keep your arms and legs?" I ask her, and she giggles. We're both Florida girls, and we know that the springs belong to the gators at night. So we move to a little wooden bench and settle for looking instead of diving.

It's so quiet for a few minutes. Only the gentle sound of bubbles breaking on the surface of the water. The call of an owl somewhere not too far off.

"What was your sister's name?" Rio finally asks me.

"Dani." The name feels strange on my lips. I almost never say her name out loud, even though I hear the echo of it inside my head pretty much every minute of every day. I search out the green of Rio's eyes for just a second, but they're so intense that I have to look back out at the water. "Her name was Dani."

"What was she like?" Rio asks. She's slipped off her flip-flops and she's drawing circles in the damp grass with one toe.

I'm relieved that her first question isn't about what happened. How she died. That's what people usually ask when they're looking to satisfy their own morbid curiosity.

"She was three years older than me," I begin. "My mom and dad were always busy fighting. So it was just me and Dani most of the time." I shrug.

There's more I'd like to say, but I can't find the words. Talking about Dani feels a little bit like trying to open a jar that's been sitting on a pantry shelf for years. The lid is stuck tight, and maybe you don't really want to open it anyway. Because how do you even know what's in there?

"How old were you when she died?"

"Ten," I say, and I slip off my flip-flops, too, so I can pull my knees up and hug them tight to my chest on the bench. "She was thirteen."

"Was she sick?"

There's the ache.

The hurt. The guilt.

I feel it leaking out around the edges of my soul. Seeping between the cracks, the way water pours out of the spring vent. I'm trying to breathe and plug the holes, both at the same time, so I can seal everything up inside me before it oozes out onto the grass.

"She was killed in a hit-and-run accident."

Rio is quiet for a long minute. "A school counselor told me something once," she finally says. "I mean, usually those counselors are awful, but this one said something that stuck with me. She said that the people we love most become an actual physical part of us. That they get ingrained in our synapses. They're literally imprinted on our brains forever in the pathways where memories are created. And that never goes away."

"That's nice," I say. "I don't believe in ghosts or the afterlife or anything. You know? So I like thinking that maybe part of her lives on in my brain. Like that."

Rio brushes away the curtain of dark bangs that has fallen across her face. "What *do* you believe in, Tru?" I'm not sure what she means, and for the briefest moment, I have the feeling we aren't alone out here. That someone is watching us. Hovering in the shadows. Waiting to hear my answer to Rio's question. She leans in closer, and the feeling evaporates. There's nobody but us in the whole world. "If you don't believe in ghosts or anything. Or the afterlife. What *do* you believe in?"

That stumps me. My brain stalls and I almost feel drunk again. Or high. "I don't know," I admit. "I've never thought about it, I guess."

Rio has her eyes fixed on me now, and it's like standing naked in a spotlight.

"Well think about it," she tells me. "It's more important to know what you *do* believe in than what you don't."

"What do you believe in?" I ask her, and Rio shrugs.

"That's what I'm here to figure out." A breeze moves through the tops of the pines. And the palms. I hear them whispering to each other. Secret conversations all around, tonight.

"Ready to head back?" Rio asks me.

I want to say no, but instead I say, "We probably should."

We start down the little trail toward the homestead.

It's so dark once we move back into the trees that the moon might as well have been stolen. There's no soft glow to see by. Only Rio's tiny flashlight.

We're about halfway to the camp when I feel a rock stuck in my flip-flop. I try to kick it loose, but I can't. I try to ignore it, but it hurts to walk. I crouch down to pull it out.

It only takes a second. Maybe two. But when I stand back up, I'm alone. The world is completely black.

"Rio?" I whisper her name into the night, but nothing comes back to me except the call of the cicadas. I'm still. Rooted in place. I've gotten turned around somehow. I'm unsure of which way I was moving on the path. My head is all fuzzy and I can't think straight. "Rio," I say again. A little louder this time.

There's still nothing.

I tell myself it's fine, that I know this path like the back of my hand. I've walked it a million times.

This is just like diving.

Stay calm.

Control your breathing and your heart rate.

Don't panic.

But I taste something like fear on my tongue.

It's been such a long time since I've been afraid of the dark like this. I remember something Dani used to tell me sometimes, when I'd crawl into bed with her in the middle of the night. *There's nothing out there in the dark that isn't out there in the daytime, Tru.*

That never gave me much comfort. It just confirmed that the world is full of scary things, all the time. The monsters are always there, even in the sunshine.

Behind me, a twig snaps. I count to three. And then another snap.

Closer this time.

"Rio? Is that you?" My voice is hoarse. Strained. I couldn't say why I'm whispering.

Nobody whispers back.

I take a few steps, but I have no idea if I'm moving closer to East and the others. Or farther away. I listen to the scratch-scratch sound of my own footsteps on the sandy path.

And the occasional snapping of twigs. The rustling of leaves in the scrub.

The hair on my neck stands up. I'm being watched.

"Rio." I whisper her name. Even though I'm sure she isn't there. "East?"

There's the unmistakable sound of footsteps coming toward me. Down the trail. Not an armadillo or a possum. The unmistakable crunch of boots on gravel. Human footsteps. Slow and steady.

Then they stop.

My legs turn to Jell-O and my heart moves up into my mouth. It sits there, beating wildly on my tongue. Hammering against the backsides of my teeth like it wants to be set free.

Everything goes still. There's no more pounding. My heart has stopped completely.

Because someone is breathing in the dark. Someone close enough to touch.

Someone so near that I can feel the warmth of their breath on my cheek.

"Tru! You okay?"

I whirl around and Rio is hurrying down the path from the

opposite direction. The tiny glow of her flashlight is barely enough to light up her face. I can see that it's her. And my heart starts to beat again.

I look back over my shoulder, into the dark. If Rio is coming from that way, who was following me on the trail?

East or Paz, maybe?

Or Dill?

Maybe someone woke up and came looking for us.

But why didn't they answer me when I called out?

I'm quiet for a few seconds, listening for that breathing. Rio is watching me with a strange look on her face.

"I was almost back to camp before I realized you weren't behind me," she says. I'm still looking over my shoulder. "You okay?"

"Yeah," I say, and I give myself a little shake to clear my head and snap myself out of it. "I'm good."

We make our way back to the homestead. East and Paz are still passed out on the cots exactly where we left them, and when Rio aims her little flashlight at Dill and Derry's tent, I can see that it's zipped up tight.

None of them came after us.

The fire is dying again, and there's no wood left to burn. Rio and I sit close together on the upside-down five-gallon buckets. Despite the heat, I'm cold. My teeth won't stop chattering.

"Tru?" Rio is studying me. "You sure you're okay?"

"Did you hear anything out there?" I ask her. "Or did you see anything?" I hesitate. "Or anybody?"

"No," she tells me. She holds my gaze and some kind of recognition floats across her face. Then it's gone. "Why?"

"I could have sworn there was someone out there with me," I tell her. "On the trail. In the scrub. Someone besides you." Rio's pale skin glows like a ghost in the dark. "I know that sounds stupid. Like I'm making things up. Or letting my imagination get the best of me. Or whatever. But—"

"It doesn't." Rio shakes her head. "It doesn't sound stupid." She picks up the stick again. Pokes at the coals. But they refuse to give us any light this time. Or warmth. They're already dead. I watch Rio stare into the dark, then turn to look at me. "Have you ever heard of the Glades Reaper?"

SEVEN

"OF COURSE I know the Glades Reaper," I tell her. "But he didn't work this area. He wasn't—"

"But what if he did," Rio says. "What if he was?"

I shiver hard in the swampy heat. "There was never a confirmed Glades Reaper kill north of Lake Okeechobee."

"Right." Rio nods. "Confirmed."

"Wait." Now it's my turn to interrupt. "You think the Glades Reaper killed Bailey and Celeste? Or that the Glades Reaper is out there somewhere now?"

"Both," Rio says with the kind of certainty that I've never felt about anything in my life. "But not somewhere. Here."

"I don't—" Everything is so strange tonight. But I can't shake the terror I felt on the trail. Footsteps. The sound of someone breathing in the dark. "What makes you think that?"

Rio pushes her hair back away from her eyes. I can see her wheels turning. Like she's trying to figure out how to explain it.

"I've always had this idea in the back of my mind," she finally says. "That what happened back there at the clearing twenty years ago had to do with what happened down there in south Florida. All those murdered girls . . ." She trails off. Turns back to look at the dead, black coals. "I know things sometimes. I can feel them. And I feel like he was here." She stops. "Is here."

"What do you mean? Like, you're psychic or something? That doesn't—"

"No. That's not it. Tru. Listen." She puts the stick down and takes a deep breath. "Everybody knows he killed girls. In pairs. That was his thing, right?"

I nod. There were fourteen Glades Reaper victims down south. Seven blood-soaked murder sites stretching from the tip of Florida, where he gutted two sets of girls inside the borders of Everglades National Park, up to the southern part of Okeechobee County, where he decapitated two cross-country running partners who were out early one morning preparing for a race. Best friends. Sisters. Teammates. Co-workers. Lovers. It didn't seem to matter to him, as long as he could take out two girls at the same time.

Two beautiful birds with one stone.

"But Bailey and Celeste didn't fit his pattern," I remind her. They looked into all that at the time. I've read that much in the newspaper articles written about the Hidden Glen killings. "The Glades Reaper was ruled out. He took his time with his victims. Tied them up. Tortured them first. And he posed the bodies for shock value after he was finished." He considered himself an artist; that's what all the profilers said at the time. I shake my head. "With Bailey and Celeste, it was a surprise attack. A crime of opportunity. Heat of the moment."

Bailey and Celeste were the work of an amateur. That's the conclusion all the investigators came to. Somebody who'd never killed before. Not the experienced serial killer who'd spent so much time terrorizing our neighbors to the south.

The Glades Reaper was active years before Bailey and Celeste died in the scrub that night. And years after. His last known kill was just a decade or so ago. I was old enough to hear about the last one on the news. Then it all just stopped. There were no more murders after that.

At least not that anybody knows about.

"I know it doesn't make sense." Rio chews on her lip for a second. "There's a lot of shit in my life that doesn't make sense. That's why I came here. To see if I could maybe figure out what happened that night." A deep sigh escapes from her lips. The sound is immediately absorbed into the night. "To see if I could maybe make sense of this one thing. You know?"

"Yeah," I say. "I do know." I'm spinning out. Inside my own head.

It's almost like Rio is reminding me of something I already knew, instead of telling me something completely shocking and implausible.

"Look." Rio reaches into the pocket of her shorts. "I want to show you something." She pulls out a piece of paper and starts to unfold it.

"Tru?" East's sleep-coated voice sounds confused. Like a little boy who's woken up unsure of where his mother is. "We gotta get home," he says. When I turn back over my shoulder to look at him, he's sitting up on our cot. Shirtless. Rubbing his eyes. Running his fingers through those tousled blond waves. "Mom's got the early shift. She's gonna need me there to watch Seth."

Rio slips that piece of paper back into her pocket. We wake

up Paz and gather our things. We're being so quiet. Trying not to wake up Dill and Derry. It's 3:00 a.m. Dark as the grave. And just as silent. Even the bugs and the frogs have finally gone to sleep.

"You think Dill and Derry would care if I crashed here for the rest of the night?" Rio asks me. She's perched on the edge of one of the cots. "It's a lot more comfortable than the ground."

"They won't care," I tell her. "But I'm warning you, Dill wakes up super early. Like five o'clock."

"I don't mind early," Rio says. "I'll be glad for the bed." For a second, I want to ask her to come home with me. Her being out here in the dark, exposed to the night, scares me. But she's already crawled back on her cot. And her eyes are sliding closed.

East and Paz and I say our goodbyes and we make our way back down the trail toward the main spring and the parking lot. East and Paz both have bright flashlights. I keep a good grip on East's hand the entire time.

I listen. But I don't hear any breathing. Just our own footsteps on the sandy trail.

After I drop East off at his place and Paz at his brother's, I head on home. The house is dark except for the flicker of the silent television. Mom is passed out on the couch.

I ease the door closed and tiptoe up the stairs. I need a shower, but I don't take one. I collapse on top of my comforter and let the cool of the AC wash over me like spring water as I pull my favorite memory out of my pocket. I close my eyes and picture it. Me standing just over my sister's shoulder. Her drawing that graceful galloping horse. Pencil in hand. The quiet scratch of the lead.

I let myself drift off to sleep, because I want to be up early. I may not know enough about the Glades Reaper to say for sure whether Rio might be onto something with her theory. But I know somebody who will.

It's the sound of the Weed eater that wakes me up right after sunrise the next morning. I haul myself out of bed and dig around on the floor for my flip-flops. I throw on my sunglasses, because my head is pounding like crazy, and I head out to the front yard.

Jon Boy is wearing baggy dress pants and an ancient Mount Orange Comets T-shirt. REESE is printed in huge letters across the back. He's got on his gardening boots, so I know he means business, and he's currently attacking a big patch of nut grass that's taken over the area around our mailbox. I lift my arm in a wave and he shuts off the Weed eater. Then he swipes at his forehead with the back of his arm and wipes it on his shirt. It doesn't do him any good, though. As early as it is, he's already totally soaked through with sweat everywhere.

"Mornin'," I tell him, and I offer up a cold Sprite that I grabbed out of the fridge on my way through the kitchen. Mom keeps them around to mix with her vodka.

"Mornin', Trulee Bear," he tells me. "You're up awful early."

"Sorta hard to sleep with somebody making all sorts of racket right outside my window."

"Sorry." Jon Boy grins at me and downs the drink I brought him. "Just tryin' to get this done before I head into the office. Supposed to rain in a bit." He glances up at the overcast sky and hands me back the empty can. "No rest for the wicked," he tells me with a little wink.

I'm not sure if he means him. Or me.

"You busy later this evening?" I ask. "I got something I wanna pick your brain about."

"I got to drive to Gainesville this evening," he tells me. "To pick up a new camera lens." He gives me a long look. "What's up, Trulee Bear? Is it somethin' we can talk about at the office today?" Jon Boy's phone makes a dinging noise in his pocket, and he takes it out to read a text. "Actually," he tells me, "something just came up for me this morning. Gotta run take a meeting with somebody."

"A meeting?" I almost laugh out loud. "With who?" Jon Boy isn't usually in demand at a lot of meetings.

"Nobody important or interesting. I can promise you that." He pulls out a red bandanna to mop up the sweat that's running down his neck. "There's not gonna be much going on at the office. You wanna just take the day off, and then we can meet at my place on my lunch break?" He jerks his head toward his little house, a few hundred yards away. "I got some eggs I need to use before they go bad."

"Sure," I tell him, and I'm glad to have the day off, even though I've only worked two days so far this summer. I leave him to his Weed eating and head back to the house.

When I push open the front door, Mom is standing in front of the open freezer staring at the contents like she's waiting for some kind of sign. "You want waffles?" I ask her.

She raises an eyebrow at me. "That depends. You asking me to make waffles? Or are you offering to make them yourself?"

"I'll make them," I tell her. I hunt down some Advil for my head. Mom keeps it stashed under her pillow for easy access. Then I text East and tell him to bring Seth over for breakfast.

Thirty minutes later we're all sitting around our table eating waffles with syrup and powdered sugar. Seth is going on and on about some video game he's obsessed with, and my mom is laughing at him. Acting all interested. Letting him have her bacon. I think she likes having a little kid around again.

East smiles and rubs my calf with his foot under the table. "Got my dorm assignment letter yesterday," he announces. "It was waitin' on me when I got home this mornin'."

My mom stops listening to Seth and turns to look at me. "Did you get yours, Trulee? I've been keeping an eye out for it."

"Not yet," I tell her. I have to fight to keep from throwing up my breakfast. I know I won't be able to keep my secret much longer.

I honestly don't know why I never finished the FSU application. I started to feel so buried alive by the whole idea. It's not that I hate the idea of going to FSU with East. It's more that I don't really *love* the idea, either.

It was the path everyone figured we'd take, so that became the plan. It was never the future I chose, though, and I'm starting to think maybe what I really want is to actually *choose* something. For once in my life. Just for myself.

Mom frowns. "We should call the admissions office if it doesn't come this week."

"Yeah," I say. I reach for more syrup. "I will."

East leans across the table and covers my hand with his. He squeezes and something in my chest tightens in his strong grip.

Mom smiles at both of us. It's nice to see her happy. I wish it wasn't over a lie.

"I'm glad you're going somewhere together," she tells us. "You two have something really special." She looks back down at her plate. "Kevin and I were high school sweethearts." I cringe because it's strange to hear her call my dad by name. Besides, that's not actually the most encouraging comparison. I guess she gets that because she looks back up and turns on her hundred-watt real estate agent smile. "You two, though. You're soulmates. You'll do better than us." She nods. Takes a drink of orange juice. I can smell the vodka she's added. "Y'all are gonna make it."

East gives my hand another squeeze.

I know that's what he's hoping for. The same thing my mom's hoping for. East's mom, too. That we'll go to FSU together. College degrees. We'll get married. Kids. East wants three. At least. Plus a couple of dogs. The whole nine yards. Because East and I are perfect for each other. And we've loved each other since we were babies, practically. This has all been part of the plan since we were in third grade. Maybe even longer.

So how do I really know that's the life that I want, and not the life everyone else wants for me?

Mom's talking again. "College is such an exciting time. You learn so much about yourself." I'm not sure how she knows that. My mom did a semester and a half of community college, and then dropped out because she was pregnant. She smiles again, but it's a sad smile. Suddenly, I know where this is going. These moments always throw me sideways, like a sharp curve in the road. Even before she says it, my wheels are already slipping on gravel. "I wish Dani could have had that experience."

I take a bite of waffle and chew it like a million times. My gaze is locked on the syrup bottle. The sticky powdered sugar fingerprints that Seth has left along the edge of the table. There's the low rumble of thunder from outside.

The rain is getting closer.

It's East who changes the subject. "So," he says, "Rio seems pretty cool, Tru." He drops his hand to my bare thigh. Gives me another little squeeze. His way of telling me that he saved me on purpose. East knows how hard it is for me to talk about Dani.

My mom looks confused. "Who's Rio?"

"A girl we met out at the springs," I say. "A diver."

Mom sighs and I figure I'm about to get another lecture about diving and how dangerous it is. How it'll kill her if she has to bury another daughter. But Seth knocks over his milk and I spring into action to grab some paper towels.

The rest of breakfast is easy. Chitchat and nibbles of bacon. After East and Seth leave, I say I'll handle the cleanup so Mom can get ready for work. I wouldn't have offered if I'd realized that powdered sugar is the equivalent of kitchen glitter. That stuff is everywhere.

By the time I'm finished, it's almost nine o'clock. My head still hurts, so I crawl back into bed, and when I wake up at almost noon, I look out the window and see Jon Boy's truck parked in his driveway. I drag myself out from under the covers and brush my hair, then find my flip-flops and start across the patchy lawn for our lunch date.

I pat the mailbox manatee on his chipped head as I make my way up the stepping-stone path to his front door. Overhead, the sky is dark, and I hear the low growl of thunder again. I think about that other thunderstorm.

The one that moved through the scrub just before Bailey and Celeste were murdered.

In Florida, you can keep track of pretty much everything that happens by keeping track of the storms.

I glance at the clouds and move a little faster up the front steps, but I hesitate before I knock on the door. I haven't figured out exactly how I'm going to bring this up. I don't get any time to think about it, though, because I hear Jon Boy yell from inside. "Come on in, Trulee Bear! Door's open."

It's been a while since I've been inside Jon Boy's house, and I realize that he keeps it just as cold at home as he does at the office.

So much for it being about the newspapers.

"Good timing." He's standing in the kitchen holding a little bowl. "I was just makin' lunch. Egg salad. You want some?"

"I'm good," I tell him, and I wrinkle up my nose. I've never liked egg salad. The smell makes me sick. Plus I'm still stuffed from the waffles. I move a couple of *National Geographic*s from one of the tall barstools and climb up to have a seat.

I'm staring at a picture of Jon Boy and Reese as teenagers that hangs above the bar. They're on a boat. Both wearing swim trunks. The two of them grinning from ear to ear. Reese is holding up a giant fish with one hand and he's beaming straight at the camera. Jon Boy is looking at his big brother like he's some kind of God.

I recognize that expression on his face. It's the same one I'm wearing in the picture of me and Dani that hangs over the television at our house.

Not too long after what happened to Dani, Reese's canoe overturned on a fishing trip and he drowned in Lake Louisa. Jon Boy's always been torn up that he wasn't there to save his big brother that day. We've never talked about it, really, but that's our unspoken bond. Jon Boy absolutely idolized his older brother. He worshiped the ground he walked on. Then he lost him. I know he still feels that loss every day. Just like I do with Dani.

At least he isn't the reason Reese is dead.

Dani was out on the road early that morning looking for me. What happened to her was my fault.

Jon Boy catches me looking at the photo of him and his brother. "I don't remember him much," I admit. "Reese. I wish I did."

Jon Boy raps a boiled egg on the counter, then rolls it back and forth under the palm of his hand before he starts peeling off the shell. "He wasn't around a whole lot while you were growing up. He worked so hard all the time. And he traveled a lot." He shakes his head. "He was always chasing some story. Or heading to some newspaper convention." I watch him reach for another egg. Rap. Roll. Peel. "The truth is, I think he was bored in Mount Orange. He had bigger dreams. You know? When he was home, he was restless. He'd walk late at night when he couldn't sleep. For miles sometimes." He's picking a bit of shell out of the bowl. "I wish we'd spent more time together those last ten years or so. I wish I'd—" He stops. "If I'd known how things were gonna end up, I'd have done things differently with Reese, because he was everything to me. I don't know if he ever knew that." He shrugs. "I guess hindsight is twenty-twenty. Isn't that what they say?"

I wish I could talk about Dani easy like that. The way Jon Boy talks about Reese. But it hurts way too much. The ache of it fills up my mouth and gets in the way of the words coming out.

There's another low rumble and Jon Boy and I both look toward the kitchen window. The sky is getting darker by the minute, but the rain hasn't started yet.

Jon Boy turns to open the fridge and I catch sight of another picture of his brother. It's a newspaper clipping stuck to the refrigerator door with a sea turtle magnet. It's not from the *Star*. The photo is faded and yellowed, but it's all in color. So it must have run in a big newspaper. Reese is beaming in a dark blue suit. Holding up a trophy.

Jon Boy catches me looking at it. "That's when he won Small-Town Newspaper Editor of the Year. They had a big ceremony down in Florida City. The *Miami Herald* covered it." He taps the photo with one finger, and I can tell how proud he is of that, even all these years later. "It was a big deal."

I think about how Mom has all Dani's awards from school saved in a box. How sometimes when I get up early, I find her passed out on the couch with that box open on the floor. *I like to see her name on things*, she told me once. *It proves she was here.*

"That's really cool," I tell him.

"He won all kinds of awards." Jon Boy shakes his head and laughs. "I can't even win the Kiwanis club turkey raffle. And I enter every year." Jon Boy is mashing up his eggs. Spooning in Duke's Mayonnaise, like the good ol' Southern boy he is. "But I know you didn't come over here for a family history lesson. What's on your mind, TB?"

I figure I better just spit it out. "I wanted to ask you about the Glades Reaper."

"Okay." Jon Boy stops. He sets down the paprika and looks at me. "Why?"

I think about lying, but Jon Boy is part newspaper reporter and part bloodhound. He can sniff out a lie easier than he can whip up an egg salad sandwich. So I decide to just lay it all out.

"Remember that podcaster who came by the newspaper office the other day?"

"Yeah." Jon Boy is still just looking at me.

"She isn't really a podcaster. Her name's Rio. I met her out at the springs. She's a free diver, but she's super interested in what happened out at Hidden Glen. The murders and all that. That's why she lied to you. So she could see your research."

"Okay." Jon Boy looks confused. And hurt, maybe. Or disappointed. "Murder isn't entertainment, Tru. Those were real girls. Real people who—"

"I know that," I snap. Jesus. Of course I know that. I'm not some kind of murder-ghoul tourist.

"You know if you have questions," he goes on, "about any-thing, you can always come to me. You don't have to—"

"I didn't know what her plan was. We'd barely met. I had no idea she was gonna show up at the *Star* pretending to be someone else. That was all her."

Jon Boy sighs. "Okay. But what does any of that have to do with the Glades Reaper?"

"She's got this idea that maybe the Glades Reaper was respon-sible for what happened to Celeste and Bailey."

"No." Jon Boy shakes his head and goes back to working on his egg salad. He's slicing a lemon. Adding a squeeze of juice. "That was all settled a long time ago. Bailey and Celeste don't fit the pattern."

"I know," I tell him. "But maybe there's something somebody missed. What if—"

"No," Jon Boy says again. "I covered some of the Glades Reaper's murders, Tru. I saw what he did." Jon Boy shudders. He twists open a jar of pickles and reaches for a knife. "What happened to Bailey and Celeste was awful. But it wasn't that. It wasn't anything like what he did." I watch him slice a pickle into little bits and toss it into the bowl. "I've never seen any-thing like what he did."

Thunder rumbles loud enough to rattle the windows and shake the pictures on the wall. Including that one of Jon Boy and Reese and the giant fish. But there's still no rain coming down outside.

"What do you mean?" I'm trying to understand why he's so

sure it couldn't have been the Reaper who went after Bailey and Celeste in the scrub all those years ago.

"The first victims I saw were the twins." Jon Boy stops chopping. "This was back before you were even born." He doesn't look at me. He's staring down at the knife in his hand while he talks. "Sisters. Beth and Emily. He grabbed them walking home from a friend's place. They didn't find 'em till almost a week later. He had the bodies set up in an empty house. The Realtor went to show it to a potential buyer, and when he opened the door, there they were. Bodies posed at the dining room table like—" He shakes his head. "The Reaper took his victims, then returned the bodies somewhere different. He set 'em up to shock people. Christ, TB. He left his last two victims sitting side by side on a park bench down in Clewiston. Holding their own heads in their laps." He finally meets my eyes. "Remember that? The nursing students. You must have been old enough to hear about that one."

I do remember. Dani and I were home alone after school when the special report came on. GLADES REAPER RETURNS was splashed across the television screen in big red letters. There were two of us. Me. And Dani. We were a set. A pair. Like all those dead girls down in south Florida.

Dani wasn't afraid. She got up and changed the channel. Then she promised me that nobody would ever hurt us. That we were both safe.

Less than six months later, she was dead. Broken and twisted and staring in the wet grass right out in front of our own house.

And I was left alone.

Jon Boy has finally finished his egg salad. I watch him pop two slices of white bread in the toaster. "Whoever killed Celeste and Bailey wanted them dead." He pauses. Puts the twist tie back on the bread wrapper and sets it carefully in a basket on the counter. "But he didn't do the things the Glades Reaper did. That's for damn sure." He's hunting for the salt and pepper shakers. A set of ceramic pelicans. "Besides, the Reaper was big on trophies. He took something from every kill site." I watch him add salt and pepper to his lunch, and it amazes me he's not dead from sodium poisoning. "Nothing was missing from the campsite out at Hidden Glen."

"Maybe he just forgot," I offer, but Jon Boy shakes his head.

"Nah. Killers like the Reaper are creatures of habit. They don't just switch things up."

"You think he could still be alive?" I ask. "The Reaper."

"I'm pretty sure he is." Jon Boy's toast pops up and he reaches over to grab it. "He's sent a couple letters over the years. To the *Herald* down in Miami."

"Seriously?" I shiver on the kitchen stool as the first drops of rain hit the window. "I've never heard anything about that."

"The *Herald* never printed 'em. Just turned 'em over to the police. They kept it quiet for the investigation. But I've got a buddy in the newsroom down there. He lets me know when they get one in. Last one wasn't that long ago. Last year sometime." He's spreading egg salad on toast now. "He hasn't killed for almost a decade, though. That we know of." I watch him slice his sandwich into two perfectly symmetrical triangles.

"But none of that has squat to do with our girls." He arches an eyebrow at me. "You can tell your new friend, Ms. Brown the pretend podcaster, that she's barking up the wrong tree. Our killer wasn't the Reaper. Our guy was a beginner. Bailey very nearly got away from him."

"Yeah," I say. "I guess you're right."

"You sure you don't want somethin' to eat before I head back to the *Star*?" he asks me. "I got plenty."

"Nah," I say. "But thanks." I hop off the stool and head to the door. "And thanks for taking care of the yard this morning. It means a lot. All the stuff you do for us."

"Just being neighborly, TB." He waves my gratitude away like it's nothing. "We gotta look out for each other, you and me."

I nod, but we both know it's more than that. Jon Boy doesn't treat me and Mom like we're neighbors.

He treats us like we're family.

The rain starts coming down hard as I'm crossing the little distance back to our house. It comes like someone turned a garden hose on, falling from a sky that's gone black as night. The first streak of lighting lights up the world when I hit our front steps, and I'm grateful to slip inside to safety.

The thunder and lightning don't last long. They never do. But the rain keeps falling in steady sheets all day. I worry about Rio. I wonder where she is and if she's safe. If she's keeping dry in all this.

I'm wanting to get back out to the springs so the two of us can talk. I want to tell her what Jon Boy said. About how it couldn't have been the Glades Reaper who got Celeste and Bailey. How it doesn't make any sense. It doesn't look like that's going to happen today, because this is the kind of rain that settles in and stays awhile.

Upstairs in my bedroom, I keep going over everything Jon Boy told me. All the details, the reasons why Rio's theory doesn't make sense.

Yet something about it feels right.

I dig the little half heart out of my backpack. I rub it with my thumb, like a good luck charm. Rain isn't the only thing Rio has to worry about out there alone at the springs.

My mind keeps going back to what happened last night on the path. I wasn't alone.

Even if Rio was wrong about the Glades Reaper, I wasn't wrong about that.

Someone—or something—is on the prowl out at Hidden Glen.

EIGHT

THE NEXT DAY is Thursday, and the weather is perfect. Sunny and clear, with enough breeze to blow away the bugs and the sweat. It's perfect diving weather, so I hurry out to the springs as soon as I'm finished at the newspaper office. Jon Boy even lets me leave a little early, I think because he catches me staring out the window so often.

Out at Hidden Glen, the parking lot is overflowing. I have to park down the road and hike in. I guess everyone is trying to make up for the miserable rain yesterday.

Derry is set up with her card table and typewriter at the main spring. She has a coffee can to hold her donations and she's ready to crank out poems for tourists. She puts down her book to tell me good morning as I make my way toward the boardwalk. I can tell by the cover that it's a mystery she's reading this time. A departure from her usual romances.

I don't have to look very hard for Rio. I find her back at the Well with Dill. They're floating on their backs in that circle of bright blue, but they pop up to wave at me when I undo the safety latch and push open the gate.

"Just in time!" Dill shouts. "New Girl and me were just gettin' ready to go below."

I pick my way across the rocks and sit down to wiggle out

of my shorts and T-shirt. I slip off my flip-flops and let my feet dangle in the cold water. Rio swims over and pulls herself up to sit beside me.

"You make it through all that rain okay?" I ask her.

"Yep." She jerks her head toward Dill. "Dill and Derry let me crash under their rain tarp."

"We're tryin' to get her to stay with us." Dill is swimming circles around the opening of the Well, warming up his muscles for the dive. "No use in her being all by herself. Not when we've got plenty of room at the homestead."

"Might as well." Rio shrugs. "It's not like I really have anywhere to go." She turns to look at me, and I'm almost blinded. She's all bright green eyes in the morning sun. "Plus I still have a lot of questions that need answers."

What Jon Boy told me is at the tip of my tongue. About how it couldn't have been the Glades Reaper who killed Celeste and Bailey. But I don't get a chance to speak.

Dill hauls himself out of the water and he's pulling on his fins. Spit-cleaning his mask. "Y'all come here to dive or make chit-chat?" he asks us. He's grinning like a little kid. Mischievous. Wound tight. Ready to go. The anticipation comes off him in waves, the way you can see steam rising up off the highway after a summer storm.

"I came to dive," I tell him.

"Me too," Rio adds.

"That's what I wanna hear, girls." Dill gives us a sideways grin. "Let's get below."

Dill goes down first while Rio and I watch from up top. It

never gets old to me, watching Dill in the water. It always makes me think of this one time when I was really little, maybe five or six, Mom and Dad took me and Dani over to Weeki Wachee Springs. They have these mermaid shows, and they perform elaborate choreographed underwater routines. Fairy tales and Greek myths. They use long air hoses to breathe so they can stay down and act out the whole story. It's like an underwater ballet. People watch them from behind glass, in this special theater cut into the side of the natural spring. And these Weeki Wachee mermaids, they're world famous. They wear bikini tops and sparkly mermaid tails. They have mermen, too, and I remember thinking how beautiful the boys were. Graceful and strong. Not like the boys I knew from school.

That's what Dill always reminds me of. A Weeki Wachee merman.

"I wish I'd had someone like Dill to teach me to dive," Rio says. "Not that it was awful learning on my own or anything." Her voice has a sad sound to it. It's something I haven't heard from her before. One more tiny piece of her puzzle. I pull my eyes away from Dill to glance in her direction. "It's just nice to have people to share stuff with, sometimes."

When Dill pops up from his dive, he swims straight to the rocks and pulls himself up to sit next to us. He gives his dark curls a good shake and water flies everywhere. He's like a Labrador retriever coming in from the rain. If Derry were here, she'd shriek and giggle and swat at him with her paperback book, then the two of them would laugh together before he leaned in for a kiss. Dill and Derry have this easy way with each other. I never saw that between my mom and dad. Not even before Dani.

"Who's next?" Dill asks, and Rio and I look at each other.

"You go," we both say at the exact same time.

"Why don't you two go together," Dill offers. "I can spot two at a time."

I hadn't realized until he said it that that's what I was hoping for. To be in the water with Rio.

To share space in all that blue.

Rio and I both prep to dive. We stretch together. Arms to the sky. Slow neck rolls. Breathe together. Our rhythms overlap and we fall into sync without even meaning to. In and out. Slow and steady. Then she gives me the tiniest smile before she slips into the water, and I follow right behind her.

Rio and I swim down and down and down. She turns back to look at me over her shoulder. Even behind her mask I can see the bright green of her eyes.

We communicate effortlessly, like we've been diving together our whole lives. A glance from her, and I know exactly where she wants to go. We take turns playing follow the leader as we explore the Well like we're both seeing it for the first time.

Below us, on the floor of the spring, bubbles stream from the vent. A desperate need to swim through that curtain of bubbles pulls me deeper.

I want it for me.

And I want it for Rio.

I want it with Rio.

I haven't even been paying attention to the depth markers

scratched into the limestone, but a quick check tells me we're at ninety feet. That's deeper than I've ever been before.

Only fifty feet or so to the bottom.

I feel it in my guts. The relentless tug of the spring floor. Like someone is reaching way down my throat to grab hold of my insides and turn me wrong side out.

Rio and I hover, weightless for a few moments, and our eyes lock on each other's.

Nothing holding us up.

And nothing holding us down.

Rio points toward the surface, and I nod. Because I know she's right. It's time to head topside.

We swim together toward the blazing opening of the Well, and when I count my fin-kicks to match my heartbeat, I'm counting Rio's, too. Because we're moving in perfect time with each other.

One.

Two.

Three.

Four.

Five.

Beating hearts in sync.

When we finally break the surface and draw that first breath together, it's like we're sharing one set of lungs. Euphoria washes over me like a tidal wave and I can't stop smiling. I'm giddy. Absolutely loopy from the diver's high.

I look down into the water. Way down. One hundred and forty feet below. To the vent.

And there she is.

Bailey.

She reaches for me, and I swear I feel the brush of her icy fingertips on my thigh, even though she's so far away.

She wants something from me.

Something she needs me to do.

I blink. Rub the water from my eyes. When I look back down, she's gone again. A trick of my oxygen-starved brain.

The crowds are starting to show up in full force, and Dill scurries across the rocks to talk to some guys he knows.

Rio and I sit side by side, feet dangling together in the water. "I talked to Jon," I tell her, because Jon Boy has threatened me with instant and painful death if I ever use his old nickname in front of anybody other than my mom. Rio turns to look at me, and it's clear she has no idea who I'm talking about. "My friend. Or my boss. The one who runs the newspaper."

"Oh," Rio says. "Mr. 'show her the file,' right?"

"Yeah. He's studied both cases, and he says there's no way the Glades Reaper killed Celeste and Bailey. Whoever murdered Celeste and Bailey did it quick and messy. He wasn't an artist. Not like the Reaper."

She reaches down into the blue of the spring to scoop up a handful of water and I watch it slip through her fingers. I like the trick of it. How it isn't really blue at all. When you cup it in your hands like that, it's crystal clear.

I remember Dill telling me and East how the colors in sunlight separate as they pass through the springs. Really pure water doesn't absorb the color blue, so all the blue light gets reflected back. That's what makes it look blue to us. *The deeper the water*, he explained, *the more light eventually gets absorbed. See those really dark places? Those are places where it's deep. And the brightest spots, those are the shallowest areas.*

I've learned more science from Dill out here than I ever learned in any classroom.

Rio's chewing on her lip. She doesn't look convinced. "There's some connection there, Tru. There has to be. I feel it."

I'm still watching that water trickle between her fingers and slide down her arm. "What has you so convinced the Reaper was involved in what happened out here that night?"

Rio looks back over her shoulder, toward the scrub and the little clearing where Celeste and Bailey set up camp on the last night of their lives. When I follow her gaze, I can almost see them. Bailey's brown ponytail. Celeste's blond curls. I swear I catch the glint of those half hearts winking in the sunlight around their necks.

"I just feel it," Rio tells me again. I think about that water dripping from her fingers. How it's bright blue in the spring, but crystal clear when you hold it in your hand, and I remind myself that things aren't always what they seem to be.

Maybe I don't know.

Maybe Jon Boy doesn't, either.

I think about what he told me. About how he figures the Reaper is still alive. How he's been sending little reminders to the newspaper down in Miami. Love notes every couple of years. Just so they don't forget about him.

If he's still alive, he has to be somewhere.

Why not here?

"You really think he's out there?" My eyes are still trained on the scrub. It's so thick and tangled. Someone could be standing back there right now. Watching us.

"Somebody's out there," Rio says. She turns to look at me. "And you sensed them the other night."

I remember my creeping terror. How it felt to know something was out there in the blackness. The heavy sound of someone breathing close.

I'd trust Jon Boy with my life. He's the smartest guy I know. I'm sure he's probably right.

But Jon Boy wasn't out here the other night. In the dark. Alone but not by myself.

The midday crowds are getting to be too much now. Even the Well isn't the sanctuary it normally is. There are too many bodies pressed close together in the water. Too many people clinging to the edges, waiting to dive. And too many spectators jockeying for spots on the rocks.

Dill and Rio and I pack up our stuff and follow the boardwalk toward the main spring. Derry has a long line of customers waiting for poems, so we don't bother her. Dill manages to find a little spot of empty ground under one of the huge old live oaks. He and Rio lounge in the shade while I trudge up to the Dive Bar to buy us ice cream.

I stand baking in the sun while kids try to make up their minds which flavor ice pop they want and families do the math to work out how many tubes they need to rent, then I get us all ice cream sandwiches and we eat them in the sweltering heat.

I'm swatting away flies and trying to catch the bits of vanilla ice cream that are dripping onto my towel. Mostly I'm thinking about the Glades Reaper and searching the crowd for anyone who might be watching us a little too closely.

After the ice cream, Derry comes over to tell us she's ready for a break. She and Dill invite us back to their campsite. "I picked some good blackberries yesterday," Derry tells us. "We can't eat 'em fast enough. They're gonna go bad."

In case the blackberries weren't enough of a draw, Dill tells us he'll roll us a fat joint we can all split.

We pick up our towels and shake them out, then Dill grabs the folding card table and Derry grabs her ancient typewriter. Rio and I follow them around the swimming area and down the path away from the springs. The two of them are walking ahead of us. Laughing together. Both of them barefoot. Glistening with sweat and spring water. Derry is holding her skirt up around her thighs with her free hand. She looks back at Rio and me and smiles, and then looks up at Dill. "If we're gonna have a house guest staying with us," she says, "we need to get a more permanent place set up for her."

"Already on it," Dill tells her. Then he throws a wink back in our direction.

We're all laughing. Everyone is happy and relaxed and glad to be spending the morning together. But when we reach the end of the trail, Dill and Derry stop. "Holy shit," Dill mutters, and he drops the card table. Derry's free hand flies to cover her mouth. I can't see what they're looking at. Not until Rio and I push our way in between them.

"Jesus." Rio's voice is a low whisper. It sits on top of the thick, humid air.

Dill and Derry's tent has been totally destroyed. There are huge gashes all in the sides. Holes that look like gaping wounds in the orange material. You can see right inside to where their sleeping bags lie twisted like bodies.

I've never seen anything like it.

That's a lie. I've actually seen something exactly like this. In those crime scene photos hidden away in that box on the top shelf. In the basement of the *Star*.

There's no blood at this scene—no oozing black—but someone has slashed Dill and Derry's tent to ribbons in the exact same way as Celeste and Bailey's.

NINE

"DILL?" I CAN hear the tears in Derry's voice. She swallows hard before she speaks again. "What happened?" She starts to walk toward the tent, but Dill grabs her by the wrist and jerks her back.

"Wait," he snaps. "All of you just wait here."

Dill creeps toward the tent. He peers inside, then walks all the way around it. We watch as he paces the whole campsite. He checks the perimeter, peering into the bushes. Lifting the tarps. Peeking into their makeshift outhouse. Looking behind the curtains that hide their rigged-up shower. Until he finally decides it's safe and waves us in from the path.

"A bear, maybe?" There's hope in Derry's voice. Like she wants some kind of animal to have done this. We do see them from time to time, little black bears wandering the scrub looking for berries.

"Nah," Dill says. His eyes are dark and brimming with fury. "This was no bear."

"Not unless bears wear boots," Rio says. She's squatting down in the sand on the far side of the camp, near the firepit. "Check this out."

Around the ring of rocks, where the sand is mixed with black ash, a set of footprints is clearly visible. The prints are large. A man's boots. There are distinct wavy lines across the heel. Definitely not Dill's because he goes barefoot twenty-four seven.

Maybe East's or Paz's, I think. From the party the other night. Then I remember all that rain. These are fresh prints.

Derry sinks down to sit on a big rock and she buries her face in her hands. She's crying, but Dill is already at work. He's pulled a big roll of gray duct tape out of the tent and he's ripping off long pieces with clenched teeth. "Here," he growls, and when he hands me the tape roll, I see his hands shaking. "Hang on to that for me."

I'm hoping he keeps it together. All that barely contained energy of his is great, as long as it's directed toward something positive. Which it is most of the time. When it's not, it can be like walking into a summer lightning storm.

I manage the tape and Rio holds the torn places together while Dill repairs them. He works with the deftness of a surgeon, the kind of skill that comes from living with old things. From patching up and making do instead of replacing.

In the end, he manages to close up all the holes, but he doesn't figure it'll be waterproof enough to withstand the Florida rain, so he pulls out a spare tarp and rigs that up between the trees, just to keep the water off the tent.

When Dill is finished, his shoulders finally relax, and he goes to sit next to Derry. He slips an arm around her shoulders. "It doesn't look like much," he tells her. "But it'll hold."

"It's beautiful," she tells him, and I can see that she means it. There's this softness in her eyes. She's looking at the tent, but I know for sure by the way she says it that she's thinking about Dill. There's so much love there.

"But why?" she asks. "Why would anyone do this?"

Dill's eyebrows are knitted together in a deep frown. It's weird to see that expression on his face. He looks so much more natural with a grin.

"I don't know," he says. He's staring at the tent. "Somebody lookin' for drugs, maybe." But he doesn't sound convinced.

Rio is staring at me, a question burning in her green eyes. Or a message. She walks away a little bit, to the edge of the clearing, and I follow her. "Do you have any idea who did this?" she whispers.

I shake my head. "Everyone loves Dill and Derry. Nobody ever messes with them."

Rio glances back over her shoulder toward the patched-up tent. "What if I'm right? What if it really is the Glades Reaper?"

"Why would the Glades Reaper do this?"

It doesn't make sense.

Rio pulls a folded piece of paper from her pocket. The same one she started to show me the other night at the campfire party. When I open it up, three words stand out against the white notebook page. FEAR THE REAPER is written in black. All caps.

"Where did you get this?" I ask her. The slanted angle of the letters gives them a wild kind of urgency. Like they're coming right off the page.

"Somebody left it for me at the murder site. The first night I spent back there. I woke up the next morning, and this was sitting under a rock right next to my head. Boot prints all around the clearing." She glances toward the campfire circle. "Exactly like the ones here."

"Why didn't you tell me this before?"

"I tried," she says. "But you were so convinced it wasn't him. I wasn't sure if I could trust you."

I stare at her.

"Holy shit." East's voice rings out loud in the thick quiet of the scrub. "What happened?"

Rio snatches the note back and shoves it into her pocket.

"Somebody fucked us over," Dill says. "Tore the tent to shreds." East drops the duffel bag he's carrying and crosses over to put a hand on Dill's shoulder. "It's cool, though," Dill tells him. "Got 'er all patched up."

It isn't cool, though. I can tell by the tight set of Dill's jaw and the simmering anger bubbling under his words.

East points to the big duffel bag on the ground. "I was bringing this out for Rio. It's an extra tent we had in the attic." He walks toward Dill and Derry's tent and runs his hands over the tape like he's examining a scar. "But it looks like maybe y'all need one, too."

Dill shakes his head. "It's all good. Let New Girl have that tent. She needs a dry place to sleep."

Derry slips her arm around Dill and squeezes. Then she lays her head on his shoulder. "This one'll hold for us," she says.

The five of us spend the next couple of hours sitting on Dill and Derry's overturned five-gallon buckets talking about everything except the fact that somebody carved up their tent like a Thanksgiving turkey. We smoke some of that weed Dill promised us. Eat some of the beef jerky I gave Derry the other night. Pass around a half bottle of wine. And we polish off those beautiful ripe blackberries. Then East helps Rio get her tent set up.

Once or twice when I glance at Dill, I see him staring at their tent. His hands are balled up into fists and his eyes are narrow slits. He catches me watching him and he gives me a grin and a wink.

I want to talk to Rio, find out more about that note.

Eventually, East gets hungry. He asks if anyone wants to go to the Dairy Barn with us for lunch. Dill and Derry say no. I figure they want to stick close to home. Keep an eye on things. But Rio's dying for a cheeseburger.

"I've been living on peanut butter and jelly for more than a week," she says.

The three of us pile into my truck, but we don't talk much. It's too hot to be running our mouths. Plus we're all still thinking about Dill and Derry and their tent.

The Dairy Barn is crammed, but we manage to find a not-so-clean booth in the corner. We all order burgers and shakes. Fries to split.

"Thanks again for the tent," Rio tells East. "You sure you don't need it?"

"Nah," he says, and he reaches for a fry. He's drawing little circles on my back with his other hand, and I relax against him. "Keep it as long as you want. I've got another one."

I honestly don't think that's true. East and his mom don't have money for a lot of extra stuff. But he's not the kind of person who's going to let someone sleep out in the open when he has a tent they can use.

A couple of guys from school walk in—buddies of East's—and he goes over to talk to them. So it's just me and Rio.

It feels so quiet. For the past few days, we've been talking nonstop whenever we're together, but away from the water, we don't know what to say to each other.

Everything's run dry.

All I can hear is the ever-present hum of the old window air conditioner above my head. It shakes and spits, working hard to keep the Florida heat and humidity at bay. After a minute, I don't just hear it. I feel it somewhere in my brain. In the rattling of my bones. I keep my focus low. I'm counting the grease spots on the tabletop. I know Rio is watching me.

Finally she says, "I know things sometimes." I know she's talking about the Reaper again. I look up and find the green of her eyes. "So I knew it was him. Way before I ever got that note."

It's warm in the Dairy Barn. The AC can hardly keep up with the heat. But I feel goose bumps pop up on my arms anyway. "How?" I ask.

I brace myself, because I can tell by the look on her face that she's about to tell me something really wild. "I told you that I heard about the Hidden Glen murders on a true-crime show. Remember?"

"Yeah."

"Well, that was a lie." She pauses, twisting a short piece of dark hair in her fingers. "At least it was kind of a lie. I did hear about the murders on a crime show. But I already knew about them." She hesitates. "I just didn't know what it was that I knew. Not until I happened to come across that show on TV." She sighs. Reaches for her shake. "Does that make sense?"

"Kind of," I say. But I'm honestly not sure what she's getting at.

"It's like, I've always seen it in my mind. What happened that night. The water. The trees. The knife slicing through the side of the tent. Again and again. All of it." She bites at her lower lip. "I've always had that knowledge. Since I was tiny. Like, I was born knowing it. But I didn't understand until I learned about Celeste and Bailey. Then all the puzzle pieces fit."

"What about the Glades Reaper?" I'm trying to make sense of what she's telling me.

"I knew about him, too." She stops. Backtracks. "Not in the same way exactly. But I remember the first time I heard about him." She's chewing on her straw. "When I heard that name for the first time, I recognized it. And when I heard about what he did." Rio shudders. "I knew in my bones he was connected to Hidden Glen. To that night." She's staring at me now. Waiting for me to respond. "You don't have to believe me. I know it sounds wild. Or impossible," she says, "but—"

"It doesn't," I tell her. "I mean, it does. Sound wild. But it doesn't sound impossible."

A few days ago I would have said the opposite. But everything has been so weird lately. I don't know what is or isn't possible at this point.

East comes back to the table then. Paz is with him now and he squeezes into the booth next to Rio and grabs what's left of our fries. "We hangin' tonight?" he asks.

"Movies at my place," East says. "Mom's working the night shift at the nursing home. So I gotta stick close."

Paz turns his big, brown puppy dog eyes on Rio. He's such a natural flirt, and usually it makes me laugh to see him work his magic on girls. "How 'bout you?" he asks. "Wanna make it an even foursome?"

"I think I'm gonna stick with Dill and Derry," she says. "After what happened, I just wanna make sure everything's cool out there tonight."

"Shit." Paz looks confused. "What happened to Dill and Derry. Everybody okay?"

"Yeah," East says. "It's a long story. We'll fill you in later."

Rio has to use the bathroom, so Paz hops up to let her out. She heads toward the HEIFERS and BULLS signs at the back of the Dairy Barn, but her backpack falls out onto the floor when Paz goes to sit back down. Some of her stuff spills onto the filthy linoleum.

When I bend to help Paz pick it up, something catches my attention. I see the corner of a manila envelope and the letters CRIM written in red ink, and I'm pretty sure I know what it is.

Rio has no business having it in her backpack. I bet that's one secret she had no intention of sharing with me.

TEN

AFTER THE DAIRY Barn, East and Paz ride along with me out to Hidden Glen Springs where we drop Rio off in the parking lot. Paz offers to walk her back to the homestead. I think he's 50 percent still trying to get somewhere with her and 50 percent genuinely concerned, since we filled him in on what happened to Dill and Derry's tent earlier. She tells him she's fine. That it's still daylight, and there are plenty of people around.

Besides, she's not afraid.

I spend the rest of the evening watching movies with the guys at East's house, but my mind is on Rio the whole time. I'm going back and forth between being pissed at her for taking those crime scene photos and being concerned about her safety.

"You okay, baby?" East's eyes are a darker green than usual. He always knows when something's up with me.

"Yeah," I tell him, and I reach up to trace the outline of his jaw with one finger. "Why?"

"I don't know," he says. "You seem distracted." He frowns. "You've been a little off lately."

I pull him in for a long kiss. My fingers travel over his forearms. His chest. And his hand cups the back of my neck. I pull his bottom lip into my mouth and nibble at it with my teeth, because I know that drives him crazy. And I figure it'll stop him asking any more questions. I love him for caring about me. I really do. But I'm not ready to talk to East about any of the things that are really eating at me.

"Jesus." Paz rolls his eyes. "Take it down a notch, you two. You have company, for Pete's sake."

"You know." East gives him a pointed look. "You could always go home. You do have a home, right?"

"Not a chance, lover boy." Paz laughs and shakes his head. "The AC's out at my place."

East sighs, and I get up to make more popcorn for all of us.

The next morning, I'm at the newspaper a good half hour before I'm supposed to be, which is probably the first time that's happened. Ever. Jon Boy checks the clock on the wall when I walk through the door. "Hey there, early bird," he tells me. I say a quick good morning as I grab Reese's old sweater off the coatrack, but I don't stop to chat. "You look like you're on a mission."

"It's a mess downstairs still. I want to make sure I get the nineties organized today," I lie. "Maybe start on the 2000s."

Jon Boy shakes his head and goes back to whatever he was doing on his laptop. "Trulee Bear," he says, "we both know you're never gonna finish all that before you head off to school in the fall."

I freeze for a second. One foot on the creaky basement stairs. I know I need to start telling people that I'm not going to FSU in August. That I never even finished the application. It's just over two months away.

I have to tell Mom.

I have to tell East.

I have to say it out loud. To someone.

And I have to figure out what the hell I *am* going to do. Because I don't think I'm staying here, in Mount Orange. That's a realization that's been growing in me slowly. Like a little seed that's just started to sprout.

I head down into the basement and flick the switch on the wall. It shocks me and I curse. The light buzzes, but it's not as loud today as the humming in my brain. Jon Boy was onto something. I am on a mission.

I drag a folding chair over to the back shelf and climb on top to pull down that box. The one with all Jon Boy's research. I tell myself that maybe I'm wrong. That maybe I didn't see what I saw in Rio's backpack.

But when I set the box on the floor and dig through it, I find exactly what I knew I'd find.

Or I guess I don't find what I knew I wouldn't find.

The crime scene photos are gone. Rio stole them.

I should be pissed as hell. And I am. What I can't quite work out is why I feel so goddamn hurt.

Betrayed. Or used. Or whatever.

I manage to fake work my way through the rest of the morning. I shuffle boxes around. Stack and restack some newspapers. Scrub out the coffeepot that Jon Boy never bothers to wash.

The entire time I'm trying to figure out what I'm going to say to Rio when I see her.

Around noon, Jon Boy calls me upstairs for a lunch break. He offers me half his tuna sandwich and a little bag of Fritos.

We enjoy our sad picnic in his cramped and cluttered office, under the giant portrait of his brother, Reese, that hangs over the desk. Like it is still his space. Not Jon Boy's.

"I was thinking about that conversation we had the other evening," he tells me between bites. I wait while he reaches for a bottle of sweet tea. "You're outta here in a couple months. You know?" He unscrews the cap on the tea and takes a long swig. "You gotta stop thinkin' about the Reaper and Hidden Glen. You gotta be lookin' forward now. Not back."

It hits me as a little ironic that the guy who still drinks out of his dead brother's coffee mug is telling me I need to move on. I'm wearing that sweater with Reese's name tag pinned to the front.

Jon Boy used to have an editor name tag of his own. I remember it pinned on the front of his shirt, but he must have lost it, because I haven't seen it in forever. I guess he never bothered to get a new one. He's content to live in an imaginary world where Reese is still alive and well, and where he might come back any moment to grab the sweater hanging in the corner and resume his work as editor of the *Star*.

The phone rings and Jon Boy reaches over to answer it. "*Mount Orange Star*," he says around the bit of tuna sandwich that's still in his mouth. Then his face turns serious, and he covers the phone with one hand to whisper in my direction.

"Why don't you head on out for the day, TB? Take the afternoon off." He winks at me. "A reward for comin' in early."

"Sure," I say, and I swallow the last of my sandwich.

I hop in my truck and make a beeline for the springs. I'm looking for Rio. It's time for her to answer a few questions.

I pull into the parking lot and spot her before I even get out of the car. She's stretched out on a towel at the main swimming area with Derry. I don't see Dill, but I figure he must be out in the water somewhere.

Rio looks up as I'm crossing the grass in their direction. She nudges Derry, who glances up from her reading to give me a warm smile.

"Hey, Tru." Rio's voice has that slow and sweet Tennessee honey in it on this steamy afternoon. And it immediately takes the edge off my anger, whether I want it to or not.

It riles me up, that ability she has to disarm me, in spite of myself and my better judgment.

Even now that I know she's a thief.

She gives me a little grin, and more of my hostility evaporates in the swampy heat. I'm trying to hang on to that anger. I'm clawing for it with my fingernails. But it floats away like campfire smoke.

Rio sits up and tucks her long legs underneath her, to make room for me on the blanket she and Derry are sharing.

I look out toward the spring and Dill is waving at me from the shallows. I watch him showing off for some kids. Teaching them to do handstands and somersaults under the water while their parents applaud and snap pictures on their phones from dry land.

"How're things at the paper?" Derry asks. "Any big news?"

I shrug. "Not really."

She lifts her hair up off her neck and fans herself with her magazine. "Well," she says, "you know what they say. No news is good news."

"How was last night?" I ask them. "Anything else happen back at the homestead?" Rio and Derry both shake their heads.

"It was quiet all night long," Rio says. "I guess whoever fucked up the tent figured he'd gotten the point across."

I'm trying to work out how to get Rio away from Derry for a few minutes so I can pin her down about the missing crime scene photos, but Dill makes it easy for me. He calls Derry down to the water's edge and she goes to sit on a rock closer to him. He acts like such a little kid sometimes, with his *watch this* and *did you see that?* ways.

She gives him the applause he's craving, and then he tries to drag her into the water to cool off. She protests, but he won't take no for an answer, so she laughs and gives in. I watch her slip out of her flowy skirt and wrap her long, honey-colored hair higher on her head to keep it dry. She's wearing just a tank top and underwear when Dill helps her into the spring. She doesn't care a bit. The two of them bob up and down in the deep blue. Nose to nose. He's pressing kisses to her forehead as she clings to him. They're so oblivious to everything and everyone else around them.

I wonder what that must feel like. To be that consumed with love.

The only thing I feel that intensely is the need to dive.

"I'm glad last night was quiet," I tell Rio. "I was worried—"

"He'll be back," Rio says. "I didn't tell Dill and Derry that. I didn't show 'em that note or anything. No use in getting 'em all worked up." She hesitates and reaches down to scratch at a bug bite. "I'm pretty sure it's me he's after. I'm the one who's been poking around out here. Asking questions. Stirring shit up."

I decide not to waste any more time. "There's an envelope missing from the research box at the *Star*," I tell her. "The one we were digging through the other day." Rio is focused on Dill and Derry down in the water. "Crime scene photos. From the Hidden Glen murders." She won't look at me, and I feel my anger creeping back in. "Rio." My voice has a sharpness to it that makes me kind of proud. She finally turns to face me. "Did you take them?"

She stares at me for a long minute. I can see her mind spinning behind her eyes. I figure she's trying to come up with a lie, so it surprises me when she hits me with the truth instead.

"Yeah. I did."

I'm stunned for a second, but then I remember I'm pissed. "Jesus!" I tell her. "You could get me in big trouble. What if my boss found out?" It feels a teensy bit disingenuous to call Jon Boy my boss, but that's what he is. Isn't he? "I told him the truth about you. I told him we were friends. That you weren't really a true-crime podcaster."

"Well what the fuck did you do that for?" Rio's the one who looks surprised now. "He didn't need to know that."

"Because I'm not a liar," I say.

Rio's lip twitches and she drags her fingers through her hair. Then she breaks into a crooked grin. "I guess I got what I deserved. Expecting a girl named Tru to lie for me."

"If he finds out those photos are missing, he's gonna think either I let you take 'em or I took 'em myself."

The grin melts off Rio's face.

"I'm sorry. I swear to God, I'm not a liar, either. Most of the time," she says.

"That's why you showed up at the newspaper pretending to be someone else," I counter. "Because you're such a truth teller."

Rio rolls her eyes. "I said most of the time." She reaches down to pick up a tiny lizard that's scampering across the blanket. We watch it work its way over her fingers and up her arm. "The thing is, I was afraid if I asked to see that research again, the answer would be no." She takes a long, deep breath. "And I really needed to see it."

"Why is this all so important to you?" I demand.

Rio sets the lizard back in the grass before she turns to look at me. "Why is it so important to you?"

"Because it's my town," I tell her. "My history."

Rio nods. She doesn't take her eyes off mine. "It's my history, too. That's why I needed to get a look at the photos from that night," she goes on. "I needed to see if I had it right."

"You wanted to see if the photos matched up with what was in your head."

"I didn't think about getting you in trouble. I figured nobody ever looked at that stuff."

"Were you right?" I ask her. "About the details."

Rio nods again. "I've always seen stripes. I never knew what they were. I just had this image in my head of horizontal stripes." I must look confused because she clarifies for me. "Celeste's tank top." She pulls the manila envelope out of her bag and slides out one of the photos. "It's all horizontal stripes. See?"

Rio's right. I can't tell what color they are, because it's a black-and-white photo, but Celeste's tank top is all sideways stripes.

I tear my eyes away from the dead girl and look over at Rio. She's staring down at the picture of Celeste in my hand. Body tangled in the sleeping bag. One muddy foot poking out. Blood smeared everywhere. Black when it should be red. The tent slashed into a hundred gaping smiles.

Just like Dill and Derry's tent.

"They never found the knife," she says. "Did they?"

"Just the tip. It broke off. They found it during the autopsy." Lodged in Celeste's liver.

"You think he took it with him?" she asks. "The murder weapon."

"Probably," I say. "It doesn't seem like the kind of thing you'd wanna leave lying around."

"It's weird to think maybe it's out there in somebody's base-ment," Rio says. She reaches up to brush the hair out of her face, and her arm grazes mine. The lightest sensation of skin on skin. My arm tingles, like I've felt that touch a million times. "In a box," she adds with a little shiver. "Or whatever."

I have this wild urge to reach out and take her hand, and it's like I know exactly the way our fingers will lace together. The way I know with East.

Rio pulls at me like nobody—nothing—else ever has.

Except the bottom of Elijah's Well.

I glance down at the photo again, and that's when I notice it. I hadn't realized it the first time I saw the picture—because I was so unsettled by the blood, and the body—but there's no gold half heart around Celeste's neck.

"Where's her best-friends locket?" I say out loud. Rio squints at me, confused. "They wore them all the time. Both of them." I pull out my phone and flip to the pictures Rio snapped in the *Star* basement the other day. "See. Look at these newspaper photos." I show her their senior pictures from all the articles. "They both wore a half heart around their necks. All the time." I glance back down at the black-and-white image in my hand. "Celeste would have had hers on that night, too."

Rio is frowning. She pulls the other photo out of the manila envelope and studies it. "Bailey doesn't have hers on, either," she says.

"Hers was found later. At the crime scene."

I don't tell her that it was years later. Or that I was the one who found it.

I definitely don't tell her it's a few feet away, tucked in my backpack.

"Maybe she left it at home that night," Rio tells me.

"Maybe," I say, but I'm not convinced. I've looked back at the high school yearbook from that year. In every single photo, Bailey and Celeste have those matching necklaces on. Band practices. Basketball games. Study hall. The senior trip to Orlando. Every picture.

"Or maybe he took it," Rio adds. "The Reaper."

I think about what Jon Boy told me, how the Reaper always took a trophy. A souvenir. He said nothing was taken from the Hidden Glen campsite.

What if he was wrong about that?

I hand the photo of Celeste back to Rio and she studies it for a second before she says, "You can have them back. So you won't get in trouble." Her words have the sound of an apology. "But we should take pics of them. Before we return them." I hand her my phone and she snaps photos of both eight-by-tens before she slips them into the manila envelope and hands it back to me. I tuck it into my backpack and zip it up tight.

The crowds are continuing to grow. It's too loud, all the laughing and music and kids shouting to each other. I need a little space. Some room to breathe.

"You wanna see another spring?" I ask her. "A secret one?" My face flushes because I sound like such a little kid. "I mean, it's not deep enough to dive or anything like that. But it's cool." I hesitate. "If you haven't been there yet. I thought—"

"Tru. Stop." Rio's face is all lit up and her eyes flash almost as bright as when she first came up from her dive the other day. She arches one eyebrow at me. "You had me at secret spring."

We tell Dill and Derry we're going for a walk, and I lead Rio around the main spring and down off the boardwalk. A narrow, sandy trail meanders through the tall grass back toward the scrub, halfway between the Well and Dill and Derry's homestead.

I try to ask a little more about her family, where she came

from. Because right now, it's like she dropped out of the sky and landed in the middle of Hidden Glen Springs. But Rio refuses to give me any real information. She dances. Evades. Dives deep into her own mind and swims away.

Maybe she isn't a liar by nature. But she's definitely a hider.

I guess two can play that game, though.

We come to a fork, and Rio starts down the overgrown path to the right. There's no sign to mark the trail we're on. Nothing that indicates there's anything at all worth seeing up ahead.

"How did you know which way to go?" I ask her, and she stops walking. I see her look around like she's trying to figure that out herself.

"I don't know," she says, and she takes off walking again. I have to hurry to catch up. Her legs are so much longer than mine. "A lucky guess."

From the fork, the path winds another two hundred yards or so farther into the tangle of trees before it dead-ends at a sparkling pool. It's dark and shaded here. The spring is small and shallow. No more than four feet at its deepest. There's no grassy lawn to relax on, like at the main spring. No rocky places to sit and soak up the sun, either, like back at the Well. There's just a thick tangle of trees and shrubs fighting for space right up to the edge of the water. So it's not as popular as its sisters. I've always thought it was beautiful, though. It's hidden and private and wilder than the other springs. Like something left over from prehistory.

A set of three metal steps leads down into the water, so I slide off my flip-flops and settle on the top step with my feet in the cold of the spring.

Rio kicks off her shoes and sits beside me. "Wow," she breathes. Her voice sounds loud in the close-pressed silence of the thick scrub. "It really is a secret spring."

We're sitting shoulder to shoulder in the sticky heat.

"This one is delicate. Fragile, I guess. The ecology of it. They don't want a lot of people back here. Locals all know about it, of course. Not many of them come back here, though."

"Does it have a name?" Rio asks, and I nod.

"It's called Yucha Spring," I tell her. "It's a Timucuan word."

"What's it mean?"

"Two." I'm staring at our faces reflected on the surface of the water. "It means two." I point toward the bubbles streaming from twin cracks in the rock. "See? Two separate vents."

"Two," Rio repeats. She reaches down and stirs at our reflections with one finger. Our features disappear, then re-form as the water settles. Two sets of eyes stare up at us. One dark blue and one bright green. "It's beautiful here."

I barely hear the faraway sounds of people down at the main spring. We're a million miles away from all that, like we've gone back in time.

"Yeah," I say. "I come back here a lot. When I need to be alone."

I reach down and grab a floating stick. I try to break it in half, but it's too waterlogged. It only bends. I toss it back out into the middle of the spring and watch it make its way toward us again.

"It seems like a good spot for that," Rio tells me.

"It's kind of my private place."

Rio's expression is unreadable, but her eyes are shining. "And you shared it with me."

"I guess I did." Something tickles at me, like a fly walking across the back of my neck. But when I reach up to brush it away, there's nothing there.

The stick has made its way back to us, so I pick it up and toss it out into the middle of the spring again. A solo game of fetch.

Suddenly Rio gets to her feet. She grabs me by the hand and pulls me up, too. "Come on," she says. "I'm tired of looking."

She leads me down the stairs into the water, and I hiss when the cold stings my thighs. Something about going in wearing shorts and a T-shirt makes it feel even icier.

Rio lets go of my hand and dives below the surface of the shallow water, and I follow her. We don't have masks, but the water is clear. When I open my eyes, I see Rio swimming beside me.

We spend a long time exploring the shallow spring together. We're below the surface more than we're above it. We're searching for treasures. Polished rocks and little shells that flash silver in the sunlight. Every time Rio finds something beautiful, she shows it to me before she gives it back to the spring.

I find a little sliver of broken shell. The soft inside is lined with pink. *These are her favorite*, I think. *The smooth ones with all the pink*. I'm breaking the surface with the treasure clutched in my fist before I have time to wonder how I knew that.

When I present it to her, she lets out a long breath. "I love these," she whispers. Her voice is suddenly low and thick. As if she's about to cry. She cups water into her hands and splashes her face, then plucks the shell from my fingers. Her eyes are the color of eelgrass and she's smiling a smile that warms like a memory.

I swear that every time I look at her, she's more a part of the spring. More a part of me.

When we finally finish exploring, we float on our backs together. Our ears are below the surface, so the calling birds and the shouts of people down at the main spring are all muffled. The sounds bleed together.

There's the hushed music of bubbles escaping the vent.

The whooshing noise automatic doors make when they open and close.

Our heartbeats. Maybe.

For a second, I see myself as Bailey. Floating on my back in the middle of the Well. My hair floats out around me like the tendrils of an aquatic plant, and blood colors the water as dark as midnight.

I tense. But then I hear Rio breathing softly beside me.

And I'm Tru again.

When we're tired of floating, we stand together in the waist-deep pool, in our little circle of blue. "It's so quiet back here," Rio says. "The main spring is always so crowded."

I shrug. "It's summer vacation. What can you do?"

"Is it less crowded in the winter?" she asks me. "Wakulla Springs always clears out when the temps drop. Winter's the best time to dive up there. But it's never empty."

"You can't swim here for most of the winter," I tell her.

"How come?"

"Manatees," I explain. "When the water temperature in the river drops, the manatees come up the run into the springs here to stay warm. It's a designated refuge, so nobody is allowed in the water when the manatees are in. You can come and see them, though. Some days you can count more than a hundred of them in the main spring."

Rio loses her balance, and she reaches out to grab my arm. I'm a little unsteady, too. Like the sand is shifting under my feet. It reminds me of walking through one of those fun house mazes where the floor slants at weird angles.

"We get manatees up at Wakulla. But not like that." She's watching me and it takes me a second to realize she still has her hand on my arm. "Maybe I'll get to see them here this winter." She frowns. "But I guess you won't be here, will you?"

I come so close to telling her I'm not going to FSU. I'm tired of holding that lie, and Rio feels like the person I should tell. She reaches up to brush the water out of my eyes. In that moment, I want to tell her all my secrets. Every single one. But a sound stops me. A sharp snap in the scrub. Rio and I freeze. We're listening. Not moving.

Another snap.

Then another.

And another.

Too big to be a rabbit. Or a possum.

The sound is deliberate. Even. Not like the scurrying of an animal wandering through the undergrowth.

Rio and I stand completely still as the sound shifts around the little spring. It started near the stairs, but now it's moved halfway around the circle. No one should be back there. There's no path. No trail on that side of the spring. There's only thick, twisting scrub.

Under the water, Rio slips her hand around mine. Our fingers weave together. She squeezes hard.

There's another snap. I see the swaying of branches. Something big is circling us. Something tall.

Something distinctly human.

"Shhh," Rio whispers so softly I can barely make it out.

"Hey! There you are!" I spin around to see East jogging down the path toward us. He stops at the little stairs. "Dill and Derry said y'all went for a walk. I figured you might be back here."

I look at Rio, and she's still staring across to the backside of the spring. To where those footsteps stopped.

"Yeah," I say. "I—"

Rio lets go of my hand and I move toward the steps. Toward East. He reaches out to pull me from the water.

Our fingers interlock. Just like mine and Rio's.

"We need to go," he tells me in a low voice. "Your mom is sick. At work. They need somebody to pick her up."

"Shit," I say. "Shit." East pulls a towel out of my backpack and hands it to me. I wipe my hands before I dig my phone out of the front pocket. Four missed calls from Realty One. I turn back to look at Rio. She's still frozen in the middle of the spring. "We gotta go," I tell her.

"Yeah," she says. "Okay." She makes her way to the steps, and

I hand her my towel. We both pick up our backpacks and follow East down the trail.

We leave Rio at the main spring with Dill and Derry, and when we get to the parking lot, East pulls me in for a hug. "Hey," he says. "Look at me, Tru." He puts a finger under my chin and tilts my face up toward his so I can't avoid his eyes. "You're not alone. Okay? Whatever's going on with your mom, I'll help. I promise."

"I love you," I tell him. I mean it so much. My protector.

It almost burns a hole in my chest to look at him.

He touches my face and I run my eyes over his chest. The way that T-shirt fits him ought to be illegal.

I think about how perfect he is.

I think about how perfect everyone says he is for me.

Then he leans in for a kiss, and I realize that East has almost the greenest eyes that I have ever seen.

ELEVEN

EAST AND I find Mom passed out on the couch in the break-room at Realty One. The only other human in the office today is Donald, a guy who looks like he should be an assistant principal somewhere. He gives us a sad smile, then leans against the door-frame and watches, sipping his coffee from a Styrofoam cup, as we guide her out the back door and into my truck.

East knows the drill. He helps me drag Mom into the house and waits while I get her tucked into bed. Then we curl up on the couch to watch a movie and he holds me until he has to go home and watch Seth so his mom can go to work.

Later, I make myself a grilled cheese sandwich and eat it in the silent house while trying not to stare at that picture of Dani and me. Then I head upstairs and unzip the pocket of my back-pack to let Bailey's half heart slip into my hand.

I rub it with my thumb like a good luck charm and wonder where the other half is.

Who has it.

I flip on the light and drag my backpack up onto the bed with me; the manila envelope isn't inside.

I dump everything out on my rumpled comforter.

Towel.

Mask.

Fins.

Hairbrush.

Water bottle.

A million hair ties.

A couple of random seashells and a shit ton of sand.

No crime scene photos.

How is that possible? I slipped them into my backpack my-self when Rio handed them to me. I know I did.

Someone stole the photos. When we were at Yucha Springs. That's the only explanation.

Rio stole them from Jon Boy.

Then someone stole them from me.

I push the backpack and all my stuff off onto the floor and turn off the light, but I don't sleep. I lie there, wondering if someone is looking at those crime scene photos right now.

And if they have the other half of a tarnished gold heart clutched tight in their hand.

The same way I do.

Mom's asleep when I get out of bed the next morning, which means she's going to be late. I tell myself that's not my problem.

I bang on her door, though. Three good hard knocks. She answers with a muffled "I'm up." So I figure I've done my duty.

When I get to the *Star* offices for work, Jon Boy doesn't greet me when I walk in, but I hear voices coming from his office. He sticks his head out to give me a quick hello, then closes his of-fice door.

I don't really have the mental energy to wonder who it is he's talking to. I'm too busy going over and over the fact that somebody stole those crime scene photos out of my backpack while Rio and I were swimming.

I head down the stairs to the basement and try to do some actual organizing, but my mind is on that box on the top shelf at the back of the basement. And the photos I know aren't inside.

At noon, Jon Boy sends me to the Dairy Barn to get us lunch, and Knox is standing outside smoking a cigarette when I come back.

He tips his cowboy hat when he sees me. Knox likes to put on like he's this pillar of society now. That he's cleaned up his act and all that. Holier than thou. He's front row at First Baptist every Sunday.

I wonder how he'd act if he knew that East told me he got pissed and broke a window out at his mama's place. Drunk off his ass and being rowdy. Just like old times.

Knox doesn't say a word as I head back into the newspaper office with my bag of burgers and fries. He also sure as shit doesn't bother himself to open the door for me as I try to juggle two large shakes. So much for being this town's knight in shining armor.

After work, East is waiting for me in the parking lot out at Hidden Glen. He's sitting on the split rail fence, and he gives me the most adorable grin when I hop out of the truck. Normally, that might distract me a little bit. But today, all I can think about is slipping into the springs.

"Hey," he whispers in my ear as his hands go around my waist. "I've been missing you today." He pulls me in for a long, slow kiss. His fingers are in my hair. Sliding up and down my arms. Then snaking around under my shirt to caress my lower back.

"I missed you, too," I tell him, but I'm already reaching back into the truck for my dive bag. East chuckles.

"God, you're impatient," he says. But he's smiling, and the way his dimples twitch when he grins reminds me of when we were kids. I suddenly miss that other version of us. Back when we were just best friends. Running free through the scrub, hunting for cicada shells and racing our bikes down the dirt road between our houses.

My chest hurts a little bit thinking about it.

So I make myself slow down and I take the time to kiss him back. Like he deserves.

"I love you, truly. Truly, dear," he murmurs in tune. Our old song.

"I love you, too, East," I say.

I do love him.

I really do.

We love each other.

His teeth are on my earlobe now.

We love each other so much.

We always have.

His lips are on my neck.

Ever since we were kids.

I was his very first kiss.

He thinks he was mine.

When I finally pull away and grab my dive bag, East sighs.

Then he reaches up to tuck a stand of hair behind my ear. "I know what you need," he tells me. "I can see it in your eyes."

He holds my hand as we follow the boardwalk up the run to the Well, and there are only a couple of people there. No Dill or Derry.

No Rio.

I'm wondering where she is. There's so much we have to figure out.

But I can't wait for her. I need to get below. So East and I take turns diving the Well, and I push myself a little more each time, going just a foot deeper and a few seconds longer on every dive. The last time I come up, I'm light-headed and disoriented.

"That's enough, Tru," East says. "You need to take a break."

But it isn't enough, because thoughts about Rio and those missing crime scene photos and Dani and FSU flood my brain as soon as the perfect stillness of the last dive fades.

We wander back toward the main spring and find a spot under one of the big, old live oaks that ring the swimming area. He points out a line of eight turtles, the ones we call river cooters, basking on a log in the sunshine. One by one, they plop into the water and swim away. Then we watch a couple of long-necked anhingas perched on the rocks with their wings all spread out, waiting for their feathers to dry after diving for fish. We even spot a little alligator resting at the edge of the run, almost completely hidden in the duckweed, only his eyes and the ridges along his tail giving him away.

We used to spend all day every day out here in the summers.

We'd chase lizards and frogs and make mud pies and climb trees until we were filthy. Then we'd take turns pushing each other off the jumping platform and letting the cold water wash us clean again.

I don't know why those days are on my mind so much this afternoon.

"Remember playing here when we were little?" I ask, and East reaches for my hand.

"You were my very first friend," he tells me. "It's always been you and me, Tru."

He's right. Ever since the very first day of preschool. I asked to borrow his purple crayon, and we never looked back.

Paz shows up just then. He grumbles and curses when we ask about the red teeth marks on his ankle. "Damn shih tzu had his way with me," he says, and he begs East to come swim with him. Says he's dying of heatstroke from walking dogs all day. East gives me a grin and a shrug and the two of them head for the jumping platform. I watch them push and shove at each other, until Paz goes over the edge into the water with a surprised shriek, and East cannonballs in right behind him.

It isn't long before I catch sight of Rio coming out of the scrub, where the trail back to Dill and Derry's homestead disappears into the trees. Maybe she can feel me watching her, because she stops and scans the crowd at the swimming area until her eyes land on me. Then she raises a hand to wave.

When she reaches my spot under the big tree, she drops to the ground beside me. Her fingers are stained purple, and she tells me she's been helping Derry hunt for blackberries most of the day, and that Dill taught her how to use the bark of a gumbo-limbo tree to soothe the places where she got all scraped up traipsing through the thick scrub. She's smiling, and I see something hiding in her eyes. Some emotion she hasn't given words to yet. I think maybe she's finally going to tell me something about her family. Or her past. But all she says is "It's nice, having people." The way she leans against my shoulder lets me know she's including me in that thought, not just Dill and Derry.

I hate to ruin the mood, but I figure I better tell her my news.

"Somebody took the crime scene photos out of my backpack." Rio's smile fades. "While we were swimming back at Yucha Spring yesterday."

"Holy shit," Rio whispers. Her frown deepens. "I really am gonna get you fired."

"Nah," I say. "You won't. I mean, Jon Boy is gonna be pissed as hell. But he won't fire me. He's practically family."

"Who would steal those photos?" Rio asks. She's chewing on her lip and staring out at the water where East and Paz are horsing around like a couple of kids. "Do you have any ideas?"

"I don't know. Whoever was trying to scare me on the trail, I guess."

Rio nods. "Same person who tore into Dill and Derry's tent."

"Probably," I say.

"Definitely," she tells me. "Same person who left me that note when I first got here. 'Fear the Reaper.'"

I'm starting to feel like I can't breathe on land.

Like I'm suffocating.

I turn to Rio. "Will you dive with me?"

"You know I will." Her eyes are so green today, and I notice that her face is flushed. From the heat.

I yell to East that I'm going back to dive the Well with Rio. I can tell by the way he winces that he doesn't like it. But he doesn't say anything. He's not the kind of guy to try to tell me what to do. Which is why it's weird that I haven't been able to work up the courage to tell him I don't want to follow him to Florida State this fall.

It's hard, veering off the path. Even if nobody ever asked me which path I wanted to take in the first place, sending my life careening around an unexpected curve seems really terrifying.

Maybe it's easier to keep moving straight ahead.

I follow Rio up the boardwalk to the Well. It's late in the day, and we're the only two inside the safety fence.

She lets me go down first, and I follow the light and the shadow as they dance together under the surface. I let them lead me deeper and deeper, until I become part of the spring. The closer I get to the bottom, the harder it is to tell where I stop and the water begins.

I start to think that maybe I'm made of water.

No more muscles or skin. Or bones.

I'm only water and sunlight.

I catch a glimpse of Bailey. Floating hair like pond tendrils.

Reaching for me. Begging me to just keep going.

When I look again, there's nothing there.

Of course. It was just a trick. Sunlight and shadow dancing together under the water.

I push myself harder and deeper and longer than I ever have before, and my body splinters into shards of pure ecstasy.

I don't make it to the bottom, though, so my itch doesn't get scratched. It doesn't go away. I need to get even deeper next time.

Go farther.

Last longer.

When it's Rio's turn, I stand on the rocks above and watch her like she's a Weeki Wachee mermaid and I'm her captivated audience. She moves like someone who's performing ballet without even realizing they're dancing.

When she comes up, she tells me I look hot. And it makes me snort. So I let her pull me into the water with her.

We float and bob. Diving is everything to me, so I forget sometimes how good it feels to simply relax in the water. Topside. Like a normal person.

When we're good and waterlogged, we haul ourselves out to sit on the rocks.

"Was your sister a diver, too?" Rio asks me.

"No," I tell her. "Dani was really different from me. I mean, we were close, you know. But she was an artist. That was her thing. She loved to paint. And draw. Flowers and cats and all kinds of stuff." I hear the words spilling out of me. The spatter of syllables as they hit the rocks, like an overflowing fountain. It's like the spring water dissolved whatever stone has been lodged in my throat all these years. I can't stop talking. "She hated being outside. Too hot. Too many bugs." I stop and stare down at my toes. Chipped black nail polish. "She did teach me to swim, though. Mom and Dad couldn't afford swimming lessons."

"Why didn't your mom and dad teach you?" Rio asks, and I sigh. Because that's a good question.

"My mom is—" I stop. I'm not sure what I want to say. "She has her own issues. And my dad is pretty much useless. Even before Dani died, they weren't exactly winning any parenting awards." Rio is quiet, and I'm wondering if this is a doorway that she's propped open for me. I decide to step through. "What about your mom and dad?"

At first I think she isn't going to answer. But then she does.

"I haven't seen my mom in years. And as for my dad . . ." Rio shrugs. "Your guess is as good as mine."

"You never knew him?"

She shakes her head. "My mom wouldn't ever talk about him. I don't even know his name." She leans down to trail her fingers through the water. "She told me he was dead. But who knows if that's even true. Most of the shit she told me wasn't."

"A lot of people lie about a lot of things," I say. "Don't they?"

Rio looks over at me, her dark lashes sweeping low across her eyes. "I know I told you I wasn't a liar," she says. "But I am." She scoots a little closer to me on the rock. Some kind of warning fires off in my brain, but, before I have time to process it, I feel the press of her thigh against mine. "I don't want to be, though. Maybe you can help me be more honest." She laughs. "My new friend, Tru."

She's holding me hostage with those eyes. And the pressure of her thigh against mine.

I can't talk. Or breathe. Or think.

Something deep inside tells me to run. But I don't move. I just stare down at my toes, chipped black. When I finally look back up, Rio's face is inches from mine.

The loud clank of metal on metal makes us both jump. A couple of older guys I recognize from the dive club have pushed open the safety gate. They shout a friendly hello as they drop their gear on the rocks on the other side of the spring.

That's all it takes. A clank. And a shout.

The spell has been broken. Rio is staring at her own reflection. I don't know where to let my eyes rest. Or what to say. It's Rio who breaks the silence between us.

"Let's go back to the campsite."

"To Dill and Derry's?" I ask, and Rio shakes her head. She turns to look over her shoulder. Back into the scrub.

I hesitate. It's almost dusk, and somebody cut up Dill and Derry's tent.

Stole those photos.

Stalked me in the dark.

Left Rio that *Fear the Reaper* note.

"Come on," she pleads. "I haven't been back there since I started staying at the homestead."

I agree and we pull on our shorts and T-shirts so we can head out through the gate. My stomach flip-flops and my heart is beating loud as Rio and I stand side by side, just outside the tree line. I turn to look at her, and for a split second, she doesn't look quite like herself. I mean, I see her. Long legs, perfect skin, and eyes that light up the dark. But there's someone else there, too. Someone who only shows at the very edges.

An echo.

It's shadowy in the scrub. The trees are blocking out what's left of the light. We move through the thick tangle, back toward the clearing. It feels like we're walking back in time. Like the distance between the Well and the campsite is measured in years, not feet or yards.

With every step, I pause. Listen for the snap of twigs. Look for swaying branches. Anything that might hint we aren't alone out here.

But there's only the pounding of my heart.

The quiet sound of Rio's breathing beside me.

We're almost to the clearing. A few more steps. Push aside a branch. Knock down a spiderweb.

And then we're there. Standing on hallowed, haunted ground. The clearing where Bailey and Celeste died. My eyes find the spot where the tent stood. The place marked on Jon Boy's map by that blood-red X.

I see their tent so clearly. The zipper on the door. The places where the fabric has been faded by the Florida sun. The way one of the poles is bent just a little.

The zipper sticks. You have to be gentle with it.

"Tru." Rio's voice is unsteady.

I turn in the direction she's looking. Toward the skinny pine tree to the east of the crime scene. Where the killer might have stood that night.

Something is tacked up there.

We move closer, and we both realize what it is at the exact same moment.

We don't move.

We don't speak.

We just stare.

Rio reaches for my hand. Her fingers clutch tight around mine.

Stuck to the tree are two glossy eight-by-ten photos. In one, Celeste lies bleeding and tangled in her sleeping bag. In the other, Bailey floats faceup in the Well.

Except the faces aren't right.

"It's us," Rio whispers. Her own face has been cut out and glued to Celeste's body.

And Bailey has my shoulder-length red hair. My blue-black eyes.

Now it's us bleeding out in the scrub.

Our turn to die.

TWELVE

RIO PULLS THE photos off the tree. Our faces are cut from printed images. They're candid snapshots. Taken out here at the springs. Rio and me sitting side by side under the big live oak at the main swimming area. They're grainy. You can tell they were taken from far away and then zoomed in close.

Someone is stalking us.

There's a rustling in the leaves behind us and Rio and I whirl around to face a giant raccoon staring at us from the edge of the clearing.

"We need to go," I say, and Rio slides the photos into her backpack.

When we reach the main spring, Paz and East are sitting in the grass, waiting for us. They've made plans to grab a pizza, then spend the evening at Paz's house playing video games. They ask me if I want to come, but I'm too freaked out to spend the whole night pretending everything's fine.

I tell myself I shouldn't be keeping more secrets, especially not from East, but that doesn't stop me from kissing him goodbye, then turning to Rio and saying, "You wanna come to my place for a while?"

It's Saturday, dollar beer night at the Wild Clover, which means Mom won't be home.

"Yeah," she says. "I don't want to be here right now."

We make our way up toward my truck, and it's mostly quiet on the ride. I switch the headlights on as we pull out onto the highway, to fight back against the looming darkness, and Rio slides the crime scene photos out of her backpack. She's staring at our faces on those dead bodies.

I think about what I know about the girl sitting beside me in my truck. And it isn't much.

She was born in Nashville, Tennessee. But she grew up in Crawfordville, Florida. Near Tallahassee.

Her mom said her dad was dead. But her mom is a liar.

She spent some time in foster care.

That's it.

I park in the carport and Rio follows me up the steps and in the front door of our house.

When I flip the lights on, Rio sees the big photo over the television. "That's you and Dani?" she asks, and I nod. She turns to study me with serious eyes. "You look like her."

"It's weird," I say, "being older now than she ever was."

I find some microwave dinners in the freezer and heat them up for us. Lasagna for me. Meatloaf for Rio. We eat them right out of the plastic containers at the kitchen table.

We're sitting in my air-conditioned house, but really, we're still back at the springs, standing in that clearing. Sweat rolling down our backs while we stare at those photos tacked up on that pine tree.

When I clear away the dinner stuff, Rio pulls those photos

out again. We lay them on the kitchen table and study them under the bright light.

"These were taken yesterday," she tells me.

"Yeah." I recognize what we're wearing.

"Do you remember seeing anybody out there? Anybody with a camera?"

"No," I tell her. "But they were probably taken on a phone. Right? Nobody uses a real camera anymore. And everybody has a phone on them."

"I don't know," Rio says. She picks up the photo of Celeste and studies her own face up close. "These look like they were taken from really far away. I think it had to be a real camera. The kind with a serious zoom."

Maybe she's right. I don't know anything about cameras, except that I don't remember seeing anybody with one.

Rio carefully peels our cutout faces off the photographs. She keeps the faces, slipping them into her back pocket, but she hands the crime scene photos back to me. So I can put them back in the research box.

I don't bother to point out that we're still missing the manila envelope they're supposed to be in.

My phone rings then, and my heart sinks when I see a familiar number pop up on the screen. "Shit," I say. "I have to answer this."

It's Billy. The manager out at the Wild Clover. Mom's had enough for tonight, he tells me, even though it's only a few minutes after nine o'clock. She needs a ride home. ASAP.

"There's something I have to take care of," I tell Rio. She looks intrigued, but she doesn't ask any questions. She just follows me back out to the truck without a word.

When we pull into the Wild Clover parking lot, Rio raises an eyebrow at me. The music from inside the bar seeps into my truck. A couple of people are leaning against the outside wall, smoking cigarettes under the blinking neon sign.

"My mom," I explain. "She needs a ride home. She drinks." I shrug. "Too much sometimes."

Rio doesn't look at all fazed. "I'll come too," she says. "In case you need help."

The guy checking IDs at the door doesn't stop us from entering. In fact, he barely glances in my direction. I see him giving Rio a good look over, though. "Evenin', Tru," he tells me. "Your mama's inside. A couple of guys was givin' 'er a hard time. Figured she'd be better off at home, state she's in."

Billy is behind the counter, but he points toward a corner table, and there's Mom all slumped over with her head on her arms. Spilled beer drips from the edge of the table and puddles on the sticky floor.

I manage to shake her awake enough to haul her to her feet. I slip my arm around her waist, and Rio does the same on the other side, and together we drag her out the door and somehow manage to get her up into my truck.

Mom's crowded onto the bench seat, sandwiched in between me and Rio, but we're over halfway home before she seems to realize there's a stranger sitting right next to her.

"Who's this?" she asks me, and Rio gives me a little grin.

"A new friend," I say, and that seems to be enough to satisfy her curiosity. She leans back and passes out for the rest of the short drive.

When we get her inside the house, Mom glances up at the big, framed photograph over the television. Two little girls she used to know.

Neither one of them exist anymore.

It's no wonder she stops and stares at it. Everyone who comes in the door does the same thing. You can't not look at it. It fills up the whole wall behind the TV.

Sometimes it seems to fill up the whole living room.

The whole house, even.

Nights like this, I'd swear it fills up my whole life.

Rio waits on the couch while I get Mom ready for bed. It takes a while, but once I get her settled, I grab a bottle of cheap wine from the fridge and Rio and I move out to sit on the front porch steps. We stare across the road to where the flickering lights of a television glow in the front window of Mr. and Mrs. Binger's place.

"Does that happen a lot?" Rio finally asks. "With your mom?"

I shrug and swat at a mosquito, but I'm too late. It's already drawn blood. "I don't know." I'm busy trying to get the screw cap off the wine. "Define 'a lot.'"

"My mom never drank," Rio says. I can feel those green eyes on me. "She did plenty of drugs, though." She reaches up to brush her hair away from her face. "Meth, among other things. Still does, I'm sure. Unless she's dead and nobody bothered to tell me."

"My mom's not that bad," I say. The wine is finally open, so I take a long drink before I hand the bottle to Rio. "She's been through a lot."

"So have you," Rio reminds me. She tips the bottle up and makes a face as the sticky sweet liquid runs down her throat. Then she holds the bottle up to look at the label. "Peach, huh?"

"Sorry," I say. "It's all we have at the moment." She's close enough that I can feel her breathing.

"What do you think she's gonna do when you go off to college next year?" she asks me.

"I'm not going." I take the bottle back and take another swig. It really is disgusting. That's why Mom hasn't downed it yet. But at least it's wet. And cool.

"You gonna stay here?" Rio asks. "To look out for your mom?"

"Nah," I say. "I don't have any idea what I'm gonna do. But I'm getting the hell out of this place."

"Your boyfriend know that?" Rio's tone is teasing as she reaches for the wine, but I can tell the question is a serious one.

"Nope," I say.

"There's a lot of stuff he doesn't know, huh?"

"There's a lot of stuff nobody knows."

It's quiet for a few long seconds while we pass that bottle back and forth. I'm starting to feel the wine a little. I'm a long way from drunk, but I'm definitely more relaxed.

"Why haven't you told anybody you're not going to FSU?" Rio finally asks.

"I don't know," I admit. "I'm scared to shake things up. You know? To admit that maybe I want something different."

"Even if you don't know what it is."

I nod. "Yeah."

Rio takes a long look at me, then passes me the half-empty bottle. "You know why we dive, Tru? The real reason?" She picks up a little bit of gravel and pitches it out into the dark. Like she's playing baseball. "Because that's how we find out who we are. What we're made of. We dive down deep. As far as we can. For as long as we can. Till we almost can't see the sun anymore. And then we hold our breath and kick like hell till we make it back to the surface."

"That's pretty deep," I tell her. "No pun intended."

Rio snorts, and I do, too. The sound floats up and away into the night like sparks from a fire.

"Okay, well, the truth is Dill told me that last night," she admits, and she takes the bottle back. I watch her swallow another long drink of wine. She barely makes a face this time. "But I thought it was pretty good."

A car hurtles down the dirt road in front of the house. Headlights and flying dust. Radio blasting some twangy country song.

In an instant I'm thinking about Dani. The change in mood feels like the shift in the air just before an afternoon thunderstorm. Rio can feel it, too, because she's looking at me again. "What?" she finally asks.

"That's where it happened," I say, and I point to the drainage ditch that runs alongside the road, on the other side of the white fence with the peeling paint. "Right there is where Dani died. It was dark. Like this. Really late when she got hit. Maybe three or four o'clock in the morning. But people drive too fast out here. We didn't find her—I didn't find her—until the next morning."

Rio is staring out at the ditch now. She lets out a long, low whistle. "You found her?"

I nod. Swallow more peach wine. The sweetness of it makes me gag. "She'd been dead a couple hours already."

Grass in her hair.

Dew on her skin.

"What was she doing walking along the road in the middle of the night?"

I tip the bottle up one more time, but it's empty. I only get a drop or two.

"She was out looking for me."

I hand the bottle back to Rio, and she sets it on the steps beside her. We sit there for a minute, breathing together. Almost like we're getting ready to go below.

It's amazing to me how Rio knows when to ask questions. And when not to. I've never met anybody who could read me like that. Even East isn't as good as she is.

"What do you think happened to her?" she finally asks me. She runs her fingers through her dark hair. "To Dani."

"Somebody hit her," I say. "Like I told you. Then they took off."

"No, I mean, what do you think happened to her after that?"

I'm confused for a second, but then I catch on to what she's saying. "You mean, like, after she died?" Rio nods.

"I don't know," I admit. "I've never really thought about it. Nothing, I guess."

"What if you're wrong?" Rio is staring at me now. Her eyes are wide. Sincere. She moves a little closer and I hold my breath. "What if we get another chance. At least sometimes."

"I don't know," I say. "I'm not really religious or anything."

I only halfway remember the funeral. We were all in such a daze. But I know the preacher said a lot of stuff about Dani being in heaven.

It sounded nice. All that shit about angels and living forever in some kind of paradise.

None of it rang true to me, though.

"I'm not, either," Rio says. "But what if . . ."

"What if, what?"

"What if sometimes we get to come back? Maybe not every bit of us. Not every time. But parts of us. Like, the most important parts." I raise one eyebrow. It sounds so wild. Even if I am kind of drunk. "I'm serious," she adds.

"You're talking about reincarnation."

"Kind of," Rio says. "I guess. But different cultures and religions have different names for it. Or different ideas about how it might work." She pauses. "There are documented cases and everything. Like there was this three-year-old kid not long ago, in Indiana or somewhere, who claimed he was the screenwriter for *Gone with the Wind*. Nobody believed him at first. But he knew all this stuff about Hollywood and working in the movie industry. The making of that specific movie. The most obscure little facts. And he was right. About all of it."

"It's a nice idea," I tell her. "I'd like to think that maybe Dani got another chance."

Rio reaches over to brush her fingers through my hair, and my chest squeezes like some kind of mini–heart attack. I panic. My stomach is in my throat. I don't know what to do. Or how to react. My instinct is to jump and run. But instead, I freeze up, and she pulls her hand away.

"What if Celeste and Bailey got another chance, too?"

"What do you mean?"

"I keep lying to you, Tru. I know that. But I don't wanna lie anymore."

"Okay." I'm having trouble following her. I don't know if it's the peach wine, or this twisting conversation.

"I told you I heard about the Hidden Glen murders on a crime show, but then I told you that was a lie. That I'd always known about them. Remember? I said that I knew things. Details about what happened that night."

"Yeah. Okay . . ."

"But neither is really true. The real truth is that I didn't just know about the murders out at Hidden Glen. I remembered them."

"What do you mean you remembered them?"

"I was there."

I shake my head. There's no way that's possible. Bailey and Celeste were murdered two years before we were even born.

"Tru, listen." Rio reaches for my hand. Her words are calm. Slow and even. Like I'm super dense and she's trying to make me understand algebra. "My earliest memory isn't something that happened in my life. At least not this one." Rio takes a deep breath. "My earliest memory is waking up confused. With a knife ripping through the side of a tent."

"You can't—" I start, but Rio stops me by reaching up with her free hand and stroking my cheek.

I'm not prepared for that. Suddenly I can't remember how to swallow. My head is spinning. I feel dizzy and drunk.

A little bit off balance.

Rio squeezes my hand and I look up at her face.

"I think I'm Celeste," she tells me.

"Jesus," I say. "Rio. Stop." I'm practically begging her. "You can't mean that."

"I know that sounds wild. And it isn't all clear. Parts of it are. But there are parts that are muddy and confused. The thing is, I swear to God, I remember that night."

"The night you died," I say. And it sounds so bizarre when I hear it out loud.

But Rio shakes her head.

"The night we died."

THIRTEEN

"WAIT A SECOND," I manage to spit out. "You think I'm—"

"I know you are."

"Bailey." I can't wrap my head around it.

"Yeah," Rio says. I open my mouth to say something, but my brain won't work. "Tru, I remember reaching for you and—"

"No," I say, and I shake my head. "No. Maybe you remember reaching for somebody. But—"

"You think I'm lying." Rio's eyes have gone all dark now.

"No," I tell her. "I don't think you're lying. I just think—"

"That I'm making it up."

"Jesus! Give me a damn second," I tell her. "I don't know what I think."

"That's how I know it's the Reaper," Rio says. "For real."

"Because you remember it."

"Yeah. I mean, I don't remember him, really. The guy who . . ." She hesitates.

"The guy who killed you." I shake my head. "Killed us. Whatever."

"Yeah. I don't remember seeing his face or anything. I only remember that the Glades Reaper was involved. Somehow. I remembered that name. I knew it before I even heard it. Almost like it had been right on the tip of my tongue from the very beginning."

"Because you remembered it. From a past life." Rio nods. Everything is spinning and I feel really close to throwing up. "I gotta lie down," I say, and I pull my hand away from Rio. "Can you just stay here tonight?" There's no way I can drive her back out to the springs.

"Sure," she says. "A couch beats a cot, any night."

Rio follows me into the living room, and I dig an extra pillow and blanket out of the hall closet and toss them to her. Then I flip off the light and turn to head upstairs.

"Tru." When I look back over my shoulder, Rio is still standing in the middle of the living room. It's mostly dark, a little light coming from the open bathroom door. I can't really see her face. Only the shape of her. And for second, she's someone else again. Someone with beautiful blond curls.

Someone who told me jokes and made me laugh.

Someone who used to trail their fingertips up and down my arm at night. When we were curled up together in her bed. The lightest touch of hot-pink painted nails.

The way it made me shiver.

Does that tickle?

I sway on my feet and grab for the handrail. I must be drunk.

"You feel it," she says. "I know you do."

"I don't know what I feel," I tell her. That's the closest I can get to the truth tonight.

Upstairs, I surrender to the heaviness I'm feeling and fall into bed, and it's almost like falling backward into the spring. I drift down and down and down until I hit bottom. I'm so exhausted, but sleep is elusive. I keep going over and over everything. Even with my eyes closed, I see our faces on those crime scene photos. I'm wondering who it is that's stalking us. Trying to scare us. And why.

I'm thinking about what Rio said.

That she's Celeste.

And I'm Bailey.

I get up and pull the half heart out of my backpack so I can crawl back into bed with it clutched in my hand. I rub it with my thumb.

It helps, but it's not enough to let me slip into sleep.

Not until I pull out my secret weapon. That special memory of me and Dani. The one that never lets me down.

I close my eyes and lose myself in the movements of her artist's hand.

That overwhelming sense of peace is the last thing I remember until sun streaming in the window wakes me up early the next morning.

It's after six o'clock. Sunday. Mom will be getting up soon. Hopefully. She has another open house this afternoon, and she's supposed to go in and get everything set up. I want to get Rio out of here before that happens. There's no way Mom's gonna remember meeting her last night, and I'm not in the mood to deal with questions about who she is and what she's doing here.

I take a few minutes to brush my fuzzy teeth before I head

down to wake Rio up. But when I get downstairs, the blanket is folded neatly on the couch, and my houseguest is nowhere to be seen.

I'm wondering if she took off on foot. Headed back to the springs on her own. I open the front door, and she's sitting on the porch steps, staring out at the road.

"Mornin'," she says, without so much as turning around to look at me.

"Have you been up long?"

She shakes her head. "A few minutes. I heard water running upstairs, so I figured you were awake."

"You sleep okay?" I ask her.

"I actually did," she says. "It was nice to have air-conditioning."

I sit down beside her, but I don't say anything. We just stare at the road together. The air is wet and sticky. Thick. Like a brick wall between us.

"What you said last night," I start. But Rio stops me.

"You don't have to believe me."

"I want to believe you." My head is starting to ache. "There are things about it that make sense. But I can't."

"Well fuck you," Rio says. The words are harsh, but she sounds more hurt than angry. It still gets my back up, though.

"Who the hell do you think you are?" I demand, and I push myself up to my feet. "You blow into town like some kind of ghost. Don't tell me shit about yourself but ask a million questions about me. Then you lay your wild theories in my lap and expect me to believe you? When I've known you less than a week? Why would I?"

"You're right." Rio shrugs. "There's absolutely no reason you should believe me." She stands up, too. "Give me a ride back out to the springs?"

"Yeah," I say. "Sure." Now I'm confused. Because are we mad at each other or not?

We both start for the truck, and as soon as I swing the door open, I freeze. Rio's already pulled herself up and into her seat. She's ready to go.

I'm standing there. Stuck. I can't get in.

"What?" she says, and I blink. "Hey. Earth to Tru."

"Where did that come from?"

I point at a gold half heart. Tarnished. Old and all scratched up. It's swinging back and forth slightly as it dangles from a black ribbon that's been slipped over the rearview mirror.

Rio sees what I'm staring at. "Oh my God." Her eyes get huge. She turns back to look at me. "Is that what I think it is?"

I pull myself up into the truck seat and close the door, but I still can't make my mouth work right. I lift the locket off the rearview mirror with shaking hands. I hold the little half heart in my palm and rub at it with my thumb. The shape and the feel are familiar. I know the weight of it.

This one is the opposite of the one I have in my backpack.

"It's Celeste's," I say. "Somebody replaced the gold chain with a ribbon. But it's hers. For sure."

"What the fuck." Rio sounds as stunned as I feel.

"Did you see anybody out here this morning? Messing around the truck?"

"No," Rio says, and she glances around. "Nobody." She

reaches out to take the locket from me, and her hand is shaking even worse than mine. The moment she lays her fingers on it, she flinches, as if a shock of electric current runs through her whole body. "There's a *C* on the back." Her voice quivers, but it isn't a question. She flips it over, to be certain, and, sure enough, there's a *C* engraved there. But I already knew there would be. It's the exact same fancy script as the *B* on my hidden half.

"He wants us to know he's watching us," I say.

"What?" Rio looks up from the locket in her palm to stare at me.

"Whoever had that locket took it from around Celeste's neck that night. He's leaving us hints. That note you got. The photos. This locket." I take a deep breath. But I can't get any oxygen. The air inside the truck cabin is too hot, stifling, like the air inside an oven. Or a tomb. "Whoever killed Celeste and Bailey that night, he wants us to know he's watching us."

"Then there's only one thing we can do," Rio says. "We have to figure out who it was that murdered us." I don't argue with her about that last part because it doesn't matter right now. The only thing that matters is that twenty years ago, some homicidal maniac murdered two teenage girls in the scrub. And now he's sneaking around stealing our shit and leaving us creepy-ass presents. "Can I keep this?" Rio asks, but she's already slipping the half heart into her pocket.

"Yeah," I say. It's only fair. After all, I've been holding on to Bailey's for years.

I manage the short drive out to Hidden Glen Springs in a fog. I couldn't tell you how we got there, but it isn't long before I'm pulling into a parking spot.

"I have to go to work," I tell Rio. "Jon Boy needs my help with some last-minute ad layouts for next week. Tomorrow's the printer deadline. But I'll come back this afternoon."

"Okay." There's a fire burning inside her eyes again. "That gives me a couple hours to come up with a plan."

She opens the door and starts to slide out, but I reach over and lay a hand on her arm. "Be careful," I tell her.

She doesn't pull away.

I don't take my hand back.

"I'm not scared, Tru," she says. "I'm pissed. Somebody's fucking with us."

"A killer is fucking with us, Rio. Stick with Dill and Derry today. Okay? Until I get back."

She smiles at me then, and it almost knocks the wind out of me. This fluttery feeling in the pit of my stomach, it snuck up on me. I wasn't prepared. It's been a really long time since I felt that with East.

If I ever felt it with East.

I'm trying to remember.

Rio slides out of the truck and shuts the door, then walks around to the driver's side and leans into the open window. Her mouth is so close to mine. "You be careful, too, Trulee," she drawls in that honey-sweet Southern accent. Then she turns and heads down toward the swimming area. "I'll see you later, alligator."

I glance at my watch. Shit. I'm already late, and I still need to run home before I show up to the *Star*. I can't go into work with greasy hair, smelling like nasty peach wine.

I make it back to the house, hoping to slip upstairs and jump in the shower without any interaction with Mom. But no such luck. She's standing in the kitchen making coffee when I push open the front door.

"Morning," I say as I keep walking.

"Trulee. Wait." I stop with one hand on the stair railing and turn to her. Last night's smeared eye makeup and pillow lines on her face. "Did you bring me home last night?"

"Yeah," I say. "Billy called."

Her face turns red, and it makes me feel better that at least she still has the decency to be ashamed. She doesn't apologize or anything, though. She just says, "I'm gonna need you to drop me off at the Clover so I can get my car, then."

"Yeah," I say. "No problem. Let me take a quick shower."

"You sleep on the couch last night?" Mom's looking at the neatly folded blanket and the pillow.

"Oh," I say. "Yeah. It was hot upstairs." Mom nods and turns back to her coffee, and I take the opportunity to escape.

I'm clean, dried, dressed, and back downstairs ready to go in less than fifteen minutes. Mom's not ready yet, of course. I can hear her hair dryer going in her bathroom.

The door to the hall closet is open. I must have left it that way when I grabbed the pillow and blanket for Rio last night. I see a big box on the top shelf. It's marked DANI.

I know what's inside. It's all the paper stuff Mom kept. School award certificates. Report cards. Lots of loose photos. A bunch of Dani's drawings.

I'm stuck there in the hallway. Staring at that box. I've looked through it before, always searching for the same thing. That drawing of the horse.

I've never been able to find it.

If I could just have that drawing. It scares me to think that the memory will fade, that I'll lose it eventually. And if I do, I'll lose Dani.

I cross to the closet and pull the box down off the shelf. I figure I'll take one more quick look. In case I missed it somehow. Maybe it was stuck to another piece of paper. Or maybe she drew it on the back of something else.

I'm sliding the box back onto the shelf when Mom comes out and says she's ready, so we head out to the truck. On the way to the Wild Clover, she's busy scrolling through missed messages on her phone.

"I was looking for something," I say. "I thought it might be in that box. The one in the closet. Dani's stuff."

That gets Mom's attention and she turns to look at me. "What were you looking for?"

"A drawing," I say, and Mom sighs.

"Well, there are probably a hundred drawings in that box. Dani always had a pencil in her hand." She turns back to her phone.

"I'm looking for a specific one I remember. It's a horse. With wildflowers all braided into its mane."

Mom frowns and shakes her head. "I don't think so. Dani

never drew horses. Tons of cats." She laughs a little. "Pigs and bunny rabbits. Every other animal you can imagine. But never horses." She turns to look out the window. "I'd remember a horse like that."

She's wrong, but I don't bother to argue with her. There's no point. She doesn't know where that drawing is.

Maybe she never even saw it.

Or maybe she did, and the memory of it was stolen. By time. And vodka.

I drop Mom off at her car, the only one sitting sad and lonely outside the Wild Clover on a Sunday morning. I watch her amble the walk of shame across the parking lot before she turns to wave at me. Then I head to the *Star*.

It feels like this day has been a million years long, and it's only just started. Already, all I can think about is diving. It's a constant buzzing in the back of my brain. I'm craving the water in a way that's so much more than mental. There's a deep ache in my bones. A hollowness in the pit of my stomach.

A need.

"Hey there, TB!" Jon Boy chirps. "Thanks for comin' in this morning. You know I hate messing with those graphic layouts." He's leaning over the counter studying the *New York Times* when I walk in the door, and he pushes his glasses up on his nose to grin at me.

"No problem," I tell him. "I'm gonna run downstairs real quick before I get started. I think I left my headphones down there."

Jon Boy doesn't even look up from the paper as he nods, so I snatch Reese's sweater and make a beeline for the stairs. I have those crime scene photos stashed in my backpack, and it's like I can feel them burning me through the nylon material.

I need to get them back in the box where they belong, before I break down and spill the beans about Rio stealing them in the first place.

And someone else stealing them a second time, then returning them with our own faces superimposed on two dead girls.

"Whoa," Jon Boy shouts over his shoulder. "Where's the fire?" I stop and turn back toward him, because the last thing I want is to make him suspicious. But I guess he can see some weirdness on my face, because he says, "Hey. You okay this morning?"

"Yeah," I tell him. I'm playing with the name tag on Reese's old sweater. He was a big guy. Tall, like Jon Boy. So the sweater's huge on me, hanging way down past my knees. It's always scratchy and itchy, but today, all I notice is how dirty it is. Cuffs ringed with grime. "I got a call from Billy last night. Out at the Wild Clover. He needed me to pick Mom up."

"Shit." Jon Boy shakes his head. "I was hoping things were getting better."

"Yeah," I say. "Me too."

He folds up the *Times* and sticks it under his arm. "I'll stop by to see her this evening. Just to say hi."

"Thanks," I tell him. "I'm gonna grab those headphones."

"Sure, Trulee Bear." He winks at me. "Take your time. I'm paying you by the hour, remember."

As soon as I'm alone in the basement, I take the crime scene photos out of my backpack and sneak them back in the box where they belong. Other than the fact that they're missing their manila envelope, you can't even tell they've been on an adventure.

I look around the dimly lit basement, searching for an extra manila envelope to put the photos in. If I could find a red marker, I could probably fake Jon Boy's all-caps lettering. Unfortunately, all I see are stacks and stacks of moldy newspapers.

Back in the corner are a few shelves filled with junk. One of them is almost completely taken up with Reese's trophies, including the one for Small-Town Newspaper Editor of the Year. I remember the faded photo stuck on Jon Boy's fridge.

The other shelf is crammed with a mix of old office supplies and clutter. A bunch of dusty books about journalism. A desk plate with Jon Boy's father's name on it. Stacks of dusty legal pads and boxes of pencils. Dried-up ink bottles. Jars and jars of rubber bands. A clunky old typewriter. And an old-school rotary phone. There's even a microphone and tape recorder that look like they're straight out of a 1950s detective movie. Jon Boy could open a damn antique shop if he ever gets tired of being a newspaper editor.

But, of course, I can't find one single envelope.

As I'm walking back toward the stairs, though, I happen to spot a little brown corner sticking out of one of the old newspaper stacks. I grab it and pull it free. And sure enough . . . it's a beat-up manila envelope.

Exactly what I'm looking for.

When I open it up, a brittle old Florida map falls into my lap.

It's folded all wrong, which means Jon Boy must have been the one to fold it, but when I open it up and smooth it out, I see the words *Glades Reaper Kills* scrawled across the top. There are seven little circles drawn on the map in black marker.

Everglades City. Belle Glade. Clewiston. Florida City. Copeland. Plus the two inside the borders of the huge national park.

When I look a little closer, I see that all the locations are actually circled twice. Once in black. And once in a fading red that's turned light orange with age.

None of those circles are north of Lake Okeechobee, but I knew that already. The Reaper never worked north of there. And, like Jon Boy said, serial killers are pretty set in their ways. They usually don't just wake up one morning and decide to shake things up by killing more than two hundred miles north of their territory.

But Rio is so certain.

I remembered that name. Like I said, I knew it before I even heard it. Almost like it had been right on the tip of my tongue from the very beginning.

I lay the old map aside, then slide the crime scene photos into the manila envelope. I run upstairs and grab a red marker so I can write across the front of the envelope in Jon Boy's messy lettering. Then I admire my work for a second before I return everything to its rightful place.

As I'm putting that box back on the shelf, my eyes fall to the one beside it. The one labeled GLADES REAPER. I'm guessing that map belongs there.

I pull the box down and open the lid, expecting to find a bunch of newspaper articles and notes. But there's nothing. The box is completely empty. Whatever was in there must have been tossed out years ago. After Jon Boy gave up on it.

I almost slip the map into the empty box, but I decide to stick it in my backpack instead. I figure nobody will miss it, and maybe there's something useful there. If I look hard enough.

Jon Boy is still poring over the paper when I come trudging up the stairs. "Find 'em?" he asks, and I'm confused for a second. "Your headphones."

"Oh. Yeah," I lie. "Right where I left them."

He turns his attention back to the paper, and I head to the breakroom to use the ancient desktop computer in there to work on this week's ad layouts. The clicking and dragging soothes me some. I lean into the monotony of it and try to forget about everything else.

Around noon, Jon Boy calls to me. "I'm heading out to lunch at the Dairy Barn. Want me to bring you back anything?"

"A cheeseburger!" I shout. "And a strawberry shake!"

"You got it," he says, and I hear the little bell over the door jingle. I stop and stretch. My back aches from perching on the stool and leaning over the keyboard. I figure I've earned a break, so I start for the bathroom. As I step out of the breakroom, I glance out through the big front windows in time to see Jon Boy climbing into a familiar truck.

Knox is in the driver's seat. He doesn't look particularly happy. That ridiculous cowboy hat is pushed way back on his head, revealing narrow eyes and a tight-set jaw. It makes me wonder what's up, because, usually, spending any time with our mayor is the last thing on Jon Boy's to-do list.

It's less than an hour later when I hear the bell jingle again. I jog up the stairs to see who it is, but it's only Jon Boy coming back. He's got a Dairy Barn bag in his hand. His good mood is gone.

"Got your burger. But I forgot the shake. Sorry, TB."

"It's cool," I say. "No worries."

Jon Boy pulls the rolling chair out of his office and sinks down into it so he can dig his own burger out of the bag while I get comfy on the floor behind the counter. It reminds me of when I was little. He'd sit up in the chair in our living room and read to me, or tell me a story, and I'd sit on the floor at his feet.

"Want some ketchup?" he asks. I shake my head.

"Good." He rolls his eyes. "Because there isn't any in this damn bag."

I swallow a bit of burger. "Was that Knox you left with?"

Jon Boy grunts. "Yep. The mayor himself." I wait while he takes a bite of burger. Then he reaches for Reese's mug on the counter so he can wash it down with what's left of this morning's coffee. "He's got some bug up his ass about the elections board. Wants me to write a story about it. It's all in his head, but somehow, I got myself in the middle of it. Part of the price you pay for being editor of a small-town newspaper."

My hand finds Reese's EDITOR name tag on the front of the sweater I'm wearing, and I run my fingers over it. "How come you don't wear your name tag anymore?" I ask Jon Boy.

He gives me a funny look. "I never had one. Seemed kind of silly. I mean, everyone in town knows who I am."

"Huh." I decide to let it go, but I swear he's wrong. Like Mom was wrong about Dani's horse. I can practically see it pinned to the front of a blue shirt. But maybe I'm thinking of Reese's tag. I decide right then that I'm gonna get Jon Boy an EDITOR name tag for Christmas. He's the one running the *Star* now, and he should be proud of all the work he does around here.

"I was thinking," I tell him. "About Knox. And the murders out at Hidden Glen."

"Trulee." Jon Boy reaches for another sip of cold coffee from Reese's old mug. "You gotta move past that. You're on your way outta this shit town." He gives me a long look. "On to bigger and better things."

"No," I say. "I know. It's just, you know Knox was a suspect." I look around for a napkin and Jon Boy hands me one from the bottom of the crumpled-up bag. "You ever think maybe he actually did it?" East would be pissed if he knew I was having this conversation. But East also knows his uncle has a nasty temper and an ego bigger than his ridiculous cowboy hat. "He was dating Celeste at the time. Right? Isn't it always the boyfriend?"

Jon Boy laughs. "Between you and me, I don't think he has the brains to pull off something like that and not get caught. Besides," he adds, "if Knox did do it, that arrogant asshole wouldn't be able to keep himself from bragging about it. He's so full of himself that he announces it to the world every time he takes a shit. Then he expects me to run a damn story on it."

"Who did it, then?" I ask the question more to myself than to Jon Boy. "And why?"

Jon Boy sighs. "If I could figure that out, Trulee Bear, I'd be working for the FBI, not the *Star*." He picks up his dead brother's mug and wraps his fingers around it, like he expects the cold coffee to keep him warm. "Most people would probably say it was either love or hate that led to what happened out there that night. And honestly, more bad things get done in the name of love."

That has me thinking of Knox again, and whether he loved Celeste enough to want her dead for some reason.

"Do you think we'll ever know the truth?" I ask.

"Some things aren't ours to know." Jon Boy wads up his burger wrapper and tosses it toward the trash, but he doesn't even get close. "That's a thing I've had to make peace with." He groans and pushes himself up out of the chair to grab the wrapper off the floor and throw it in the can behind the counter. Then he leans against the wall and looks at me. "If you're seriously asking my opinion, though, I always figured it had to be a stranger. Someone random." He's looking out the big front windows now, watching an old Buick lumber down Main Street. Or maybe he's just staring at his reflection. It's hard to tell. "Someone passing through town. Our boy probably hopped off the highway, did his thing, and then hopped back on the highway and headed out of state. That's probably why he was never caught. Why he never killed again, at least around here."

That's a theory that makes sense. Random stranger. Random victims. Random crime.

A thrill kill.

Except he did come back.

He is stalking me and Rio now. "So why couldn't it have been the Reaper?" I ask him, and he sighs. "I mean, I know you said it doesn't fit the pattern, but—"

"Because nobody wants it to be, Tru. That's the real truth. We're Floridians, and we know too much about lightning."

"Huh?" I'm not following him at all.

"You remember that house on Cherry Street?" he asks me. "The little one that burned down twice."

I nod.

"It got hit by lightning both times. After the second strike they got wise and didn't rebuild it." He takes a deep breath. "Sometimes lightning does strike twice."

"You're scared he might come back."

"If the Glades Reaper paid us a visit, there's always the chance he might pay us another one someday. And none of us can live with that."

"Why'd it have to be here?" I don't mean to let the thought slip from between my lips. "Why not someplace else? The next stop on the highway."

Jon Boy shrugs. "I don't think there is a why. That's the truly terrifying part." He's still staring out toward the front windows. Our view on Main Street. Those green awnings and flower boxes overflowing with pink blooms. Tiny downtown Mount Orange. "We've never been the same. What happened out there that night altered the DNA of this whole town. Forever. You can see it in the way we don't trust each other. The way we're always looking at people like maybe they could be secret monsters."

"But some people are secret monsters," I remind him.

"See, that's what I mean." He turns to look at me, and his eyes are so sad. "I mean, look at you, Trulee Bear. You weren't even alive back then, and it's got you all messed up." I don't know what to say to that, because he doesn't even know how right he is. "Did you know Celeste's mama keeps her room exactly like it was? Comin' up on twenty years, and she hasn't so much as touched a thing in there. It's like she's hoping, maybe, somehow, Celeste is gonna come home."

That hits me like a two-by-four in the chest. I remember finally helping Mom pack up Dani's stuff more than a year after she died. The hardest thing I've ever done. But walking past that permanently silent room every day, the one with the hot-pink bedspread and the Kelly Clarkson posters, would have hurt more.

Jon Boy reaches for Reese's mug again. He stares down into it like he's trying to read the coffee stains on the bottom, the way psychics read tea leaves. "I swear," he says. "It's like this whole town's been holding its breath all these years. Waiting."

"What do you think we're all waiting for?" I ask, and Jon Boy cocks his head to one side, like he can't believe I had to ask. He lets out a long breath.

"We're waiting for it to happen again."

FOURTEEN

BY THE TIME I make it out to the springs that afternoon, I'm close to exploding. If I don't get to go below soon, my heart might pound its way out of my ribs.

I pull into the parking lot and shut off the truck. I need a minute to think about what we should do. I look around, wondering if whoever left that locket in my truck is out there in the crowd of people gathered around the swimming area.

Is he watching me right now? My skin prickles and fear gnaws at my bones like a rat. My hands shake on the steering wheel.

Maybe the best thing is to talk to the police. If Rio's poking around out here scared someone—scared them bad enough that they really are after us, whether it's the Glades Reaper or not— we're gonna need help.

East knocks on the window and I almost jump through the roof. "I love you, truly. Truly, dear," he sings from the other side of the glass, and I roll down the window to kiss him. He leans into the truck, just like Rio did this morning.

An ache wells up from deep inside me.

East's lips are soft, and he tastes like snow cone. Grape, today.

"How was work?" he asks me.

"Boring," I answer, and East pulls me in for another kiss.

Everything about him is warm and comforting, like stepping out of the shower and into the softest robe. Suddenly, he's all I want.

I need him even more than I need to dive.

East opens the door and pulls me out of the truck. I let him tuck me against his chest and I sink into the safety of his arms as he leans down to press a kiss to the top of my head.

"Can you stick around for a while?" I ask, but he shakes his head.

"I was heading home. Mom needs my help with some yard work. I've been putting her off for days. Come by later tonight, though," he tells me. "If you can."

I nod and untangle myself from his arms, and I promise to see him later.

When he's gone, I start down toward the boardwalk. I glance at the people gathered around the swimming area. Some young guys from the dive club. A middle-aged man who's trying to lure his wife into the water. A couple of tourists struggling with their rented snorkel equipment.

Nobody looks like a serial killer.

Back at the Well, Dill and Rio are already in the water. They're floating in circles while Derry watches from a shady spot.

When they see me, Rio makes her way over to the rocks and crawls up to sit beside me. She doesn't leave any space between us, the pressure of her thigh against mine.

Like yesterday.

Only today, she's cool from the water. She smells like the springs.

Dill has climbed up onto the rocks and I see him studying the two of us. "Y'all wanna go down together again?" He gives his head a good shake, and water flies in all directions. Derry squeals and swats him with her book.

"Yeah," I say, and a grin spreads across Rio's face. "We'll go together."

We both stand up and stretch. Then we dig out our gear and start our prep. We're side by side.

Breathing in tandem.

Finding that shared rhythm is so easy with Rio. We're naturally tuned to the same frequency.

I think about what she told me last night. How she thinks we're Celeste and Bailey.

Bailey and Celeste.

And for a second, I wonder . . . *what if?*

Then we're in the water.

Rio moves through the spring, and I follow her.

We go down and down and down, and I'm shedding little pieces of myself on the descent, scattering parts of myself like penny candy tossed from a parade float.

Until all that is left of me is the air in my lungs.

One single breath.

And a million shades of blue.

The sound of my own heartbeat in my ears.

And Rio.

That's all that exists.

She turns back to look at me over her shoulder. Even with her mask on, I see the question in her eyes.

Deeper?

I nod.

We swim down together.

A clawing desperation pulls me closer and closer to the bottom, and I glance at the depth markers scratched into the limestone. One hundred and ten feet. Only thirty feet to the bottom.

I'm so close.

Rio has stopped swimming. She's motionless. Suspended in the water.

At first I think maybe she's in trouble, but then I see she's staring at something. I follow her eyes and I see it, too. Something shiny is winking at us from a little ledge. Maybe another fifteen feet below where we are now.

I can't tell what it is, but it doesn't look like it should be there.

I need it.

All of a sudden that tug is so strong, like having someone reach down my throat, grab a big handful of guts, and yank me inside out.

I start to move toward whatever it is.

Rio shakes her head and points toward the surface. I know she's right.

We're out of time.

Out of air.

Out of options.

If we don't head up right now, things are going to get really dangerous really fast.

We start our ascent together.

I count our fin-kicks. We're moving in sync.

One.

Two.

Three.

Four.

Five.

I know our hearts are beating in time, too.

We're barely going to make it. My lungs ache. They burn. I fight my rising panic.

Almost there, I tell myself.

Then we break the surface at the exact same time and pull in that first breath together, and I'm shattered into the tiniest possible pieces.

Broken down into the most basic molecules.

My insides are made of stardust. Everything expands.

I'm an entire galaxy.

In this moment, I can do anything.

Rio is grinning at me. We lock eyes.

Dill is standing on the rocks, frowning at us both. "Too deep," he says, and he shakes his head. "Way too deep." I know he's thinking about last week. How he had to jump in and haul me to the surface. "And way too long."

But today isn't like that day.

I made it today.

I'm okay. Way more than okay.

"I'm fine," I promise him. I'm treading water, wiping my eyes dry so I can see more clearly. "I'm—"

"You're not fine, Tru." Dill's voice is sharp. He looks from me to Rio. "Neither one of you is fine. You're both pushing too hard. Taking too many risks."

I hadn't even noticed Derry standing behind him, looking down into the water. "You're gonna get yourselves killed," she warns us. Her voice is harder than I've ever heard it, and it stops me cold. She's twisting one of her Mountain Dew can rings around one finger. "I don't want to sit here and watch you die." She stops and looks up at Dill, then back out at us. "Any of you."

"Yeah," I say. "Okay." I shrink a bit. This feels like having a friend over and getting yelled at by your parents in front of them.

"We'll be more careful," Rio promises, and Dill and Derry relax a little bit. The two of them sit back down. Dill stretches out on the rocks, and Derry picks her book back up.

Rio and I don't get out of the Well, though. It's so hot today, staying wet seems like the best plan. We bob and float, enjoy being in the water together.

But we both glance back down toward the bottom every so often. To the little ledge where something silver winked at us in the depths.

When we get tired, the two of us lie back on the rocks to-gether. Eyes closed. Faces turned up to the sun. I sneak a peak in Rio's direction, and it hits me like a freight train how stun-ning she is. Just knock-you-on-your-ass gorgeous. The sudden realization of it sucks the breath right out of my chest.

The lines and curves of her body.

Perfect skin against the bright blue backdrop of the water.

That coal-dark hair shining in the late afternoon light. Full lips and long eyelashes.

I realize that I've seen East like this a million times—a hundred million times—but it's always been different. I mean, I've always known he was beautiful—the way you know a sculpture in a museum is beautiful—but looking at him has never really undone a piece way down deep inside me, the way looking at Rio does.

"What are you staring at?" Her eyes are still closed, but that low Southern accent ripples into my ear.

I don't acknowledge her question, though. Because I feel like she already knows the answer.

Instead, I lay out an idea, one that came to me earlier, when we were down below.

"I have a plan," I tell her. "Something we can try." I've got Rio's attention now. She opens her eyes and sits up.

"What kind of plan?" she whispers.

"I found out today that Celeste's mom has kept her room the same all these years. Exactly the way it was on the night she died. Never touched a thing."

"Okay," she says.

"We could go there. See if there's anything that might give us some idea of who did this to them."

"And who's doing it to us," Rio adds. I nod, but she frowns. "Didn't they go over that room with a fine-tooth comb back in the day?"

I shrug. "Probably. But would a bunch of men searching a

teenage girl's room even know what to look for?"

Or where to look?

I see Rio glance back down toward the bottom of the spring. Toward that little ledge. And whatever that thing is that doesn't belong there.

"So we're gonna walk up to the door and what?" she asks. "Ring the bell. Ask if we can see Celeste's room?"

"I don't know," I say. "Something like that, I guess."

"Y'all ready to head out?" We both turn in the direction of Dill's voice. "I could use a nap." He winks at us, and his usual grin is back. There's not a trace of that sharpness in his voice now, and I feel bad for worrying him. And Derry.

"Yeah," Rio says. "We're coming."

The two of us stand up and start pulling on our clothes.

I'm trying not to stare as Rio slips on her shorts, but I can't help noticing the way the little beads of water slide down her neck.

Her back.

And her legs.

The way her wet hair is clinging to her face.

She catches me, and I immediately turn bright red. Rio has her T-shirt in her hand, like she was about to pull it on over her bikini top. But instead, she shoves it into her backpack. I look away. Grab my own T-shirt and pull it on over my head.

When I look back, Rio gives me that little smirk of hers. One corner of her mouth pulls into an almost-grin, and I feel my cheeks burn from the heat of it.

She and Derry start toward the gate. They're talking about how hot it is. The most miserable day of the summer so far.

Too hot to be alive, almost.

Dill and I are still gathering up our things and stuffing them into our bags.

Sweat is dripping down my face, and I wipe it away with the hem of my T-shirt. Dill is watching me, but he's not saying anything, like words would get hung up in all that mugginess.

I glance toward the bottom of the Well one more time.

"What's going on with you lately?" Dill finally asks me. "Something's up. I can tell." I've just finished cinching my backpack closed, and the two of us start across the rocks, trailing Derry and Rio.

"Do you ever wish you could be something totally different?" I ask him.

He looks serious for a second, then says, "I'd love to be a polar bear."

"Come on," I tell him. "That's not what I mean." But it makes me laugh.

"No, I mean it," he insists. "It's so damn hot. I'd kill to be a polar bear, living up in the Arctic and floating around on a big ol' chunk of ice." He looks at me. Holds the gate open so I can go through. "Why?"

"No reason." I shrug. "Just conversation."

"Well," he says, "I'm sticking with polar bear, then." He throws an arm around my shoulders as we follow Derry and Rio down the boardwalk toward the main spring. "Besides the ice part," he whispers, "the best thing about being a polar bear's gotta be that polar bears don't care what other polar bears think of them. They just eat fish and hunt seals and make more polar bears and live their lives making themselves happy. They do what feels good, right? And they don't give a shit about anyone else's opinion."

"No polar bears in Florida," I tell him. "Outside of SeaWorld."

"Maybe not," he says. "But it's still a nice thing to think about." He's grinning at me. "Expectations are meant to be shattered, Tru."

I don't feel jealous very often. That's not me. But right then, I'm jealous of Dill. Because that's the thing about Dill. He really means that. He's always doing the unexpected, and he gets away with it somehow. People love him for it. He shatters expectations all the time. But me . . . I feel more comfortable just living up to them. Keeping things easy.

When we reach the swimming area, Dill and Derry ask if we want to come on back to their place for a smoke. Rio tells them that we're heading to the Dairy Barn for milkshakes.

Dill gives me a little grin, and he starts to whistle as he and Derry head toward their campsite and Rio and I start across the grass, up toward the parking area.

We climb into my stifling truck. She's still wearing her shorts and bikini top, and everything feels unsteady.

Precariously balanced, like I'm standing on the edge of a cliff higher than any we have in Florida.

Rio reaches across and runs her fingers through my hair, and the fluttery feeling in my stomach almost knocks me down.

Whoever called this feeling "butterflies" was so wrong. This feels more like I've swallowed a bunch of bald eagles. Feathers and talons and all. I don't let myself freeze up, though. I don't move away. I make myself stay relaxed. I stop fighting and allow myself to lean into her touch. I keep my breathing nice and slow and steady, like diving. I know she's testing me, and I don't want her to stop.

Rio's smile is brighter than the sun blinding me through the windshield.

"Are we really doing this?" she asks me, and I'm not sure if she's talking about the visit to Celeste's house or something else.

I answer her anyway.

"I guess so."

"Cool," Rio says, and she drops her hand to her lap. We're both grinning now. Even in the sweltering damp heat of a June afternoon, I can almost feel the icy-cold sting of crystal-clear spring water.

It makes me feel just a little bit like a Florida polar bear.

FIFTEEN

ON THE DRIVE to Celeste's house, the giddiness starts to fade right along with the daylight, and cold, hard dread wells up in its place.

When we stop in front of the little yellow house on Brandywine Avenue, Rio pulls her T-shirt back on. "Is this it?" she asks me.

"Yeah. Bailey's family moved away not long after the murders, but Celeste's mom and dad never did. I used to ride my bike by here all the time, hoping I'd catch a glimpse of them." I pause, remembering how East used to complain when I made him come along. Which was pretty much always.

Rio is staring out the window at the neat flower bed. The carport with the blue Toyota parked underneath. "I thought I'd recognize it," she admits. "But I don't."

We get out of the truck and start up the walk, but I haven't really figured out what we're going to say yet.

Maybe nobody will be home.

We stand outside on the porch, in the suffocating heat, for a solid two minutes, trying to work up the nerve to knock. I have this feeling that reminds me of when I was six and Dani paid me five dollars to jump off the high dive at the pool. I stood up there forever, torn between wanting to jump and wanting to climb back down the ladder, until Logan Kellerman finally got fed up waiting his turn and pushed me off.

Where's Logan Kellerman when I need him?

It's Rio who gives up and rings the bell. I see the curtains move in the front window, and then Celeste's mother answers the door. It's the first time in forever that I've seen her up close. Usually, I just glimpse her from a distance.

She looks so different than she did in the old newspaper articles that came out just after the murders. Not just older. Her face is sharper. More hollowed out.

I think of my own mom, and how she became a different person after Dani.

How I did, too.

I remember the way Celeste's mom was studying me downtown, the afternoon of the memorial, and suddenly I'm wondering if she's been watching me my whole life. The way I've been watching her.

"Yes?" Celeste's mother is eyeing us like she's expecting us to try to sell her something.

"Hi," Rio starts. "We have kind of a strange question to ask. I was—" She hesitates. Looks at me. "We were—"

"I work at the *Star*," I say. "I've been doing some research into what happened to your daughter. And to Bailey. For the anniversary coming up. The twentieth. And I was hoping we could see Celeste's room."

"I know it's a weird thing to ask," Rio jumps in. "But we're—" She stops and looks at me again.

"You're curious," the woman says.

"Yeah," Rio admits.

I expect that to make Celeste's mother angry, but it doesn't. In fact, she seems to relax a little bit.

"How old are you two?" she asks us.

"Eighteen," Rio tells her.

She studies us for a moment, then some kind of light comes on behind her eyes. She's staring at me. "You're the Langstaff girl, aren't you?" she asks. I nod, and she steps back out of the doorway to let us through. "Come on in."

The house is neat on the inside. Sparsely decorated, a few photos on the walls. Pictures of Celeste, mostly. They all stop senior year. There should be pictures of her as a young woman. Posing with a husband, maybe. A kid or two.

"Thanks," I tell her. "We really appreciate it. We won't stay long. I promise."

The woman is looking at me again. "I remember what happened to your sister. Such a tragedy." She gives me a small smile. "I suppose you know a thing or two about living with holes."

"Yes, ma'am," I say, and Rio reaches over to give my hand a quick squeeze as the woman leads us down the little hallway.

"Honestly, I'm glad to let you see Celeste's room. My husband won't go in there anymore, so it's nice to have someone to show it to." Her face falls and she lets out a breath. "Almost nobody around here remembers her."

"That's not true," I assure her. "Everyone in town remembers Celeste and Bailey."

The woman shakes her head. "They remember how she died. But they don't remember who she was before. They don't really care about that part."

"That's why you don't usually come to the memorials," I say. "Isn't it?"

Celeste's mother nods. "It's not about the girls anymore. It's about being a stop on some kind of macabre murder map. All people want are the gory details." She shudders and braces herself on a chair for support. "I went to this last one, though. The twentieth. I guess I thought it might be different this year." She stops and looks at me again. "I saw you there."

"I saw you, too," I admit.

"But it wasn't different," she finishes. "It was just more theater. Nobody really cares about my Celeste. They only care that she was murdered."

"We do," Rio promises her. "We care about who she was. Before all that. That's why we're here."

The woman nods, then pushes open the door to the last room at the end of the hall, and I hear Rio suck in her breath, like someone punched her in the gut. She's gone all pale, staring at the pink-and-yellow flowered bedspread. The faded sky-blue rug in the center of the floor.

My eyes are drawn to the white desk in one corner. Notebooks and pens and sticky notes and magazines are scattered across the top, like Celeste was in the middle of studying for a test, and she's popped down the hall to the kitchen for a snack.

There's a bottle of bright blue fingernail polish with the lid off. Long dried up, I'm sure. A pair of headphones are tangled with a hairbrush. An empty glass sits on top of a book. And a pack of chewing gum lies open on the edge of all that chaos. Waiting for someone to come back and unwrap a stick or two.

Above the desk are framed drawings. Beautiful pencil sketches of barns and beach scenes and trees dripping with Spanish moss.

"Celeste was an incredible artist." Her mother's voice sounds faraway inside my head. "She would have gone on to do amazing things." A cell phone rings just then, and Celeste's mother pulls it out of her pocket. "Excuse me a moment," she tells us. "It's my mother. She calls around this time every day." She steps down the hall toward the living room, and I hear her answer the call. "Hi, Mama. Yes, I'm okay. How are you feeling today?"

"Tru?" I turn back to look at Rio when she whispers my name, and I see that she's shaking.

"Hey," I say, and I cross to put my hand on her arm. "What is it?"

Her eyes are wide and all the color has drained from her face. The freckles scattered across her nose stand out like spatters of blood.

Down the hall, I hear Celeste's mother sigh. "No, Mama. Don't send those people any money. It's a scam. I told you that already."

"You remember this room," I say. "Don't you?"

Rio nods, and the look on her face is enough to convince me that, whether it's true or not, she absolutely believes it. This isn't a joke to her. Or a lie.

Rio points to one of the bedposts. The top left. "If you screw that knob off, the post is hollow." Her voice is hoarse. "There's a—"

"There's a hiding spot in there," I finish.

Nobody knows about this but us. It's our secret.

Rio nods once, but she doesn't move. I can still hear Celeste's mother talking down the hall, so I cross over to the bedpost and unscrew the knob on top, then peer down into the hollow post. There are two rolled-up pieces of paper tucked inside. I pull them out and screw the knob back on. I've barely finished twisting when Celeste's mother steps back into the room, so I shove the papers into my pocket and turn to face her.

"Sorry," the woman says, and she shakes her head. "My mother wants to send money to some person who sent her an email." I'm nodding along when something catches my eye. A framed drawing that hangs over the nightstand beside the bed. "I've told her a million times—"

"That drawing." I'm pointing to it now. My heart has stopped beating. The whole world has gone silent. "Who did it?"

Celeste's mother moves to stand beside me, and we stare at the artwork together. "It's one of Celeste's," she tells me. "Her favorite one she ever did. She entered it in a countywide art contest her freshman year and won first place." She reaches out to run her fingers over a faded blue ribbon that hangs on the edge of the frame. "She was so proud."

I'm blinking in disbelief, open mouthed.

It's a drawing of a horse in full gallop. Muscled legs. Long tail. Fierce eyes.

Wildflowers woven into his flowing mane.

Dani's drawing.

My knees buckle, and I sway on my feet. Rio reaches out

an arm to steady me. "Thank you so much for letting us look around," she says. "We really appreciate it."

Celeste's mother smiles and leads us back down the little hallway toward the front door. "You can come back and visit," she tells us. The loneliness in her voice almost kills me. It sounds like making a wish for something you know you'll never have again.

Rio surprises all of us by throwing her arms around Celeste's mother and pulling her in for a long hug.

"We will," she says. "I promise."

We step out onto the front porch, and I'm surprised that it's almost dark. Not that the sun going down has had any effect on the oppressive heat. I'm sweating. Sick. Dizzy and wobbly on my feet.

Rio doesn't look like she's faring much better.

Somehow, we both make it to the truck. I dig the keys out from under the seat and start the engine so we can crank up the AC, but I don't trust myself to drive yet. I lean my head back against the headrest and try to take a good breath. But I'm shaking too hard.

"You okay?" Rio asks me, and I manage to nod.

"Yeah. You?"

She shrugs. "I don't really know. I guess it's nice to know I had a mother who loved me. Once upon a time."

I try to think of something to say to that. There are questions I should ask her. But I can't. I'm too busy trying to make sense of what I just saw.

That horse.

My very favorite memory.

Framed and hanging on the wall of Celeste's museum-like bedroom.

I'm racking my brain, trying to think if maybe I could have seen a picture of that drawing somewhere. Maybe online? Celeste's mom said it won a contest. Maybe I saw it in a newspaper article and made the whole memory up.

But I know that's not true. Because I don't just remember the drawing. I remember watching someone draw it. I remember someone's hand moving across the page. Taking time with every single one of those tiny, intricate wildflowers. Petal by petal.

Someone who I've always thought was Dani, but who must have been Celeste.

If I was standing behind her, over her shoulder, watching her work, that must mean that I'm—

I'm going to throw up. I reach out to grab the door handle, in case I need to push it open and vomit onto the sidewalk.

"What about the papers?" Rio's voice pulls me out of my tailspin. I'd forgotten she was sitting over there.

I pull the crumpled papers from my pocket and smooth them out on the steering wheel.

They're short little notes. Typed on plain white paper turned yellow from age.

Can't stop thinking about you. Wish we could be together tonight.

and

      You're the most delicious secret I've ever had.

"Celeste had a secret admirer," Rio says.

"That's what it looks like," I say. "She was dating Knox at the time. The two of them were actually supposed to get married that next fall." I'm staring at the crumpled paper in my hand. "But I'm guessing Knox didn't write these."

Rio smirks. "That's where the 'secret' part comes in." She thinks for a minute. "But what if what's-his-name—"

"Knox."

"Yeah. What if he found out, and what if he was pissed?" Rio looks at me. "Pissed enough to kill her for cheating on him."

I'm so confused. "I thought you said it was the Glades Reaper."

"It was," she tells me. "I'm sure of that. Or at least I'm sure he had something to do with it. But if Celeste had a secret boyfriend, maybe that has something to do with it, too."

"How come you only remember bits and pieces?" I ask her, but I'm also asking myself.

Rio shrugs. "I think it's kind of like painting over wallpaper. In some spots, the paint is good and thick, and you can't see the wallpaper. You'd never know it was under there." She twists her hair around her fingers as she stares at the little yellow house in the falling dark. We watch the porch light flick on. "But in some spots, for whatever reason, the paint goes on thinner. So maybe a little bit of the wallpaper pattern shows through in those spots. Or maybe in other places, something happens to damage the paint. A little bit of color gets scuffed. Or scraped away. And surprise, there's that wallpaper again. Little red cherries showing through."

That makes sense, I guess.

Or at least as much sense as anything makes at the moment.

I start the truck and turn on the headlights, then pull away from the curb. Rio watches Celeste's house in the rearview mirror until we turn the corner.

"What are we going to do?" I ask her. "I don't like you being out at the springs. Whoever stole those photos and left them at the campsite with our faces on them, they're watching us. And they know you're out there."

"They know where you are, too," she reminds me. "They left that locket in your truck. At your house."

"We should go to the police," I tell her. It's obviously the thing to do.

Whatever—whoever—we're up against, it's too much for us to handle on our own.

"No," Rio says flatly. "No police."

"Why not? We can't—"

"The police aren't gonna do shit," Rio says. There's a bitterness to her voice that's new. "Aren't they the ones who let it go unsolved this whole time? Now, what? We hand over those crime scene photos and a locket we think is Celeste's, a couple of secret love notes, and BAM. Suddenly they're gonna have an answer?" She shakes her head. "No way. All they're gonna do is make things worse. These small-town cops, they don't know their ass from their elbow. They won't even ask the right questions. They never do." She leans back against the seat and looks out the window. "Did they do anything about what happened to your sister?"

"No," I admit, and I remember how they treated my mom and dad like criminals. Asking all sorts of wild questions. Making accusations. Pushing their way into our home at the worst moment of our lives. "Okay. No police. So what's our plan, then? Hang around and wait to see if we end up dead?"

Rio turns to look at me. "How do you feel about camping?"

Something tickles at the back of my neck again. That fly walking across my skin. And the hair on my arms stands up.

I've been camping a hundred times. With East, mostly. But the idea of camping with Rio—at Hidden Glen Springs—ties my insides up in knots.

"I don't know . . ." I tell her.

"What if we stay out there together? Tonight. At the murder site. Just you and me. The way it was the night—"

"You want to lure him out."

"I mean, whatever works, right? If he knows we're out there alone, the two of us, maybe he'll make a move."

"And maybe we'll end up dead," I say.

"No way." Rio sounds way too sure of herself. Too cocky for her own good. For our own good. "This time, we'll be ready."

"Okay," I agree, because I know that if I refuse, she'll camp by herself.

Rio's watching me, and she reaches over to lay a warm hand on my thigh. Her skin against mine is so hot and I suck in a quick breath. "Besides," she adds with a little smirk, "it could be fun."

As long as we survive.

We stop by my place and Rio waits in the truck while I slip in

to grab a few things, and to leave Mom a note saying I'm camping with Dill and Derry out at the springs. I'm hoping she'll be
able to make it home from the Wild Clover on her own tonight.
Otherwise, Jon Boy will have to rescue her.

I dig around in the cluttered garage until I find the tiny tent
Mom bought me when we thought I was going to join Girl
Scouts. I figure that will save us from having to walk back to
Dill and Derry's place to take down the tent Rio's been using
there. Then I gather water bottles from the fridge, a couple of
flashlights from the emergency kit, two sleeping bags and pil-
lows. Bug spray. Some granola bars.

All the essentials you might need to fight off a serial killer.

I also grab the baseball bat that leans in the corner of our hall
closet. Mom bought it a couple of years ago, when some guy
she dated for a hot second and then dumped was coming by the
house at all hours, giving her trouble. A few good swings at his
head and we never saw him again.

Rio's lost in thought when I get to back to the truck. I wonder
if she's thinking about Celeste's room the way I'm thinking
about that drawing of the horse.

When she turns to look at me, I see what's around her neck.
She's wearing Celeste's locket. That half heart. Tied with a black
ribbon for mourning.

Black for remembrance.

I imagine its other half burning a hole in my backpack pocket.

The ride out to Hidden Glen Springs is nothing but more
quiet and more darkness. The roads are deserted and the whole

world seems to have shrunk down to just the seat of my truck. Rio looks at me once and says, "It's gonna be okay." I'm not sure if I believe her.

Like she told me before, she lies.

When I pull into the parking area, we don't get out right away. We sit there in the truck for a few minutes, looking down at the main spring bathed in moonlight.

During the day, you can sit up here and see a hundred different shades of blue in the water down below. Blues you didn't even know existed until you see them. The bright turquoise blues of the really shallow places and the darker blues of the deep spots—and everything in between. But at night, it all looks dark and deep.

I wonder what it would be like to dive the spring at night, to hold your breath and slip into that frigid blackness without the blinding sun to tell you which direction is up. I bet it would feel like floating alone in the vastness of outer space. It reminds me of what Rio said about diving at Wakulla, the darkness that she seemed to love so much.

For a minute, I think about it. Just one quick dive in the dark. Me and Rio. Alone in all that emptiness. But at nighttime, the springs belong to the gators, and I'm a creature of the sunlight—not the moonlight.

I let that thought go, but I still feel the need to do something big. Something to mark this moment. I keep thinking about how Celeste and Bailey didn't know they were about to die that night.

What would they have done differently if they'd been aware of how little time they had left?

What truths would they have told each other?

I pull the half heart out of my backpack pocket. I cradle it in my palm and show it to Rio, and she gasps when the light hits it. I flip it over with my thumb so she can see the fancy *B* on the back. The exact same curling script as the *C* on her half.

"Where did you get that?" she asks. Rio's fingers move to the locket hanging around her own neck.

"I found it a couple of years ago. Back at the campsite."

"And you kept it?"

"Yeah." I'm staring down at the half heart in my hand. "I had to."

"Tru—"

"I believe you," I tell her. "I do. I believe you." She doesn't ask me what changed my mind, and I'm grateful. I'm not ready to talk about that horse yet. Not only am I reeling because Rio is right, about her being Celeste and about me being Bailey, but also I've lost the biggest piece of Dani I had left.

That memory never really was what I thought it was.

I'm learning that about a lot of things in my life.

Rio takes the tarnished locket from around her neck and holds it up toward me. I take the one in my palm and we fit them back together.

They match up perfectly.

One whole heart in the moonlight.

"So," Rio says, "you ready?"

It's been so long. Twenty years this summer. Bailey and Celeste deserve answers.

We deserve answers.

"Yeah." I nod. "Definitely. Let's go camping."

SIXTEEN

WE HAVE TO use flashlights to see our way back to the clearing behind Elijah's Well, because it's fully dark now. Rio and I share the load of supplies I've brought with me.

We don't talk much. There's too much to think about, too much to listen for. And to carry. But the silence between us becomes heavy. It's easy to hear every tiny rustle of leaves.

Every snapping twig.

The scrub is full of noises at night.

We're setting up the little tent by the light of a flashlight I'm holding between my teeth when Rio asks, "When are you planning to tell everyone you're not going to FSU with East this fall?"

I take the flashlight out of my mouth and set it on a rock. "I don't know. Soon. I guess." I'm trying to fit two bent tentpoles together. Wondering how the hell they got messed up when I swear we only used this stupid tent like one time. "Orientation is coming up next month. So before then. Obviously."

"You sure you don't wanna go?" Rio brushes her hair out of her eyes. She's holding the canvas up for me so I can wedge the bent pole into place.

"I'm sure," I tell her, and I sit back on my heels to peer up at the stars through the canopy of trees. "At some point I've gotta have the guts to say, 'This is what I want.' Right?"

Or at least to say *this isn't what I want.*

Our voices are low, almost whispers, and we both freeze when we hear a loud rustling at the edge of the clearing. We only start to breathe again when a fat raccoon waddles out of the dark to peer at us. He refuses to leave until I unwrap a granola bar and toss it in his direction.

"Seems like you're doing okay in the guts department," Rio says. "Camping out in the woods with an almost-stranger. Trying to bait a serial killer out of hiding."

"You're not an almost-stranger," I remind her with a little smirk of my own. "Remember. We've known each other before."

We've known each other always, maybe. What if it's always been her and me? What if there are other stories with happier endings?

It leans a little, but the tent is set up, so Rio and I grab our backpacks and the sleeping bags and crawl inside on our hands and knees.

The space is so small. We have to maneuver around each other to spread our sleeping bags out edge to edge. We'll be sleeping right up against each other. No room between us.

Once we get situated, we zip up the tent to keep the bugs out and then we sit on the sleeping bags with our flashlights on. I know that means we're clearly visible, that our silhouettes can be seen by anyone who might be hanging around outside. Watching us from the dark.

But the idea is to draw out whoever is stalking us. Not hide from him.

Besides, I figure he won't show himself until we turn the flashlights off.

Until he thinks we've fallen asleep. Just like Celeste and Bailey.

I sit with the baseball bat laid across my lap, and Rio unzips her backpack to pull out a short piece of heavy metal pipe.

"Where'd you get that?" I whisper.

"I picked it up somewhere," she says. "You learn to be prepared when you're on your own."

This feels like another window. A doorway into her story.

"You mentioned your foster dad the other day," I start. "And your mom. Something about her being on drugs." A stick is poking me from under the tent, and I shift a little bit. Closer to Rio. "But that's all I know about you."

That and she's a freaking amazing diver. And she has eyes the color of the eelgrass that grows along the edges of the spring run.

Plus, her laugh turns me a little bit inside out and the sound of her voice is my favorite new song.

Rio's quiet for a second. A rustling outside the tent fills up the silence, and we lock eyes. Rio tightens her grip on the metal pipe, and I wrap my fingers around the baseball bat.

We wait.

More rustling.

Something is moving around out there in the night, outside our tent.

"Probably that raccoon," I whisper, and Rio nods. But she has that pipe ready.

Whatever is out there, it's moving around to the other side of our tent now. We hold our breath and listen, frozen, as it works its way around us in a slow circle. Cracking twigs. Rustling leaves. The rhythmic sound of breathing. Something brushes against the outside of our tent and Rio raises the pipe.

I'm ready for a knife, ripping through canvas.

The thick night air flooding through the gaping wound.

But the rustling sound moves farther away, and then it's gone.

I'm shaking. Rio reaches out and puts a hand on my knee. Her touch is gentle. But not tentative. There's nothing shy about it.

I listen to the wind moving through the tops of the pines, and it sounds like a honey-soft whisper.

"Possum, maybe," Rio says.

"Yeah," I say. "Probably."

We're both breathing again. Neither of us loosens our grip on our weapon of choice.

And Rio doesn't take her hand off my leg.

"Something happened when I was little," Rio says, and it takes me a minute to remember that I'd started to ask about her past.

"To you?"

"No. My little brother." She finally moves her hand to brush the hair away from where it's clinging to her cheek. It's hot. And our breath in the tent is making it humid.

"I didn't know you have a little brother," I tell her.

She looks down at the metal pipe in her lap. "I don't. Not anymore." There's so much emptiness in her voice. A sound I'm well acquainted with.

It's grief.

"He died." I exhale the words into the closeness of the tent, and they get muffled. Almost swallowed up by the heat and the sleeping bags. Our bodies.

Rio and I don't need a past life to connect us. We have plenty to draw us together in this one.

Rio nods. "I was six and he was four." Her hair has fallen across her face, and I wish that I could see her eyes. "It was an accident. But DHS came for me anyway. And, yeah, my mom was on drugs. All kinds of shit. She'd get me back every few years after that. For a month or two. Until she'd fuck up again." She shrugs. "So I mostly grew up in foster homes."

"What was his name?" I know the power of the question. The need to say the name out loud. The pain of it, too.

"Evan," she tells me, and I can tell by the way she says it that she hasn't felt his name in her mouth for a really, really long time. She lifts her chin to look at me, and her eyes connect with mine, my own sorrow reflected in the sheen of hers. "I wanted to tell you, when I found out about Dani. I—" She stops, and I wait for her to go on. But she doesn't.

This time it's me who touches her. I don't even think about it as I cup my hand on her cheek.

She leans into my touch and my stomach is in knots. My heart is pounding so much harder now than it was when that possum—or whatever—was rooting around outside our tent. I was pretty sure that was a small animal of some kind.

But this? I have no idea what this is.

"I knew you felt it." One corner of Rio's mouth twitches up in that damn smirky way she has, and it throws me even more off balance. Her face turns serious then. "I knew it as soon as I saw you." I realize I'm stroking her cheek with my thumb. "I knew we were connected. That it was supposed to be you and me." She leans in closer. "That it had always been you and me."

I reach out and touch that half-heart locket. The one hanging around Rio's neck.

Rio is watching me. Long eyelashes sweeping low.

Parted lips.

God. Her eyes.

This is what I think a car accident must feel like. Not the actual crash part, but that sliver of a second just before—when you realize what's about to happen, but it's too late to hit the brakes.

Rio leans in even closer. Her hand curves around the back of my head and pulls me toward her. I exhale. Try to relax.

One more breath and her lips are so close now.

And then we both freeze, because the sound of whistling is floating on the thick night air. It's a clear sound.

Close.

Just beyond the clearing. In the dark.

"He's here," Rio says, and she pulls back to tighten her grip on that metal pipe again. "Turn off the flashlights." She's crouching in the tent. Ready.

"No," I say. "Wait." Because I can hear the song now. It's a tune I know.

I love you, truly.

"It's East," I tell her. We listen for a few more seconds.

Truly, dear.

"Are you sure?" she asks me.

"Yeah," I say. "Wait here." I reach to unzip the tent. But Rio stops me with a hand on my arm.

"Don't go out there, Tru." There's an edge of panic in her voice. "Please."

"It's okay," I promise. "It's East."

I pick up the baseball bat. Just in case, then I unzip the tent and step out into the dark, using my flashlight to scan the scrub.

"East?" I say. My voice sounds so loud.

"Tru?" The reply comes back to me beyond the reach of my flashlight. "It's me." When East steps out of the clearing into my light, I drop my baseball bat and my legs turn to Jell-O. "Hey," he says. "Whoa." He's instantly at my side, wrapping me up in his arms. "I didn't mean to scare you. That's why I was whistling our song. I wanted you to know it was me."

"It worked," I tell him.

He leans down to kiss me, and I have a flash of Rio.

Green eyes.

Full lips just a breath away from mine.

"What are you doing here?" I ask when East pulls away.

"I got worried," he says. "You said you were gonna come by. And then you didn't. I tried your phone a couple times. Then when you didn't pick up, I went by the house. Your mom said you were camping out at Dill and Derry's. But you weren't there. And Rio wasn't, either. So . . ." He stops and shrugs. "I figured maybe you guys would be here."

Rio is crawling out of the tent behind me now.

"Hey," she says.

"Hey." East nods at her. His eyes narrow like he knows something's up. "You guys okay out here?"

"Yeah," Rio says. "Actually, we're totally fine."

East's hand goes around mine. "Do you care if I talk to Tru alone?" He gives Rio an apologetic smile.

She shrugs.

East leads me away from the tent, toward Elijah's Well. I glance back through the thick scrub, and the glow of Rio's flashlight splinters through the growth.

"What's up?" I ask him, and he sighs.

"Listen," he says. "I don't wanna tell you what to do or anything. But do you really think it's a good idea being out here alone. With her?"

That throws me. I wasn't expecting it.

"Rio?"

"Yeah," he says. "It's just . . ." He stops and reaches out to tuck a strand of hair behind my ear. "We don't know much about her. You know? And this place . . ." He glances back toward the clearing. "I don't like it, Tru. It scares me."

I don't want to lie to him anymore. About anything. All I want is for things to be simple between us, the way they were when we were little kids.

Before we were a couple.

Before I was lying about FSU.

Keeping too many secrets.

"East," I start, but a sudden shriek cuts through the dark. I whirl around and look back toward the clearing, but Rio's flashlight has gone out. There's nothing but a sea of blackness.

"Rio?" I yell her name, but there's no reply.

Then someone bursts out of the trees to our left and I scream.

"Fuck!" East is startled. He tries to jerk me out of the way, but we aren't fast enough. The shape, dressed all in black, slams into me and I fall hard. Stickers dig into my palms and I cry out.

Whoever jumped out at us is tearing through the scrub. Running toward the Well. Moving fast. "What the fuck?" East says. "Stay here, Tru!" Then he takes off running. His flashlight beam bounces as he hurtles through the tangled undergrowth.

"East! Wait!" He's already gone. "Be careful!"

He has no idea who it is he might be chasing through the dark.

I scramble for my own flashlight and move as fast as I can back toward the clearing.

"Rio?" I'm calling her name, frantic. "Rio? Are you okay?"

She's moaning, crumpled in a little ball in the clearing. I drop to my knees in the sand.

"What happened? Where are you hurt?"

"He hit me with something." She reaches for my hand. "Right on the back of the fucking head."

"The baseball bat," I say. "I dropped it outside the tent."

It isn't there anymore.

My arms go around Rio's shoulders and I pull her against me.

"Jesus," I say. "Are you bleeding?" It's hard to tell with only the flashlight. My fingers are working through her hair. I'm trying to be so gentle, but she flinches and sucks in air through her teeth when I find the huge lump that's already forming.

At least there's nothing wet. No blood.

"Did you get a look at him?" I ask her, but she shakes her head.

"It happened so fast. Did you?"

"No. But East went after him." Terror washes over my skin again. If anything happens to East because he was out here looking for me, I'll never survive it.

I've been down that particular road once before.

"It worked," Rio tells me, and I see just the faintest hint of that smirk. "We drew him out of hiding."

"Yeah," I say. "But we still don't know who the fuck he is."

Rio reaches out to run her fingers over my face. "We'll figure it out, Tru. I promise. There's no way I'm going to let him separate us again."

I pull Rio to her feet, and we stand there for a second. I figure I'll start packing up our stuff. *East will be back any minute*, I tell myself. There's no way we're spending the rest of the night out here. When East comes back, he can walk us to my truck. Rio can sleep on my couch again.

Maybe she can stay there the rest of the summer.

My flashlight hits the tent and I gasp. So does Rio.

The tent has been slashed to ribbons. Big holes in one side gape and smile like toothless mouths. Like someone is laughing at us.

"Who was that?" I ask. "Who the hell is fucking with us?"

"We just met the Glades Reaper, Tru." Rio's voice is certain. It's so clear that she believes that. One hundred percent.

It doesn't matter, though. At least not tonight. All that matters is we're both still alive.

This time, at least we survived the camping trip.

SEVENTEEN

ABOUT THE TIME my worry turns to absolute dread, I hear East's voice. "Tru. You guys okay?" I see the beam of his flashlight moving toward us through the trees.

"Yeah," I yell in his direction. "We're fine."

When he makes his way back into the clearing, I aim my flashlight at him.

His arms and legs are scratched and bloody. Torn by thorns and brambles, and his T-shirt is ripped.

But he seems okay.

Whole.

"Did you catch him?" Rio asks.

"No. He slipped away from me." East is staring at her. "Who the hell was that?" He shifts his gaze to me. "Tru, what the fuck is going on?"

"We need to get out of here," I say. "I'll explain everything. I promise."

East sighs and mumbles something under his breath, but he helps us gather up our gear. I cram the tent and the already-bent poles back in the bag and jerk hard on the zipper. No use being careful with it now. It's totally shredded.

The three of us make our way through the scrub. "Stick close to me," East tells us. Rio keeps the pipe clutched tight in her hands.

When we reach the main spring, the thick trees recede, and I'm instantly relieved. We're out in the open now. The world is lit by moonlight.

No place for anybody to hide.

Let him come after us out here if he wants to. Where we can see him coming.

If he's not too chickenshit.

We're almost to the end of the boardwalk when I trip over something lying across my path. It's the baseball bat. The shadow in black must have taken it with him, then dropped it when he reached this spot.

I pick up the bat and look around, peering into the darkness at the edges of the spring, but there's no sign of whoever attacked Rio.

We hike up the lawn toward the parking area. Just my truck and East's in the gravel lot.

"Was there another car or anything?" I ask him. "When you got here?"

He shakes his head. "Only your truck."

Hidden Glen Springs is three miles out of town. There's nothing else around here. Nowhere to hide a car nearby. I'm trying to work out where the man who attacked us came from.

And how he got away.

We load the stuff into the back of my truck, and when we're finished, Rio climbs into the passenger seat and closes the door.

East puts his hands on both sides of my face. "Tru," he says. "Whatever's going on, you can tell me. You know that."

"I don't know what's going on," I tell him, and that's definitely not a lie. "It's all confusing."

He leans in to press his lips to my forehead. "Come to my place tonight," he whispers. "Get her someplace safe. Then come to me." His voice is pleading. I glance at Rio. She's sitting in the truck, staring straight ahead. Being careful not to turn her head to look at us. "Or. Fuck. Bring her with you. I just need to know you're okay tonight."

If I go with him—stay with him—nothing can hurt me.

Nothing has to change.

I'll feel safe.

But maybe feeling safe isn't the most important thing in the world.

"I can't," I tell him. "Not tonight."

"Tru—"

"I'll explain it all tomorrow. I promise. But tonight, I need you to trust me."

East reaches out to smooth my hair. He brushes his knuckles over my cheekbone, and I shiver.

"It's not you I don't trust." He glances at Rio, and I wonder if she's watching him in the rearview mirror.

I kiss East goodnight, and he tells me to be careful. Then I climb into the truck with Rio. "We should go to the emergency room," I say. "You could have a concussion or something."

"No. No doctors. No fucking police. Let's just go to your place."

I want to ask her what we're going to do. Now that we know for sure that somebody is really after us.

Somebody who wants to do more than just scare us.

But I don't because Rio's head has to be pounding like crazy. Plus I figure she doesn't have any more answers than I do.

Mom's car isn't in the driveway when I get home, and I cross my fingers that she'll be out the rest of the night. Maybe she'll find some guy to go home with.

I pull the pillow and blanket out of the hall closet and get Rio settled. I make a ziplock baggie full of ice for the lump on her head. But I don't go upstairs. Instead, I curl up on the other end of the couch and flip on the TV.

Rio gives me that little smirk when my foot touches hers under the blanket.

"You shouldn't go to sleep," I tell her. "In case you have a concussion or something."

"Right." She pulls the blanket up over both of us. "Better safe than sorry."

We spend the night watching black-and-white monster movies.

Dracula.

The Wolfman.

Them!

We've done this a hundred nights before. But never before tonight.

At one point, I get up to make popcorn. We share the bowl, occasionally brushing hands as we reach in for another fistful. Maybe our fingers linger on each other's a little too long. Like some swoony moment from a silly rom-com.

Once, Rio slips a hand under the blanket to rest on my thigh. Her fingers play over my skin. Just for a second or two. The lightest touch.

There's an almost-memory there. Those fingers on my body.

The paint is thin in that spot, and the wallpaper is peeking through.

I keep thinking about that moment in the tent, right before we heard East whistling. Practically lip to lip. One breath separating us.

We never get back to that place, and I don't know if I'm relieved or disappointed about that.

Both, I guess.

I tell myself it's not a big deal, because we don't really talk about anything the rest of the night. I tell her some boring stuff about East and Paz. She doesn't mention anything else about her mom. Or Evan. We make jokes. Try to make each other laugh. It's easier than it should be, given what just happened to us. Things should be serious. Somber. Maybe we're a little bit giddy from surviving. The adrenaline rush of that.

Turns out Rio loves silly puns. And warm blankets. Sometimes we talk about diving. Or about Dill and Derry. I tell her a little more about Dani. That's about it.

It's nothing.

But it doesn't feel like nothing. It's starting to feel an awful lot like something. Even if I can't figure out exactly what.

The next morning, I take Rio back out to the springs before Mom has a chance to come stumbling home. I make her promise to stick close to Dill and Derry, and I tell her that I'll come back out as soon as I can.

It's Memorial Day, so I don't have to work. That means I can head home to crash for a couple of hours. Mom comes home in a good mood. It must have been an okay night. She wakes me up and assigns me a list of chores to do while she's out taking photos for a new listing, so I'm pretty much trapped at home. It's okay, though, because it's started to rain. I figure Rio is spending the day holed up in her little tent, or under the rain tarp, right next to Dill and Derry.

East calls me late that afternoon. There's a party he wants me to go to with him. "Please, Tru," he begs, "come with me." I know what he really wants. He wants me to let him in. He wants to know what's going on, an explanation for what happened last night. I've spent most of the day trying to figure out what to tell him, and I still don't have any ideas.

There's nothing that's going to make any of it easier for him to hear. Or understand. I know that. I agree to the party, though, because I owe him that much.

It's almost dark when East picks me up. The rain has stopped, but it's all wet and steamy, like the inside of a bathroom when somebody leaves a hot shower running too long.

I climb into his truck, and East slides a warm palm up my thigh. Immediately, I'm thinking of Rio again. Her soft hand slipping under the blanket. "Hey," he says. "You okay?"

"Yeah," I tell him. "I'm good." He shakes his head and sighs, and I know he can feel the lie, but I'm not ready to talk about what happened out at Hidden Glen last night. I just need to get through this party. A couple of hours. I can do that. Then I can head out to the springs and check on Rio.

The festivities are out behind the old Paradise Motor Court, right off the highway, in a back lot that's littered with broken bottles and cigarette butts. Not the most scenic location, but it's outside the city limits, so nobody really cares what we get up to back there.

By the time East and I show up, there's already a big crowd. I spot Paz camped out on the hood of his brother's car with one arm around some girl. She's laughing at everything he says. When he sees us, he raises his beer in a tipsy salute.

We find a spot to park, and East puts the tailgate down on the truck so we can use it as a bench. He puts his arm around my waist and pulls me close, and I snuggle against him. Partly out of habit, and partly because it feels good.

One of the guys from the baseball team comes up and puts a cold beer in my hand. He's got one for East, too. After that, there's another one. And another one after that. It doesn't take long before I'm mostly drunk. Everybody has their radios tuned to the same station and we're all singing along and telling stories. Laughing and carrying on and giving each other a hard time. One of the marching band kids—the skinny one who plays the tuba—has some weed, and the joint gets passed around a couple of times.

Whatever happened at Hidden Glen Springs last night keeps getting hazier and hazier. The fear I felt when Rio got attacked is fading. And everything else about last night is dissipating right along with it. Even that almost-kiss. In the tent. I try to remember the way that moment felt, but I can't.

And maybe I like it that way.

East leans down to kiss me in the moonlight. His hand is warm on my knee. He nuzzles my neck. "I'm glad you came," he murmurs in my ear. "You look really hot tonight." His hand moves a little farther up my thigh.

In that moment, I see my whole life laid out in front of me. It's all so clear. All I have to do is choose it. A life with East. FSU. Then a little house somewhere. Mount Orange, probably. I know he'd choose to come back here, if he had the option.

This is home.

His home.

Our home.

A big lemon tree in the side yard.

The two of us playing cards with Paz and his girl on Friday nights.

A couple of kids eventually.

It's all perfect. Absolutely perfect.

It's what we had planned.

What everyone had planned for us.

East pulls me in for another kiss, and, for a second, the fog lifts and I feel Rio again. I remember everything with a blinding clarity that's crystal clear as spring water. Her hand on my skin. The electricity of it. Our lips so close that we're sharing the same breath. I'm almost knocked down by this weak-in-the-knees hunger that I've never felt with East. No matter how much I love him.

The burn starts low in my stomach, but I feel the heat of it creeping up my body, inch by inch, marking its territory. The intensity of it forces the air out of my lungs and leaves me shaking. It steals my voice and makes my vision blurry.

"Hey," East says. "What is it?"

"Can we get out of here?" I ask. "Take a walk, maybe?"

Everything is suddenly too loud. Too close. Too crowded.

"Sure." He snags an old blanket from behind the seat of his truck, then leads me across the field toward the tree line.

Paz stops eating that sophomore girl's face long enough to give us a big grin and a totally subtle thumbs-up. East looks at me and rolls his eyes.

At the edge of the field, we leave the chaos of the party behind and step into the trees, where we stop to share another kiss. East slips his arms around my waist and I'm dizzy. My brain is slow and fuzzy. I'm reeling from all the beer. And the weed.

From thinking about Rio.

We walk farther back into the dark, with only the moon and our cell phones to light our path, until the music and laughter from the party become a blended murmur of indistinct sound. When we find a little clearing, East stops and spreads the blanket on the ground.

His mouth is on my neck. Nibbling and sucking. I let him lower me to the blanket. Then his tongue is in my throat and he's already fumbling with the clasp on my bra. I kiss him back hard, and I reach down lower to feel him through the rough denim of his jeans. East grits his teeth and moans my name. He whispers that he loves me. And I whisper it back.

"I love you, too, East."

Shoes off.

Shirts off.

Jeans off.

I love you.

Bra off. Finally.

And underwear. Until we're both naked and clinging to each other on this blanket in the woods. And I'm trying to make out the muffled words to a song I can just barely hear. But East's got his hands on me again.

And then his mouth.

My fingers are tangled in his blond waves. But I'm thinking about Rio's dark hair.

The taste of cheap beer clings to my teeth. I hear a cheer go up from the party crowd and I wonder what we missed. I hadn't even realized my eyes were closed, but, when I open them, I can just barely see the rusted-out motel sign through the trees, standing sentinel on its long pole in the moonlight. The word *Paradise* is still easy to make out. Only it's missing the *e* at the end. That fell off years ago.

And suddenly I feel so utterly alone. I'm drifting away. All by myself. Even though East has me all wrapped up in his arms. Covered with his own body.

I don't have to say anything. He can sense it. He knows. Not about Rio and me, not that part. He sees that I'm frozen, that the wind has shifted.

That this isn't going to happen tonight.

"Come here," he says, and he rolls over onto his back. His voice is low and sexy. Gentle, but thick with gravel. My head is on his chest and he's stroking my shoulders. We're still naked, but East pulls the corner of the blanket up and over both of us.

I shiver and he holds me tighter, pressing his lips against my forehead without saying a word. I love him—this boy who shared his crayons with me on the first day of preschool. The one person who somehow, single-handedly kept my head above water when Dani died. This guy I kissed for the first time when we were both twelve years old. I wonder what it is that this drop-dead gorgeous human with a heart the size of the big scrub sees in me, when he obviously deserves so much better.

"I love you, East," I tell him. I barely get the words out. But it's 100 percent true.

"I love you, too, Tru. Talk to me. Please."

"Can we just stay here for a little bit?" I ask him.

"Yeah," he says. "Sure, baby. Anything you need." He wraps both arms around me and the familiar rhythm of our hearts beating so close together lulls us both to sleep.

Hours later, I clutch at the blanket and sit up with a gasp. It takes a second for me to remember where we are. East is still fast asleep, and I stare at him while dread settles on me like a boulder, because I know these are the last moments of us. I give him a little shake. "We better get going," I mumble. "It's really late."

"Shit." He rubs at his eyes as I pull on my T-shirt. Then my underwear and shorts. I stuff my bra down in my pocket. East takes my cue. He gets up and gets dressed, too.

I watch him moving in the moonlight, and I remember him at four years old with a buzzed haircut and at six with that awful mullet. At nine, when he wore that Dale Earnhardt shirt for a year straight. And at twelve with braces. Our first kiss. I do the math in my head. He's been my boyfriend for six years but my best friend for more than fourteen. My whole body starts to shake, because I'm about to separate myself from the one person who has been my partner in everything for literally as long as I can remember.

East pulls me toward him and wraps his arms around me. "Tru, what is it?" He kisses the top of my head. His hands are on my cheeks. "You're scaring me." I know it's selfish, but I let him hold me and stroke my hair for a few minutes, like I'm trying to soak up as much of him as I can. Then I take a deep breath and look him in the eye.

"Being with you like this . . . it isn't working for me. I'm so sorry, East, but it's not what I want anymore."

He's staring at me, trying to process what I'm saying. "You're breaking up with me?" he finally asks, and from the way he says it, it's clear he doesn't quite believe it, that he thinks there must be some misunderstanding. But I nod, and I hear all the air leave his lungs. He looks like I've hauled off and punched him in the face.

"Why, Tru?" he asks. I don't answer, because there are so many reasons running through my head. I don't even know how to sort them all out. "Is there another guy?" he presses, and I can answer that one truthfully, so I do.

"No, East, I swear. There isn't. There has never been any other guy for me. Not ever."

"Then what'd I do wrong?"

"It isn't anything you did or didn't do. I promise. You're perfect, East. You're . . ." My throat tightens up and I feel like I might be sick.

I've totally blindsided him. I've taken myself by surprise, too. This wasn't on my agenda for the night.

"Why, then?" he asks, and his voice is so gentle. So careful. I'd feel better if he was mad. If he'd scream and curse. Throw things. "I don't understand, Tru."

"I know," I whisper. "I don't, either. Not really. I just can't do this anymore. That's all." I reach for his hand, but he pulls away from me, and that hurts really bad—like having someone jerk a chair out from under you just as you're about to sit down. "I'm so sorry, East."

"This is really sudden," he says. "I just—"

"It really isn't," I admit. "Not for me." There are so many things I wish I could make him understand. "I don't have any idea what I want to do. Or what kind of life I want. Who I really wanna be." I pause, because I'm not sure if I should say the next part. But at this point, it seems silly to hold anything back. "I never even sent my application in to FSU."

"You don't wanna go to college?" He seems almost more surprised about that than anything else.

"I don't know," I tell him. "Maybe. Someday. Once I get things figured out."

"I thought you loved me." His voice cracks, and it feels like someone has sawed me in half.

"I do love you. This has nothing to do with you. I swear! It's all about me," I tell him. "I love you with my whole heart, East. I love you so fucking much. Just not like that."

"You mean the way I love you."

"Yeah," I say. "I guess that's what I mean."

The music from the party is quieter than before. Just barely audible over the rustling of the swaying trees.

"We've been together a long time," East says finally, and I nod. "We've been together forever."

"You were my first friend," I tell him.

He won't look at me now. "You were my first friend, too, Trulee."

"I still love you like that," I promise. "I always will."

"I gotta go home," he says, and I help him gather up the blanket. Shake out the pine needles. Then we move back through the dark trees together, toward the sound of the music. East doesn't talk, but he keeps his hand on my lower back.

Just that little bit of connection. So I know he doesn't hate me.

Or maybe old habits die hard.

Only a few cars are left in the overgrown lot. Most of the crowd is long gone, and we don't stop to talk to any of the hard-core partiers who are still hanging around. Paz shouts and waves us over, but East ignores him. The two of us climb into his truck and shut out the crowd.

"You okay to drive?" I ask him. My head feels surprisingly clear, but I'm not sure how much East had to drink.

"Yeah," he mutters. "I only had like three beers, and I slept those off. Plus getting dumped has a way of sobering you up."

The ride back to my place is silent, and when he pulls into the driveway, I have this moment of crushing fear. It descends on me like some kind of toxic cloud. The remnants of an atomic blast. It burns my throat and poisons my lungs. Stings my eyes.

What if I've thrown the best part of my life away? Ruined everything. Because, what I did, there's no way to undo that. No way to take it back. Even if I wanted to. It would never be the same between us.

"I'm sorry," I tell him again. It's the only thing I know to say.

"Me too," he tells me. I start to open the door. "Tru. Wait." I turn back and East is gripping the steering wheel with both hands. He's looking straight ahead. Not at me. "You need to tell me what's going on with you."

"I don't—" He gives his head a little shake.

"I don't mean with us." He turns to look at me, and his eyes are so sad. "I mean with you. Whatever it is, I wanna help."

"When I figure it out," I say, "I'll let you know."

Then I get out of the truck and head inside, and I don't let myself look back.

It's after one o'clock in the morning, but in the kitchen, Mom is making herself a grilled cheese sandwich. Her purse and shoes are lying in the middle of the floor, so I figure she just got home.

"Hey," she tells me when I walk in. "Where you been?"

"At a party with East," I say.

"You hungry?" she asks me. There's a hopeful cadence in her voice, and I kind of hate to disappoint her, but I shake my head.

"Came home to grab my keys. We're heading out to the springs to spend the night. At the homestead."

"I feel like we hardly see each other anymore." Mom leans against the kitchen doorframe. She's sipping from a glass of something that smells like whiskey. "But I know how it is. When you're young."

I head up the stairs to grab my truck keys, and when I come back down, Mom is still leaning in the doorway. She's staring at that big picture of me and Dani.

"Mom, what do you want for me?"

She takes a long drink and turns to look at me. "Tru, I've never wanted anything from you, other than for you to do your very best."

I shake my head. "No, Mom. What do you want *for* me?"

She thinks about it for a second. Takes another long drink. I hear the clinking of her ice cubes. "I want you to be happy."

"Is that really all?" I ask her.

"Yes," she says. "That's really all. That's everything."

I nod. "'Night, Mom. I love you."

"I love you back, Tru," she says. "Be careful out there."

EIGHTEEN

I'M NOT SCARED until I pull into the deserted parking lot out at Hidden Glen. It's dark. No lights out here. There used to be, but the county took them down a long time ago. They were hoping it would cut down on the partying. I guess they figured nobody would want to get drunk and hook up in the pitch black. At the site of a famous double murder. They were pretty much right about that. People took the hint and the nighttime parties moved to other places. So in the middle of the night, even on a holiday, it's empty and still at the springs.

I take a deep breath, and I reach down to grab the baseball bat from under the seat where I stashed it, then open the door and step out into the night.

I flick on the flashlight and start down toward the main spring. I'm moving fast, but I don't let myself run. I'm trying to stay calm.

Counting my footsteps.

Trying to match them to my heartbeat, just like diving.

But my heart is pounding so fast, and I can't control my breathing. If this were a dive, I'd be in serious trouble right now.

Honestly, I may be in serious trouble anyway.

It was stupid of me to come back out here in the dark,

especially after what happened last night. When I know now that somebody out there has it in for Rio. Probably me, too.

But after what happened with East, I know where I need to be.

Who I need to be with.

I glance toward the dark circle of the swimming area as I skirt around it on the boardwalk. It's beautiful, but it doesn't pull on my soul the way the deepest part of the Well does.

I pause for a moment before I step off the boardwalk to take the trail back to Dill and Derry's campsite. I scan the thick scrub with my flashlight, but the beam doesn't penetrate far into the tangle. Anyone could be out there.

Watching.

Waiting.

I hold the baseball bat at the ready, in front of my chest, and I step as lightly as I can so I can hear if anything else is moving out there, beyond the reach of my light.

It's not far. The length of a football field, maybe less.

The scrub gathers in around me. Sharp thorns. Grabbing branches. The closeness of the scrawny trees.

Tonight it feels like being eaten alive.

Four or five times I think maybe I hear something, but when I stop there's never anything there.

Finally I see the glow of Dill and Derry's campfire up ahead, and I stop for a second, at the edge of the homestead. Dill, Derry, and Rio are gathered around the fire. They're sitting on those overturned buckets, talking to each other. But I can't make out the words.

They look cozy. Safe. The brightness of the fire is inviting, and the hum of their voices puts me at ease, but they haven't heard me approaching on the path. They're so vulnerable out there. It would be so easy to take them by surprise.

They'd never see me coming.

"Hey," I say, and they all whirl around to stare at me.

"Holy shit, girl!" Dill is instantly on his feet. "You scared the piss out of us!"

Rio is moving in my direction. "What are you doing out here this late, Tru?" She takes my hand and leads me toward the fire. Our shoulders are touching, and she lowers her voice. "You shouldn't be out in the dark by yourself. Not after last night."

"I broke up with East," I whisper. "I had to be here."

Rio's eyes go wide with surprise. She starts to say something, but Dill and Derry are watching us. When I glance in their direction, they turn back toward the fire to give us some privacy.

"Wow," Rio says. "That's major. You okay?"

"I don't know," I tell her. "I don't know anything." I'm trembling now.

Rio puts her hand on the back of my neck and pulls me into her body. Her skin is soft and she smells like spring water. Somehow, even with the rain, she managed to get in a dive today.

I breathe her in and feel my heart rate start to drop back down to something more normal.

Almost like I'm diving.

Rio's fingers are in my hair, and my cheek is pressed into the curve of her neck. We're both a little tentative—hovering on the threshold of something, skirting the edges.

It makes me hungry, because being held by Rio feels like having been ravenous my whole life, without ever having known
what it was I really wanted to eat—and then finally, one day,
opening the fridge and figuring it out.

Holy shit.

This.

This is what I've been starving for.

It makes me wonder what that kiss would have been like.
Alone in that tent.

Then I remember that we weren't alone.

Someone was watching from the shadows.

Just like Dill and Derry are watching us now. Even if they're
trying to pretend they aren't.

Rio leads me over to the fire and Dill and Derry turn around
to smile at me, like they've only just realized I was there. Derry
is poking at the fire with a stick, holding her long skirt back
out of the way, but I see Dill glance toward our hands. Fingers
laced together.

"Drag up a bucket, Tru," he tells me with a grin. "It's a nice
night to be a polar bear." Then he pulls out his rolling papers
and gets down to business.

We spend the next couple of hours sitting around the fire.
Dill and Derry are telling stories about some of the crazy things
they've done. I've heard them all before, but Rio hasn't.

Every time Dill and Derry look away, Rio and I reach for each
other.

The brush of fingers.

My bare leg against hers.

We're searching the dark on the other side of the campfire. Peering between the flames to look for a shadow. Any movement. A hint that he's out there.

We both know he is. He must be.

Even the weed isn't enough to take the edge off that fear.

Finally Dill just looks at me and says, "You two wanna tell us what's going on?"

"Dill." Derry swats him on the arm. "Leave 'em alone. They'll tell us when they're ready."

Rio looks at me, then at Dill and Derry. "If we tell you something really wild, will you try to believe us?"

Dill runs a hand through his tangled curls and passes the joint to Rio.

"Kid," he says. "Just try us."

"Do you believe in past lives?" Rio asks, and she reaches for my hand.

I brace myself for some kind of smart-ass remark from Dill, but Derry pipes up instead. "I do," she tells us. "My sister was born with this funny little birthmark on her chest, and she always used to tell us it was where she got shot, the first time she died. This was when she was really little. Before she even knew what that meant."

Rio is rubbing the back of my hand with her thumb, and I think I might die if she ever stops.

"What if I told you," Rio starts, "that Tru and I are connected like that. Through a past life." She looks from Derry back to Dill. "Would that be too hard to believe?"

"What kind of past life?" Dill leans in toward us. I can't tell if he believes this at all, but I know he's interested. Curious. That's how Dill is. He wants to understand everything there is to know in the world.

"What if I told you that I was Celeste? And that Tru was Bailey."

Everything stops while Dill and Derry register what Rio just said, like when the rain is beating down on the roof of your car and then you pass under a bridge, and, for a split second, everything is sudden, deafening nothingness.

Derry finally breaks the silence, and I can hear the rain on the roof again. "Oh my God." Her hand flies up to cover her mouth, and her eyes are wide in the firelight. "Oh my God."

"Holy shit." Dill doesn't say the words. He exhales them slowly with a cloud of smoke. "You're fuckin' with us."

"There's all this stuff," I say. "It's hard to explain. But it makes sense."

"Are you sure?" Derry asks me. "How can you be sure, Tru?"

Rio is watching me, still stroking my hand.

"There's this memory I've always had. Something from when I was really little, I thought. This memory of Dani drawing a horse. This one specific horse. But it turns out it wasn't Dani's drawing. It was Celeste's. I saw it in her room."

"The horse with the flowers in his mane," Rio says, and I nod.

"That's when I knew. For sure. But." I turn toward Rio, and I feel my face flush. The heat of the fire. Rio's touch. Dill's and Derry's eyes on us. It's all too much. "I felt it before that. I think I knew when I saw you that first time."

"Yeah," Rio says. "I knew who I was before. I'd figured that much out. That's why I came here asking all those questions. Digging around." She runs her fingers over the skin of my wrist. "But I didn't know about you. Not until I saw you that first day. Then it hit me. You had to be Bailey." Her eyes are lit on fire. "You were the piece of the puzzle I was missing."

"Whoa," Dill says, and he pulls more smoke into his lungs. Holds it. Lets it slip between his lips. Then he passes the joint to me. "Take a hit," he tells me. "That's a pretty intense story."

"That's not even the weirdest part," Rio tells him.

"We think Rio asking questions got somebody scared," I explain, and Rio squeezes my hand. "Really scared."

We fill Dill and Derry in on everything's that happened. How somebody was following me on the trail. Those crime scene photos, stolen and then returned with our faces on the dead girls' bodies. Derry scoots closer to Dill.

We tell them about the locket, too. The one someone left in my truck. Rio and I both show them our halves, made whole again in the palm of my trembling hand.

"It gives me chills," Derry whispers, and Dill slips an arm around her shoulders.

We go over the trip to Celeste's house. The gut punch of seeing that pink-and-yellow bedroom.

That horse with the flowers. How it had the same effect on me.

The secret hiding spot we both knew was there. Two typed love notes from a secret admirer.

We end with what happened last night, the grand finale, at least so far. The attack in the dark.

Derry insists on looking at Rio's head. They both flinch when she finds the huge lump on her skull. Dill's eyes flash bright blue and angry.

"Jesus Christ, Tru!" He's pacing circles around the fire. "Y'all could've gotten killed back there. Again!" He picks up a discarded beer bottle and tosses it into the fire hard enough to shatter it. "Is that what you want?" Derry holds out a hand to him, and Dill sinks back down to sit on one of the buckets. "Who do you think it was?"

That's when Rio mentions the Glades Reaper, and I see Dill and Derry both recoil like someone spit on them. Derry clutches at Dill's arm.

Rio tells them how she always knew that name. Even before she knew her own. How she's been sure from the very beginning that it's him who's out there. How someone left that note for her, the first night she spent back in the scrub. The whole time she's talking, I see Dill studying my face.

"You don't think that's right. Do you, Tru?"

"I don't know," I say. "I mean, I guess it could be. Jon Boy told me the Reaper's still alive, that he sends letters to the paper down in Miami sometimes. But they don't publish them."

"Who do you think it is that's been after you?" Derry's voice is so soft. I can barely hear it over the crackling of the fire. "If you don't think it's the Reaper. Who killed Celeste and Bailey?"

"I don't know," I admit. "Whoever wrote those love notes, maybe. A secret boyfriend. Or maybe Knox found out and was pissed."

Any of those possibilities seem so much more likely to me than a serial killer.

I can't make it make sense. No matter how hard I try. It seems almost right. Like I can remember something about that name, too. Something that links him with the murders.

But the pieces don't quite fit.

It's almost always someone you know. That's what they say.

"From now on, neither one of you goes anywhere alone out here. Day or night." Dill pins me down with his blazing eyes. "You got that, Tru?"

"Yeah," I say. "Okay."

He shifts his gaze to Rio. "Got it?"

"Yeah. I got it," she tells him. "You don't have to get all bossy." But I can tell she likes that he cares.

"We didn't mean to get you guys involved in this," I say, and Dill glances back toward their tent.

"That fucker out there, he got us involved in this the minute he destroyed our home." He reaches out and gives my shoulder a squeeze. "And the minute he went after our family."

"We weren't here that night," Derry says, and then she pauses. "The night the girls died." Her voice sounds like she's reaching way back into the past, digging around for a memory the way people look for a lost shoe in the bottom of a closet. "We'd gone to stay at my parents' place, and I always wondered why Bailey and Celeste picked that night to go camping. I mean, the weather was so awful. If they had just stayed home—" She stops and shakes her head. "The storm passed quick, but it was intense. I've never heard thunder that loud." She's watching the campfire send embers up toward the night sky. They look like escaping stars. "When we came back out here that next day, Hidden Glen was swarming with police. Crawling with all kinds of people." She looks a little embarrassed. "We thought maybe it was our weed. We always had a little patch growing." She turns to Dill. "Remember how we thought that? Until we saw them bringing out the body bags." She closes her eyes, like that might help block out the memory. "I remember not being able to go back there, to the Well, for a really long time. I kept imagining it. Those girls. Dead." Derry opens her eyes. "I've never been able to get it out of my mind."

I know exactly what she means. Only I don't have to imagine it. I've seen the photos. Rio slips an arm around my waist. She pulls me to her, and I rest my head on her shoulder.

"So, what else is going on here?" Dill asks us, and he gestures back and forth between the two of us.

Rio and I both grin. My smile fades fast, though, and hurt comes rushing in.

Guilt.

"I broke up with East tonight," I tell them.

"Awww, shit. Poor guy." Dill sucks in his breath in a long, low whistle. "How'd he take it?" he asks me.

"Okay, I guess. I don't really know."

"Give him some time," Derry tells me. "He loves you so much."

"Did you tell him about this?" Dill gestures back and forth between me and Rio again, and I shake my head. "Why not?" he asks. "Seems like he deserves the truth."

That stings. Because I know he's right.

"A lot of reasons," I admit. "Partly because I figured it might make it worse for him. But mostly because I know it'll be this completely huge thing. I can't deal with that right now."

"Your mom doesn't know?" Derry asks.

"No," I say. "There's not any reason to tell her."

"You think she'll freak out?" Dill asks.

"No," I tell him. "Not really. But once I tell her, everything's different. The world is upside down, at least for a little while. Until we sort it all out again." I blow out a big breath and look down toward my feet. A bug is crawling on my ankle, and I reach down to flick it away. "It's like, for eighteen years, she's had this road map of my life all drawn up in her head, you know? And, when I tell her, she's going to have to make a whole new map, with no warning. Totally on the fly." I lift my head and look at them. "It will be nothing but uncharted territory."

"Here there be dragons," Derry says.

"What?" I ask her.

"Here there be dragons," she says again. "It's something medieval mapmakers used to put on their maps to mark uncharted oceans. To show that they didn't know what was out there— but that it might be something really scary." She looks at me, and her eyes are gentle. "But they were wrong, Tru. It turns out there weren't any sea monsters. It was just more water."

Dill reaches over and gives my leg a slap. "You've never been afraid of the water, sister." He stands up and stretches, then tells us he'll be right back. We watch him disappear into their tent. I can see him through the door, squatting down low. He's digging around in one of the big plastic tubs they keep their stuff in.

Derry gets up and moves to the edge of the clearing. The fire has gotten hungry and she's searching through the wood they have stacked there, looking for something the right size. Every few seconds, I see her raise her head and look into the dark.

"Do you think you'll go to college?" Rio asks me in our moment alone. "Not with East. I know you said you don't wanna do that. But do you think you'll go at all?"

"Maybe." I shrug. "Who knows?"

"What do you want to study?" she asks. "If you go."

"Something in environmental science," I say. "Ecology, maybe." I reach for Rio's hand, and she raises one eyebrow at me.

"You're aware I'm totally imagining you in a sexy park ranger uniform right now. Something in a dark chocolate brown. Really short shorts."

She tugs on my arm. Pulls me onto her lap. Now we're sharing a bucket and her hair is so beautiful in the glow of the fire.

I blush and shake my head. "You're picturing a UPS man. Not a park ranger." She laughs again, and the sound lights me up. I'm pretty sure, if you looked up the word *sexy* in an online dictionary, you'd find an audio file of that throaty little giggle of Rio's.

"What about you?" I ask her. "What do you want to do with your life?" She looks at me like that's a thing she's never considered before. "You should start thinking about it," I tell her. "We know our past was shitty. We deserve to have a future."

Derry comes back with the wood and gets the fire burning

bright again. She notices me sitting in Rio's lap, but she doesn't say a word about it. Neither does Dill when he comes out of the tent. He's holding another joint in one hand and something else in the other, but I can't tell what it is until he holds it up for us to see by the light of the fire.

It's a gun. An old-looking one. Like you see in cowboy movies. Some kind of revolver, I think.

"Dill!" Derry warns. "Be careful with that!"

"I wanted to show y'all that we're safe here." He raises the gun and points it up toward the sky. Then he shouts into the darkness, "You hear that, motherfucker? You don't wanna mess with us!"

"Put that away," Derry scolds him. "Before somebody gets hurt." Then she turns to me and Rio. "Stay with us tonight, Tru. You can't walk back to your truck alone."

"Yeah," I say. "I was planning on it." Beside me, Rio is looking off into the night. Toward the trail that leads back to the springs.

"Shhh," she tells us, and everyone immediately falls silent.

Then we hear it. The sound of footsteps. Jogging. Someone is moving fast up the path in our direction.

"Fuck." Dill stands up and aims that old gun of his into the dark. I wonder if he's ever actually fired it. If he has any idea at all what he's doing.

Or if it's even loaded.

Rio wraps her arms tight around my waist and Derry moves to stand right behind us, one hand on each of our shoulders.

"I'm not goddamn playin' around," Dill shouts. "Whoever's

out there, stop. Right fuckin' now. Before I blow your brains out."

"Hey! Take it easy!" Dill lowers the gun, because we both know that voice. "It's me." East steps out of the dark and into the circle of light around the fire. "I just—" He stops when he notices me. And Rio. I see the exact moment he realizes that I'm sitting on her lap. That her arms are around my waist. Her chin tucked into my shoulder. The way our legs are intertwined. "I came to get fucked up."

"East," I start.

His mouth opens and closes. He looks from me and Rio to the gun dangling from Dill's hand. "Somebody please tell me what the hell is going on," he says.

Dill was right. East has never been less than honest with me about anything. Not once in his whole life. He deserves that same respect, at the very least.

"Okay," I promise him. "I'll tell you everything." Rio reaches out to take the joint that Dill is still holding in his other hand. She passes it up to East.

"Take this," she tells him. "You're gonna need it. Trust me."

NINETEEN

EAST SINKS ONTO one of the big, overturned buckets and I untangle myself from Rio so I can sit next to him. I wait for Dill to relight the joint and I let East get one good inhale. To soften the blow of what he's about to hear.

Dill slaps me on the back. "Just like getting into the spring, Tru. Quick and all at once is the best way when the water's cold. You wade in slow, and it makes it worse."

I know he's right. He always is. I take a big breath myself and then I let it all come spilling out.

How I was drawn to Rio as soon as I saw her.

How it felt like we'd known each other for years. Like I'd been waiting for her somehow. Without even realizing it.

East passes the joint to Derry, but he doesn't say a word. His hands are balled up into tight fists and he's staring at the toes of his boots. I know this hurts. That it's hard for him to hear.

It's hard for me to say.

"And you know how fascinated I've always been with the Hidden Glen murders," I add. "How I've never been able to get past what happened to Celeste and Bailey that night." I reach out and touch East. A quick hand on his arm. I can see him trying to connect all the dots that I'm laying out like bread crumbs.

"But what does that have to do with anything?" he asks.

I look at Rio and she takes over for me. She explains how she knew about the murders out here, even as a really little kid living up in Tennessee. The facts she had.

The things she remembered.

"Wait." East raises his head to look at us. "What do you mean 'remembered'? All that shit went down before any of us were born."

"Yeah," Rio says. "Exactly."

East is more confused than ever.

"What do you know about past lives?" Derry asks him. She's brushing that long, honey-colored hair out of her face, and her eyes are so serious. I'm glad she's the one who brings it up, because she says it so gently and with so much care. I see the dawn of understanding spark in East's eyes.

"Wait." He stands up and stares down at Rio. "You can't be serious." He's looking at me now. "She thinks she's—what?— like the ghost of Celeste or something?"

"Not a ghost," Rio corrects him. "It's a past life."

"This is fuckin' crazy." East looks across the fire at Dill and Derry. Then at me. "I can't believe you guys are sitting here like this is a normal thing to say."

"I didn't believe it, either," I say. "Not at first."

I tell him about that memory. The horse. That shuts him up for a second, because he knows what that memory has always meant to me. I've told him about it a million times. How that memory is my safe place. He's helped me search the house for that drawing more times than I could count.

"You're seriously telling me you think you're Bailey. Were Bailey. Whatever." He's shaking his head. "No. There's no way. There's gotta be some other explanation." East is back on his bucket, and he leans forward to take both my hands in his. "Listen to me, Tru. Please. I understand if you want something different. Don't want me. Whatever. I mean, it kills me." I see him blink back tears. "But I can understand it. I can take it. If I have to." He shakes his head. "The rest of it . . . no." He throws a quick look in Rio's direction. "I don't know who this girl is. But she sure as shit isn't Celeste."

"Don't be so certain," Dill tells him as he fires up the joint for another round. "'There are more things in heaven and earth, Horatio, than are dreamt of in your philosophy.'"

"Don't," East warns him. "Come on, Dill. Just don't. Don't quote the Bible to me right now, man."

I don't bother to tell him that it's Shakespeare. *Hamlet*. We read it in English IV last fall.

Or at least I did.

"There's more," Rio says. Together we map out the rest of it. The weird things that have happened, from the strange and threatening to the downright dangerous, ending with the attack. Last night. At the murder site.

"The guy I chased through the woods." East sounds like this is the last straw. "You're telling me I was hot on the heels of the Glades Reaper?"

"It's a lot to take in," Derry says, and she passes the joint back to him.

"I don't know for sure." I glance at Rio. "But we know that Rio scared somebody with her digging around. Whoever is after us is most likely the same person who killed Celeste and Bailey."

"So now—what?—he's gotta kill you." East lets out a little laugh. It escapes from his mouth on accident with the smoke he's exhaling. "Again?"

"Something like that," Rio says.

East stands up. "I can't listen to this anymore." He hands the joint over to Dill. "Y'all have fun out here. I'm goin' home."

"Wait." I grab him by the hand. "Don't go back into the scrub alone. Please." I'm scared to let go of him. "Stay here tonight. With us."

East looks from me to Rio, and he shakes his head. "Nah. I gotta go."

"Careful out there, brother," Dill warns him. "Watch yourself."

East gives me a look. "Honestly," he says, "I don't think anything else could possibly hurt me tonight."

Then he stomps off into the dark.

Dill, Derry, Rio, and I sit there, huddled up to the light of the fire and stare after him for a few seconds.

"He'll be fine," Rio finally says. "It's not him the Reaper wants."

I hope she's right.

Dill and Derry drag Rio's little tent closer to their big one. Then Dill tells us all goodnight. He throws another couple of logs on the fire. Gets it going real good. Then he settles down on a bucket with that gun on his knee. I realize he intends to stay out there until morning.

It chokes me up a little, thinking about how much he loves us. Derry, of course. But me, too. And even Rio, I think. How he'll sit up all night looking out for us.

Our protector.

I've always wished Derry was my mom, but for the very first time, it makes me wish a little bit that Dill was my dad. Or even that my dad was my dad, in any of the ways that really matter.

Inside the tiny, borrowed tent that East gave Rio, there's barely enough room for the two of us. I left my sleeping bag in the truck, so Rio unzips hers and spreads it across the floor of the tent like a carpet.

There's a little battery-operated lantern hanging from a loop at the top of the tent, and Rio reaches up to turn it on so we can switch off our flashlights. It's still got to be at least ninety degrees. We're both dripping with sweat. Hair sticking to our faces. So we strip down to our underwear and bras. And even though it's not much different from the swimsuits we've already seen each other in, we're each trying so hard not to stare.

There isn't much room to maneuver, and I bump my head against the lantern and start it swinging like crazy. Rio laughs at me, and we both lie back on top of the sleeping bag watching the weird shadows bouncing around the tent from the swinging lantern above us. Soon, though, the lantern stops swinging, and the light stands still.

Rio rolls over on her side to face me, then props herself up on one elbow and trails her fingers down my arm. I break out in goose bumps, ninety degrees or not.

The tingle it sends down my spine is one of recognition.

Not surprise.

"You're gorgeous, Tru," she tells me, and I blush. I've never felt gorgeous. Not even with East. He's always made me feel loved and wanted. But I never felt beautiful with him, even though he always told me I was.

When Rio says it, it's different. For the first time, I feel it. Just a little bit.

"Do you think we were more than friends?" I ask her. "Before?"

"I don't know," she says. "Maybe. Or maybe we wanted to be."

"I'm glad we found our way back to each other," I tell her, and I wrap my fingers around her hand.

"We always will," Rio says. "I really believe that."

She reaches up to turn off the little lantern and the last thing we hear before we drift off to sleep holding hands is the sound of Dill whistling quietly to himself just a few feet away.

When daylight first starts to creep in, I slip on my clothes and sneak out of the tent. Dill is still awake. The fire is coals now, and he's bending low, cracking eggs over a cast-iron skillet. "Did some yard work for this old guy last week," he tells me. "Got paid in chicken eggs."

My heart squeezes because it makes me think of East, and how he always made breakfast on our camping trips. He'd get up early and by the time I'd crawl out of the tent, there'd be sausage and bacon and fried potatoes with onions. Scrambled eggs with big chunks of tomatoes and green peppers mixed in.

I hope East is okay this morning. I'm not someone who prays, but I offer that thought up to the sky and I let it drift toward the clouds with the smoke from Dill's fire.

I hope you're okay. And I hope you know how much I love you.

I know he isn't okay, though. None of us are.

When Rio and Derry come out of the tents, drawn by the smell of Dill's cooking, we gather around what's left of the fire to eat breakfast while we chart a course for the day. The plan is for me to drop Rio and Derry off at the local library, and then I'll head home to have another conversation with Jon Boy. I already texted him that I wasn't coming into work this morning, but I asked him to meet me at his house on his lunch break. I was shocked when he actually replied and said that would be fine. Most of the time his phone is dead. He never remembers to charge the damn thing.

But before we can do any of that, we have to dive. This morning I feel like I might tear apart at my seams if I don't make it to the water soon. I need that calm to soothe my nerves and clean the wounds last night left me with. The breakup with East. That broken, confused look in his eyes when he took off into the night.

I want to wash away the stale smell of sweat that's settled on my skin.

I need to remember how to breathe.

Rio and I change into our swimsuits, then we help Dill get the breakfast things cleaned up while Derry takes some laundry down off the clothesline they have strung up between two pine trees.

"Dill." Derry's voice is worried. She's standing across the

clearing with a couple of long skirts folded over her arm. "Come here." Dill puts down the cast-iron skillet he's been scrubbing and moves in her direction. Rio and I exchange glances and follow him. "Look at this."

In the sand behind the clothesline are a few trampled clumps of grass and some very obvious boot prints. Someone stood back there recently. Walked back and forth behind the cover of the hanging skirts and faded beach towels.

"Fuck." Dill rubs at his eyes, like he can't believe what he's seeing. I know he has to be beyond exhausted. He didn't sleep a wink last night. Sitting up. Keeping vigil.

Now he knows there was someone out here, just beyond the clearing. Watching the watchman.

"Those are the same boot prints I saw around the fire," Rio says. She points to the wavy lines on the heel. "After someone cut up the tent."

The same ones she found all around the clearing when someone left her that note.

Fear the Reaper.

"Fuck!" Dill grabs the beach towels off the line. He yanks them down with such force that the clothespins go flying and I have to duck to avoid getting hit in the face.

Derry slips one arm around Rio and the other around me.

"Are we still gonna dive?" I ask. I know it's stupid. We have much bigger worries at the moment. But I'm unraveling and only the pressure of the water can hold me together.

Dill looks back down at those footprints. "I'm gonna stick back here today. Keep an eye on things." I see him glance toward the bucket by the fire. The one with the old gun resting on top. "But you three go on." He looks from me to Rio. "You two keep a close eye on each other. Down below and up top."

"We will," Rio promises. She reaches for my hand as we start for the path.

It's already close to a hundred degrees. A record breaker, the radio promised. Cars are lined up pulling into the parking lot. The scorching heat means there will be lots of annoying tourists in the water. Normally, that would be awful. But today I don't mind sharing space with sunburned bald guys wearing Ray-Bans and kids in hand-me-down swim trunks. I figure, the more people around, the better.

I see Derry checking out the crowd that is already starting to gather at the main spring, and it hits me that she should be setting up her card table and typewriter today. She'd be making good money with her poems on demand. She's stuck babysitting me and Rio instead. If she resents it, though, she definitely doesn't let on.

Back at the Well, Derry settles under a tree with her book while Rio and I prepare to dive. Before I start my breathe-up, I see Rio take a good look around. She's studying the faces. I figure she's wondering the same thing I am.

Is he here?

Is he watching us right this very minute?

As soon as I slip into the water, I am calmer. Soothed. It doesn't take long for that magnet to start pulling on me. It's impossible to ignore that hard tug this morning.

I know Rio feels it, too.

We take turns going down over and over and over. We get deeper every time. Stay under longer. We still can't reach whatever it is that's winking at us from that little ledge. And it's frustrating for both of us.

Finally Derry looks up from her book and says, "I'm calling it. That's all for this morning. You've had enough."

Rio and I get dried off and gather our things, but my eyes stay locked on the bottom of the Well. Toward that little ledge. Whatever is down there, I need to bring it to the surface.

Derry's right, though. I'm light-headed. Dizzy. A little disoriented. I need a break. So the three of us head up to my truck.

In town, I drop Derry and Rio at the tiny Mount Orange community library so they can do some research into the Glades Reaper murders. And so Derry can return the stack of books she's brought along. I head toward my place to shower. After that, I'm going next door to see Jon Boy and fill him in on everything. Since we're not keeping things a secret anymore, he might as well be the next one to know what's really going on. He probably knows more about the Hidden Glen murders than anyone alive. Maybe he can tell us something we don't know. Something that will tie everything together and make it all make sense.

I'm pulling into the driveway when I get a text from East. **Can we talk? It's important.**

I hesitate for a second before I text him back. I'm so anxious for a shower. And clean clothes. I'm sweaty and sticky and gross. Plus, if he wants to talk about us, I don't think I can handle that this morning.

Not on top of everything else.

I can't blow him off, though. It's East. So I reply, When and
where?

His response is immediate. Knox's place. Now if you can.

A warning bell goes off in my head. I'm really not in the
mood to deal with our cowboy-hat-wearing mayor today. I'm
wondering why on earth East would want to meet at Knox's
house anyway. I mean, sure, Knox is family, and East rarely says
a word against him. Not even when Knox gifts him with a black
eye for popping off. But they aren't close. Not by a long shot.

Another text from East. Please?

I respond with Sure. I don't want to, but I can't make myself
say no to him. I back my truck out of the driveway and head
toward Knox's McMansion on the edge of town. When I pull
up, East is waiting for me on the front porch.

"Hey," he tells me when I climb out of the truck and start up
the steps in his direction. "Thanks for coming." East is fidgeting. Nervous. He comes down the steps to meet me, then takes
my hand and leads me off the sidewalk and around the corner
of the house toward Knox's workshop. "Let's talk back here. It's
more private."

The warning bell inside my brain is a full-on five alarm now.

East pulls open the door to a metal shed that stands off to the
side of the house. Against the back wall, cardboard boxes filled
with Knox's old junk are stacked almost to the ceiling. A 1969
Ford Mustang sits up on blocks inside—his prized possession—
surrounded by parts and tools. Knox has been working on fix-
ing that car up for as long as I can remember, and sometimes East

helps him. I wonder if maybe that's why he called me over here. Maybe he was here working on the car. Then it hits me that it's Tuesday. He should be at the Sno Shack making rainbow snow cones for kids who pay him with spare change they dug out of their mothers' purses.

So why isn't he?

It's about ten million degrees today, and I'm grateful for the little air conditioner rattling in the one tiny window. But despite the cool air in the shed, I'm starting to sweat. East and I stand there looking at each other for a few long, uncomfortable seconds before I give in and ask what's up.

"Sit down, Tru," he tells me, and he points at a stool. So I do, and East pulls up another stool so we're sitting knee to knee. "I have some stuff to tell you."

"Okay," I say. "I'm listening."

East takes a deep breath. He rubs the palms of his hands on his shorts. "I did some checking around," he says. "And I found a few things out. Stuff you should know."

"About what?"

East takes a deep breath. "About Rio."

That's not what I was expecting at all.

"Why were you checking up on Rio?" My voice has an edge to it, and I see the change in East's face. He's even more wary now.

"I wasn't checking up on her exactly. I talked to a few guys I know. Divers up at Wakulla Springs." He reaches down to pick up one of Knox's empty cigarette packs, then he crumples the box in his fist and tosses it into the trash on the other side of the shed. "And they had some stuff to say."

"Why would you do that?" I stand up to go. "I didn't want to hurt you, East, but I was trying to do the right thing. For both of us." East looks like I kicked him. "You had no right to go poking around into Rio's past like that just because you're jealous."

"Jealous? I'm not jealous, Tru." He stops. Runs his hands through his hair. "I mean. Shit. Of course I'm jealous. But I'm also worried about you. This girl—a total stranger—blows into town and says a bunch of impossible shit, and you believe every word out of her goddamn mouth like it's coming straight from the Bible? You don't even know her."

"I know the past lives part sounds wild," I tell him. "I know that. And maybe you can't wrap your head around it. But I believe her."

I trust my own memory. That hand moving over the paper, slowly revealing the shape of a running horse.

Wildflowers in its mane.

"It's not just that part," East says. "It's everything. Everything out of her mouth is a lie."

"I gotta go," I say. I'm not listening to this anymore. I turn and head toward the door of the little shed.

"Wait." East jumps up and grabs my hand. "Tru, please." His eyes have gone all dark. I've never seen East look this serious. This desperate. "Let me talk. I deserve that much. After everything."

I can't really argue with that, so I sigh and sit back down on my stool. East settles back on his. "Okay," I tell him. "Five minutes."

"Okay." East runs a hand through his hair again. Those soft blond waves. I have to remind myself not to reach out and do the same. It's such a habit, loving East. "So. The first thing I found out is that her name's not Rio. It's Erin."

"So?" I say. "Lots of people have nicknames."

"Yeah. That's true. But there's a lot more."

"Like?" I'm losing patience fast.

"Like she was in the foster system. Something about her mom being on drugs, they said."

"None of that's Rio's fault," I counter. "Besides, she already told me about that."

"Yeah," East says. "But Rio—or Erin, whatever—she got kicked out of a couple of foster homes. She'd get caught lying. Or stealing. Like, from her foster families, but also shoplifting and stuff like that."

"Okay." I mean, that's not great. But it's not major stuff, either.

"The guys I talked to didn't have a lot of details. So that's why I came over here this morning. I figured Knox might know some people up in Wakulla County. I asked him if he'd make some phone calls. Find out the real scoop on this girl."

"You did what?" I'm instantly on my feet again.

So much for just calling a couple of divers he happens to know.

It pisses me off that East enlisted the help of his piece-of-shit uncle to dig into Rio's history, all because I had the nerve to break up with him. The guts to think that I might want something different.

"Tru. She took off from her last foster home. A couple weeks ago. Just after graduation. She stole a bunch of money from those people. That's what Knox found out. A couple thousand dollars in cash. Some jewelry, too. They decided not to press charges, but—"

"Jesus, East." I throw up my hands. "I don't care! I don't care about any of this."

"Just listen a minute, Tru. That stuff you told me last night. About Dill and Derry's slashed-up tent. The crime scene photos. The locket in your truck." He's looking right into my eyes now. "What if she's involved in it somehow? What if she made this whole Bailey and Celeste thing up for some reason, and she's playing some part in all this stuff that's happening?"

"That doesn't make any sense," I tell him. "What possible reason would she have for doing that?"

I hate that I'm already running through everything in my head. Checking to see if that could be true.

"I don't know," East says. "I don't know her like you do." It's hard to miss the accusation in his eyes. "Maybe she just likes the drama of it. Maybe she's just one of those people who loves causing chaos. Maybe it's some kind of game to her. People like that—"

"People like what?"

"She's a thief, Tru."

"No. Rio's not like that," I say. "She isn't—"

"She's a liar. You don't know what she's like or isn't like. You barely know her. It's been like, what? A little over a week?" I want to say that he's wrong. That I've known her a lifetime. That the minute I saw her, I remembered her. But now, sitting here in this shed with East, looking into those familiar eyes and hearing his voice, I'm second-guessing myself. "I'm just asking," he says. "Is it possible?"

"You were out there at the campsite. You took off after whoever that was that knocked me down. Are you saying you think Rio let you chase her through the scrub and then somehow doubled back and hit herself over the head? That's impossible. How could she have done that?"

She couldn't have taken those pictures out of my backpack, either. We were together in Yucha Spring the whole time. No way she could have taken the photos of us that were taped to the faces, either. The locket . . . she could have slipped that into my truck while I was sleeping. But where would she have gotten it in the first place? I guess maybe she could have slashed up Dill and Derry's tent. But the rest of it? No way.

East is quiet for a second. I see his wheels spinning. "What if she has someone helping her?" he asks.

"I know I hurt you, East." I take a step back. Away from him. "But I really thought you'd be on my side."

"You didn't hurt me, Tru." East looks away from me, down toward the oil-stained floor of the shed. "You broke my heart." He looks back up to find my eyes. "I'm always gonna be on your side. But I want you to believe me, too. Because in all those years, I've never lied to you. Not once. Not ever."

"East—"

"I don't know what I think is really going on. But I know she's a liar and a thief. I don't trust her. And you shouldn't, either."

That's the final straw.

"You don't get to tell me what I should or shouldn't do, East."

Nobody does. Not anymore.

East stares at me for a second, like I'm a stranger. "I thought you should know. She isn't the person you think she is, Tru. She isn't honest."

"Is that all?" I ask him.

"Yeah," he says. "That's all."

East gives me one last look, then turns and heads out the door of the shed, leaving me standing there with his uncle's old Mustang and the boxes of junk, inhaling the mechanic's grease and stale cigarette smoke, wondering what the hell just happened.

I give my head a good shake, and I start to head back to my truck. But a shiny glint catches my eye. Something caught on one of the door hinges.

When I take a closer look, I see it's a chain.

Delicate.

Tarnished.

With a broken clasp. As if it had been yanked from around someone's neck.

I stare at it for a second before I pull it off the hinge to study it up close. When I hold it up to the sunlight coming in the open door, my hand is shaking. Because I recognize this chain.

The length.

The style.

The weight of it in my hand.

The interlocking pattern of the links.

It's all the exact same as the broken chain that goes with the half-heart locket of Bailey's.

Which means this one has to be Celeste's.

I think about how that locket showed up in my truck tied on a black ribbon, the chain missing.

Now here's the chain in Knox's workshop. There's only one explanation for that, so far as I can see. Knox must've torn it from Celeste's neck, and he's been holding on to it all these years.

A souvenir.

I look toward those old boxes stacked again the back wall. Overstuffed and water stained. Filled with decades' worth of junk. Old clothes. Papers. Scraps and bits.

One of the boxes has been pulled off the top of the pile. It's sitting on the floor of the shed, its flaps ripped open. Like someone was in a hurry to find something they'd stashed inside a long time ago.

I slip the chain into my pocket and step out of the shed to head for my truck. As I come around the corner of the house, Knox steps right out in front of me.

"In a hurry, Tru?" He's grinning at me. I take a step back. "That's a shame. I told East to ask you to stay to lunch." He takes a second to pull out a cigarette and light it up. When I don't say anything, his grin just gets broader. "Your new friend's been feeding you a load of bullshit. He tell you that?"

"I gotta go," I say. "Mom needs me at home." I move to step around Knox, but he moves with me so he's still blocking my path.

"Tru, darlin'." Butter wouldn't melt in his mouth. "We both

know your mama's still passed out from whatever nonsense she got up to last night."

"Fuck you," I say, and I move to go around him again. This time, I manage to get by, but he reaches out quick—like the strike of a cottonmouth—and grabs me by the wrist so hard I yelp. "Let me go, asshole!" I hiss the words through clenched teeth. If he wants to be a snake, I guess I can be one, too.

Knox throws his head back and laughs when I try to pull away from him. I feel my face get red. "I heard y'all been pestering Celeste's mama, even. That poor woman's been through enough." Knox narrows his little pig eyes at me. "You tell your friend she needs to move on. There's nothing for her in Mount Orange."

I jerk back hard, desperate to get away, and Knox releases his grip on my wrist. I stumble backward until I slam hard into the side of the house.

"You better watch your back, Trulee," Knox tells me as I start toward my truck, but I don't give him the satisfaction of a response. I've watched him bully East for years, and every other member of his family, including his own mother. I've seen him berate city clerks and city council members. I've watched him terrorize everyone who crosses him. But I'll be damned if I'm going to be one of Knox's victims.

"No," I mutter to myself as I climb into the truck and slam the door. "You better watch yours." Then I reverse out of his driveway with squealing tires and head for home.

With that broken gold chain burning a hole in my pocket.

TWENTY

I PULL INTO the driveway at home, and when I get out of the truck, I slam the door again. So hard this time that Jon Boy comes out on his front porch to see what's up.

"Easy there, Trulee Bear," he shouts. "You're gonna shake that truck apart." His voice is teasing, but when he sees me marching across the patchy lawn in his direction, his smile slips away.

Jon Boy leads me up the steps and into the house. He kicks off his boots and I sink down onto his old sofa. I'm still shaking from my run-in with Knox. Jon Boy is eyeballing me from the kitchen where he's leaning on the counter. "You need a glass of water or anything? Or some lunch?"

"No," I say. "I need to ask some questions. And I need you to tell me the truth."

"Okay. I can do that," he says. "Hit me with your best shot."

"Did you know Celeste had a secret boyfriend? Someone she was hiding from Knox?" Jon Boy's eyes get a little wider, but other than that he doesn't really react. He comes around the counter to sit on the ottoman across from me. "Someone who wrote her love letters?"

"I mean, there were some rumors at the time," he admits. "But nothing was ever proven." He hands me the glass of ice water he got for me, even though I told him I didn't need one. "Why?"

"Okay, but if she did have one—some sort of secret love or something—any idea who it might have been?"

Jon Boy shakes his head. "No idea. We didn't run in the same circles." I drain the glass of water and hand it back to him. I know what he means by the "same circles." He means Celeste and Bailey were popular and he was a big nerd. "What's this about, Tru?"

"I'm ninety percent sure Knox killed the girls. I think he found out Celeste had somebody else, and he went out there that night to settle things." I'm talking too fast. I make myself take a breath. "Maybe he didn't mean to. Maybe things got out of hand, but—"

"Whoa. Slow down." Jon Boy sighs. "Tru, I know you wanna figure this out. I get that. I really do. But you can't accuse—" I pull the broken chain out of my pocket and hand it to him.

I see the color drain right out of his face.

"It's Celeste's," I tell him. "The one that went with her best-friends locket. I found it in Knox's shed."

"Tru," Jon Boy says, "maybe that's what it looks like. But there's no way to know what this is. It's just a broken chain. Not the missing link."

"I can know," I tell him. "And I do know. Because I have Bailey's to compare it to." I take the chain and slip it back into my pocket. "Will you promise to listen and not say anything until I'm finished?"

Jon Boy nods. "Yeah. Sure, TB. I'll listen. I promise."

He keeps his word. He listens to my whole story. In fact, even after I stop talking, he sits there for a long time with his mouth open.

"So," I tell him. "I was hoping you could help me figure out who's doing this. Who it is that's after us. If it's really Knox, like I think—"

Jon Boy shakes his head. "Knox isn't a murderer. I mean, he's a hothead. Sure. And he would've been pissed if that's true about Celeste having a boyfriend on the side. But murder?" Jon Boy shakes his head again. "Nah."

"But you believe me?" I ask. "About all the other stuff I told you."

"Yeah, Tru." Jon Boy reaches out and squeezes my arm. "I won't pretend I understand any of it. But I can accept there are things beyond my comprehension." He glances up toward that photo of him and Reese. The one with the fish. "Besides, I like the idea of coming back new." He looks at me and smiles. "Everyone deserves a second chance."

"You've spent longer than anyone else looking at the evidence. Is there anything you can remember about the murders? Anything I don't know yet?"

Jon Boy frowns for a second before he gets up and disappears into his bedroom. He comes back with a sealed manila envelope and hands it to me.

"Look in here," he tells me. "Whenever you're ready."

"What's in here?"

"Private photos I took out at the crime scene." He sits back down on the ottoman across from me and drops his head to his hands. "I lied to you, TB."

"What?" I can't quite comprehend what he's saying. I've

known Jon Boy my whole life and I don't think I've ever known him to lie to anybody. "Why?"

"I told you there was no way the Glades Reaper was the one who killed Celeste and Bailey. But that was a lie. I didn't want you to be scared. Because you've gotta live your life here. In this town." He swallows hard, then gets up and crosses to the kitchen sink to get himself a drink of water. "But you're grown now. And you need to know what it is you're up against. Who you're going toe-to-toe with out there at Hidden Glen."

I look down at the envelope in my hands. "Why did you keep this to yourself all these years? Separate from that stuff at the *Star*?"

Jon Boy's cheeks are on fire. "Nobody else believed the Reaper was responsible. Anytime I mentioned it, I took a lot of flak. I was the butt of a lot of jokes back in the day." He takes a long drink of water. "The truth is, I was hoping I'd come across something else eventually. Some pieces of the puzzle that would prove me right. I didn't want anyone else to beat me to the scoop, especially not with information from my own research. So I kept some of it to myself. Held a little bit back. An insurance policy, I guess."

I glance down at my watch and see that it's a few minutes until one o'clock. "Shit," I say. "I have to go." I need to pick Rio and Derry up at the library.

"Let me know if you find anything," Jon Boy says. "And Trulee, watch your back. I don't know what that chain is or why Knox had it, but you're dealing with someone way scarier than Knox."

When I pull up to the library, Rio and Derry are waiting under a tree. I watch them for a few seconds before they notice my truck. They're laughing together. Flushed from the heat. Derry in her long, swirling skirt. Rio in her shorts and tank top. Both of them are beautiful and sunlit. There's a tightness around their jawlines, though, a wariness in their eyes. A tendency to look back over their shoulders into the shrubbery that indicates there's something running like an electric current under this lazy summer afternoon.

I honk and they head in my direction and climb into the truck. We're shoulder to shoulder. Rio in the middle. Her arm warm against mine.

"Find out anything interesting?" I ask them.

"It was a lot to read," Derry says. She's holding a new stack of paperback romance novels. "We combed through pretty much every newspaper and magazine article ever published about the Glades Reaper. From papers all over the world." She shudders. "Really sick stuff."

"Anything stand out?" I ask. I'm trying to stay focused. Not let myself get distracted by Rio's hand on my thigh.

The heat of her skin.

The burn of that gold chain in my pocket.

The way all that stuff East said bubbles in my brain.

"You mean other than the crazy stuff he did with the bodies?" It's Rio's turn to shudder now. "He posed those twins around the dinner table."

"Beth and Emily," I say, and Rio shoots me a look. "Jon Boy mentioned them the other day."

"Did you know he left a calling card?" Derry asks, and I almost stop the truck. That's a detail I hadn't heard before.

"What kind of calling card?" I ask.

"A pair of unsmoked cigarettes," Rio tells me. She sounds so proud of herself. "Different brands. But always menthols. Crossed to make an X."

"Why?" I wonder.

"Nobody really knows," Derry says. "There was some speculation maybe he was a smoker. Or maybe a smoker who'd quit. There's no way to say for sure." She leans forward to lower her face toward the air conditioner vent. "In some cultures, it's tradition for cigarettes to be left as offerings. Like on religious altars and stuff like that. Offering up tobacco to the Gods. Or to the spirits of the dead." She closes her eyes and enjoys the stream of cool air. "Maybe it was something like that?"

I pull out onto the highway and point the truck toward Hidden Glen. Rio asks me for my phone, and I dig it out of my pocket and hand it to her. "I wanna look through the pictures I took that day at the newspaper office," she explains.

I know what she's looking for in her photos of Jon Boy's research. She's looking for something about cigarettes. Unsmoked. Two menthols.

She won't find it. I've pored over those notes for years. Memorized the details.

If there'd been any mention of cigarettes, I would have seen it.

Which means Rio's probably wrong about her theory. Jon Boy's wrong, too.

Our killer can't be the Glades Reaper.

Knox is still my number one suspect. No matter what anybody else says. That gold chain feels heavy in my pocket. I need to tell Rio about it.

And I need to ask her some hard questions.

At the springs, every spot is taken, so I park on the side of the road. When we get out of the truck, I grab my backpack. It's got Jon Boy's envelope in it. I pull the broken chain out of my pocket and drop it into the glove box when Derry and Rio aren't looking.

It's the only real evidence we have, and I don't want to risk losing it.

Dill was clear about nobody being alone, so Rio and I walk back to the homestead with Derry, even though it's so crowded today that she would have been fine without us. There's not a single rock or patch of grass that doesn't have a towel spread over it, and the swimming area is so jam-packed that you can't even see the water. Just bodies. Even the trails are swarming with people, hot as it is. We pass five or six groups, mostly families with sweaty, complaining kids, on the hike back to Dill and Derry's place.

Before we get too close, I shout out a greeting to let Dill know it's us coming down the path. I don't want to take any chances with his excitable trigger finger.

He's sitting on a bucket by the firepit, working on untangling the line on one of their fishing poles. "Y'all find out anything useful?" he asks us.

"Not really," Derry tells him. "But at least the library's air-conditioned."

I feel bad for not sharing my new information. But I need to talk to Rio alone first, and there's only one place I can think of that might be deserted on this miserably hot day.

"You wanna take a walk back to Yucha Spring?" I ask Rio.

"Yeah," she says with a little grin. "That sounds good to me."

We tell Dill and Derry that we're going for a swim, and they remind us to stick together. Even in the crowd. Not to take our eyes off each other for a second. We promise that we won't.

The heat is so miserable that we haven't gotten very far before our shirts are sticking to us like skins. All I can think about is getting in the water.

Being cool.

We take the overgrown trail toward Yucha, and I groan when I hear voices up ahead.

"Dammit," Rio whispers.

There's a little family at my supposed-to-be-private spot. A mom is standing waist deep in the water while two kids, a boy and a girl, argue over a pink float ring.

"Steph, let your brother use it," the mom says in an exasperated tone. "You've had it all afternoon."

"No," the little girl counters. "He already popped his."

I can tell by their accents they aren't from around here.

Tourists.

The mom gives up and turns back toward the little steps to sit down. She jumps when she sees Rio and me.

"It's okay for us to be here, right?" she asks us. "I didn't see a keep-out sign or anything. And it's so crowded at that other place."

"Oh yeah," I say, and an idea pops into my head. "This is the best place to be. People don't come back here to swim, really. Because of the gators."

"Gators?" the mom asks. "You mean alligators?"

"Yeah," Rio says, and she points to the leaf debris on the bottom of the spring. "Because of the leaves. All the trees overhead. You know? You can't even see the gators back here. They could be right there. Camouflaged. Just under the leaves." She bends down with her hands on her knees to talk to the kids. "Y'all are so brave," she tells them with a sweet smile.

"Snakes, too," I add with a grimace. "Cottonmouths." It's a little over the top, but I'm having fun now.

"Snakes?" We have the little girl's attention. Steph, or whatever her name is.

The mom takes an uneasy look around. Then she calls the kids out of the water. "Stephanie! Weston! Let's go get some ice cream," she says. "From that concession stand we saw."

The three of them gather up their things and head back down the trail toward the main spring.

Rio and I grin at each other, then settle on the steps and pull our sweat-soaked T-shirts off so we can sit in our bikini tops, dipping our hands in the spring and bringing the cold water up to splash against our chests and arms.

I watch a water strider bug do its Olympic skating routine on the surface of the spring. A breeze moves through the trees, and I lift my face to find it.

Rio leans against my shoulder. I don't want to ruin the moment.

But there are things we need to talk about.

"There's something wrong," she says. "Isn't there?"

I watch our reflections in the water.

"I talked to East," I admit. "He told me some stuff."

Rio looks surprised. "Something about the murders?"

I shake my head, then turn to look her in the eye. "Something about you."

"About me?" The change that comes over Rio happens so fast. There's this caution that settles across her face like a mask. "East doesn't know anything about me, Tru."

"He talked to a few people. Up at Wakulla. Divers he knows."

"Shit." Rio's shoulders slump.

"He says you got in some trouble up there." Rio gets up and wades out into the middle of the spring. She's facing away from me. Staring deep into the trees on the other side. "Why didn't you tell me?"

She turns back to look at me. "It was all a stupid misunderstanding. The money was supposed to be a graduation present."

I stand up and step down into the cold water, but I don't move to where she is. "I want you to be honest with me. We're partners now. Right? Dive buddies."

That little smirk creeps across her lips. Only it doesn't seem as cute as it usually does. "Dive buddies? Is that what we are?" I don't say anything. "Okay, Tru. Whatever."

"I deserve the truth," I tell her, and her face hardens.

"I'm not gonna detail all the ways I fucked up. I don't owe you the story of my terrible childhood," she tells me. "It's none of your business."

"Seems like nothing about you is my business," I say.

"Yeah, well." Rio drags her fingers across the surface of the spring. The water ripples and flows with her touch. It's so clear and bright, like melted diamonds. "Maybe that's because there's stuff you wouldn't want to know."

"Try me," I tell her. "You don't have any idea what I can handle." I take a step in her direction, toward the center of the spring. "You told me we were meant to be together. That you believed that. You made me believe it. So let me in, Rio." I take another step farther out into the water. "Tell me the truth about whatever happened up there at Wakulla."

"Like you've told me the whole truth about what happened to Dani?"

I stop. She might as well have laid into me with that piece of pipe she's been dragging around in her backpack.

A white-hot anger builds up inside me. My fury lets me forget my promise to Dill and I leave Rio standing there alone in the middle of Yucha Spring.

I march up the little metal steps and grab my backpack, then head back down the path toward the main swimming area. I'm still dripping when I hit the boardwalk. I run right into East and Paz. They're carrying their dive bags, looking for an empty spot.

They both look me up and down, but neither of them says a word. I must look a little wild. Dressed in my clothes and soaking wet. All red faced and angry.

Right now, I don't care about any of that.

"You guys wanna dive?" I ask them, and I know how desperate I sound. I might as well be asking them if they want to do a line of cocaine in the back room of some party. Like something out of an eighties movie.

East and Paz look at each other, then Paz says, "Sure, Tru. We can dive with you."

"Let's go back to the Well," East suggests. "Too many people here."

I glance back toward the path to Yucha Spring. I'd kind of hoped Rio would follow me. But she hasn't.

I'm the one who's been following her. Ever since that first day we met. But not anymore. If she changes her mind, she'll know where to find me.

"Come on," I say, and I start toward the Well. East and Paz fall into step behind me. It feels good to be leading. "Let's get below."

TWENTY-ONE

EAST AND PAZ let me go down first, and, somewhere in the cold rocky deepness of that blue limestone hole, I find the calm that I crave. I don't get as deep as I want on my first run. Or on my second. I don't quite make it to that ledge. Whatever is down there calls out to me, winking just out of reach. I can see it, but I can't grab it. I try to push that out of my mind, though, and focus on being in the water.

Diving is medicine. Meditation. Prayer.

I feel like, if I can just get deep enough, all this confusion will be washed away. And I can start over.

Figure out what's true.

Make sense of it all.

East goes down after me, and I stand on the rocks with Paz to watch.

"East told me what happened," Paz says after a few quiet minutes pass between us. "That y'all broke up." He hasn't taken his eyes off East. He's doing his job, being the rescue buddy.

"Is he okay?" I ask.

"Not really," Paz says. "Are you okay, Tru?"

I swat at a bug crawling on my arm. "I think so. I'm dealing with a lot of shit right now. It's confusing."

Paz nods. "Life is confusing as fuck." It's quiet for another long second. "I figured you two would be together forever."

"Everybody did," I say.

Including me.

On the other side of the Well, a boy about our age picks up a girl and throws her into the spring. She squeals and hits the water with a splash, then comes up laughing. The musical sound of it reminds me of Rio.

"Have you ever been in love?" I ask Paz. I know he's had girlfriends. Lots of 'em. But none of the girls he's dated have ever been anything serious.

Paz shakes his head. "I thought I might be once. With Lyra Nazari. Sophomore year. Man," he says. "Remember her?"

I nod.

"It turned out I wasn't lovesick. I just had the flu."

"Right," I say, and I smile. Because Paz is still Paz. There's comfort in his goofiness, even if I did break up with his best friend.

"East loves you, Tru," he tells me. "Like, really, really loves you."

"I'll always love East, but I wasn't in love with him." I shrug. "It's hard to explain."

Paz nods like he gets it. "I guess it's hard to know what that other kind of love feels like," he tells me, "until you feel it for the first time. Up till then, you're just guessing."

When East comes up from his dive, we decide to call it a day. It's getting late in the afternoon, and the crowds show no sign of thinning out. There are too many people.

It's overwhelming.

East and Paz walk me back up toward my truck, but Paz stops halfway up to the parking lot.

"What's your uncle doing out here?" Paz asks East.

We look toward the Dive Bar and I catch sight of someone leaning on the end of the counter wearing a big, stupid-looking cowboy hat. Even though he's never sat on a horse in his life.

East shrugs, but when Knox raises a hand to wave at him, East waves back. Even from a hundred yards away, I see the malicious little smile playing at the corners of Knox's mouth. I know that's for me.

He thinks he's scared me. But he's wrong about that. I'm done being afraid.

We reach the parking lot, and Paz heads over to his car to give East and me a moment alone.

"Did you talk to Rio?" East asks. "About all that stuff I told you."

"Kind of," I say, and East stares at me and shakes his head.

"Whatever's going on out here, she's mixed up in it. And she's got you mixed up in it, too."

"You're wrong, East. I think I know who's been messing with us. And it isn't Rio." I don't tell him that I'm pretty certain his uncle is a murderer. That I found a dead girl's broken chain in his shed, that it's sitting in the glove box of my truck right now. That seems like a conversation for another day.

"Well, be careful anyway, Tru." East's voice gets all thick. "I can lose us. That part of us. You know." He starts to reach out and touch my cheek, but he stops himself. "I wouldn't survive if anything happened to you."

"It would kill me to lose you, too," I say. Even this new distance between us hurts me so much.

I look down and realize I'm wearing his old soccer shirt. Number thirty-seven. Mount Orange Comets. I pull it off over my head so that I'm standing there in my swimsuit top.

"You want this back?" I ask him.

"Nah." He shakes his head. "It's cool. You can keep it."

"Do you hate me?" I ask him.

East shakes his head. "I could never hate you, Tru. That'd be like hating a part of my own heart."

There are tears on my cheeks, and I don't even know how they got there, but I wipe them on East's old shirt, and then pull it back over my head. He's all blond hair and summer sunshine and broad shoulders. He's home. And I'm suddenly so, so homesick. "Can you forgive me?"

He smiles a little. "I'm working on it. But it's gonna take a while."

I know that's so much more than I deserve.

We say goodbye and I climb into the truck. As soon as I close the door, I notice the extra towels I keep behind the seat have been tossed onto the floorboards. Everything's been dumped out of the glove box. Insurance papers. Ketchup packets snagged from the Dairy Barn. An old Florida map that Dill gave me, with all the freshwater springs circled in orange highlighter, has been crumpled up and shoved under the driver's seat with my keys.

I know before I even peer into the glove box that the broken gold chain won't be there anymore.

The only evidence we had, stolen in broad daylight.

I start the truck up to get the AC going and I head home. I don't know what else to do.

When I pull out of the parking lot, I see Knox leaning against the split rail fence, watching me.

He raises one finger in a lazy, good-old-boy wave as I drive away. I want to hit him with my truck.

The whole way home, I'm fuming. It can't be a coincidence, Knox showing up at the springs just when someone's ransacked my truck and taken the one piece of evidence that could maybe connect him to Celeste's and Bailey's murders.

I bet you anything that, if I did run over him, when I went through his pockets, I'd find that damn gold chain.

I'm worried about Rio again. I left her alone back there at Yucha Spring and I know I shouldn't have done that.

Especially not with Knox wandering around.

But it's too late to go back now.

Mom's sitting on the couch watching television when I get home. She has a glass of red wine in one hand and a real estate magazine in the other, the kind with full-page pictures of big fancy houses with screened-in lanais and pools with fountains and state-of-the-art "media rooms."

We don't really have houses like that in Mount Orange, so she'll never get a chance to sell one. But they don't put glossy pictures of two-bedroom trailers in *Real Estate Monthly*.

I mumble a hello and head straight for the stairs.

"Trulee," she says. "Wait. Come here for a second." She pats the spot right next to her. Like I'm some kind of puppy.

I sigh and take the spot at the opposite end of the couch, even though watching whatever soap opera she has on is the last thing in the world I want to do.

"You okay?" she asks me.

"Yeah," I tell her. "I'm good. Why?"

She's looking at me like she's trying to decide if she believes me.

"I ran into East's mom at the Food 4 Less this morning."

"Oh," I say. I now know where this is going.

"She told me you guys broke up."

She doesn't seem mad, like I thought she'd be. She asks me what happened, and I tell her that nothing happened, I just realized I didn't want to be with East like that anymore. That it didn't feel right. Mom is confused by that. She gives me an awkward little pat on the knee and tells me that maybe I'll change my mind, because I'm young, and sometimes it's hard to know what you want.

"Your dad and I broke up twice before we got married," she says. I nod and try to ignore her, because the irony is, for absolutely the first time in my whole life, I know exactly what it is I want—and, as hard as it might be for my mom to accept, it isn't East.

"I gotta take a shower," I say, and she looks at me and shakes her head. "I'm really fine. I promise."

"You're just like your dad," she tells me, and she takes a long drink of wine. "You'd never tell anyone, even if there was something bothering you."

I get up and leave her on the couch.

It's not until I make it upstairs and toss my backpack onto my bed that I remember the envelope Jon Boy gave me earlier this afternoon. His secret evidence. Whatever Jon Boy's been hanging on to all these years might be the only hope we have.

I crawl up on top of my comforter and pull the envelope out of my bag, and when I slide my fingernail under the seal, a photo falls into my hands.

Two cigarettes lie against the base of a pine tree. They're crossed in the shape of an X, one on top of the other. They're resting in a patch of three tiny purple flowers that are growing wild, right at the edge of the scrub behind the Well. A little green stripe is visible at the end of the filters.

Holy shit.

The calling card of the Glades Reaper. Captured right there in Jon Boy's photo.

That green stripe is so familiar. I've seen it somewhere before.

I have this flashback to being in Knox's shed with East earlier today. Him picking up that empty cigarette pack and crumpling it in his fist. Then tossing it in the trash.

A gold-and-black package with a green stripe running across the bottom.

The cigarettes in the picture are Dodgers, just like our mayor smokes.

The room starts to spin.

Everything blurs and blends together.

What if I'm right about it being Knox and Rio's right about it being the Glades Reaper?

Maybe the answer to all of this is that, yeah, Knox killed Celeste and Bailey because he was jealous of Celeste's new love.

But he also killed all those girls down in south Florida. Because he's the fucking Glades Reaper.

I pick up the phone and call East, and he answers on the first ring.

"What are you doing?" I ask him. "Right now."

"Watching Seth," he says. "Why?"

"I need you to meet me out at Hidden Glen. As soon as you can."

East is quiet for a minute, and I think that maybe, for the first time in our lives, he's about to turn his back on me. But then he says, "It'll have to be after nine. When Mom gets home."

"Okay," I say. "That's fine. I'll meet you there after nine."

"What's this about, Tru?"

"There's something out there. Something that might help me prove who's behind all the stuff that's been happening to Rio and me. And I need you to help me get it."

I don't tell him that I'm almost 100 percent convinced now that his uncle is not only a double murderer, but also the most notorious serial killer in Florida history. If I'm gonna lay a bit of news on him, I want to do it face-to-face.

"Okay," East says. "I'll be there. But wait in the truck for me. Okay? And keep the doors locked until I get there."

"Yeah. Okay," I tell him. "Thanks." I start to hang up, but then I remember to add one important instruction. "And East—"

"Yeah?"

"Bring your dive light."

TWENTY-TWO

I KEEP MY promise to East. I sit in the truck with the doors locked until I see his car pull into the Hidden Glen parking lot at 9:22.

When he gets out of the truck, he has a baseball bat clutched in one hand. The Mount Orange weapon of choice, I guess. We throw our dive bags over our shoulders and start down toward the boardwalk together. We both pause at the split rail fence. We're looking down at the main spring, all laid out in the moonlight.

It's quiet for a few long seconds. We've stood right here together so many times. But this time is so different.

Everything is so different.

"Are you in love with her?" East finally asks me.

"I don't know," I admit. "I think maybe I could be."

"After a week?"

"It's been more than a week."

"Right," he says. "Your past life. Or whatever."

"You don't have to believe it," I tell him. "I know how it sounds. But when I'm with Rio, it's like, I get this incredible clarity. It's the same feeling I get from diving. Only I've never been able to find that feeling on land before." I hesitate because I don't want to hurt him, but I need him to understand. "Not until Rio." I hear East let out a long, slow breath. It sounds like giving up. "I'm sorry," I say. "I should have told you, right at the beginning. I should have been honest."

"Maybe you could have handled it better." He shrugs. "But you aren't obligated to sacrifice your own happiness for the sake of anybody else's." He shifts his eyes out toward the spring again. "You don't owe that to anyone. Not even me."

We start down the sloping lawn, and I'm so grateful to have him beside me. I won't ever be ready to let go of East, not completely anyway.

I hope he feels the same way.

We're both on high alert as we make our way back to Elijah's Well. Listening. Scanning the shadows. East keeps the bat ready.

The Well is dark and deserted, sitting right at the edge of the big scrub. It feels like the edge of the world. A bead of sweat rolls down my back, between my shoulder blades, and I shiver. The scrawny pine trees bend in the little whisper of a breeze that rolls through. They're crammed so close together, and they're so toothpick thin, that their trunks clank against each other like wind chimes. It's an eerie kind of music, but it seems to fit the night we're having.

East and I walk the perimeter to look for gators on the rocks and in the water. We're using our flashlights to check for the night shine of their glowing eyes. Red pinpricks that give them away. It's a lot less likely to come across one back here than it would be at the main spring, because of the chain-link safety fence. But alligators can climb if they want to. I've seen them hauled out of the Well more than once.

While we're doing our safety check, I tell East about the shiny thing on the ledge. How it's been eating away at me since Rio and I first saw it. How I think if I can get it, I can solve this whole puzzle.

East doesn't say anything to that; he just looks down into the depths—and the dark—with a worried look on his face.

When we're sure the coast is clear of reptiles with big teeth, we pull out our gear. I'm going down, while East stays up top to keep watch, so I get my fins and mask on. Then East gives me one of the dive lights he brought. I strap it to my wrist and flip it on. It's bright. Steady and reassuring. Once I'm in the water, it'll light everything up like daytime.

The air is alive with buzzing insects and with an energy that's hard to describe—the thrumming of electricity you can feel deep in your bones before something really big happens.

"What do you think is down there, Tru?" East's question is hard to answer, because I don't have any idea what it is that's sitting down there on that ledge calling to me.

"Maybe nothing," I tell him. "But I have to try."

East and I both look around. We're peering back into the trees. Toward the murder site.

"All this scrub here," East tells me, "it's what's left of a chain of islands. Did you know that? The backbone of an ancient archipelago. Twenty-five million years ago, this was all ocean."

"I guess a lot can change in twenty-five million years," I say. I think about how much has changed for me, just in the last few weeks.

How much has changed for East, too.

I go into my breathe-up, and it feels so new to be doing it bathed in moonlight. The stillness of the night makes it easier to find the stillness inside my own mind. I'm so anxious to get below that I'm tempted to just go for it. But I need this to be a really good dive, so I take the time to prepare, the way Dill taught me years ago.

Once I'm under the water, the Well is so alive. I've never seen this many fish. They're still, like party decorations suspended by strings from some invisible ceiling. I move down and down and down, keeping my movements smooth and easy. Anything jerky or chaotic will send East into a panic up top. He'll be in the water after me in a heartbeat. The last thing I want is for him to haul me out of here before I get my shiny prize.

In the dark, the Well seems bottomless.

Everything shrinks down so small. There's only what exists in the beam of my light.

Nothing else.

I don't push myself too hard the first time down. When I come up, I take some time to float and reset, on my back, hair drifting out around me, like Bailey, and then I get below again. This time I get deep. Really deep. And that beautiful euphoria comes. I'm turned completely inside out so that the rawest parts of my soul are exposed to the moonlight and the Well. The water washes all my wounds clean, seals them shut to heal.

I forget East waiting up top with his broken heart.

I forget Rio and the secrets she's keeping.

I even forget that there's someone after us. Someone lurking in the night.

I forget me.

At least for a second.

Then I feel that hard tug. I aim my dive light down into the deepest part of the spring, and I see that shiny thing winking at me from the ledge. I remember why I'm here.

I pinch my nose and blow out to equalize. I swim down. And down.

One hundred fifteen feet.

One hundred twenty.

One twenty-five.

I know I'm going to make it this time. I can almost reach it. If I stretch.

Another foot.

I wrap my fingers around something hard and shiny that's half-buried in leaves and pine needles and dirt.

When I pull it free, I'm holding the handle of a knife.

A long knife. With a broken tip.

My heart stops and everything freezes. I'm hanging in the water like one of those sleeping fish.

Still.

This is what I was meant to find.

I know it's time to start for the surface. Past time. I point my face up toward the moonlight filtering through the deep water. I flag my light, twice, to tell East I'm okay. That's the signal we agreed on.

I start my ascent.

That's when she grabs me.

Bailey. Hair like weeds in the water.

Her fingers clamp around my wrist, and when I turn to the side, there she is.

Wide eyes.

Open mouth.

Speaking to me in the language of bubbles.

My heart starts to beat again. It's racing now.

She's pulling hard on me. Trying to drag me down to the very bottom of the Well.

I'm out of oxygen.

Out of time.

And I know we're playing tug-of-war with my life. So I kick hard for the surface. I give it everything I have. I refuse to let my panic get the best of me.

Bailey is trying to take me down. I feel the pressure of her fingers. Hard and cold. Sharp bone against my skin.

I give one last good yank, and I'm free. When I pull loose from her grasp, I drop the knife. It slips from my fingers. I grab for it, but I miss. And I watch it sink down into the darkness.

It's another fifteen feet to the bottom.

I'll never make it.

Bailey is sinking back now. I watch her and the knife both disappear into the blackness below me. Then I kick like hell for the surface. Because there's nothing else I can do.

My chest burns.

For a few seconds, I held the knife that killed Celeste and Bailey.

I'm swimming hard for the surface. Trying to keep it together.

About the time I decide I'm definitely not going to make it, my head breaks the surface and I'm sucking in air.

"Tru!" East is shouting at me.

I can't talk yet. I'm too busy breathing. But I wave to let him know I'm all right.

Then I swim to the side and let him pull me up onto the rocks.

"Did you get it?" he asks me. "Whatever it was you were after?"

"Yeah." I nod. I'm lying back on the rocks. "A knife. With a broken tip."

"Holy fuck," East whispers.

"I know."

"Where is it?" he asks me, and I close my eyes and sigh.

"I dropped it," I tell him. I don't explain why.

I expect East to tell me there's no way I'm gonna get that knife off the bottom of the Well. That it'd be suicide to even try. Fifteen more feet may not seem like much. But I pushed myself as far as I could tonight.

I don't know if I have any more left in me.

He doesn't say anything, though, because his focus is off in the scrub. He's staring at something, and when I turn to see what, I notice a light moving slow through the trees.

East puts a finger to his lips, and it occurs to me that he's being silly. Whoever is out there already knows we're here. We're sitting on this rock. Completely exposed. With a dive light bright enough to blind someone.

I get to my feet, but East grabs my hand. "Where are you going?" he whispers.

"To see who's back there." I'm so tired of being afraid. I want this to end. If we don't find out who's doing this, it never will.

And if it's Knox, I want East here when I find that out.

East picks up his baseball bat and wraps his fingers tight around it. It hits me again how he still has my back, in spite of everything I've put him through.

We switch off our light and move as quietly as we can toward the safety gate. There's enough moonlight for us to see our way across the rocks.

We stop at the gate, and I ease the latch open. Then we sneak through as quietly as possible and head toward the tree line.

That light is weaving through the scrub. I hear the snapping of twigs—the rustling of leaves—as whoever is out there makes their way toward the clearing where Celeste and Bailey's tent stood all those years ago.

East and I keep moving. We're pressed close together, like the skinny pines and palms surrounding us.

We stop and peer into the clearing.

I see the shine of moonlight on dark hair.

It's Rio.

Just Rio.

I let myself relax, and I take a step forward. Call her name. She whirls to face us. Hits us with her flashlight beam.

And then she screams.

"There's somebody behind you!"

I hear a heavy thud. East grunts and goes sprawling onto the sand. "Tru!" he shouts at me. "Run!"

Someone grabs for me, but I manage to tear away. I stumble into the clearing, fighting to stay on my feet.

Rio is instantly there; she grabs me by the wrist and jerks me to her. Then we're flying through the scrub. Pushing our way through the thick undergrowth. Thorns and brambles tear at my skin. The pain makes my eyes water.

From somewhere back behind us, I hear East's voice, loud and angry in the dark. "Jesus fucking Christ!" he shouts. "It's you, isn't it?"

"East!" I yell his name. Start to go back. But Rio yanks me hard.

"Come on!"

Rio and I are hand in hand.

Celeste and I.

Running through the scrub.

From the tent. To the spring. If we can make it to the water, maybe we'll be safe.

But we aren't running to the water. We're running deeper into the trees. Someone is right behind us now. I hear them crashing through the thick brush. Panting. Snarling. Breathing like a wild animal.

I glance over my shoulder, and I don't see anything, only darkness. But I know he's there.

The killer.

We've played this game before. The three of us. I know it as sure as I know anything.

Her hand in mine.

Fighting the trees.

Escaping through the dark.

Rio and I keep running. Like we've been running forever.

Almost twenty years now.

You can't run from the Reaper.

I hear those words so clear. I'm not sure if someone whispered them to me right now. Or if someone said them to me decades ago.

Rio gets her feet tangled and goes down. Hard and fast. I fall right on top of her.

We hold tight to each other. Waiting for the end. For the knife.

For something.

But there's just silence.

We stay there for a long time. Afraid to move. Or speak. There's nothing. No snapping twigs. No rustling leaves.

No breathing in the dark.

Finally, Rio switches on her flashlight.

"Whcrc the hell are we?" she whispers. I don't know. I have no idea how much ground we covered. How far we are from the clearing.

From East.

"Tru? Rio? Is that you?" Someone is calling our names. It isn't East. It's Derry. "Where are you?"

"Here!" I say, and Derry steps out of the trees with a little flashlight. She's got her long skirt tied up. Her hair is wild. She's flushed and sweating, like she's been running. She drops to her knees in the sand when she sees us.

"Oh my God," she says. "Dill! I've got them!" She reaches out to run her hands over our faces. Our arms. The tops of our heads. "Are you hurt?"

"We're okay," Rio says.

"What are you doing out here?" I ask. I'm not sure if I'm talking to Rio or Derry.

"We woke up," Derry says. "Dill and me." She turns toward Rio. "We saw that you were gone. When you didn't come right back, we came looking for you." She reaches up to pull her hair back with a tie that's around her wrist. "Dill!" she shouts again. "We saw the light back here. Figured it was you."

Dill steps out of the trees into our flashlight circle. No shirt. No shoes. Legs and chest torn up from the brambles. He has his gun stuck into the waistband of his shorts and a thick piece of wood in one hand. "Holy shit," he says when he sees the three of us. "But what the fuck did I say? Nobody goes anywhere alone!"

"We're not alone," Rio offers. She reaches for my hand. Squeezes hard. "Not anymore."

"Come on," Dill growls. "That's enough excitement for tonight." We get to our feet and follow him back through the scrub toward the boardwalk.

"Did y'all see East?" I ask them. "He was at the clearing with me when someone surprised us."

Dill and Derry look at each other.

"We came through the old campsite a few minutes ago," Dill says. "Looking for you. There wasn't any sign of East."

Sure enough, when we reach the spot where Bailey and

Celeste died, East is nowhere to be found. I yell his name into the dark.

Wait for a response.

There's nothing.

Nothing in the clearing.

Nothing in the trees around us.

It's too quiet.

Dead still.

A deep and unshakable dread wells up in my chest. It only takes a few seconds for it to bleed out into my entire body.

"Maybe he went back up to the truck," Derry says. "To wait for you."

"Maybe," I say. But I know he wouldn't do that. East would never, ever leave me alone.

The way I left him.

"East!" I'm still calling for him when we hit the boardwalk, searching the tree line with my flashlight beam. I'm not leaving without him. He could be out there somewhere. Hurt.

The four of us make our way around the Well. It's so dark. I shine my light across the rocks.

The surface of the water.

I almost miss him, but then I catch the glint of the flashlight on soft blond hair.

He's facedown in the spring. Floating. It takes me a split second to register that something's not right.

That he shouldn't be like that.

I can't move. Don't want to move. If I don't go any closer, I won't have to see. If I don't see, it won't be real.

"East!" Dill runs toward the safety gate and throws open the latch. I hear the clang of the gate against the fence.

I hear the splash as Dill hits the water.

That's all I hear. After that it all unfolds without sound. Like a silent movie.

Rio and I are in the water right behind Dill. But he already has East. He flips him over. Drags him to the edge. Gets him up onto the rocks.

Dill checks to see if East is breathing. He's not.

And neither am I.

Then I see Dill start CPR.

Rio climbs out of the spring and stands with Derry, huddled together. Hands over their mouths. Derry is crying.

Rio is staring at East's unmoving chest.

"Come on, man!" Dill pleads between rescue breaths. "Come on East, buddy!" I'm squeezing East's hands. Running my fingers through his hair. I don't remember getting out of the water. "Talk to him," Dill tells me. "Let him know you're here."

But I'm frozen, because I see a single cigarette. Dodger brand. The bright green stripe at the end is a dead giveaway. It's sitting on a rock right at the water's edge. Someone placed it there. Carefully. Just so. To keep it from rolling into the Well. Everything is muffled. Like I'm deep below the surface. "Tru! Come on! Talk to him, goddammit!"

Dill's command snaps me out of it.

"I'm here, East," I tell him. "I'm right here. And I love you so much." I'm choking. Sobbing. Trying to get the words out. Doing my best to keep it together. "Please, East. Baby."

Derry digs my phone out of my backpack. I see her mouth moving. She's talking to someone.

East still isn't breathing.

It's been too long.

Way too long.

His eyes are open. Staring up at the dark sky. Unblinking.

Just like Dani.

I know what that means.

Dill keeps trying. He doesn't give up. Even after we hear the sirens screeching into the parking lot. Even after we hear the pounding of feet on the boardwalk.

Rio grabs my arm and pulls me away so the EMTs can do their thing. Dill moves to the side and lets them take over. I wish I could hear the things they're shouting to each other.

I wish I could tell them how he's my best friend. My first friend. The beautiful blond boy laid out on the rocks.

But my voice won't work.

My bones have turned to dust.

Rio's holding me up. Keeping me on my feet while we watch them work. Nothing about what I'm seeing makes any sense.

It can't be East lying there motionless like that.

I can't hear anything. Not until the EMTs stop. Not until there's no more frantic activity.

Until one of them says it's time to call it and announces the time.

Then all the sound comes rushing back at once. And I hear myself scream.

TWENTY-THREE

I TELL THE sheriff everything I know. But my head is so messed up, I can barely get the words out. I know I'm making a jumbled mess of it. I try to explain how someone's been leaving us threatening messages. The photos of the dead girls with our faces on them. How someone cut up Dill and Derry's tent. How Rio got attacked in the woods. I don't mention the locket. I don't want him to ask us for it.

Rio stands next to me while I do the talking. She doesn't ever let go of my hand.

Once I lay it all out, except the reincarnation part because I figure he doesn't need to know that, I realize the sheriff hasn't written down a single thing I said. No notes. No questions except, "So you're tellin' me you saw someone put your boyfriend in the Well tonight?"

"No," Rio tells him. "We didn't see it. We weren't here when it happened, but—"

He cuts her off. "It's dangerous out here. Swimming at night. A guy all alone. You get a cramp. Or you slip on the rocks. You hit your head. It's all over." He glances at the deputy and shakes his head. "It's a damn shame kids don't have more sense."

"Aw, shit," one of the sheriff's men says. "You know who this is, boss?" He's leaning over East's body. "It's the mayor's god-damn nephew."

"Jesus Christ," the sheriff says, and he turns to glare at me and Rio. "The mayor's going to want to know what happened here."

"We know what happened to him," Rio insists.

Now the sheriff is finally paying some attention to her. "You're that girl from up in Wakulla County." He narrows his eyes and I feel Rio stiffen beside me. "Mayor gave us a call today. Told us to keep an eye out." He takes a step closer. "Heard you're a little bit of a troublemaker." He's smirking at her, but she glares right back at him. She isn't going to let him push either one of us around. "You stick around town for a few days at least. In case I have questions for you."

The paramedics take East's body away.

Derry and Rio circle their arms around me.

Dill sits on the rocks where East died, pulling at his tangled black curls.

And that's it. The sheriff and his sidekick deputy leave us standing there in the dark.

I couldn't tell you how I got home. Who drove me. Someone tracks my mom down. She spends the night sitting on the edge of my bed with one hand on my back while I stare at the wall. Shaking uncontrollably.

All I can think about is what must be going on at East's house. His mom. And Seth.

Oh God oh God oh God.

Seth.

He's almost the same age as I was when Dani died.

❧

The next week is a blur. I don't eat. I don't sleep. I can't get out of bed.

East's funeral is on Wednesday. June 9. It's the twentieth anniversary of Celeste's and Bailey's murders. Now the date is marked by another Mount Orange tragedy. It's strange driving to the church, seeing ribbons tied to every tree in town. All the lampposts. The flower memorials and teddy bears. At first, I think they're all for East.

The services are held in the high school gym. None of the churches in Mount Orange are big enough for the crowd. Everyone from the school. All the dive club guys.

Everyone in town, basically.

East's mother asks Paz and me to sit with her and Seth up front. "You're family," she tells us. I can't look her in the eye.

Knox and his mama, East's granny, are down on the other end of the row. Knox's face is hard, and he's staring straight ahead. He doesn't so much as glance at me. I don't know what I'd do if he dared to speak to me today.

I'm trying to look anywhere but at the casket laid out in front of us. I'm staring at the unlit scoreboard. The flickering exit sign over the far door.

Literally anywhere but at East's still face.

He looks too pale. And his hair is too perfect.

When I look back over my shoulder, I see Dill and Derry and Rio standing along the back wall. Dill is wearing a dark blue suit, and it seems so strange to see him in that. It's a long way from new looking, and it doesn't quite fit him. I wonder where he got it. I wish I could see his feet. I wonder if he's wearing shoes.

I turn back toward the front. There's this rock in my chest where my heart is supposed to be. I can't feel anything except an aching emptiness that stretches out like an ocean.

Guilt.

So much guilt.

When the service is over, people hug me. I recognize them, but I don't know who they are. These people I've known my whole life. Their faces. Their names. I can't keep them straight. They murmur words like "Tragic accident . . ."

"So young . . ."

"I'm so sorry . . ."

And . . . "He loved you."

When it's all over, Mom goes to get the car. She tells me to wait out front. That she'll pull up to get me. I'm looking around for Rio. And Dill and Derry.

They've slipped away, and I'm not surprised. I figure Dill probably had about all he could take of real clothes.

I'm waiting in the blazing sun, wondering if I'm going to pass out. Then I see them bringing East down the front steps. Paz and some of his other buddies are carrying the casket. I stare as they load him into the back of the hearse. I want to climb in with him. To hang on and not let them take him away from me.

But I don't do any of that. I stand there, one single phrase repeating over and over in my head.

I'm sorry.

I'm sorry.

I'm sorry.

I'm sorry.

"Trulee Bear." Jon Boy slips an arm around my shoulders and I let him pull me against him. I wrap my arms around his middle and cling to him like a baby. "What happened out there, it wasn't a diving accident, was it?" His voice is a low whisper.

"There was a cigarette," I tell him. "I found it by the Well. Where East—" I can't finish that sentence.

"Just one?" Jon Boy asks, and he frowns.

"Yeah," I tell him. "One victim. One cigarette. That makes sense, right?"

"Listen." Jon Boy squeezes me hard. "I want you to let all this go, TB. Just drop it. Drop the whole thing." I'm staring at him. "Drop it and walk away." He's pleading with me now. "Run away. Go to Tampa. Or Jacksonville. Go to the damn moon if you want. Leave and start over and never look back. Because if you don't let this go, you're gonna end up dead." He stops for a shaky breath. "And this town has had enough death to last it a really long time."

"You can't run from the Reaper," I tell him.

"What did you say?" It's his turn to stare at me now. "Where did you hear that?"

"Never mind," I tell him. "It doesn't matter."

"Hey. Tru." I turn to look back over my shoulder and Knox is glaring at me. He's standing there squinting into the sun. Sweating through his cheap suit. "This is on you," he tells me. My stomach drops and I feel woozy again, because he's right. My heart is hammering so loud I can barely hear Jon Boy's response.

"Give it a rest," he says. "She just walked out of her best friend's funeral."

"Her best friend?" Knox scoffs. "I thought he was her fuckin' boyfriend." He takes a step in my direction, but Jon Boy steps in between us.

"Nobody's causing a scene. Not here. Not today."

"Fine," Knox says, but he's glaring at Jon Boy. "Watch yourself, Trulee. And you better watch that friend of yours, too." He takes a few steps away, then turns back to stare at me. "That fucking nephew of mine got lucky. If he'd lived, he probably would've married you, and this whole town knows you're gonna end up just like your goddamn mother."

Jon Boy and I stare after Knox as he crosses the parking lot and climbs into the car with his mama. They turn on their headlights to join the funeral procession.

I'm shaking so hard my teeth are chattering.

"Don't let him rattle you," Jon Boy tells me.

I'm not rattled. I'm enraged. My blood is on fire and my guts are boiling. As soon as Rio and I get the proof we need, it's all over for Knox. We're gonna be the ones to take him down for what he did to Celeste and Bailey. And to all those other girls down south of here.

For what he did to East. His own flesh and blood.

Mom pulls up then, and Jon Boy helps me into the car. He tells us he'll see us out at the cemetery.

Somehow, I make it through the part of the day I've been

dreading the most. The part where they put East in the ground. I close my eyes when they lower his casket into that dark hole. Close my ears when his mom starts to sob. I manage to stay on my feet when Seth wraps his skinny arms around my waist and asks if I'll still come over to visit.

After, I drop Mom at home and change into my swimsuit. I pull East's old soccer shirt over the top, then I head straight for the springs.

Rio is sitting on the split rail fence. I wonder how long she's been there.

"It wasn't an accident," she says. "We both know that."

It's the first time we've talked since Dill pulled East out of the Well.

There are things she doesn't know yet.

I dig that envelope out of my backpack and hand it to Rio. Jon Boy's photo. The one he's been keeping to himself all these years. The two crossed cigarettes resting in between those three tiny purple flowers that are growing wild at the edge of the scrub.

"The Reaper's calling card," she says, and I nod.

"There was a cigarette back at the Well. That night. When East—" I stop and take a deep breath, because I can't make myself say the word *died*. "I wish I'd grabbed it. But I didn't think about it."

I need to tell her about the knife, too. That shining thing we saw winking at us from the ledge in the Well.

She doesn't even know that I managed to grab it. That night. With East.

Then dropped it straight to the bottom.

My head has been so jumbled up since East died. Everything is muddy and awful. I find Rio's eyes to try to explain that to her, but all that comes out is a choked sob.

"I'm so sorry, Tru. I know how much you loved him." Rio pulls me into her arms. She wraps me up tight and I finally come undone.

When I pull myself together, Rio digs something out of her pocket. It's a folded-up piece of newspaper. "I have something to show you, too. I saw this newspaper when I was walking through town with Dill and Derry earlier. Today's *Miami Herald*."

The headline starts my mind reeling.

DO YOU RECOGNIZE THESE MESSAGES
FROM A SERIAL KILLER?

I only read the first paragraph of the article.

For the past decade, reporters at this newspaper have received periodic correspondence from a writer claiming to be the infamous Glades Reaper. In an effort to maintain public calm and to avoid hampering an ongoing investigation, we have not printed any of these letters to date. However, at this time, the FBI has asked us to release the following samples, in the hopes that someone might recognize the writer. We believe these letters to be legitimate, as they contain detailed information about the crimes that has never been released to the public. Those details have been redacted here.

"Holy shit," I say. "They printed them."

"It's how they finally caught the Unabomber," Rio says. "It's a smart move."

The letters don't look like much. Most of the words are blacked out. Only a few lines of each have been left visible. And taken on their own, they don't seem to make much sense. The only line that really stands out to me is:

You can't run from the Reaper.

That's the exact phrase that came into my head as Rio and I were tearing through the scrub on the night East died. It just popped into my mind. Out of nowhere. Almost like I'd heard it spoken out loud.

There's something else about those typed lines that's eating at me. I dig through my backpack. I'm looking for the secret love notes we pulled out of the hiding spot in Celeste's room.

"Rio," I say. "Look at this." I hand her the notes. "Look at the lowercase *r*'s." *You're the most delicious secret I've ever had.* "See that? Look at the way the bottom half of the letter is missing. Every lowercase *r* in those two love notes is the same way."

"The key is messed up," she tells me.

"Now look at this," I tell her, and I hand her back the newspaper article she just showed me. "'You can't run from the Reaper.' See that? The lowercase *r* in *run* is exactly the same."

Rio looks up at me. "Whoever wrote these love notes to Celeste—"

"Wrote these letters to the *Miami Herald*."

"Knox wasn't the Reaper." The realization lands on me with the speed and weight of an avalanche barreling down a mountain. "Celeste's secret boyfriend was."

"That's probably why they were out here that night," Rio says. "Even though there was a storm warning." I'm watching her make the connections, the fire in her eyes igniting. "They were out there so Celeste could meet her secret boyfriend. Without Knox finding out."

"Only Celeste didn't know the guy she had fallen in love with was the Glades Reaper." I shiver in the heat. I'm covered in sweat. "She didn't realize she had an appointment with death."

Rio takes my hand, and we start down the lawn toward the main spring. We'd been standing there in the blazing sun forever, exposed in the parking lot. I figure I'm about five minutes away from heatstroke, and I hadn't even realized it.

I think back over the last few days, and I realize there's still so much Rio doesn't know. This week so far has been a blur of misery and pain, and so much has gotten pushed aside. I fill her in on the gold chain I found in Knox's shed. How he smokes the same brand of cigarettes as the ones the Reaper left. How those two things had me convinced it was him.

I was wrong about that. "I don't know why he had that chain," I say. "Or where he got it. But I don't think he killed Celeste." Something strange moves in my chest. "Maybe he really loved her. He never married or anything. After what happened to Celeste." I think about Knox, and his miserable, mean heart. "Maybe it killed him inside to lose her."

We haven't talked about where we're going, but somehow, we both know. We've skirted around the swimming area, and we're heading back toward Yucha Spring. I'm glad when we step off the boardwalk and onto the overgrown trail. I've seen the looks people were sneaking in my direction. I've heard the whispers.

They all wonder how I'm doing, and what really happened

out here that night. If I'll fall apart at the seams. They mean well, but their curiosity isn't welcome. I don't want their pity. I've been through all this before.

"I don't get it," I say. "How could Celeste not realize she'd fallen in love with a monster?"

"People lie," Rio says. "Or they hide." She's quiet for a few seconds. There's nothing but the sound of our feet on the sandy path. "You wanted to know what happened," she says. "Up at Wakulla Springs. And I didn't want to talk about it."

"It doesn't matter," I say. "You were right. You don't owe me your story." We've reached the spring, and we kick off our flip-flops and settle on the steps together. "It's not like I've been completely honest with you, either. Like you said."

"You're talking about what happened to Dani," Rio says, and I nod.

I miss my sister so much. It's a physical kind of missing, the kind that makes you feel like all your bones are breaking and all your insides are being wadded up into a tight little ball. I wonder what it would be like if she were still here. If we'd still be close.

If I would have trusted her with any of this.

"I wanted to tell you," I say. "But it's hard. Because what happened to Dani is like what happened to East. It's the same."

Rio looks so confused. "How is it the same?"

"Because it was my fault," I tell Rio. "What happened to her. And what happened to East is my fault." I've never said those words out loud before. "My parents had a big fight that night. And I was upset. I ran out of the house. I used to do that sometimes, when things were bad. I'd run and hide somewhere until the yelling stopped." Rio is stroking my back. Then my arms. Her fingers on my skin. Like she used to do when I had trouble falling asleep, all those nights we spent together. "That's why Dani was out there that night. Walking along the road." I choke back the tears that are threatening to spill over again. "She was looking for me. I was hiding in the garage, though. I heard her calling my name. Walking up and down the road. But I didn't call back. I didn't let her know where I was. She kept walking up and down the road, looking in the bushes. And then she wasn't calling anymore. So I went to sleep. There in the garage. And the next morning—"

"Oh, Tru." Rio's breath is on my cheek. Her hand on my back. Her hair brushing my shoulder.

"The two people I loved most in the world are both dead because they were trying to help me."

It's quiet for a second, then Rio says, "Evan, my little brother, he died in a fire. And it's my fault he didn't make it out."

"What?" I turn to look at Rio.

"I was six. He was four. And my mom was gone a lot. She was into drugs. Who knows what all. But this one night she finally came home, and we were so hungry. I begged her to make us some mac and cheese, because that was Evan's favorite. And she was so fucked up. But I kept begging. Saying we were starving. She did, but she passed out on the couch while it was cooking. The next thing I knew, there were flames. I tried to wake her up. Because I didn't know what to do. Then everything happened so fast. The kitchen filled up with smoke. Evan ran to hide somewhere. 'Cause he was just a baby. So when the firemen came in—some neighbor must have called them—they found my mom passed out in the living room, and me hunkered down in the hallway. But they didn't know to look for Evan. Mom was too fucked up to tell them she had a four-year-old." She stops and lets out a long breath. "And I didn't think to tell them." She turns to look at me and there are tears on her cheeks. It's the first time I've seen her cry. "I don't know why I didn't tell them he was in there. Why I didn't—"

"You were six," I tell her. "You must have been terrified."

"He was four," she tells me. "I was supposed to take care of him."

I slide my arm around Rio's shoulders and pull her against me. "Your mom was supposed to take care of you both."

Rio reaches down into the water to stir at our reflections with one finger. We disappear in a swirl, and then reappear when the surface stills.

But for a half second in between, I see two other girls.

One with a brown ponytail and one with blond curls.

"I love you," I say. The words fall out of my mouth. I can't call it an accident, because I've been thinking it for a while now.

Rio looks a little stunned, but she smiles. "I love you, too. But you already knew that."

Something inside me cracks wide open, my hurt spilling out. I'm sobbing. Everything is so raw and exposed. Rio puts her hand on the back of my head and pulls my forehead down to rest against hers. She's stroking the sides of my face. Running her fingers through my hair. I hear myself choke out her name. "Shhhhhhh, Tru. It's okay," she says. "I'm here." She's whispering quiet soothing words against my ear. More breath than sound. "I love you," she tells me. And I whisper it back to her over and over and over and over.

I can't get control of myself. The levee has burst and there's no going back now. All I can do is sob.

I'm so destroyed. For all of us.

Me and Rio.

Celeste and Bailey.

Dani and Evan.

And East.

"I can't breathe," I say. I'm gasping. I feel panic rising up to tear at me with pointy fingernails. I'm hyperventilating. "I can't—" I clench my hands into fists. White knuckled and afraid.

"Sit down there," Rio tells me, and she points at the second step. The one just below where we're sitting now. "Come on," she says. "Trust me."

I move down, so that the water covers the tops of my hips, and I let my feet rest in the sand. Rio scoots back a little, to make room, and then shifts so I'm sitting between her legs, her knees on either side of my body. She pulls my T-shirt off over my head and tosses it up onto the railing.

She takes hers off, too.

I'm shaking. Sitting there in my bikini top. Hiccupping and trying hard to pull in air. But my lungs won't cooperate.

"Rio, I'm scared." I force the words out between fits of gasping and choking.

She slides her arms around me and pulls me back against her. "Relax," she tells me, and I settle back against her body. "Lay your head back on me and close your eyes." I do, and she lets one palm rest against my chest, and the other on my stomach. Then she puts her mouth against my ear. "Let your body turn to liquid," she whispers. "Relax every single muscle. Let me hold you up." I feel the tension draining out of my arms and legs, and my body gets heavier as I settle into Rio more deeply. My breathing eases a little. And some of the panic slips away. "That's it, Tru," she whispers. "I have you. Just let it all go." There's a long exhale of breath.

Hers.

Then mine.

"Okay," she tells me. "I'm going to take some really slow, deep breaths, and I want you to match me. You breathe when I breathe. In and out. Nice and slow." I copy her, pulling air into my lungs, filling all the space that I can before I let it go. We breath in on a five count, and out on a five count. Rio presses her hands more firmly against the solid square of my rib cage and the soft curve of my stomach so she can feel each breath.

In again for five. And out again for five.

We're breathing up together. Preparing to dive.

The sun is warm on the top of my head, and I feel Rio's chest expanding and contracting behind me with each exchange of air.

I realize I'm not gasping anymore.

"Can you feel me?" she whispers in my ear. I murmur something that I hope sounds like yes.

We stay that way for a long time, eyes closed, sharing each breath. Inhaling and exhaling together until we build up a slow, steady, easy rhythm. In for five and out for five. Over and over.

After a while, it's like we're inside the same body, like we've melted completely into each other. She's the air inside my lungs, and I'm the air in hers. With each unhurried breath, Rio fills up all the space inside me.

And then there's no more room for fear.

Or guilt.

Or pain.

She slides her hands down to my waist. Then my hips, exploring my angles and curves as we breathe together. She dips her hands into the blue pool and little dribbles of spring water fall like cool rain across my shoulders.

My neck.

My stomach.

The tops of my thighs.

She pulls me back harder against her and my eyes open in surprise.

"Just breathe with me, Tru," she whispers. "Don't tense up." Her lips are on my neck now. She's pressing tiny kisses into my collarbone. It's almost more than I can stand. "I want you to stay completely relaxed. No matter what. Okay?" I nod, and Rio takes my chin in her hands and turns my face to the side.

Our lips meet.

Then our tongues.

I don't think either one of us is breathing at all anymore.

I feel a hundred things at once. The cold of the water. The warm sun on my hair. My toes in the sand.

The heat of Rio's mouth.

The pressure of her tongue against mine.

The sharpness of her teeth.

She's stealing my breath—and then giving it back to me—over and over and over.

Rio deepens the kiss. Her hands are tangled in my hair, and I feel her working at my knots. All the tied-up places. Gently tugging at threads one by one until she's completely untied me from the inside out.

We finally pull apart, and I come up for air, and boom! There it is. Just like diving. That thunderbolt moment of clarity wrapped in a blanket of euphoria.

"Nothing holding you up," she says.

"And nothing holding you down," I finish.

Rio's eyes are blazing green. Her hands are on my face. Her thumbs against my cheekbones. She murmurs that she loves me, pressing the words against my lips like a different kind of kiss.

Her face is flushed, and her damp hair clings to her forehead. I don't know how I'm supposed to see her like this and ever recover from it. It's like all my insides are being squeezed into this one pinprick-sized spot somewhere in the deepest pit of my stomach.

I pull her face down toward mine and kiss her again—slow and gentle and easy. Like we have all the time in the world.

I won't let anyone take this away from us.

I won't let what happened to East be meaningless.

"Are you ready to dive?" I ask her, and Rio nods.

"Are you?"

"Yeah," I tell her. "There's something waiting for us at the bottom of the Well."

TWENTY-FOUR

ON THE WALK back to Elijah's Well, I fill Rio in about the knife with the missing tip. How I managed to snag it off the ledge, then dropped it and watched it sink into the darkness.

I even tell her about Bailey, that I've seen her in the water a handful of times now, the first time before Rio and I even met, when Dill had to rescue me.

"She was trying to show you that knife," Rio says. "She wanted you to find it."

"Yeah," I say. "That's the only explanation I can figure out. But I still don't know if she was real. Or a trick of my own mind."

Rio thinks about that for a second. "Maybe she's some part of yourself. The Bailey part of you. The bit of her that's left. Like the wallpaper. Remember? Maybe somehow the water washes some of the paint away."

"So the wallpaper shows through."

Rio nods. "Maybe that's the real magic of the springs," she says.

We've reached the chain-link safety fence, and I freeze when Rio lifts the latch to swing the gate open.

That memorial plaque for Celeste and Bailey is shining in the sun. Now I wonder if there will be one for East, too.

My stomach lurches.

I can't look at the spot on the rocks where Dill laid East that night.

Can't think about him in the water.

Or what happened to him before that.

Was he afraid?

Did he know he was going to die?

I keep hearing his voice. The last words I ever heard him say. *It's you, isn't it?*

I have the urge to run.

I can't do this. I can't be here.

Rio puts one hand on my chest. Then she takes my hand and puts it on her own chest. She takes a slow, deep breath and lets it out. I do the same.

"Feel that?" she asks, and I nod. "All we have to do is keep breathing together, Tru."

Rio asks if I want her to go in. To try to get the knife. But I tell her I need to do it. I know where I dropped it, where it should be.

This is something I need to do.

For myself.

For East.

For Bailey.

I start my breathe-up routine. I take my time. I do it exactly the way I know Dill would. I don't cut corners. I wait until I'm good and ready. Until I can't feel my bones and my insides have turned to warm jelly.

The whole time, I feel Rio breathing right beside me. I'm not alone.

As soon as I hit the water, I know that I have a good start. I find a rhythm and settle into it, pushing myself deeper and deeper. Elijah's Well is alive with light and movement and color, and the beauty of that other world below the surface works its magic on my soul, just like it always does. I swim down and down and down and down.

I'm doing as little work as possible. Keeping my movements tiny. Conserving my air.

I equalize and go even deeper, because I haven't found what I'm looking for yet—but I know I must be close.

Then I'm there, the place divers call "the doorway to the deep." At thirty-five or forty feet, your own natural buoyancy stops pushing you up toward the surface. Instead, everything reverses, and the water starts pulling you down. Once you hit that spot, descending gets easier, because you don't have to swim down anymore. You put your arms to your sides, like a skydiver, and let yourself free-fall effortlessly toward the bottom. It feels like stepping off a cliff and plummeting straight down in slow motion.

I ride that column of water toward the bottom of Elijah's Well, and for every foot I slip down, I feel another piece of me gone, until I'm not made of muscle or bone or skin—or need or fear or memory—anymore. I'm only liquid.

My body is liquid.

My brain is liquid.

The whole world is cold blue liquid.

Down and down and down.

Until the entire universe is liquid.

I feel my feet hit the sandy bottom, and the sudden solidness takes me totally by surprise. One hundred and forty feet down. Thirteen stories below the surface of the world.

My time down here is measured in microseconds.

The Well gives me a gift. There's something cold and hard under my foot. I reach down and pull the knife from the sand. I grip the handle tight.

This time I won't let go. No matter what.

Then instinct takes over. My feet push off and my legs kick hard, propelling me back up toward safety. I count my fin-kicks, like Dill taught me, to fight the rising panic, and I watch as the circle of sunlight gets bigger and brighter, until I eventually burst through, and my brain tells my burning lungs to suck in air to keep me alive.

I pull myself over to the rocks and collapse on my back in the sun. I don't feel the burn in my lungs or the ache in my muscles anymore. I don't feel the rough bits of limestone under my back. I'm only breath.

Breath and bone-deep calm.

I open my eyes and Rio is staring at my hand. The one with the knife gripped tight in my fist.

"You did it!" She leans down and presses her lips to mine, and I reach up to brush the hair away from her eyes.

"We did," I tell her.

I sit up on the rock and stare down at the murder weapon in my hand. It's a big hunting knife. Silver with a serrated edge and a black grip.

A broken tip.

"How hard do you have to stab someone to break a knife like that?" Rio asks, and I have no idea.

I think about that tip, lodged in Celeste's liver.

I'd been hoping that holding the knife would trigger a feeling. A memory that would make it all clear, that would tell us who it belonged to.

Who threw it in the spring to hide it.

But there's nothing like that. It's just a plain-looking hunting knife.

I can tell Rio's disappointed, too. "This could have belonged to anyone," she says. I know she's right.

I sigh and flip the knife over in my palm to check out the other side.

And I immediately wish I hadn't.

I take it all back.

Every single bit of it.

I don't want to see. Don't want to know. Don't want to think about the name that's scratched deep into the black grip there.

Four letters that spell out the end of whatever was left of my world.

D-I-L-L.

TWENTY-FIVE

MY MIND REFUSES to believe what my eyes are telling me.

"Oh God." Rio sounds like she's going to throw up. "No. No no no no no. Please. Not Dill."

I know exactly how she feels. I wanted to know so bad. Now all I want is to unknow.

My mind races through everything. And it all fits. Dill could have been the one.

He could have left that *Fear the Reaper* note.

Could've stalked me on the trail that night. Then doubled back and beat us to the homestead. He knows this scrub like the back of his hand. He's fast. Nimble and strong. And his night vision is panther sharp.

He could've fucked up his own tent.

Could've stolen those crime scene pics and then left them on that tree.

He could've put that locket in my car.

He could've attacked Rio that night at the campsite. That's why there was no car in the parking lot.

He could've made those tracks himself. Maybe he got the boots wherever he got that dark blue suit. The one he wore to East's funeral.

East.

Dill could've killed him that night. Could've done whatever he did, and then stepped out of the scrub to lead me and Derry and Rio out of there to safety, like nothing had happened.

After all, wasn't it always Dill warning me not to dive too deep?

Maybe that's because he knew what was down there. Hidden in the muck at the bottom of the Well.

"Dill is the Glades Reaper," Rio says. "He sneaked off from Derry's folks' place somehow. During the storm. And he killed Bailey and Celeste that night."

I wish she hadn't said it out loud. If we don't say it out loud, then maybe it isn't the truth.

The hunting knife in my hand says otherwise.

I'm racking my brain, trying to figure out something— anything—I know about Dill before Derry. His childhood. Where he grew up. What he did before Derry found him and dragged him back to Mount Orange with her. But there's nothing. Not one single thing I know about his life before he landed back at the homestead.

Except that Derry met him down south somewhere. I never thought to ask where. That could mean Fort Myers or Fort Lauderdale. The Keys, maybe.

It could also mean Miami.

Or Everglades City.

Glades Reaper territory.

I thought Rio was secretive, but I never realized how much Dill was hiding all these years.

He's so mesmerizing—so charming—that I never noticed I didn't know a damn thing about him.

Except he was a drifter.

That he used to smoke cigarettes.

He's from south Florida.

None of those facts reassures me any.

I remember that folded-up map in my backpack, the one with the Reaper kills circled in black and red. I pull it out and unfold it for Rio. "Look," I tell her. "All these circles. Every single circle is a dead girl. Seven crime scenes. Two victims at each one." I turn to stare at Rio. "That's fourteen circles."

"Do we really think Dill did all this?" Rio's voice is shaking. She's staring wide eyed at the map.

"I need to get out of here," I say, and I stick the crumpled map into my backpack. I can't look at it anymore. "I need to think."

"Yeah." She reaches for my hand. Our fingers intertwine.

Everything is so tangled up these days.

"Can you come home with me for a while? You can't go back to the homestead. Not until we figure some things out."

"Yeah," Rio says. "I need to be with you."

We wander back toward the main spring in a daze. I barely register where I am or what I'm doing. I only know Rio has me by the hand, and that gives me a little bit of comfort.

At the main swimming area, Derry has her card table and typewriter set up. A long line of customers waits for their poems.

"Fuck," Rio says, and she points in Derry's direction. "Those love notes. And the Reaper letters to the *Miami Herald*. Both of them were written on an old-fashioned typewriter with a broken lowercase *r* key."

"Shit," I say. Because it keeps getting worse and worse. "How many people do you even know who have typewriters like that?"

"Have you ever seen one of Derry's typed poems?"

"I don't know," I say. "Probably. I don't remember."

"Dill must've used it to write those love notes to Celeste," Rio says. "And to write the Reaper letters to the newspaper."

It all makes sense. They would've run into each other out here at Hidden Glen. They must have known each other. Dill would've been almost thirty years old at the time. Celeste was only eighteen.

No wonder they kept it a secret.

But Dill was—is—handsome and charismatic and smart. So different from any of the boys she would've known.

So different from Knox.

Dill is the answer to everything.

He's the Glades Reaper.

Celeste's secret boyfriend.

The Mount Orange boogeyman. The person who sliced open Bailey and Celeste's tent that night and changed this town forever.

I feel like I might pass out, so I bend at the waist and put my hands on my knees. It's a diver's trick. One that helps when you're light-headed after a trip down.

A trick that Dill taught me.

"We need to get a look at that typewriter," Rio says, and I nod. Because I know she's right. But right now, all I need to do is get out of here. Before Dill shows up. He's got to be close by.

We make it up to the truck and the drive to my house is

totally silent. When we pull up, Mom's car is in the driveway. I was hoping she would've already headed out to the Wild Clover for the night, but no such luck.

When I walk in with Rio, Mom's sitting on the couch watching television, and for the first time since I can remember, there isn't a glass in her hand.

"Hey," she tells me. "I thought I'd stick close this evening. Just in case you needed anything. I didn't want you to be alone tonight." She stops and looks a little embarrassed when she notices Rio standing behind me. "But you aren't alone."

"Mom," I say, "this is my friend Rio. She's gonna spend the night tonight. If that's okay."

"Oh. Yeah." Mom nods a little too enthusiastically. "Of course, baby. Your friends are always welcome here." Rio steps up beside me and smiles. "I saw you at the funeral today," Mom tells her. "You were a friend of East's, too."

"I was," Rio says. "He was a good guy." She reaches for my hand and I let her wrap her fingers tight around mine.

Mom is staring at Rio now, and I figure she's trying to work out why she seems so familiar. She's wondering if she knows her from someplace else. She doesn't remember Rio helping me drag her out of the Wild Clover.

I start up the stairs with Rio. We're still holding hands.

"I ordered pizza," Mom calls after me. "It'll be here soon. I'll call you down when it's ready."

"Okay," I say. "That sounds good." Even though the idea of food makes me queasy. My stomach is so unsettled.

Rio tells Mom thanks for letting her stay, and Mom just nods and turns back to the television. When I look over my shoulder as we reach the top of the stairs, I see that she's watching us.

Rio and I spend the rest of the evening upstairs in my little room. She's looking at all my things. She never had a real room of her own, she tells me.

Mom calls us down for pizza and we take a couple of slices upstairs. Neither of us touch them.

We stay up all night, going over everything again and again and again. From the very beginning. And we always come back to the same conclusion.

All roads lead to Dill.

Finally, sometime after four o'clock in the morning, we both get too sleepy to sit and talk anymore. Our brains are tired. Our hearts are so broken. Our bodies refuse to cooperate.

We stretch out on top of my comforter together. I flip off the overhead light, but I leave my little bedside lamp on. The glow is soft and warm. Like moonlight.

It reminds me of being out at the springs.

My eyes are closed when Rio says, "Do you still wanna know about the money? The cash I got in trouble for taking. Up at Wakulla?"

I force my eyes open to look at her. We're both lying on our sides. Facing each other. Just a couple of inches between our bodies. She's so beautiful. "I don't need to know any of that," I tell her. "It doesn't matter."

"What if I want to tell it?" she asks me. She's trailing her fingertips up and down my arm now.

It's my favorite little Celeste trick. The most magical thing she does. Nights when she sleeps over. Our legs tangled in my sheets together. Her fingertips moving over my arms. The lightest touch. Like the kiss of a feather. Nothing else has ever felt as good.

"Then I want to hear it," I say. "I'm listening."

"I lied to you. I took it. I didn't know what else to do. I couldn't stay there. Those people were way worse than my mom ever was." She sighs in the almost-dark. "I needed to get away. I was about to turn eighteen anyway. I didn't know what was gonna happen to me after that."

Celeste's fingers are still moving over my skin.

Rio's fingers.

I can feel her trembling. "It's okay," I whisper.

"I was scared," she says. "I freaked out."

"So what happened?"

"They tracked me down. Hauled me into the station in handcuffs. It was a whole thing. I admitted I stole it. But they didn't ask the right questions. They never asked me why."

No wonder she didn't want to get the police involved with everything out here.

"Oh, Rio," I whisper. She pulls me into her arms and we curl up together. My head on her shoulder. We fit so perfectly.

Two halves of the same metal heart, forged together.

"My caseworker somehow convinced them not to press charges. They let me go. That's when I headed down here." She hesitates. Her fingers stop moving on my arm. "It was the only place that I could think of that felt like home. Even though I'd never set foot in Hidden Glen before."

"I'm so sorry," I tell her. "You should've had such a different life."

Rio shakes her head. "Don't feel sorry for me. That's not what I want. I want you to know me."

She tilts my chin up and pulls my mouth toward hers. Rio's kiss is long and slow and deep. I can feel the heat of her hands on my stomach. My thigh. It's hot enough to almost burn. But not quite. Just a few degrees below the flash point.

When she pulls away, she brushes her lips against my temple, and then my neck, before she opens up her eyes to look at me.

That's all I can stand.

I pull her over on top of me so I can feel the weight of her body pressing me down into the soft mattress. She looks surprised for a minute, then kisses me again. I try to keep breathing while I kiss her back. But it's hard. We're all lips and teeth and necks and shoulders. Earlobes.

Tangled hair.

Searching fingers pressed to skin.

Rio whispers my name, and I whisper hers back to her. I can't be sure if I called her Rio or Celeste. Both are on the tip of my tongue.

We're night and day. Light and dark. Sunlight and shadow dancing together. Just like in the springs.

Rio pulls me into her arms again and strokes my hair. Outside, the sun is starting to come up. I can see a golden-pink sky through my window.

"What if it was Derry?" Rio asks. Her voice is thick and faraway.

"Derry didn't kill anybody," I murmur. "That doesn't make any sense."

"No," she says. "I know Dill was the murderer. The Reaper. He wrote those letters to the paper." She stops. Wading through the river of her own thoughts as she brushes her fingers through my hair. "But what if it was Derry who wrote the love notes? On her typewriter. What if she was Bailey's secret love? And that's what got Dill so mad. Maybe he found out about that. And maybe that's why he went after them that night."

"Maybe," I say. It makes as much sense as anything else.

"Have you ever kissed a girl before?" Rio whispers the question into my ear just as my eyes fall closed. Her breath tickles and I'm suddenly covered in goose bumps.

"Once," I tell her. "A long time ago. Way back before East, even."

"Was it your first kiss?" she asks.

"Yeah." I smile against her shoulder. "My first kiss."

I was not quite twelve. But that's a story for another time. It's nice to have some good secrets. Pieces of yourself you can hand out at the right moment.

I know there will be a right moment for us.

My hand is lying across Rio's collarbone. I rub her half heart with my thumb. The one hanging around her neck on the black ribbon.

I can't say how much time has passed when I sit up in bed. We must have fallen asleep, because Rio is snoring quietly beside me.

The sound of her breathing in the almost-dark sparks against a piece of flint that's buried deep in my brain, and a blazing memory erupts to the surface with a jolt ferocious enough to almost knock me off the bed. A knife slices through the dark.

It rips our tent in two.

All the night comes rushing in when I scream.

I'm running through the woods. Only I'm not me.

Not Tru.

I'm Bailey. Brown hair. Longer legs. And Celeste is running beside me. Her blond curls are tangled. Matted with blood.

We won't let go of each other's hands. We run together. Or we die together. But we won't be separated.

Not until strong arms grab me from out of nowhere.

I feel the sting of the knife as it slides across my throat.

The warmth of my own blood as it starts to flow.

I hear Celeste scream my name.

But there's no sound when I scream hers back.

Then I'm in the water.

The last thing I remember is watching from Elijah's Well as someone carries Celeste away from me.

She isn't kicking. Isn't fighting. I want to tell her not to give up. It's too late for me, but it might not be for her.

I can't tell her that, though. I'm already dead.

TWENTY-SIX

WE SLEEP LATE the next day, but it feels so good to be curled up in bed with Rio. Nothing else in the whole world feels good right now, but this moment—waking up with her hair spilling across my pillow—does.

It's after one in the afternoon before I finally untangle myself and crawl out to go pee. I head downstairs to look for Mom, and I'm relieved when I find out she's gone to work. I was afraid she might stay home this morning.

She's left a plate of muffins on the kitchen table, though. They aren't homemade. The Food 4 Less box is in the trash can. I don't care. She's left a note, too.

For you and your friend. I love you.

When I make it back upstairs with the muffins, Rio's awake. She's pulled out that map. The one of the Reaper kills. She has it spread out on my bed and she's studying it, but when she sees me, she smiles. There's something a little awkward about her. Like she doesn't quite know what to do or say.

That's totally new. She's always so confident. It makes me happy to see her a little thrown. A tiny bit off balance. That's the way she always makes me feel.

I crawl up on top of the bed and we sit there cross-legged, knees touching.

"All those girls." She's looking at the map again. "All those girls, Tru." Her voice breaks and she looks back down at the map one more time before she folds it up and sticks it back in my backpack. "We can't let him get away with this. It isn't just about us anymore. What he did to us back then." She shivers. "I don't want you and me to be two more circles on the map."

"I remembered something last night," I tell her. Rio reaches for a blueberry muffin. She nibbles at it while she waits for me to collect my thoughts. "I remember running. That night. With you." I reach for Rio's hand. "I don't think Celeste died first in the tent like everyone believes. I think we both ran. And I think Dill chased us down. He slit my throat and threw me in the Well. Then he took you back to the campsite and finished the job."

Rio thinks for a minute, then leans across the bed and grabs my phone off the little table. She's scrolling through the pictures until she comes to the crime scene photos. Her face turns even paler than usual, and she holds up the screen to show it to me.

"Look," she says. She zooms in on Celeste's foot. Covered in mud and sticking out of the sleeping bag at an odd angle. "It stormed earlier that night," she reminds me. "The rain came down in buckets. If he killed her—me—first—in the tent—her feet wouldn't have been muddy. Nobody crawls into a tent to go to sleep with their feet covered in mud like that."

I was right. That muddy foot. It seems like such a huge thing for the investigators to have missed. How could they not have seen that something was off?

"We ran through the woods together," I say.

"Yeah," she tells me. "We ran together."

All this time, the whole sequence has been wrong. It didn't happen the way everyone thinks it did.

"Maybe Dill took you back to the tent because he loved you," I say. "Maybe he didn't want to leave your body out there. Exposed like that. The way he did mine. It sounds sick. But maybe that's why he tucked you back into the sleeping bag. Out of some fucked-up kind of tenderness."

"Yeah," Rio says. "Maybe." She sets the last of her muffin on my nightstand and reaches for my hand. "What we have to figure out now is, what are we going to do next?"

We spend the rest of the day coming up with a plan. Before we head out to the springs, I let Rio take a shower, and she stays in there a long time. I wonder how long it's been since she's had a real, hot shower with clean towels and a bath mat and everything.

The ride out to Hidden Glen is silent. We're both trying not to think about the things that are going to happen.

Or how we might end up dead.

Again.

When we pull into the parking lot at Hidden Glen that evening, the sun is just sinking down below the horizon. We sit in my truck and watch the color drain from the sky, and then the grass and the water, until all the blues and greens have turned to grays.

We walk back toward the homestead hand in hand. We don't

talk. We barely breathe. When we get close, I hear Dill whistling to himself. That dead-sailor sea shanty he loves so much.

We yell a hello to let him know it's us, and he yells back. When we step out of the scrub and into the clearing around the firepit, Dill gets up to give me a hug. He wraps me up in his arms and squeezes me so tight, I think my ribs might break. "Hey, Tru," he tells me. "God. What a week."

He has no idea how much worse it's about to get.

I remember then that I haven't seen Dill since East's funeral. Him standing in the back. That blue suit that didn't fit. It feels like someone is cutting me into the tiniest pieces with the dullest scissors.

I watch over his shoulder as Rio moves around behind him. She picks up his old gun. He's left it lying on one of the five-gallon buckets. I watch as she slips it behind her back.

"Where's Derry?" I ask when Dill finally lets me go. I'm looking around, but she doesn't seem to be anywhere, and I feel the beginnings of panic. We need Derry here. She's our insurance policy. We figured Dill wouldn't hurt us with Derry watching.

The plan was to sit them both down and confront Dill with the knife. See what he had to say.

"She spent the night with her folks. Out at their trailer." He looks sad. "I think she needed a break. After everything."

I glance at Rio, because the plan is already falling apart. But we're too far into it to back down now. I don't want to, anyway. I'm not sure I'll ever have the courage to try again if we give up and go home now.

At least Rio has the gun.

"Sit down for a second, Dill," I say. "There's something we want to talk to you about."

"Okay." Dill runs his fingers through his tangled black curls. He sits down on one of the buckets. His knee won't stop bouncing. He's fidgeting. Wary. He looks from Rio to me. "Tru. What's up?"

I take a few steps back away from him. I pull that knife out of my backpack and hold it up for him to see.

"Holy shit," he whispers. "Where did you get that?" He starts to stand up, but Rio tells him to sit back down.

"Stay where you are," she says.

Dill turns to look at her again. This time she's holding that gun of his out in front of her body. Pointing it right at his chest.

"Whoa." Dill puts his hands in the air like a little kid playing cops and robbers. "Whoa whoa whoa." He looks so genuinely confused. "What the fuck is this?"

"It's the knife you killed Celeste and Bailey with, asshole." Rio's voice quivers with rage. But her hands are steady. That gun never wavers.

Dill stands up again, and Rio and I both shout at him to sit down. So he does. My heart is beating so fast, and I feel like my stomach is full of sawdust.

"Tru." He's looking at me now. "You don't believe that, do you? You don't think I killed those girls."

I hesitate. Suddenly this whole thing seems so impossible.

But that knife.

With the broken tip.

Dill's name carved into the grip.

"We think you did a lot more than that," Rio says. "We think you killed all those girls down south, too. All the Reaper murders. That was you. Wasn't it?"

"Jesus!" Dill's eyes bounce back and forth between us. "No fuckin' way! You think I'm a serial killer?" He looks at me like I'm some kind of space alien. "Tru, have you lost your goddamn mind?"

"Were you in love with Celeste?" Rio's voice has a coldness to it I've never heard before. There's none of that honey warmth tonight. "We found the love notes you wrote her."

"What?" Dill wrinkles up his forehead. He shakes his head hard. "Celeste was just a kid."

"I remembered where they were hidden. In the bedpost in my room. They have the same messed-up *r* key as the Glades Reaper letters they published in the paper yesterday."

While Rio is talking, I slip into Dill and Derry's tent. I'm looking for Derry's typewriter. The little suitcase she carries it in. I throw around the blankets on the cot. Dig through the tubs. It's not here.

"Where's Derry's typewriter?" I ask him when I come out.

Dill drops his head to his hands. "She took it with her," he says. "Out to her folks' house." He raises his head to stare me down. "But, Tru, I swear to God. You've known me almost your whole life." He looks like I'm the one who's just killed him. "Why would you believe a thing this girl tells you?" He jerks his head toward Rio. "Who the hell is she to come in here fillin' your head with this shit?"

I swing wide around Dill to go and stand next to Rio. "I wish I didn't believe it," I say. "But it's the only explanation that makes sense."

Rio turns to glance at me for the shortest second, and in that moment, Dill lunges at us as quick as a panther. There's a blur of movement, and Rio goes down hard. The gun goes flying from her hand and it lands in the scrub. Beyond the edge of the clearing.

Dill rolls to the side, then he's on his feet in an instant. He's scrambling through the brush, trying to find the gun. But it's dark and overgrown.

Rio's on her feet now, too. She grabs my hand and jerks me up hard.

"Come on!" she hisses. "We gotta get outta here."

Then we're running.

Again.

It's always us. Always running.

Always through the dark of the big scrub.

Brambles and thorns and sand.

Always us being hunted.

Only, this time, it isn't a faceless killer. It's Dill.

Dill who killed Bailey and Celeste.

Dill who killed East.

I think it would be better to let him go ahead and kill me. It would have to be less painful than knowing what I know now.

It takes Dill a few minutes to find the gun, so we have a good head start on him. We're moving fast down the trail toward the

main spring. I hear him yelling for us. Telling us to stop running. That he only wants to talk to us.

I wonder if that's what he told us last time.

Rio and I burst out of the scrub in a dead run. Dill is getting
closer. He's hot on our heels now. We glance around but there's
nowhere left to go. It's wide open all the way around us. No
good places to hide. We'll never make it up to the parking lot
and into my truck.

Not before Dill reaches us with that gun.

Rio and I look at each other, and we both know there's only
one place to hide.

And that's in the deep.

I scan the spring and the shoreline on the other side, looking
for telltale eyeshine. Four or five sets of red glowing pinpricks
look back at me without blinking. Gators on the bank opposite
us. A lot of them.

"Tru!" Dill's voice is so loud. "God fucking dammit!" So
angry now. So close. We don't have any choice; take our chance
with the gators, or with the Glades Reaper.

It doesn't seem fair that Dill could kill us twice.

But if we don't do something, I know he will.

Rio and I scramble down the rocks into the water. We wait.
Just until we see Dill come into the clearing. Then we dive.

Deep.

Before he has a chance to see us.

There's a moon tonight. But it doesn't penetrate far into the
water. Once we're down below, he won't be able to tell we're there.

The trick is, we can't see anything, either. No masks. No lights.

We're diving blind in the pitch dark.

As soon as we start down, I'm already disoriented.

Rio and I are holding hands. If we get separated, we'll never find each other in all this vast inkiness. We swim with one arm each, like a weird version of the three-legged races they used to make us do in elementary school PE class. It was supposed to teach us how to work together, I think. I always ended up falling on my face.

I have no idea how long we've been below.

Or how deep we are. Not until my feet hit the bottom. I've never been so grateful. Because now at least I know for sure which way is up.

We're at twelve feet. Fourteen, maybe. Depending on what part of the main spring we're in.

I couldn't even tell you.

My lungs burn. We didn't have time to breathe up. And we'd been running.

We have no stored oxygen. We won't be able to stay down here long.

I'm already feeling the desperate hunger for air.

I'm waiting for the attack. God only knows how many gators we're sharing the water with. They're fast. Like torpedoes with teeth. We won't see it coming. It'll hit us hard and rip us apart.

I feel Rio take my other hand. There are so many ways we could die tonight. Time is all distorted in my head.

Rio is on the move. She's pulling me with her. I think about what Paz told me once, about his granddad sponge diving off the coast of Cuba. *Nothing but him and his lungs against the whole ocean.* Or something like that. That's exactly how I feel tonight.

It's me and Rio in a spring that's grown as large as the Atlantic.

Something hard scrapes against my arms. We've finally reached the spring wall. Rio is tugging me up now. Toward the surface.

Toward air.

Thinking about breathing makes my lungs even more greedy. She squeezes my hand hard. We cling to the wall. If we can use the edge of the spring for cover, maybe we can surface long enough to get a breath without Dill seeing us.

If we're quiet.

If we're careful.

If we're lucky.

As soon as we break the surface, I'm breathing in. I'm trying to be so quiet. Small sips of air instead of the huge gulps my body craves. We're clinging to the rocks at the very edge. Making ourselves as still and small as possible. Our mouths barely above the waterline. Everything else below.

I scan the edges of the spring in the moonlight.

One set of red pinpricks has moved into the water. I watch it swim slowly along the far edge of the spring.

There's no sign of Dill. No sound. No movement.

Rio and I lock eyes. We're pressed nose to nose in the cold water. I'm shivering hard. I can't seem to get enough air to stop my lungs from spasming.

But the pressure of her forehead against mine calms me.

The feeling of her hand in mine.

Rio touches me. And I can breathe.

There's no way that kind of calm comes from a couple of weeks of knowing each other.

This is a connection that spans lifetimes. It's a love that has existed for longer than we've been alive, even.

That's when Dill appears on the edge of the spring, right above us. The gun is an inch above Rio's head before we even know he's there.

"Get out of the water." His voice is calm. "I'm not gonna hurt you. Tru, you know that. I just want to talk about whatever the hell is going on here."

Rio pushes off hard from the edge of the spring wall. She's moving backward through the water. Dill bends down with a speed that takes me by surprise. He grabs a fistful of my hair. I scream when he tries to lift me out of the spring. I'm kicking and clawing at the air. Trying to get a grip on his arm but my fingers are slippery. "Shut up, Tru! Stop screaming!"

Rio has me then. She grabs my arm and yanks me hard away. We leave Dill standing on the edge of the spring with a clump of my hair in one hand and that gun in the other.

We've moving back toward the middle of the spring. I'm waiting for him to level that gun at us. Ready to dive again.

"Goddammit!" Dill explodes in a fit of white-hot rage. The noise he makes then isn't like any human noise I've ever heard. A growl that's wild and desperate and caged. "I swear to God, Rio! I will kill you! You think I'm a murderer? Wait until I get my hands on you! You come in here and ruin everything!"

"It wasn't her!" I yell. "It was me!" I hear the choked sob in my voice. I hate myself for crying, but I can't stop. "I found your knife! At the bottom of Elijah's Well. I'm the one you left there to die! You slit my throat and let me bleed out in the water! It was me!"

Dill explodes. Arms to the sky. He's waving that gun around. A stream of words I can't understand.

Then he points it straight at us. "Get out of the water," he tells us. "I'm not messing around anymore. I'm not a killer. I swear to God! But if you two don't get out of the goddamn water—"

There's a horrible cracking sound. Bone splintering. And Dill just drops. He crumples like he's nothing more than laundry. Just empty clothes.

Rio and I both scream.

Jon Boy is standing on the edge of the spring. He's holding a huge rock in his hand.

"TB!" he shouts. "Get out of there. Now!" He turns on a flashlight and aims it at the water just behind us. I glance back over my shoulder long enough to see a big gator slide into the water on the far edge of the spring.

"Swim!" Rio yells, and the two of us head for Jon Boy as fast as we can. We hit the rocks and he leans down to offer us a hand. We crawl out and stand dripping in the dark.

Dill is lying in a heap with his head hanging over the edge of the spring. The spreading pool of blood around his head is painted black in the moonlight. It's running into the water. It gives me the weirdest feeling of déjà vu.

But there's something wrong about the blood, too. Something

I can't quite get my mind around because I'm completely in shock.

Jon Boy is staring at Dill.

And I'm staring at Jon Boy.

"W-What are you doing here?" I stammer. I'm suddenly shaking all over. I have to chew the words up—bite them into tiny pieces with my teeth—before I can spit them out through my clenched jaw.

"Your mom asked me to come look for you," he tells me. "She was worried." He hasn't taken his eyes off Dill. "I heard what you said. About finding the knife with his name on it." He finally turns to look at me. "Is that true?"

"Yeah," Rio says. "With the broken tip. But there's more than that."

It seems like so much to explain. The love notes and those Reaper letters with the broken *r*. All the rest of it. How he used to be a smoker. Used to live down south. That sudden rage of his. How he had the opportunity and ability to do all of it. Everything that's happened to us.

I don't have it in me to connect those dots again.

Not tonight. Maybe not ever.

Rio fills him in, though, and Jon Boy's face goes white as a ghost in the moonlight. "Dill was never even a suspect," he says. "For the Hidden Glen murders, or the Reaper killings."

"Is he dead?" I ask. I don't know what I want the answer to be.

"I don't know," Jon Boy says. "I can't——" His voice is shaking almost as bad as my legs are. I sink down to my knees in the grass.

Rio bends down low. She puts her hands on Dill's neck. Then she looks at me. "If he isn't dead, he will be soon. He barely has a pulse."

"We need to call someone," I say. "An ambulance. The sheriff."

"Oh God." Jon Boy covers his mouth.

Everything is wrong.

I'm on land now. But I still can't catch my breath. The world is spinning. It's like things are moving too fast and too slow. Both at the same time.

"Tru?" The soft voice from the edge of the darkness makes my heart sink. "What's going on?"

Derry stands not even ten feet away. She has a flashlight. And a backpack. Her little typewriter suitcase.

"I thought you were at your folks' place," Rio manages to say.

"I came back," Derry tells us. "It's been such a weird week . . ." Her voice trails off. "With East. And everything. Turns out, I only wanted to be with Dill."

Nobody moves. Nobody says a word. But I see the exact moment she notices Dill's body on the ground behind us.

"Dill!" she screams his name. Then she's pushing between me and Rio. Shoving us aside. Cradling Dill's head in her lap. There's blood all over her long skirt. Her hands. She's running her fingers through his hair. "What happened?" she's screaming at me now. "Tru? What happened to him?"

I drop to my knees and crawl over to where she is so I can put my arms around her shoulders. "I'm so sorry," I say. "Derry, I'm so sorry. He went after me and Rio. Jon Boy hit him with—"

"Oh God," Jon Boy moans again. He's pale and shaking, as if he might pass out.

"What?" Derry looks at me like I might as well be speaking a foreign language. Like the sounds coming out of my mouth don't make sense. "No," she says. "No. No. NO!"

"He killed Celeste and Bailey," Rio says. She's standing there staring at the three of us. Me and Derry and Dill. "Tru found his knife at the bottom of the Well. The murder weapon. With his name carved into the side. And the broken tip. Just like the autopsy report said."

"We think maybe—" I pause, because it seems so cruel to tell her. But she has a right to know who she's been sleeping next to all this time. "We're pretty sure Dill was the Glades Reaper."

Derry throws her head back and wails then. I've only heard that sound twice in my life before tonight.

The first time was when my mother came running out of the house and found me standing on the side of the road staring down at Dani's broken body.

The second was when I saw East floating facedown in the Well.

"No." She repeats the word over and over and over until it sounds like nonsense. Just a strangled sound.

"I need to call the sheriff," Jon Boy mumbles. "I gotta call this in—like you said, Tru." He's feeling around in his pants pockets for his cell phone. "Call an ambulance." He stops. Confused. "Or something." He pulls out his phone and curses. "Shit! My goddamn phone is dead." I dig mine out of my pocket and hand it up to him. He steps away and I hear him talking, and his voice is frantic.

I can't hear the exact words he's saying over Derry's sobbing. She's covered in blood. Rocking back and forth. Clutching Dill's head to her chest. It takes me a few seconds to understand what she's mumbling to herself. But then the words become clear. "It's my fault. My fault. Oh God, Dill. I'm sorry. My fault. My fault."

"What's your fault?" Rio kneels down beside Derry, and her voice is gentle.

"I found the knife," Derry tells us. "A few days after—" She stops. Strokes Dill's pale cheek. "After the girls died."

"What do you mean, you found it?" I ask.

"My daddy gave it to Dill. For his birthday that year. It was a gift. And then it disappeared." It takes her a while to get it all out. Between sobs. She stops every few words to plant a kiss on Dill's forehead. Or to run her hands up and down his arms, like she's trying to warm him up. It's more than I can stand. So I look away. Out toward the water. The gators are still patrolling. "Somebody stole it out of Dill's dive bag. Then the thing happened with Celeste and Bailey, and it was maybe a week later, I was back in the scrub hunting blackberries. And there was the knife. I found it in the undergrowth. Covered in blood." She tilts her head back and stares at the sky. "I panicked. I got rid of it. The only way I could think of. I threw it in the Well. And I knew it was a mistake as soon as I did it."

"Derry," I say.

She turns those honey-colored eyes on me. "Dill didn't kill those girls, Tru. You should've known that. He didn't have that in him. But I figured, if anybody ever found that knife, that's all it would take to have them convinced he was a murderer." She's gasping for air. I'm afraid she's going to hyperventilate. Or go into shock. That maybe we'll need that ambulance Jon Boy's calling for her, since it probably won't do Dill any good. "All these years that knife has been down there, and I've been waiting for someone to find it. Holding my breath. Worrying about what would happen if they did." She stops. "I never imagined it would be you."

Jon Boy steps back over to where we are. "The ambulance is coming. And the sheriff's crew." He looks up at the stars. Out at the spring. Anywhere but at Dill. "They're gonna want to see that knife."

"It's back at the homestead," I say. I dropped it when Dill lunged at us.

"We can go get it," Rio offers.

I look at Derry. She barely even seems to know I'm here, but I don't want to leave her. Jon Boy tells me it's okay. That he'll stay with her. Wait for the ambulance. He's watching her rock back and forth with this stricken look on his face. For the first time, it occurs to me to wonder what's going to happen to him.

He's likely just killed a man. Even if that man was a serial killer—even if he was pointing a gun at me and Rio—I know Jon Boy well enough to know what kind of toll this is going to take on him.

For a second, I'm rooted to the spot. I have this feeling like if I just stay put, maybe nothing else awful will happen.

Then Rio's taking my hand. She's helping me to my feet. And she's leading me toward the trail back into the scrub. Toward the homestead.

My feet won't move, and Rio lays her hands on both sides of my face. She looks right into my eyes and tells me, "It's okay, Tru. It's safe now."

So I let her lead me into the darkness.

Then I remember she's a liar.

TWENTY-SEVEN

SOMEHOW, I MANAGE to stay upright for the walk back to the homestead. It's so dark. Our flashlights barely make enough light for us to see by. I can't make sense of what just happened. I can't connect the broken, bleeding shape on the ground back there with Dill.

Not my Dill.

Dill, who taught me to dive.

Dill, who kept me safe.

Dill, who loved us all so much.

It's like my brain can't handle it, so it shuts down.

Rio and I don't talk, but she keeps a tight grip on my hand. That's the only thing that keeps me moving. Back at the homestead, I find the knife lying on the ground near the fire. Rio grabs it and slips it into my backpack, then we stand in the clearing and take one last look around.

This is our last time here. We both know that.

I'm in no shape to say goodbye.

I let Rio take my hand again and lead me through the scrub, down the path, back toward the main spring.

When we step out into the clearing, though, nobody's there.

Nobody except Dill, his chest barely rising with a breath. Surrounded by all that black oozing over the rocks and into the water.

But there's no Jon Boy.

And no Derry.

I see their footprints. Jon Boy's boots. Derry's sandals. That's the only thing that proves they were ever really there.

That and Dill's crushed skull.

"What the fuck?" Rio says. "Where are they?"

I'm looking up toward the parking lot. But I don't see Jon Boy or Derry anywhere.

I don't hear any sirens yet.

"I don't know," I whisper. Suddenly all the hair on my neck is standing straight up. I know somebody is out there watching us. From just beyond the tree line.

"Come on." Rio is leading me up toward the parking area. When we get to my truck, she freezes. She shines her light at my tires.

They've been slashed, all four of them.

Somebody didn't want any of us to be able to leave here tonight.

"You think Dill did this?" I ask Rio.

"When?" she asks me. "We surprised him at the homestead. Then he came after us at the spring. He didn't have time to do this."

Suddenly I'm remembering that sleep-coated question Rio asked me a million years ago in my room.

Or maybe it was just early this morning.

What if it was Derry?

She hadn't meant to suggest Derry was the killer. She'd only imagined Derry as Celeste's possible secret love.

But what if she was more than that?

I'm staring at my truck. "Give me your phone," Rio says. "We need to call somebody. Make sure they're coming. It's been too long."

I reach for my phone, but it's not in my pocket. Jon Boy never gave it back to me after he called for help. There's no way to reach anyone.

It's like Rio and I are suddenly the only two people on earth.

We turn and start back down to the springs. We have to find Jon Boy. Get that phone.

We stop halfway down the lawn.

There's something floating just at the edge of the swimming area.

I know what it is—who it is—as soon as my flashlight beam hits him.

"Jon Boy!" I scream his name and start down toward the spring. He's floating facedown. Just like East. He must have been there when we came back from the homestead. We didn't see him. It's so dark out here at night.

Rio sprints after me and grabs my hand. We're halfway between the parking lot and the water now. She points toward Dill's body. "Where's the gun?" she whispers.

It was lying beside him when he dropped. But it's gone now. Which means someone has it.

That someone can only be Derry.

Rio realizes it at the same time I do.

"We were wrong," she whispers. "Derry killed the girls." Rio spins around to face me. "Maybe she was jealous of Dill and Celeste. Or, fuck, maybe she really was the one in love with Celeste. Not Dill. Maybe Celeste broke it off or something. And Derry used Dill's knife. That's why she threw it in the Well."

"That's why she kept saying it was her fault." But I stop. That still doesn't make sense. "What about the Glades Reaper? Derry wasn't a serial killer."

"I don't know!" Rio says. "None of it makes sense anymore." Her eyes are wild and desperate.

"That could still be Dill," I say. I need that part to be right. "If Derry wrote those love notes to Celeste on her typewriter—"

"Maybe she didn't even know about the Reaper letters," Rio finished. "Didn't realize that it was Dill."

"Or maybe she did know," I say. "Maybe she knew the whole time."

There's a noise from the other side of Jon Boy's truck. Up in the parking lot. The quiet crunch of feet on gravel. Rio and I freeze.

"We've gotta hide," she whispers.

The two of us are running again, toward the trail that leads back to the Well. We need to get out of the open. Because Derry has that gun. She's the only one left.

I glance back up toward the parking lot and I see the glint of honey-colored hair in the moonlight.

I pull Rio into the tall grass. We stay off the boardwalk. So our feet don't make noise on the wood.

When we reach the Well, we skirt around the safety fence and we're about to step into the scrub when something catches my eye. Flowers. I see them so bright and plain. In the beam of Rio's flashlight.

Like someone has hit them with a spotlight.

And I stop. Frozen. A thought is firing off in my brain. Some idea is trying to form. It sparks over and over and over, waiting to ignite.

"Stop!" I whisper. "Wait! Wait!" I know Rio thinks I've lost my mind when I bend down to examine the little cluster of three purple flowers that are growing at the base of a pine tree. My mind is spinning. Still working hard to put something together. An answer I can't put my finger on.

"What?" Rio says. She's looking back over her shoulder. Biting her lip. "Tru. Come on! Derry is—"

Then it hits me. Like a rock to the head. And everything cracks open. I'm bleeding to death.

"Derry isn't coming after us," I say. My words are flat. All hollow.

"What?"

"That photo of the cigarette that Jon Boy gave me." I'm talking so fast. The idea has just barely formed in my brain. I can't let it slip away. "The Reaper's calling card. The photo that proves he was here. That the Glades Reaper killed Celeste and Bailey. This is where it was taken."

"Okay . . ." Rio whispers. "But what does—"

"No," I say. "This is exactly where it was taken." Three perfect flowers.

Same size. Same color. Same formation.

The size of the tree is the same.

Everything is exactly the same.

"It's a recent picture," I say.

"What are you trying to say?"

"He just took it. These little flowers don't last long. It couldn't have been taken more than a week ago. It wasn't an old picture at all."

"Why would he give you a new picture and tell you it was an old picture?"

"I don't know," I say. I feel like screaming. Because I don't know anything. "And there's something about the blood in the water," I say. "Something I can't quite figure out."

"Tru, what are you talking about?"

"The blood around Bailey's body—around my body—in that crime scene photo." I'm thinking about the blood dripping from Dill's crushed skull into the water of the main spring. How the black of the blood was dispersed by the water almost immediately. I remember seeing it pooled and dark on the rocks. But not in the water.

The spring took the blood and spread it out so you couldn't see it anymore.

That happened almost immediately.

"Rio," I tell her. "Those crime scene photos. They weren't taken the next morning by the crime lab techs. They were taken right after the murders." Lit up by the flash of a powerful camera. "They were taken by—"

"By the murderer," she finishes, and I nod. "Right after he killed Bailey and Celeste."

"That dirty foot of Celeste's," Rio says. "What if he washed her down? Wiped her feet clean after he carried her back to the tent. That's why the mud isn't mentioned in any of the reports."

I sway on my feet and Rio slips an arm around my shoulders.

Jon Boy faked that cigarette photo so we'd believe the Glades Reaper was responsible for Celeste's and Bailey's murders. So we wouldn't be looking closer to home.

My mind is racing now. I think about those boot prints. The ones around Dill's body. Back at the main spring. I picture them in the moonlight.

Derry's sandals.

Jon Boy's boot prints.

Wavy lines on the heel.

The prints match the ones from the homestead. Around the firepit after the tent got slashed. Behind the clothesline that morning after someone was watching us during the night. Boots with wavy lines on the heel. With everything being so chaotic. Dill bleeding on the ground. The prints hadn't even registered.

"Jon Boy killed Bailey and Celeste." Rio breathes the words into the soft night. "He killed us, Tru."

"And I don't think that's all of it," I whisper.

A memory slams into me like a pickup truck traveling full speed down the highway.

Celeste and me. We're sitting outside the tent. I feel the weight of her hand in mine. But we aren't alone. Someone else sits with us in the afternoon light.

Longer hair.

Thicker glasses.

But the face is the same. Jon Boy is pale and shaking.

The Glades Reaper, he whispers. His voice is hushed. It carries the weight of a terrible secret. *I had to tell someone.* Celeste and I both shrink back away from him in horror. He moans. Drops his head to his hands. *What the fuck am I going to do? How can I live with that?*

I look at Rio, but she's staring back into the scrub. To where our tent stood all those years ago.

"Jon Boy told us that afternoon that he was the Glades Reaper," I tell Rio. "He confessed it to us."

Suddenly I'm thinking about the junk stored down in the *Star* basement. I remember an old typewriter sitting on a shelf. Collecting dust.

Is that what he used to write the Glades Reaper letters? I bet if I checked, I'd find it has a broken *r* key.

"That's why I remember that name," she whispers. "It was always there on the tip of my tongue. It was one of the last conversations I had before I died."

"That's why he came back that night and killed us," I say. "Because we knew his secret." I turn back toward the Well, but in my mind, I'm not standing up top looking into the water. I'm floating in the water, looking up at Jon Boy's face.

I'm dying. I know that. But I'm smiling. Because I have something clutched in my hand.

A name tag. Silver. Engraved with the words JB WESTLEY, EDITOR, *MOUNT ORANGE STAR.* I see the look on his face as I open my fist and release it into the spring.

That's what Bailey wanted me to see.

It was never Dill's knife.

She was trying to take me straight to the bottom, to where that name tag must lie covered with all these years of silt and debris.

For a second I think about going down. To see if I can find it. But then I hear a voice from behind us.

"You can't run from the Reaper."

We turn to face Jon Boy. Dripping. Breathing hard. Holding that gun of Dill's out in front of him.

"You told us that same thing that night," I say. "When you chased us through the scrub."

"You told us you were the Reaper," Rio adds. "Then you came back to kill us."

Jon Boy shakes his head. "You don't remember anything because you weren't there. That's not what I said. I never said I was the Reaper."

"That's a lie," Rio says. "We were sitting in the grass outside the tent."

"Jesus," Jon Boy says. "You aren't Celeste and Bailey." He growls in frustration.

"Why did you do it?" I ask him, and my voice sounds so much braver than I expect it to. How many people get to face down their own murderer? "If you trusted us enough to tell us the truth about the Reaper, why did you come back and kill us?"

"I did it for love," he says. "Remember, I told you not too long ago, Tru, more bad gets done in the name of love than in the name of hate."

"You wrote those love notes," I accuse. "The ones we found in Celeste's bedroom. You loved her, so you wanted to tell her the truth about yourself."

Jon Boy shakes his head. "No, I—"

"You didn't love Celeste," Rio says. "Not really. If you did, you couldn't have killed her."

"You think I did what I did because of a girl?" His voice is strung wire-tight and his mouth twists in disgust. "I didn't write any love notes. I didn't do it because I loved Celeste," Jon Boy spits. "I did it because I loved Reese."

"Who the fuck is Reese?" Rio asks.

"Oh my God," I say with sudden understanding. "Those circles on the map in the basement. Black for the Reaper kills and red—"

"Red for the locations Reese had visited on the same dates," Jon Boy admits. "Places he had stories or interviews or conferences."

"Or awards ceremonies," I add. Florida City. That damn Small-Town-Newspaper-Editor-of-the-Year trophy.

Reese was the Glades Reaper. Not Jon Boy.

All this time, I've been wearing a serial killer's sweater. It's the only thought that I can grab hold of. Everything else is slipping though my fingers.

"I didn't know until that summer," Jon Boy says. "I'd had questions. For a while. But I loved Reese so much. I didn't want to believe it. He'd go away. Disappear for days. Leave me in charge of things. And he'd be so strange when he came home. It wasn't until I found his trophies, the souvenirs he took, that I knew for sure. And I started matching up the dates and places. Making circles on that map."

"Why are you telling us all this?" I ask him. "What's the point if you're just going to kill us?"

Jon Boy sighs. "I've been trying to tell someone for the last twenty years." His eyes are empty. "All those reporters. The podcasters and interviewers and writers. The damn murder ghouls waltzing around town like they owned the place. The true-crime people. I kept thinking surely one of them would figure it out—what he did and what I did for him—and then I could rest." He stops and takes a shaky breath. "But they never did. And I wanted you to get it right, Tru. I gave you that photo, the cigarette and the flowers, because I figured if you thought it was the Glades Reaper, it wouldn't feel so personal. Maybe you'd let it go. But even when I was trying to throw you off the track, I wanted you to see it clear. Or at least some part of me did."

"You told me about it," Rio says. "You told us about it." She reaches for my hand. "That's what you said that night. Outside the tent. You came to see us. You had to tell someone. It was eating you alive. I remember that now."

A little piece of peeling wallpaper.

I'm pretty sure Reese is the Glades Reaper. I had to tell someone. What the fuck am I going to do? How can I live with that?

"We were friends," Jon Boy tells us. "Bailey had just started working at the newspaper that summer. Reese hired her. So we'd gotten to know each other. I trusted her. I didn't have anyone else. Bailey told me I had to go to the police. But I couldn't do that. She said if I didn't, she would."

"That's why you came back later and killed us," Rio says, and Jon Boy nods.

"Reese was everything to me. I wanted to stop him. But I wasn't ready to turn him in." He shakes his head. "I never would have done that. He was my brother. He trusted me."

"I trusted you, too," I accuse. All these years, we've loved each other.

Jon Boy looks like he's been stabbed. "I never wanted to hurt you!" His words come out all strangled. Choked with frustration and anger. "Why wouldn't you give up, TB?" My heart clenches when he uses my nickname. "We wanted to scare you away." Familiar eyes behind familiar glasses. "We tried so hard. But you wouldn't give up."

"Who is 'we'?" I demand.

"Me and Knox," he says. "We saw each other in the parking lot on the night of the murders. When news broke the next morning, about Bailey and Celeste, Knox came to me. He didn't think I did it, but he knew good and well that we were both in big trouble if anyone ever found out we were out there. Especially him, being the boyfriend. And he was already a suspect. So we made a pact to never tell."

"You kept each other's secrets," I say.

"Knox and I fought that night." Rio's voice sounds far away. She's twenty years in the past. She clutches her neck. "I told him I wasn't in love with him. That I was in love with someone else. And he grabbed that locket from around my neck. Ripped it off."

"You dumped him," Jon Boy tells her. Then he corrects himself. "Celeste dumped him, and they fought before I came back."

"So Knox is the one who left the locket in my truck. To scare us."

Jon Boy rolls his eyes. "I asked him to do that one thing. I knew he had it. And you'd have thought that made him a criminal mastermind. All he did was leave it in your damn truck."

"But that's not all you did. Is it? You killed East and maybe Dill," I say. "More people are dead, all to keep your brother's secret."

"It doesn't matter," Jon Boy tells us. "Nothing matters. I'd already killed the one person I loved most in the world."

"Reese," I whisper his name to the pine trees like a curse.

"I held my own brother's head under the water until he stopped breathing. And I thought that was the end of it. I sent the letters to the *Miami Herald*. I figured, if the Reaper was still alive—still writing letters—it couldn't have been Reese."

"Why did you take the pictures?" I ask him. "What made you do that?"

Jon Boy smiles a little. "I'm a reporter, Trulee Bear. It's a hard instinct to kill. That need to document."

"Bullshit," Rio tells him. "I think you had enough of him in you that you wanted a fucking souvenir. You're just as much of a monster as your brother was."

Jon Boy lunges at Rio. He hits her hard over the head with the gun and she collapses. Just like Dill. I scream her name and he elbows me hard in the face. Blood pours from my bleeding nose.

It feels warm. Sticky.

Familiar.

"Jesus, Tru!" Jon Boy snarls at me.

"Go ahead and kill me!" I dare him. "You already killed Bailey and Celeste. And your own fucking brother. What's a little more blood on your hands?"

"We both have blood on our hands, don't we?" Jon Boy's face is hard and unrecognizable. "Dani was out on the road the night she died because she was looking for you. Right?"

"I'm not the same as you! I'm not the one who killed my sister!" Rage rips the words from my throat, and for the first time ever I know the truth of that. It wasn't my fault. "I'm not the one who hit her and left her for dead!"

Jon Boy looks at me for a second, and his eyes are suddenly so sad and so familiar. Then he says, "No. That was me."

I stop cold. The world is gone in an instant. I'm not standing on anything.

I'm falling.

Falling.

Falling.

Not seeing or hearing anything. I'm not even existing any-more. Every part of me is shattered.

Disintegrated.

"Reese walked. Early mornings. I couldn't let him go on doing what he was doing, and I thought if I hit him with my car it would look like an accident. Only he wasn't out walking the morning I went looking for him. Dani was. But it was dark and I couldn't really see . . ."

The mention of her name sears hot enough to bring me back to myself. But I'm still too stunned to move or breathe.

Dani.

Oh my God. Dani.

Not Dani.

Jon Boy is the one who took her away from me. Then he came to our house the next day to sit with me.

He held my hand. Let me cry in his lap.

Jon Boy turns back to Rio. He's standing over her. Aiming that gun right at her chest. I hear him cock it. A cold metal click.

The sound of it shakes me awake. I won't lose Rio the way I lost Celeste.

I channel every bit of rage at Jon Boy. He's taken so much from me. In this life. And the one before. "I found your name tag!" I shout. "At the bottom of the Well. I tore it off your shirt. That night. Remember?"

Jon Boy turns to stare at me. His eyes are huge behind his glasses.

"How do you know that?" he whispers.

"I told you, I remember it." Rio moans from behind him in the tall grass, and I take a step backward. Toward the Well. Jon Boy follows me. "I knew it was down there. Rio and I found it. And I hid it somewhere." Another step. "If you kill us, you'll never know where that last clue is." Two steps toward the Well. I'm leading him away from Rio. "You'll live the rest of your life with that missing name tag hanging over your head." I turn to run. All I'm thinking about is leading him away from Rio. But Jon Boy is fast as lightning. He swipes at me and grabs my hair. He yanks me backward and I go down hard. He scoops me up and wraps his arms around me. I'm kicking and trying to bite him. But he's carrying me toward the Well. Around the chain-link safety fence. Up onto the boardwalk. Through the safety gate. It clangs closed behind us.

He's going to throw me into the Well again.

Just like he did when I was Bailey.

Just like he did with East.

I wonder if he'll slit my throat again. Or hit me over the head, the way he must have hit East with something.

But neither of those things happen. Instead, there's the clanking of the safety gate. Jon Boy swivels his head around to look over his shoulder, and something hits him hard across the side of the head. It sends us both flying into the water with a sudden splash.

When I come up coughing and choking, Derry is standing at the edge of the Well holding that heavy typewriter suitcase. She's staring down at Jon Boy. He's floating facedown. And the blood around his head is already spreading into the spring.

I swim to the edge and pull myself up onto the rocks. My cell phone is lying just within reach. It must have gone flying out of Jon Boy's pocket when Derry hit him.

I look at Derry and she knows what I'm about to ask.

"Dill's alive," she whispers.

I grab my phone and call for help. An ambulance. Then I scroll through the photos on my phone until I get back to the ones Rio took that first day in the *Star* basement. Her pictures of Jon Boy's interview notes. And I let out a long wail.

The answer has been on my phone the whole time. I've been

carrying it around in my pocket. Because those meticulously typed notes of Jon Boy's, they have a broken r key.

I picture that dusty typewriter again. The one in the *Star* basement. But this time I'm seeing my fingers on them.

I'm smiling. Hiding in the basement when I'm supposed to be at lunch.

There's a noise and I look up to see Rio stepping out of the scrub. She stumbles toward the chain-link fence. Her face is bloody. Battered.

But she's smiling at me.

I run to the fence and lace my fingers through hers as she collapses against it. "It was me," I tell her. "Bailey wrote those love notes to Celeste. I wrote them to you. I'd just started working at the paper. I used the same typewriter that Jon Boy used to type up his interview notes and to write the fake Glades Reaper letters."

"It was me and you," Rio says, and I hear the first sirens tearing through the quiet darkness.

"Yeah," I tell her. "Me and you. We're going to make it this time."

"Nothing holding us up," Rio tells me.

"And nothing holding us down."

EPILOGUE

MAYBE WE GET a little closer each time we go around. Remember a little more. Understand it all a little faster.

Maybe next time I won't hesitate. Won't waste any time. I'll walk right up and kiss her. Hard on the mouth. My fingers tangled in her hair.

This total stranger at the mall.

Or my boss at my first job. Day one.

The woman who squeezes past me in the produce aisle while my baby waves at her from my shopping cart. "Excuse me . . ." she'll say in a slow Southern accent that has the feeling of a memory. "The bananas."

And then she'll kiss me back.

Or she'll push me away and scream for security. In which case, I'll apologize and go on my way. Because I'll know that wasn't Rio.

And I'll keep looking. Because I know that we're meant to be together forever. In whatever life comes next, the part of me that's always me will keep seeking out the part of her that's always her.

Today, though, I don't have to look. Because Rio is standing right beside me.

There aren't a lot of people at Hidden Glen Springs on an

early November afternoon. The thick summer crowds are gone, and we didn't have to dodge any tourists on the walk back to the Well.

I shiver a little and Rio slips her arms around me. It isn't cold today. But it's not especially warm, either. I figure it's one of the last good diving days this season. Soon the manatees will start coming in, and then the springs will belong to them for the winter.

"You sure you're ready for this?" she asks me.

"Yeah," I tell her. "It's time."

"Our first time back in the water," Rio says, and I nod. "That's a big deal."

We pull on our masks and fins and stand at the edge.

I look down. All the way down to the vent.

I'm looking for Bailey. But she's not here today. I knew she wouldn't be.

Rio gives my hand a squeeze, and then I give myself over to the spring.

I let the water work its magic. I go deep. I wash myself clean. And even though there are places down inside me where I know it will never stop hurting, I let those places be soothed. At least for a little while.

I feel the pull of the bottom. I know that name tag is down there. The one with Jon Boy's name on it. But I don't feel the need to grab it today. Turns out there was plenty of other evidence in his house. Enough to prove Reese was the Glades Reaper. And that Jon Boy was the Hidden Glen killer.

Maybe I'll go searching for that name tag on the sandy bottom someday. But not today.

Today we're hunting for treasures. The little shells that flash silver in the sunlight filtering through the crystal-clear water. The ones lined with pink.

Celeste's favorites.

Rio and I swim side by side as we gather them.

One for Dani.

One for Evan.

One for Celeste.

And one for Bailey.

One for East.

One for Dill and one for Derry. They're living up near Blue Springs now, in a little trailer just outside the state park. We keep saying we'll get up there to visit them. But we haven't yet.

One for Jon Boy, even.

And one for Rio and me.

We hold them tight in our fists as we kick back toward the light.

We break the surface and breathe together.

Then we pull ourselves up onto the rocks to lie in the sun until we finally feel the warmth seeping back into our bones. After a few minutes, I open my eyes and turn to look at Rio. I rub the smooth shells and she leans down to warm my lips with a kiss.

And I keep breathing.

We keep breathing.

For all of us.

ACKNOWLEDGMENTS

Before I thank anyone else, I want to thank my mom and my sister. I could try to list all the things I'm thankful to them for, but let me just sum it up and say . . . everything. Anna Myers and Anna-Maria Lane are teachers and storytellers and wells of unquestioning love and support flavored with just the right amount of sarcasm and humor. They're the kind of tough-as-nails women I wish everyone could have in their corner.

This is a book about past lives and the mystery of those unexplainable connections we sometimes feel. My mom, to whom this book is dedicated, has always believed that when we feel that immediate pull toward someone, it might be because we've known them before in another life. I'm a skeptic in pretty much every way, but there are two things that make think maybe I'm wrong about that particular point.

The first is the way the landscape of central Florida tugs on me. I wrote this book while I was still living in Oklahoma, having spent a lot of time in Florida, but I've since moved here full time, and it definitely feels like this is where I belong. I first came to this part of Florida when I was in college, and the immediate love I felt for the dense and tangled scrub, the vast wetlands teeming with birds and alligators, the sandy orange groves spreading out beneath deep purple sunsets, and the gorgeous freshwater springs was like nothing I'd felt before. The beaches are great, and I'm an absolute Disney World fanatic, but it was the ruggedly beautiful geography of central Florida's wild interior that took immediate root in my heart and my imagination. I don't know how to explain it, other than to say this is the landscape of my soul. So maybe I lived here in a past life. Who knows?

The second is my friend and twin flame, Wes. The intensity of that immediate recognition between us left us both reeling a little bit, and we've never quite been able to pin down that feeling, other than to say that the true, deep, and unusual friendship that flared up so fast between us felt inevitable and cosmic. Like we were meant to be. And in all these many years, that feeling has never dimmed even a little bit. Wes, you told me once that if you came back in your next life as a rock, you knew for sure that I'd be the grass growing under the rock. I laughed, but I want you to know that I can think of a lot worse fates than spending eternity linked to my best friend. You're the only person who's ever made me wonder if maybe we've walked hand in hand in another life. You feel too much like home for this to be our first go-around. Thanks for being the reason I know that true love exists, and that it doesn't always looks like what we're told it will. Sometimes it looks like you and me.

This may be a book about past lives, but I wrote it in this life, and I (thankfully) had a lot of help.

To my son, Paul, thank you for holding down the fort at home. You're the grocery shopper, the puppy walker, the floor sweeper, the one who keeps things tidy and on track so that I can lock myself away and write. I love your generous heart and your sweet nature, and the way you do so much with such a beautiful, genuine willingness of spirit. You're twenty now, and the world is opening up for you in so many exciting ways. I can't wait to see all your next chapters unfold . . . but I'm also so grateful that you're still willing to curl up on the couch with me and watch scary movies.

Thank you to the rest of my extended family who are always so supportive, but this time especially to all my cousins. There's a part of all of you in me, so there's a part of you in all these books. You're all storytellers, right down the line, and I'm so glad to be a part of your stories.

To my dear writer friends, especially Lela (who's more family than friend at this point), Brenda, Catren, Valerie, Tiffany, Gaye, Tammi, Doug, Sarah (yes, I'm including you in the writer list because we all know you are one!), Alysha, Kim, and Scarlett, thanks to you all for keeping my creative flame burning by sharing your own spark. If there was ever anyone else I might possibly have known in another life, it might be Scarlett St. Clair. And if we did know each other before, I'm sure we caused a lot of beautiful chaos together.

To my agent, Pete Knapp, who I'm grateful for every single day. You're the best, and I'm so lucky to have you on my side. I feel like I won the lottery when it comes to agents.

Thanks also to the rest of the team at Park & Fine Literary and Media, particularly Stuti Telidevara, who has the answer to any question almost before I ask it, and Abigail Koons, Kathryn Toolan, and Ben Kaslow-Zieve in the Foreign Rights Department.

A huge and energetic thank-you to my editor, Rūta Rimas, who makes telling these strange, twisty stories so much easier because I know she gets me and she gets my vision, and she'll help me make it all so much clearer in the end.

To everyone else at Penguin Young Readers, including Jennifer Klonsky, Casey McIntyre, Jayne Ziemba, Felicity Vallence, Kaitlin Kneafsey, Gretchen Durning, Simone Roberts-Payne, James Akinaka, Abigail Powers, and Kristie Radwilowicz, who designed yet another swoony cover of my dreams!

Thanks so much to Berni Vann at CAA, my film and television agent; Philippa Milnes-Smith and Eleanor Lawlor at the Soho Agency; and the wonderful team at Electric Monkey/Farshore Books in the UK, particularly Sarah Levison, Lindsey Heaven, Lucy Courtenay, Laura Bird, Olivia Adams, Ellie Bavester, and Pippa Poole.

I also want to send thanks to my many friends in the SCBWI Oklahoma region. There are way too many of you to mention by name, but you all will always be my family, and I'm so grateful for all the love and encouragement you've given me.

And to my new friends in the SCBWI Florida region, thanks for welcoming me into your fabulous group and making me feel so at home!

This book is partly a love letter to the freshwater springs of central Florida. Those beautiful places captured my heart so completely from the first time I visited more than thirty years ago. Although Hidden Glen Springs is fictional, it's based in part on very real places like Silver Glen Springs, Juniper Springs, Alexander Springs, Salt Springs, Ginnie Springs, Gilchrist Blue Springs, Wekiwa Springs, Rock Springs at Kelly Park, De Leon Springs, and lots of others. If you want to know what paradise looks like, look those places up. Sadly, these wild wonderlands are endangered, and they could use your help. Check out FloridaSprings.org or FloridaSpringsCouncil.org to learn what you can do to make a difference.